Joe Speedboat

D1270454

TOMMY WIERINGA in
Aruba in the Dutch Antilles off the coast of Venezuela
before returning to the Netherlands when he was ten
years old. Kicked out of school at seventeen, he got to
university via a few diversions, studying history in
Groningen and attending the School of Journalism in
Utrecht. He has worked as a salesman, sold tickets at
railway stations, and been a magazine editor. *Joe
Speedboat* is the winner of the Bordewijk-prijs and
was nominated for the AKO Literatuurprijs, the Libris
Literatuurprijs and the Gouden Uil Literatuurprijs. *Joe
Speedboat* has been translated into thirteen languages.

SAM GARRETT studied journalism and philosophy at
the University of Oregon in the wild and woolly 1970s.
He currently divides his time between the Netherlands
and France. Winner of the Society of Authors' Vondel
Prize for Dutch translation in 2003, he has translated
into English a number of Holland's most popular
authors.

From the reviews of Joe Speedboat:

'This is such a lovely book, full of eccentricity and charm.'
Book Bag

'A wonderfully eccentric and uproariously funny novel.'
Books Quarterly

Joe Speedboat

TOMMY WIERINGA

Translated from the Dutch
by Sam Garrett

Portobello
BOOKS

First published by Portobello Books Ltd 2009
This paperback edition published 2010

Portobello Books Ltd
12 Addison Avenue
London
W11 4QR

First published in Dutch in 2005 as *Joe Speedboot* by De Bezige Bij,
Amsterdam, Netherlands.

The publication of this work has been made possible by financial
support from the Foundation for the Production and Translation of
Dutch Literature (Nederlands Literair Productie-en Vertalingenfonds).

A CIP catalogue record is available from the British Library

9 8 7 6 5 4 3 2 1

ISBN 978 1 84627 104 5

Text designed and typeset in Thesis by Lindsay Nash

Printed and bound in Great Britain by CPI Bookmarque, Croydon

For Rutger Boots

It is said that the samurai
travels a twofold Way,
that of the brush and that of the sword.

MIYAMOTO MUSASHI

Brush

It's been a warm spring. At school they're praying for me, because I've been out of it for more than two hundred days. I've got bedsores all over my body and a condom catheter taped to my flute. This, the doctor tells my parents, is the phase of the 'coma vigil': I've regained limited receptivity to my surroundings. He says I've started reacting to stimuli, pain and noise, and that's good news. Reacting to pain is a definite sign that you're alive.

They hang around my bed the whole time, Pa, Ma, Dirk and Sam. I can hear them as soon as they get out of the lift – a swarm of starlings darkening the sky. They smell of oil and stale tobacco; they've barely bothered to change out of their overalls. HERMANS & SONS, FOR ALL YOUR DEMOLITION NEEDS. Scrap is our middle name.

We demolish wrecked cars, industrial equipment and the occasional café interior, if my brother Dirk happens to be feeling pumped up. Dirk has been barred from almost every bar, shop and inn in Lomark, but not in Westerveld, not yet. He's got a girl over there. He comes home smelling of chemical violets. All you can do is feel sorry for her.

What the Hermanses talk about mostly is the weather, the same old song and dance; business is slow and the weather's to blame, no matter what the weather's like. They swear and shake their heads, first Pa, then Dirk, then Sam. Dirk clears his sinuses loudly, now he has a gob of snot in his mouth. He doesn't know where to go with it, the only thing left to do is swallow – and, bloop, there it goes.

Lately, though, there's been more to talk about in Lomark than just the weather. While I was out cold, a runaway moving van wrecked the Maandags' step-gabled house, and huge explosions off in the distance are causing the whole town to shit itself with a certain regularity. This all has to do, it seems, with someone by the name of Joe Speedboat. He's new in Lomark; I've never met him.

Whenever they start talking about Joe Speedboat, though, I prick up my ears – he sounds like a good guy if you ask me, but then no one asks me. They're sure Speedboat is the one making the bombs. Not that they've ever caught him at it, but there were never any explosions before he came, and now suddenly there are. Case closed. It's got them pretty pissed off, let me tell you. Sometimes Ma says, 'Hush now, Frankie might hear you,' but they don't pay her any mind.

'Just pop out for smoke,' Pa says.

You're not allowed to do that in here.

'Is that really his name, Speedboat?' asks Sam, my brother, two years my elder.

Sam's never the one I have to worry about.

'Nobody's name is *really* Speedboat,' says Dirk. With that big mouth of his.

Dirk, the firstborn. A real bastard. I could tell you things about him.

'Ach, the boy's just lost his father,' says Ma. 'Let him be.'

Dirk sniffs loudly.

'Speedboat, of all the stupid…'

4

It makes me itch, a nice kind of itch, the kind you can't help scratching. Joe Speedboat. Well I'll be damned.

Weeks later, the world and I are both still flat on our backs and breathless, the world because of the heat, me because of the accident. And Ma's crying. From happiness this time, for a change.

'Oh, he's back again. Sweetheart, there you are.'

She burned a candle for me every day and actually thinks that helped. In class they think *they're* the ones who did it, with their praying. Even that hypocrite Quincy Hansen joined in on it…as though I'd ever be caught dead in *his* prayers. Not that I can get out of bed or anything. I couldn't if I tried. They've still got to run tests on my spinal column; at the moment, all I can move is my right arm.

'Just enough to choke the chicken,' says Dirk.

I can't talk yet either.

'Not a whole lot ever came out anyway,' says Sam.

He looks over at Dirk to see if he's laughing, but Dirk laughs only at his own jokes. He doesn't have much choice: no one else will.

'Boys!' my mother warns.

So this is how things stand: I, Frankie Hermans, one good arm attached to forty kilos of dead meat. I've been in better situations. But Ma's tickled pink; she'd have been thankful for one good ear – as long as it listened to her, of course.

I have to get out of this place. They're driving me nuts, hanging around my bed, grousing about business and the weather. Did I ask for this? I'm telling you.

I grew a year older in my sleep, they celebrated my birthday in the hospital. Ma tells me about the cake with fourteen candles that they scoffed around my bed. My sleep lasted about 220 days and, counting the first few weeks of rehab, I'm going home now for the first time in ten months.

It's the middle of June. The miracle of my resurrection – as Ma insists on calling it – puts a lot of pressure on life at home. I have to be fed, cleaned and pushed around. Thank you all very much, but the words just won't cross my lips.

One day my brothers take me to the fair, because Ma makes them. Sam pushes the wheelchair cart; the fresh air hugs me like an old friend. While I was gone the world seems to have changed. It looks scrubbed, as though the Pope were coming to visit or something. Sam pushes me down the street in a hurry, he doesn't want people stopping him to ask questions about me. I can hear the noise of the summer fair. The shrieks, the fast patter of the carnies, the ringing of the alarm bells when you hit the mark – the noise says it all. It says hooray for the fair.

Dirk's walking out in front of us. His back is ashamed to be here. He turns into Zonstraat and passes the Sun Café, with Sam and me bringing up the rear. The fair is fading. All I can hear now are the peaks and valleys of sound. Looks like we're not going to the fair. I turn my head to look at Sam, who's ramming me down the street at racetrack speed. At the edge of the village we get to the old Hoving place. That's where we stop. Dirk is already opening the garden gate. I haven't been out here for a long time.

'Gimme a hand, wouldya?!' Sam shouts.

The cart won't roll through the high grass full of burdock and poppies. Dirk comes back, the two of them wring the cart through Rinus Hoving's garden, the garden of the late Rinus Hoving. His farm is deserted, and as long as the heirs keep fighting about what to do with it that's the way it will stay. They pick me up, cart and all, and carry me in through the pantry door. The red floor tiles are covered in a carpet of dust. I can see footprints in it. They roll me through the kitchen and down the hall, then park me in front of the sliding glass doors to the sitting room.

'Put him over by the window,' Dirk says. 'So he's got something to look at.'

'Put him over by the window yourself.'

Sam is having his doubts. Dirk's not. Dirk doesn't have doubts; he's too dumb for that.

'We can't really do this,' Sam says.

'It's his own damn fault. If she thinks I'm taking him on the Tilt-a-Whirl, she can think again.'

'She', that's Ma. Not that Dirk has any respect for her, but she has a powerful instrument at her disposal: Pa's right hand. Sam's head moves into view.

'We'll be right back, Frankie. In an hour or so.'

Then they're gone.

This is just great, dropped in some dump like a bundle of dry twigs. At least you know what you can expect from them. I'd figured something like this, I was just waiting for the facts. Facts aren't nearly as bad as suspicions. The fact of the matter is that I find myself in a darkened house that's breathing down the back of my neck. And that my view consists of a windowsill covered in dead flies, spider webs and dust balls. My fears all have one eye open now, you can't fool them, they're wide awake. And there they are, shouting to beat the band. Critters! Child molesters! Things! In a word: panic. But how long can a person stay scared if nothing happens? It starts feeling kind of weird, and when nothing keeps on happening all you can do is laugh at yourself. But wait a minute, there, that really *was* a sound! I swear, I heard a door slam, something falling over... I turn my head, which takes so much effort that I groan like some retard. Like pushing over a tree with your forehead. And there, standing in the doorway...

'Hello,' says the figure.

A boy's voice. I stare into the light coming from the kitchen behind him, and all I can see is his silhouette in the doorway. He comes over. A boy, thank God it's just a boy. He walks around in front of me and takes a long, unembarrassed look. His gaze takes in the steel braces clamped to my feet, the cart's blue upholstery (genuine leatherette, my good man), the silver tubes and the wooden lever on my right, used to steer the front wheels and propel the back wheel by sheer force of the human arm. Bought 'to grow into', after a manner of speaking. It's a real peach, never left the garage except on Sundays, you know the spiel. They say I'll be able to move around in it myself someday, but for the time being I can't even knock a fly off my own forehead.

'Hello,' the boy says again. 'Can't you talk?'

A tanned face with clear eyes. Hair cut in a Prince Valiant fringe. He turns around and looks out the window. Hoving's garden: heads of red clover, stinging nettles and the lovely poppy, so pleased to be seen but so insulted when picked that she withers in your hand.

'They dumped you here, didn't they?' the boy says, his gaze fixed on Lomark.

The top of the Ferris wheel is sticking out above the houses. He nods.

'I've heard about you. You're a Hermans, from the wrecking yard. They say Mother Mary worked a blessing on you. It doesn't look like it to me, though, if you'll excuse my saying so. I mean, if this is a blessing, what's punishment look like? Right?'

He nods, like he's in full agreement with himself.

'My name's Joe Speedboat,' he says. 'I just moved here. We live on Achterom, you know where that is?'

Broad hands, stubby fingers. Broad feet, too, which he stands on like a samurai. That's something I happen to know about, samurai. About *seppuku*, too, the Way of Dying to preserve your honour, when you stick a short sword in your guts and pull it up, from bottom left to top right. You could tell how brave someone was from the length of the cut. But I'm digressing.

I can see what it is that pisses Dirk off. It radiates off him: he's completely unafraid. Joe Speedboat, planter of bombs, ruiner of slumbers – with your cut-off jeans and your nutty dried-out leather sandals. Where have you been so long?

'Wait a minute, I need to get something,' he says.

He leaves the viewfinder and I hear him going up the stairs somewhere in the house, then footsteps above my head. Is that where he has his workshop? For his bombs and things? Speedboat's Control Room? When he comes back down he's carrying a washing-machine timer and two Black Cat batteries. He sits down on the windowsill, frowns in concentration, and hooks up the poles of the batteries. Then he attaches a little metal rod to the clock and sets the timer to zero. Suddenly he looks up.

9

'We had problems while we were moving,' he says earnestly. 'An accident. That's when my father died.'

Then he goes back to what he was doing.

The first time Lomark heard of Joe and his family was when the Scania crashed through the ancestral gabled home of the Maandag family on Brugstraat. All the way up to its ass in the front room, where son Christof was sitting in front of the tube playing a video game. He never flinched. When he finally looked up the first thing he saw was a headlight poking like an angry eye through the whirl of dust and debris. Then it gradually dawned on him that there was a truck in his house. The only sound the whole time was the *toing-toing* of the video ball bouncing across the screen.

Hanging down over the grille of the Scania was the torso of a man, his arms dangling limply like a scarecrow fallen from heaven. The man's lower body was pinned inside the cab and he was dead, clear enough. But there was still movement inside: the door on the passenger side of the cab swung open slowly and the boy Christof saw climbing down was roughly his age, twelve or thirteen. He was wearing a gold lamé shirt, sandals and a pair of knickerbockers. Your parents would have to be slightly bonkers to dress you like that, but he just peered around the room matter-of-factly, the mortar swirling down onto his head and shoulders.

'Hello,' Christof said, the joystick still in his hand.

The other boy shook his head, as though something peculiar had occurred to him.

'Who are you?' was all Christof asked him then.

'My name's Joe,' the boy said. 'Joe Speedboat.'

*

And so he came like a meteorite into our village, with its river that floods its banks in winter, its permanent web along which gossip scuttles, and its rooster, the rooster in our coat of arms, the same rooster that chased a band of Vikings from Lomark's gates a thousand years ago or so while our ancestors were in the church praying, for Christ's sake. 'It was the cock that showed its pluck,' we say around here. Something that keeps something else at arm's length, that's our symbol. But Joe came roaring in with such force that nothing could have stopped him.

The accident had left him a partial orphan; the man hanging out the windshield of the truck was his father. His mother was lying unconscious in the cab, his little sister India was staring at the soles of her father's shoes. Christof and Joe looked at each other like creatures from different galaxies – Joe stranded in his spaceship, Christof holding out his hand to make the historic first contact. Here was something that would free him from the leaden immobility of this village, where the only thing that showed any pluck was the cock, that hateful animal you ran into everywhere: on the doors of the fire engines, above the entrance to the town hall and in bronze on the market square. The rooster that was pulled around on a float during Carnival parades, that crowed at you from decorative roofing tiles beside dozens of front doors and whose incarnation at the local *patisserie* was the 'Cocky' (a crumbly dog biscuit strewn with granola flakes). On sideboards, mantelpieces and windowsills you found glass roosters, ceramic roosters and stained-glass roosters; oil-painted roosters hung on the walls. When it comes to that cock, our creativity knows no bounds.

Joe looked around in amazement at this house into which Fate (read: faulty steersmanship aggravated by violating the speed limit in a residential zone) had tossed him. In the house where he'd grown up, the one they had traded in for the house in Lomark, there were no oil-painted portraits staring at you gravely from the walls, as though you'd stolen something. And of course you'd always stolen something, which meant those faces would always keep looking like that so that you didn't have to be afraid, just give them a friendly nod and say, 'Come, come, boys, a little smile wouldn't hurt.'

The chandelier was real nice too, he thought, as was the antique refreshment trolley bearing Egon Maandag's crystal decanters filled with whiskeys of provenances from Loch Lomond to Talisker. At Joe's place all they had were squat bottles of elderberry wine, deep purple and homemade with a water seal that bubbled and belched like a gastric patient. The wine was always either not quite ripe or just a tad past its prime. 'But the flavour is really quite special, isn't it, love?' (his mother speaking to his father, never the other way around). After which they would guzzle manfully, only to flush the rotgut down the toilet the very next day; the hangovers it produced resembled nothing so much as the near-death experiences of Russian rubbing-alcohol drinkers.

Later Joe would find out that he had landed in the salon of the Maandag clan, the most important family in Lomark, owners of the asphalt plant by the river. Egon Maandag employed twenty-five men at his factory, not to mention a housemaid and at times an au pair from yet another land beyond the dykes.

Joe just stood and stared around.

Later Christof said he did that in order not to have to see the dead man hanging from the windshield. When he finally took his eyes off Christof and his surroundings, he turned and looked at his father. He reached out his hand and laid it on the back of the man's blood-smeared head. He stroked his hair gently and said something Christof couldn't make out. His shoulders shook, then he walked over to the hole the truck had knocked in the front wall. Climbing over the rubble he stepped outside, into sunlight. He walked down Brugstraat to the winter dyke, climbed over it and made for the river. Heifers were gambolling in the washlands; wilted grass left behind by winter floods hung from the barbed wire like flaxen Viking beards. Joe reached the summer dyke and the ferryboat jetty behind. Once on board he climbed up onto the railing, his legs dangling over the water, and didn't even look up when Piet Honing came out of the pilothouse to collect his fare.

That Joe and Christof would become friends was as inevitable as fish on Friday. It started with that gleam in Christof's eye when he looked so greedily at the powder-covered boy who emerged from the moving van. Sunlight poured into the salon through the shattered wall behind Joe, filling the room with the hum of a spring day. Christof had never seen anything like it. The image of the boy against that flood of light filled him with a longing to cast off his old life.

But Christof wasn't like that, and never would be. He was too skittish for that, and too much a doubter. In his longing to be just like the boy from the truck there was also the kind of envy that makes your canines ache, the vampirish urge to suck the life right out of someone.

The accident with the moving van formed them. It reinforced the stoic in Joe, and brought out something oldish in Christof, something worrisome. If Joe talked about building an airplane, Christof would say, 'Shouldn't you fix your bike first?' If the monthly air-raid sirens went off atop the bank at the very moment Joe had finished knocking together equipment that allowed him to hijack the Sunday broadcast of the evangelical community – 'Radio God', as the locals call it – and replace it with speed metal played backwards, that for Christof was a signal that building jamming stations was a bad idea. For Joe it meant that it was twelve o'clock, time for lunch.

Joe celebrated our first meeting with a doozy of a bomb, that's how I see it. The very same evening, after we had met at Hoving's farm: *tout* Lomark, straight up in bed. It's a gift. Dogs bark, lights go on, people crowd together in the street. Joe's name is on everyone's lips. In bed I lie grinning from ear to ear.

A couple of men go out for a look-see. He's blown up an electrical substation. Now the fair has no juice, and a whole lot of houses don't either.

The moon licks at the bars of my bed. I exercise my arm.

I can move again. It's unbelievable, but I can go straight ahead and I can turn corners with my cart. I move it by pulling on that lever and then pushing it away. A model PTM: Progress Through Musclepower. Otherwise I'm as spastic as it gets, things have a way of flying through the air when I try to grab them, but in the space between spasms I can sometimes get things done. I have to practice a lot, though. For the last month I've been going to school again; there's nothing wrong with my head, even though I still can't talk. I have to pick up where I left off, though, which means I'm in the same class with Joe and Christof.

The hardest part is the brakes, especially when I'm rolling down off the dyke into the washlands past the Lange Nek: that goes way too fast. Up on the dyke, the things-aren't-what-they-used-to-be men watch me go. They're almost always on that bench, their bicycles leaning on kickstands beside them. They see everything, those woody old farmers, most of whom were around during World War II. I don't look back at them. I don't like them.

The firemen are filling their tank trucks at Bethlehem Deep, the flooded sandpit down by the asphalt plant. The men wear dark overalls and white T-shirts with big arms sticking out of them. I can hear them laughing at their firefighters' jokes all the way up here, because water carries a long way. One of the firemen sees me and waves. The simp.

Above my head the poplars are hissing, in the pastures to the right of the Lange Nek a group of about ten pygmy ponies have lost their way in the high grass. They drink dark-green water from the bathtub over by the barbed wire. They probably belong to Dirty Rinus. He's been fined before for animal neglect.

Then you've got Bethlehem Asphalt, Egon Maandag's plant. Bulldozers taking bites out of the stony hills in the yard. At night you can see the factory from way off, like an orange bubble of air; when there's serious roadworks going on, the place hums around the clock. They say Bethlehem Asphalt is the economic cork keeping Lomark afloat, and every family in the village gives it their firstborn son.

I'm sopping with sweat and my arm smarts, but I'm almost at the river now. I can see the pair of big willows on the other side. Piet Honing always says, 'The ferryboat is a continuation of the road by other means,' which he seems to think is funny. Now that I can't walk anymore, he lets me cross for free. Piet once said he did that because I've seen both death and life, but he didn't go on to explain. After that first time he's never asked Joe for a penny either.

Piet pulls up to the far shore, the apron scrapes across the concrete landing. Out on the river a party boat is cruising with the current, you can hear the music and the tinkle of glasses. Can a person be jealous of a riverboat for the way it rolls? Two foamy waves travel beside it at the bow, looking like they were painted on the hull. Upstream is Germany, where hot-air balloons are floating above the hills. Hot-air balloons are OK, everyone seems to agree on that. Did you know, for instance, that those weird things that float in and out of view when you stare at something are actually proteins on the surface of your eyeballs?

Honing lowers the gate, raises the apron and pulls back on the throttle. He moves away from the shore a little and then the whole shebang comes swinging this way again. The tattered Total flags flutter in the breeze.

Beyond the hills and hot-air balloons, night is falling. The party boat has disappeared around the bend, headed God only knows where. Ships like that always seem to float downstream, while barges go the other way, to Germany, dieseling hard against the current.

Piet ties up and comes ashore: 'So, little buddy…' He grabs my cart by the handles and pushes me on board. I don't like people pushing me, but oh well. He takes me over to the alcove where he stores the road salt and the brooms.

The evening is rolling up the day like a newspaper. I smell oil and water. We thud our way to the far side, where a car is flashing its lights. Over there darkness is falling from the willows on the cows below. Cows are silly, all they do is stand around, dreaming about nothing. No, give me horses; at least when they stand around they look like they're thinking about something, thinking real hard about some horsey problem, while cows look the way the sky looks at us: big and black and empty.

The way it swings and pounds, this ferry scares the daylights out of some folks. Sometimes the water comes washing over the deck, but there's nothing to worry about. The thing's been in operation since 1928, it's just old. And it was actually built for quiet waterways, not for the river with all its strange moods. Pa says, 'That thing's a public menace. It should have gone through the cutter at Hermans & Sons a long time ago.' As though he gives a shit about public safety, not if he can't earn anything off it. But Piet keeps his ship running, cost what it may, even if it's little more than a pilothouse and a sheet-metal plate just big enough for six cars.

If you ask Piet, he'll tell you that his cable ferry was motorized when inland vessels started getting faster and faster; it became too dangerous to cross by power of the current alone. Because that's what a cable ferry actually does. It's attached by cables to three old buoys upstream, what they call the *bochtakers*. The last buoy is nailed to the riverbed with a huge anchor. At the end of the sling is the ferryboat. The ferry sweeps across the water like the drive chain of a clock, the ones with metal pinecones at the bottom. By winching in one cable and letting the other one slide, the current brings the boat to the far shore; these days, though, Piet needs the engine to keep the river monsters from rolling right over him. Sometimes the ships run up against the cables between the buoys, and Piet has some damage. Then he's closed for business for the day while he makes repairs.

Piet comes out of the pilothouse. 'And a fine evening it is, buddy.'

I look up at him and a big blob of spit gushes from my mouth. I've got litres of that stuff in me. I could raise goldfish in it. A barge, loaded with mountains of sand, is bearing down on us.

'The old landing could use a little fixing up,' Piet sighs. 'Like back in the old days, with a nice little waiting room where you could order coffee and cake. When it was cold they all used to huddle around the stove till I got there. But the bridge and that highway put an end to that. Just look at it now. Wait, though, till those roads get too packed, then we'll show 'em who's got the fastest connection around here.'

Lately he seems a little sad. The barge cuts past us. Its deck hatches are wide open, piles of sand poke up out of the hold like crests on a dragon's back. A range of hills sailing up to Germany. No wonder this country's so flat, the way we export all our hills.

There's one cloud up in the sky, in the shape of a foot. Is anybody there, I wonder. Anybody there? You know what I mean?

J oe never told anyone his real name, not even Christof, who'd become his best friend by then. We knew his last name was really Ratzinger, but his first name was a secret.

Normally, when they give you a name, you don't know any different. It's your name and you don't go whining about it. In fact, you've got nothing to say about it: you are your name, your name is you, together the two of you are one; after you die, your name lives on for a while in a few people's heads, then it fades away on your gravestone and that's that. But that wasn't enough for Joe. We're talking about back before he lived in Lomark. With that real name of his, he knew, he could never become what he wanted to be. With a name like his you could never become something or someone else. For example, you might as well have some disease that kept you from leaving the house. It was a misunderstanding, he was born with the wrong name. So when he was about ten he decided to do something about that name, that name like a club foot. He was going to be called Speedboat. Where he came up with it I don't know, but Speedboat fit him to a tee. He didn't have a first name yet, but that didn't worry him; now that he had a last name, the first one would come of its own accord.

It didn't take long. One day, as he was walking past a scaf-folding, one of those ones with a long chute on it they use to dump rubble down into a container, Joe – who wasn't called that at that moment – got some dust in his eyes and stopped to rub at them. On the scaffolding was a radio all covered in grit and paint splatters, and at that moment, from that radio, his name appeared. Happy as a child spotting its mother in a crowd, he heard his own first name for the first time: Joe. In the song 'Hey Joe' by Jimi Hendrix: 'Hey Joe, where you going with that gun in your hand / Hey Joe, I said where you going with that gun in your hand / I'm going down to shoot my old lady / You know I caught her messing 'round with another man.'

Joe it was. Joe Speedboat. A name like that you could take with you into the world.

His vocation Joe found in the little front yard of the house on Achterom. It was in the early spring after their first winter in Lomark. I was still in the hospital recovering. Joe was raking dead leaves onto a pile; fresh, cold light poured down over the rotten remains of the seasons. From beneath the leaves brownish-yellow grass appeared, and translucent snail shells. Then, from up toward Westerveld there came a sound – a sound of something ripping, something that hurt. It grew fast, in waves. The young poplar in the yard shivered nervously. Joe clutched the rake to his chest and waited, in the classic pose of parks department employees everywhere.

Then he saw them: seven glistening Opel Mantas, black as the night, with exhaust pipes vomiting fire and smoke. At their wheels were boys with grim, inbred faces and hair on the palms of their hands. Cigarette smoke was sucked from rolled-down windows, left arms rested casually on the doors, and Joe looked on in amazement as the procession passed like slow thunder. He dropped the rake and lifted his hands to cover his ears. The mufflers gleamed like trumpets, the world seemed to shrivel in all-consuming noise as the boys punched the gas with clutches to the floor, just to let everyone know they were there, so that no one might doubt it, for if it doesn't reverberate, it doesn't exist.

It was Joe's first lesson in kinetics, in the beauty of motion, as driven by the internal combustion engine.

The autocade left a bubble of silence in its wake, and in that silence Joe heard his mother's voice at the open window: 'Assholes!'

Regina Ratzinger (anyone accidentally calling her 'Mrs Speedboat' was amiably but decidedly set aright) wore out her back each morning as housekeeper to the Family Tabak, and spent each afternoon knitting herself a case of bursitis in order to supply the whole village with woollen sweaters. Those sweaters were of excellent quality, a fact that ultimately turned against her; their indestructibility meant that, once the saturation point had been reached, she barely sold a one. The sharp spike in the success of her sweaters was also due in part to the finely detailed Lomark cocks she conjured up with fine thread on the breast of each one.

Their house was full of baskets of wool, and that drew moths. At strategic spots, therefore, she had hung bait, sticky strips of cardboard laced with the aroma of mothly sex. Visitors would sometimes hear Regina Ratzinger shouting, 'A moth! A moth!', followed by a resounding smack, India's cry of 'Oh, that's mean!' and Joe's chuckle.

Not knowing Joe's real name drove Christof crazy. One day he approached Regina Ratzinger.

'Mrs Speed— Sorry, Mrs Ratzinger, what's Joe's real name?'

'I'm not allowed to say, Christof.'

'But why not? I won't tell anyone…'

'Because Joe doesn't want me to. He believes that everyone should have one secret in life, however big or however little. Sorry, Stoffy, but I can't help you.'

Christof had been named after his grandfather, whose likeness appeared in one of the paintings in the house on Brugstraat; immortalized against a backdrop of classical ruins, he looked out on the parlour the truck had destroyed. At the moment Regina called him 'Stoffy', Christof decided he wanted to be called Johnny, Johnny Maandag. Which was a fine name, absolutely, as long as you didn't know that his real name was Christof and that he had changed it in imitation of Joe Speedboat.

The name never caught on. Joe was the only one who called him that, for a while, but no one else.

During the summer holidays Christof was an almost permanent guest at Joe's house, where a more permissive atmosphere prevailed. You would always see the two of them on the same bike, Christof standing on its baggage rack like an acrobat in a Korean circus act as they went to the Spar for a bottle of Dubro or to Snackbar Phoenix for a helping of chips. That, one day, was the way they happened to pass the ruined house on Brugstraat, still hidden behind a wall of scaffolding and black plastic sheeting. Later, after the house was rebuilt, Egon Maandag sold it, saying he had never had a good night's sleep there since the accident. He had a villa built on a high stretch of ground outside Lomark, where his feet would remain dry by high water. That day, however, he emerged from behind the plastic at the front door and looked in astonishment at his son perched on the baggage carrier.

'Hi!' Christof said.

'Hello, Christof,' his father said, and those, I believe, were the only words they exchanged that summer.

Joe and Christof ate a lot of chips. The girl behind the counter at Snackbar Phoenix had a cute face and a well-rounded physique.

'What will it be today, gentlemen?'

'One chips, extra large, with extra ketchup, mayo and onions. And two forks,' Christof said. 'By the way, do you have any idea why this place is called the Phoenix?'

The girl shook her head.

'It's a mythical bird that rises from its own ashes,' Christof said. 'Kind of weird that you don't know that.'

'Oh, well, sorry,' the girl said.

She looked around interestedly, as though suddenly seeing something that hadn't been there before.

'Is this where it was last seen or something,' she asked, 'I mean, that they named it that?'

'That's right,' Joe said earnestly, 'it was on this very spot that it had its nest.'

The chips fizzed in the boiling fat, at the window there droned a bluebottle that had seen better days. While the girl scooped the chips from the fat and shook them dry, Joe and Christof stared at the synchronized shaking of her glorious backside. It exerted an almost magnetic influence. She sprinkled salt on the chips and scooped them around, and Joe and Christof firmly instilled in themselves the sight of her phenomenal hams.

'One chips with ketchup, mayo and onions for Mr Christof,' she said.

'His name's Johnny,' Joe said. 'Could you do a little more mayo on that?'

After losing a year because of the accident, now I'm back in the third class with kids I barely know. And even though I'm the oldest, if you stood me up straight I'd also be the smallest.

On the first day of school, Verhoeven, our Dutch teacher, asked us what we'd done during our summer vacation.

'What about you, Joe?' he said when half the class had had its turn. 'What have you been up to for the last few weeks?'

'Waiting, sir.'

'Waiting for what?'

'For school to begin, sir.'

Finally I'm in a position to be around him all the time. But then, one morning, Joe asks Mr Beintema for permission to go to the bathroom. A little later, from somewhere in the building, comes a thundering explosion.

'Joe,' Christof murmurs.

The jerk had been sitting on the toilet, putting together a bomb. Half his hand blown off, a trail of blood from the cubicle all the way outside, and the principal running after him. Like a wounded rat Joe tries to escape, but the principal catches up with him halfway across the yard and starts swearing like a dozen drunken tinkers. Joe isn't really listening, though; he falls to the ground as though someone's pulled the rug out from under him. An ambulance arrives, there's a whole lot of fuss and we don't see Joe again for a while. That bomb-gone-wrong put him back a bit.

Gradually, the class gets used to having me around. I'm excused from oral exams, because every answer I try to give takes at least an hour and still no one can figure it out. All very tiresome.

Particularly tiresome is the fact that I still can't still piss on my own, and somehow it happens that Engel Eleveld comes to my rescue in that regard. Engel's a unique person. He's the kind of guy you don't notice for years, almost as though he's invisible, and then suddenly you *see* him and are hopelessly overtaken by a feeling of friendship.

It was Engel's own idea. I don't know how he found out about my specific need for assistance, but all assistance is welcome. We go to the loo together, he rolls down my pants and hangs my dick in the bedpan that I always carry in the side compartment of my cart. The first few times I feel like dying of mortification, not so much when he stuffs my hose into the reservoir, but when he rinses the urinal in the sink. Amazingly enough, no one gives Engel a hard time about being my piss partner, at least not that I hear about.

You may, of course, be wondering how that goes when it comes time to take a shit, whether Engel helps me do that too. No way! Shitting I do in the privacy of my own home. Ma helps me. I tolerate no one else behind my hole.

After the explosion the toilet door at school was hung back on its hinges and the janitor tells anyone who'll listen (no one, really, but he tells them anyway) that he's never seen anything like it. What I'd like to know is what Joe was actually planning to blow up. Or whom.

When Joe comes back – his hand bandaged, stitches in his

forehead – no one talks about it anymore. The whole thing seems to be dead and buried. Really weird, as though everyone would rather forget that Joe ever did something dumb. It's not something he wears well. For myself, it makes me realize how much I'd like to see him give the world a good going over; if there's anyone who could do that, it's him.

Joe's a little quiet at first, and Christof watches over him. When Joe removes the bandages, in class with everyone there, it's Christof who keeps the curious at a slight distance.

'Joe,' he says worriedly, 'isn't that kind of dangerous?'

'Danger is where you don't expect it,' mumbles Joe, and goes on unwinding the bandage.

Then he comes over to me and holds his hand in front of my face.

'See this, Frankie? This is what stupidity looks like.'

My stomach flips. His right hand is a kind of meat platter in yellow, green and pink, loosely bound together with something like three hundred stitches. His little finger and ring finger are gone completely.

'Jeeesus, Joe!' Engel Eleveld says in awe.

Heleen van Paridon gags, but somehow succeeds in keeping her lunch down.

'A little fresh air will do it wonders, you'll see,' says Joe.

'Were you the one who made those other bombs too?' asks Quincy Hansen, the turdhead who's in my class now all over again because he's flunked twice. I'd tell my secrets to a snake before I'd talk to Quincy Hansen.

'Hey, it wasn't me,' Joe says.

'Yes it was!' shouts Heleen van Paridon.

She's kind of aggressive, if you ask me.

'No it wasn't,' says Christof, with an air of sanctimony.

Damn right, never admit a thing. What follows is a kind of

quibble, with which Joe becomes bored pretty quickly. He gets up and walks away.

'Well then who was it? Huh?' Heleen shouts at his back. 'Frankie?'

Joe turns around and looks at me, then at Heleen.

'Frankie's got more up his sleeve than you might think,' he says.

Then he's gone, Christof right behind. They all look at me. I blow spit bubbles, they laugh. Go on, laugh, laughter is good for the soul.

I don't really take part in any of it. How could I? What I do do is make sure I keep moving all the time, on the roll and on the prowl: the one-armed bandit with his bionic vision. Nothing escapes him, his eyes are peeled. He devours the world the way an anaconda bolts down a piglet. If you can't join 'em, eat 'em; how's that grab you? Over hill and dale, come rain or shine, foaming at the mouth as he goes. Standing sentry in his war wagon, wearing his poncho when the weather's mean, a sou'wester when the storm wind tugs at your shutters, or a Hawaiian shirt in the burning sun. Fear not. The Eyes have it.

I see Joe and Christof heading for the river and crawl along after them like a snail. A grinding sound comes from the link where my hand-lever imparts energy to the front wheel. It's not like I'm tagging along after them, it's not like that. This is something more active. My limits are the limits of the paved, so I guess I should be thankful for the activities of Bethlehem Asphalt. Joe puts his tackle box on the back of the bike and Christof hops up onto the crossbar. They hang out on the shore down there all the time.

Today the thistles are going to fluff, farmers worry their hay and the gulls are having a wingding. Summer has turned juicy ripe. I can choose between two routes, to the left past the sandpit and through the cornfields to the river, or to the right along the Lange Nek and through the poplars to the ferry. I take a gamble and go left, along the bumpy road that passes the Hole of Bethlehem. That pit is where the factory takes all its sand. No one knows how deep it is, but the water there stays cold as ice even in the hottest of summers, if that tells you anything.

Back of the Hole is where it all happens, that's where they come from the village at dusk on their mopeds, to kiss and stuff. You see the evidence lying all around: empty bags of weed, butt-ends, conked-out lighters, condoms.

All this is underwater in winter, which is why the road is full of holes. In spring, when the water's gone, they fill the holes with rubble and ground bricks, but that never really makes it smooth.

Flocks of sparrows fly up from the corn as I pass by, groaning from the sharp pains in my arm and shoulder; you could compare my method of locomotion to a one-armed man pushing home a dead horse. I'm not whingeing or anything, that's just the way it is. Dirk just won't lube my cart, no matter how often Ma reminds him. He'd rather go off with his sub-zero friends so they can act out their dirty little fantasies. Torturing things and stuff. He's just no good. They already put him in a home once after he tied Roelie Tabak to a tree and stuck twigs in her. When he came back it had only got worse, but then on the sly. He's a sneak, never let him out of your sight.

The sun burns on the back of my neck. All around the sand-pit are signs saying HAZARDOUS TERRAIN – DANGER OF COLLAPSING SLOPES. Perched up on one of those poles is a hangman crow, a nasty monster with a croak like the hinges on an old barn door. Slopes collapsing is exactly what happened one fall night two years ago, when the road to the ferry landing just disappeared. Gone, like that. Seems the Bethlehem Asphalt sand extractors had extracted a little too long in one place, and the hole filled itself up with the sand around it. That's what usually happens when you dig a deep hole like that, the sand around it kind of starts to roll, looking for the deepest spot. They call it 'sloughing'. But the Hole of Bethlehem is so deep and hollow that there wasn't enough sand left for it to fill itself with, and everything in the surroundings started rolling, because it had to come from somewhere. A whole stretch of the riverside and the Lange Nek chunked into the water, with a whole bunch of trees in its wake. When you come by in the morning and find the whole road gone like that, you do a double-take. Gas and electrical mains lying around, lampposts fallen over. They say it's safe now, they've stopped sucking away so much sand in one place. If you're prepared to take their word for it.

The corn is high on both sides of the gravel path, the ears almost bursting from their husks. The poles around here are all askew; whatever you set right in summer goes crooked again in winter. The path's a metre and a half wide, corn shucks lisp *Pull, Frankie, pull!* and I yank till I almost drop. My arm's going to wear out too fast this way, and once it's worn out, where will that leave me? The corn waves its fingers to cheer me on. Frankie parting the waters to escape his enemies – the sea of green closes behind him... *Go, Frankie, go!* Cornfingers urge him on – *You're almost there!*

The slope of the summer dyke is broad and gradual. If Joe and Christof aren't on the other side, I'll have come all this way for nothing. I make it to the top; my arm's about ready to fall off. Down at the bottom is a little beach, its sand yellow as the fungus nail on Pa's big toe. Swans are floating in the calm of a breakwater. Out at the end of it are two bent backs with long antennae, sounding the water for signals: Joe and Christof.

I haven't been down this way for a long time, along the water, the dyke and the fields shiny with fat grass. The spots they've just mowed are pale as a newly shaved scalp. Hundreds of lapwings are sitting on the next jetty. Joe's got a bite, he pulls a glimmering fish from the water. Christof hops around him nervously.

In fact, I'm the one who should be Joe's friend. Christof isn't good for him, he's too careful. He holds Joe back, that's how I see it. He acts as a drag on Joe's velocity, and that's not right; Joe should be allowed to soup himself up till he flies. My accident happened too soon, it disturbed the natural order of things. It should be me sitting there beside him, not Christof.

The wind at my back wafts me a little coolness, I was almost sopping in my chair. Now Christof sees me, because he suddenly stops, nudges Joe and points. They figured they were all alone, and now there's something about them like they've been caught in the act. The lapwings all take off at once, skimming the river with sloppy wingbeats. I've heard people talk about how the British bombers used to fly above the river, heading to Germany to pound it all flat. There was ack-ack here along the shore, but nothing could put a dent in that total darkening of the sun.

A lot happened around here back then. Like the stuff with the Elevelds. They used to be one of the biggest families in Lomark. September 1944 was the first time their number came up. They were all in a kind of air-raid shelter under the walnuts at the landing when an Allied juggernaut, intended for the ack-ack on the far side, landed right on top of them. One bomb, twenty-two Elevelds killed at a go. The rest of the family went to Lomark, figuring they'd be safe there. One week later the bombs came raining down again, this time on Lomark, and the first direct hit bull's-eyed their roof. The children came up the steps carrying their own intestines: 'Daddy, look!' They died on the spot. Then there were only three Elevelds left. They moved to the city, where, in the final month of the war, they got caught in a German mortar attack. Two of them were killed. By the end of the war the only one still around was Hendrik Eleveld, whom they called 'Henk the Hat'. Henk the Hat's son, Willem, is Engel's father.

It's a weird story, if you ask me. Fate vs the Elevelds: 27–0. Anyway, when you see Engel you'd do well to think about that invisible queue behind him that's commemorated each year at the war memorial.

Joe and Christof are coming up the dyke toward me. I pull hard on the parking brake.

'He's following us around,' I hear Christof say.

'Hey, Frankie,' Joe says once they're in front of me. 'You come out here all by yourself?'

'Look,' Christof says, 'like a horse with all that foam on his lips.'

He laughs. Joe comes closer and takes my arm. With his left hand, because the right one is still a mess from that bomb.

'What's up, Frankie?'

Then his eyes open wide.

'Jesus Christ, feel this, would you?'

Christof feels my arm.

'He got concrete in there or something?' he asks.

Christof raises his eyebrows, which makes him look like an owl. The way they go on about it seems a little exaggerated to me; it's not *that* special. I'm turning a little red.

'He's blushing,' Christof says.

'You mind if I take a look?' Joe asks.

He rolls my sleeve up over my bicep and whistles quietly.

'What a monster.'

Christof gives him a strange look, he doesn't really understand things like that. In fact, until now I hadn't really noticed
how big that arm was getting.

'Especially with that body of his alongside it,' Christof says.

He's right; in the last few months all my growing seems
to have gone into that one arm, it looks like the arm of a full-
grown man with bumps and veins all over it. A humongous
arm, if I may say so myself. Joe starts laughing and calls out like
a ringmaster: 'Ladies and gentlemen, in-tro-ducing…Frank the
Ar-m!'

Frank the Arm! Yeah! Christof shrugs, the demise of his own
new name a bit too fresh in his memory. Sunlight glistens off
the frame of his glasses and he squints a little. Who does he
remind me of? I can't put my finger on it. Someone from a history book maybe, but I've been reading so many of them lately
that I can't think which one. I'll have to look it up.

'Anyway, I think he's following us around,' Christof says.

As if I'm not free to go wherever I like.

'He's free to go wherever he likes,' Joe says.

'You following us, Frankie?' Christof asks.

I shake my head hard.

'See?' Joe says. 'No problem. See you around, Frankie.'

They return to their fishing rods and don't look back. They
cast out and then sit there again motionless on the basalt. I'm
dying to know what they're talking about. Or are they just sitting there, looking out over the water and saying nothing?
Those are the kinds of things I want to know. It's lonely up here.

An animal helps against loneliness. Not all animals, though. Rabbits, for example, are worthless, they're no good to anyone, they're too dopey. Dogs really irritate me too. What I wanted was a jackdaw, one of those little crows with a silvery neck and milky-blue eyes. Jackdaws are nice, and the noises they make, more than any crow or a rook, sound like human speech. Especially in the evening, when a whole colony of them would land in the chestnuts along Bleiburg and babble to each other, until it grew dark and all you heard was the occasional ka! when one of them fell off its branch. Besides, jackdaws are fairly tidy birds. You see them beside a puddle in the pasture sometimes, bending over to let the water run down their backs and wings for as long as it takes to get clean.

I knew where a couple of them were. Each spring they nested in a group of half-dead trees down by the scour-hole, a pond left behind after the dyke there collapsed a long time ago. In the olden days a broken dyke used to be a huge disaster, with people drowning by bunches. The water would come roaring in and scour out a deep hole at the spot where the dyke had collapsed. When the dyke was rebuilt it had to cut around a hole like that, which is why some of the old ones have such sharp bends in them.

The jackdaws liked to build their nests in the cracks and hollows of the trees around the pond, and late one Wednesday afternoon I got Sam to understand that I wanted him to pull a fledgling out of the nest for me.

'OK,' Sam said.

He walked behind me with one hand on the cart, talking non-stop about Sam-like idiocies. Sometimes I think he's got brain damage.

I looked out over the washlands. The river water had retreated behind the summer dykes. The trees out this way had dark rings around the trunk that showed how high the water had come that winter. Circling above them I could see little black dots. I was kind of excited. Another reason I wanted a jackdaw is because they're faithful; a jackdaw couple stays together forever, and when you've had a jackdaw from the time it was little it becomes attached to you in the same way. But you have to catch them young.

'You really expect me to go down in there?' Sam said once we were at the trees.

He muttered about for a bit, but finally clambered down the side of the dyke on hands and knees. Close to a tree with low branches he stopped and looked up, until he saw a jackdaw entering its nest. Then he started climbing. The birds flew nervously around the branches, in the perfect knowledge that this spelled bad news. I felt cold; winter was still floating between the warmer layers of spring air. It was starting to grow dark and you had to look hard to pick out objects in the distance. The trees around the scour-hole looked poisoned, as good as dead; the bark on some of them had started slipping off, leaving them cold and naked. Sam had reached a branch about a third of the way up and was still climbing clumsily. When they passed out the smarts and agility, he definitely wasn't standing at the front of the queue. In fact, he has only one real trait, which is that he's quite kind…that is, if kindness is really a trait and not just the absence of that brand of cruelty that keeps people like Dirk up and running.

Sam was only an arm's length below the nest when he suddenly stopped moving. I squinted, but couldn't make out what was wrong. After a while he started shouting, shouts that had lots of fuckingsonofabitches in them. He was panicking. It was an awfully bad place to start panicking. Situations like this made me furious. There he was, hanging motionless halfway between heaven and earth, and here I was, nailed to the road: all I could do was roll myself back to the village for help and hope that he could stick it out up there till I got back. I went as fast as I could. Till I was a long way off I could still hear the alarmed cries of the jackdaws circling around poor Sam.

I took the route into the village that went down Achterom. Joe's house was the first one in the street. The lights were on; in fact, the place was lit up like a greenhouse. I pounded on the door as hard as I could until India opened it. It was clear that she was surprised to see me. I'd never had much of a chance to take a real look at her before, but now that I did I could see that, young as she was, she was pretty good-looking. What I saw above all was that, at a certain age, she would be pretty in a very special way, and that until that day men would look at her impatiently, the way a farmer in spring eyes the tender green of his crops poking above the soil. India wasn't built like her brother, she was a lot more slender, but she had those same limpid eyes.

'What can I do for you?' she asked at last.

I gulped back the thick slime that had collected in my mouth during the dash for the village and raised my head.

'UH-UH-ZZZZJOOOOO,' I brayed.

'Joe?' she asked. 'You want to talk to Joe?'

'UH-YAAEEAAAH.'

I sounded like Chewbacca, that hairball from *Star Wars*. India went into the house, leaving the door open behind her. It was as though they were smelting ore in there, so hot and bright it was inside. The house glowed like the electric coil heater in our bathroom. 'Close the door!' someone shouted, probably the one who paid the electric bills.

'Joe! There's someone here for you!' India shouted.

Her parents had named her 'India' because that was where she was conceived, Joe told me once. Her middle name was Lakshmi. That was a goddess the Hindus said brought happiness and wisdom. I didn't know anything about Hindus, only about samurais and a couple of things along those lines. Joe's parents got married in India, he said, because they had a spiritual bond with that country. During the wedding ceremony they'd both had screaming dysentery. As a cloud of lotus blossoms descended on them, the diarrhoea was running down their legs. During the sitar concert for the bride and groom Regina Ratzinger had stayed in the toilet, emptying her bowels and weeping.

I heard Joe come thundering down the steps. Then he was standing before me, looking incredibly cheerful.

'Frankie, what's up?'

I looked up at him in silence.

'OK, what's going on, and how are you going to let me know?'

I pointed my arm wildly toward the dyke and gestured for him to come with me.

Lassie the Wonder Dog.

'Just let me get my shoes,' Joe said.

Joe pushed me. His hands seemed to be bursting with energy. It was the hour when everything turns blue, metallic blue, when all the colour drains from things and leaves them blue and hard and dark before they slowly sink into blackness.

'Is it far from here?' Joe asked.

I pointed ahead. Joe started talking about the wonders of modern physics, a subject he was wild about in those days. He had a gift for monologue, Joe did.

Suddenly, when we were about halfway there, he stopped and said, 'What's this?' He tapped his finger against the protective tube where I kept my telescope. It was a gift from Ma; she had realized early on that *looking* at things could help me shove aside depressing thoughts about my handicaps. The telescope hung at the side of my cart and was part of my expanding armoury. Joe unscrewed the cap and the telescope slid into his hand.

'Wow,' he said, raising the spyglass to his left eye.

I knew he could easily see the far side of the river and houses beyond the dyke there. It was a jewel of a telescope, a Kowa 823 with a 20–60 zoom and a 32x wide-angle lens.

'So that's what you do, huh? You keep an eye on us,' he said as he lowered it. 'But what nobody knows is what's really going on inside your head.'

He aimed the telescope at me like a pointer. My face flushed in embarrassment; the looker had been seen – I, who had thought I was invisible because no one paid attention to me for more than thirty seconds, had not escaped his gaze. Gratitude welled up in my throat – I was being seen, seen by the only person in the world who I cared to be seen by…

'Hey, it's OK, man.'

Could I help it? I was touched.

I gestured that we had to get going, for all I knew Sam might have fallen out of the tree while we were standing there. But when we got to the scour-hole he was nowhere in sight. I searched the ground beneath the trees in a panic, but he wasn't lying there, groaning with his back broken or his leg bent double. Calm seemed to have returned to the jackdaw community. Maybe Sam had made it down on his own and walked home across the fields. And now I still didn't have my jackdaw.

Joe just stood there beside me, with no idea what was going on. I tugged on his sleeve and he bent over to me.

'What are we supposed to do now?'

Using my good hand, I did my best to imitate the flapping of wings – it could just as easily have been taken for the clawing of an excavator or a hungry Pacman – and pointed to the trees. Joe looked at the birds flying back and forth, and at the sky drawing to a close behind them, then said, 'Am I right in thinking that you want a little crow?'

I grinned like a chimp.

'And you want me to get one out of a nest for you, is that what we're doing here?'

He shook his head in bemusement, but then slid down the side of the scour-hole with no further ado, climbed into a tree as nimbly as a ninja and was back in no time. In his hand was a huddled fledgling. The little bird had nervous, flashing eyes and a flat, broad beak. Pin-feathers stuck out here and there from its blue and reddish skin, between them there was a kind of greasy down. It was the ugliest thing I'd seen in a while.

'Is this what you're after?' Joe asked in disbelief.

He laid the little creature on my lap and I carefully cupped my hand around it.

'Be careful with that bone cruncher of yours.'

The jackdaw was warm and a little sticky; despite its tininess it felt like one huge pounding heart, throbbing away in the palm of my hand.

'I guess so,' Joe said with a shrug. 'I guess everyone needs something to pet.'

Grabbing the handles of the cart, he wheeled me around in the direction of Lomark. I shielded the little jackdaw carefully with my hand. He was to become my Eyes in the Sky and would go by the name of Wednesday, for the day I found him. A gentle rain started falling. I was very happy.

When I turned fifteen I let my parents know that I wanted to move into the garden house at the back of our yard. I could already do some things for myself by then, and heating up a can of hot dogs wouldn't present much of a problem. Ma was against it; Pa insulated the place and installed a gas fire, a little kitchen and a toilet. Above the door he nailed a horseshoe for good luck. After that my parents became my neighbours across the way, I showered at their place and sometimes watched TV there. Wednesday occupied a cage at the side of the house, and it was his custom during the day to ride around on my shoulder like a pirate's parrot. He had already learned to fly, he would sometimes be gone for half an hour at a time, but he always came back when I whistled.

It was there in that little house of mine that I started writing everything down. And I do mean everything. Some people find it hard to believe that I make an almost literal reproduction of this life on paper. To look at my diaries is to see time – here is what 365 days look like, this is ten times 365 days, or fifteen, or twenty. It's almost too big to see over, it's a mountain growing backwards into the past. And it's all in there – at least, if it happened when I was around or if someone told me about it. If you came by today, for example, I'd write that down. Something along the lines of: So-and-so came by, around that time and on this day. And if there was something about you that struck me, if you had weird ears or a pretty nose, I'd write that down too, and what you came here to do and how you did it. But other things as well, about how the autumn rain, for example, rinses the blond from our hair, letting the dark winter hair appear beneath, and about the river that runs through our lives the way the bloodstream runs through our bodies.

When I write I often think about the great samurai Miyamoto Musashi, who said that the samurai walks a twofold path: the way of the sword and that of the brush – the pen, in other words. The Way of the Sword is a little tough for me, so all that leaves me is the pen. I got that from *The Book of Five Rings*, *Go Rin No Sho*, which I found in the library and read to a tatter. I never brought it back.

Musashi is Kensei, the Sword Saint, who never lost a single fight in his life. His full name was Shinmen Musashi No Kami Fujiwara No Genshin, just plain Musashi to his friends. He was born in Japan in 1584 and slew his first opponent at the age of thirteen. Many fights followed, and he never lost a one of them. He was a legend in his own time, but said that he only began to grasp the tenets of strategy around the age of fifty. *The Book of Five Rings* is about how to fight like him, but it's also full of good advice, even if you're not much of a swordsman.

With the force of strategy I practiced many arts and skills –
all of them without a teacher. In writing this book I did not
make use of the teachings of Buddha or of Confucius, nor did I
consult the old chronicles of war or books of martial arts.
I took my brush in hand to explain the true spirit of this Ichi
School, as reflected in the Way of Heaven and Kwannon. It is
now the middle of the night, on the tenth day of the tenth
month: the hour of the tiger.

A few weeks after Musashi had committed his lessons to paper, he died.

Particularly useful to me has been the Strategic View, which teaches you to see things better. Musashi writes: 'Your view must be both broad and open. This is the twofold view that is called "Perceiving and Seeing". Perceiving is strong, seeing is weak. In Strategy, it is important to see things that are far away as though they were near, and to look at the things that are near from a distance.'

Isn't that something!?

I started on my diaries as a sort of retirement fund. I figured: if I write down exactly what happens, people will come to me later and ask, 'Frankie, what happened on 27 October in the year such-and-such? Would you look if you can find anything about me on that day?' And because I'd always kept track of everything and filed it away neatly, I'd be able to fetch the book they needed and find it right away. Here, 27 October, a couple of years ago, a howling southwest storm that caused a lot of damage. Trees were felled, car alarms were blaring all over the place. With spaniel-like fidelity, the club treasurer went out to rechalk the lines on the football field and was almost lifted off the ground. A white cloud came blowing from the chalk cart and mussed the lines. I admired the treasurer's dogged determination. One hour later, all outdoor sporting events all over the country were cancelled.

The hard wind turned the people out on the street into children, all wild and excited, with glistening eyes and not a worry in the world. That's what struck me most, that they didn't seem to worry about a thing, even when tiles came whipping off the roofs and their cars were damaged by flying branches. That day the ferry stuck to its moorings. The river writhed and tossed up wild, gray waves.

On 28 October, the storm was over. Then came the chainsaws.

And after I showed you that particular entry, I would take my notepad and write: *Cash please.*

But people don't care about things like that. They're not interested in what really happened. They'd rather stick to their own fairytales and nightmares, and there's no demand for the stories of Frank the Arm. They'll remain on the shelf until the day someone comes along to write the history of Lomark and recognizes them as a treasure trove that sheds a little light on the years behind us. Only then will my work be judged at its true value. Until then it's just a pile of old news at the back of a shed.

My diaries are lined up in bookcases against the back wall. I write every day. Historians and archaeologists dig things up from the depths of the past; I go around picking up the same things in the present. You could call what I do 'horizontal history'. Historians look for things that are long past, that's why they have to dig so deep: I call that 'vertical history'. The comparison came to me one day during geography class, when we were talking about strip mining and underground mining. With strip mining, you don't have to dig; the coal is close to the surface, all you really have to do is scrape it off the earth. But with underground mining you really have to go to great depths, which is why they dig tunnels into the earth.

It seemed like a useful metaphor to me.

To a certain extent, I make the historian's work unnecessary. Should they ever find my diaries, they'll take from them whatever they need, embellish on it a little and call it their own. Fancy-talking pickpockets is all they are, really, just like novelists. But what do I care as long as someday people know how it really went, all the things about Joe? The things I know, not the stuff Christof and his buddies try to claim. That's not the truth: that's lies and folklore.

Interstitial events rarely affect us directly here in Lomark. Sometimes, for example when the price of oil goes up, we know something's going on in the Middle East, and when a layer of red dust covers the cars after a rain it means there's probably been a storm in the Sahara; otherwise, most things in the world pass us right by. But when Lomark gets a new dentist, that pretty much has to be a direct result of global upheaval. In fact, we owe his arrival directly to the speech given by South Africa's President Frederik Willem de Klerk on 2 February, 1990. That was the day De Klerk lifted the ban on the African National Congress. He also announced the release of Nelson Mandela, the leader and symbol of the struggle against apartheid. 'He's a man with a vision as wide as God's eye,' Mandela's supporters say, and they put him on a par with the Great Soul of India.

In 1990 Mandela walked out the prison gates, and a few hours later he was giving his first speech in twenty-seven years. An amusing detail is that he forgot his reading glasses in his cell, and had to make do with a pair he borrowed from his wife. Three years later Mandela and De Klerk shared the Nobel Peace Prize, and in 1994 Mandela succeeded De Klerk as president of South Africa.

The country's turnaround brought huge social tensions, and

rivalry for both power and resources. Julius Jakob Eilander, dentist, and his wife Kathleen Swarth-Eilander were fourth-generation Afrikaners. They watched as their neighbours raised the walls around their villas and installed alarm systems so sensitive that a falling leaf or a rustling lizard made the sirens scream. The Eilanders didn't wait to see the country transformed. They packed and left for Europe, back to *die ou Holland*' their ancestors had left behind in the nineteenth century.

In January of 1993 they arrived at Schiphol Airport. After a few weeks with distant relatives and a few months in a holiday cottage amid pine trees and mobile homes, Julius Eilander took over the practice of Lomark's only dentist, a man who had been rigging our mouths with fillings, crowns and bridges for as long as anyone could remember.

Eilander's office is on the first floor of the building people here call the 'the White House', but which the plaque on the façade calls 'Quatres Bras'. And Julius and Kathleen have a daughter, Picolien Jane: P.J. for short. After Joe and India, she's the third exotic import at our school.

We can't believe our eyes. She wears a crown of boisterous blond curls that fall dazzlingly to her shoulders. All I can think of are oceans and foam, my diaries are full of her. Her skin is pale, her face broad, with slightly sloping blue eyes the likes of which I've never seen. Between classes the girls throng around her, running their hands over the corkscrew curls that bounce back like elastic when you tug at them. The girls all want to be P.J.'s friend. The way she talks gives everyone a thrill. Afrikaans, so close yet still so mysterious, makes you swing back and forth between hilarity and the chill that lovely language brings.

She comes, we are told, from Durban. A name that will become as magical as Nineveh or Isfahan. The sky over Durban is crisp, the salt on your skin tastes like liquorice. I think about P.J. walking through Durban; in my diary, the cockatoo cries and the monkey fiddles with his nuts. The sky there is definitely not like our own; P.J.'s eyes reflect horizons beyond ours, and secrets that truly signify something, not the fainthearted ruses we bore ourselves with. Real secrets, ones that have more to do with light than with the darkness in which we brood on festering sins with no hope of absolution, because the priest is deaf and can't hear our whispered confessions. P.J. was born of a fusion of light, her skin is as pale as potato feelers in the cellar, she seems transparent, but her hair is all flaming wheat…

There is a clear boom in presentations on South Africa.

She says, '*Wat kyk jullie so vir my?*' and that just has to be something special, for otherwise why would it make us all melt?

While our parents sit flinching in pain and fear beneath her father's lamp, as he wrenches, pounds and drills away in their mouths, we sit breathless in the light of P.J.'s countenance. Come on, say something else, make us shiver, don't hold out on us.

It was in those days that Joe first had his hair buzzed. He sat on an old engine block in the garage behind his house while Christof ran the clippers in swathes across his scalp. The thick hair floated to the ground, leaving only a shadow of itself with pale scars shining through. Now, with those slightly slanted eyes of his, he looked completely like a nomadic horseman of the steppes, an Uighur or a Hun: Joe the Hun on his tireless Mongol pony, a slab of raw meat tucked under the saddle. People sometimes asked him whether a Negro had ever played an active role in his family, or an Asian perhaps, for Joe's features were a confusing convergence of specific racial traits. Joe was all things to all men, but what I saw most of all in that strange face of his was a horseman of the steppes.

The duo Joe & Christof was expanded to include Engel Eleveld, my endearing piss mate. It started the day Joe and Engel went fishing together in a scour-hole. Joe caught a pike; there are lots of them in those pools. Engel said his father had told him that you could see Our Lord's suffering in the head of the pike. The fish's skull contains bones in the shape of a hammer, nails and a cross. They tore open the skull but couldn't find anything like that. Joe and Engel were friends ever after.

As I said earlier, Engel was one of those people you might not notice for years on end, until suddenly you saw him with a kind of light all around. That's how it was with Engel and the fairer sex as well. He never took part in the games of kissing tag, never passed love letters in class. Instead he drew aerodynamic wonders in his hardcover notebook, and made casual discoveries that would have knocked the world for a loop if only he hadn't forgotten them right away. One day Heleen van Paridon and Janna Griffioen both fell in love with him. For no apparent reason. That same week they were joined by Harriët Galama (breasts) and Ineke de Boer (even bigger breasts). After that, things took off. Former cavaliers lost both their lustre and the struggle for attention, two or three other girls also fell in love with Engel, and so, out of the blue and without having done a thing to earn it, he became the uncontested blue-ribbon stud of the schoolyard. His pockets bulged with folded scraps of paper on which shaky fingers had embossed red hearts.

To me Engel seemed as clear and spontaneous as water. Musashi, in his essay on 'Water' in *Go Rin No Sho*, once said something about that: 'With water as its basis, the spirit becomes like water. Water assumes the shape of the vessel; sometimes it is flowing, sometimes it is like a roaring sea.'

And Engel was, I have to admit, stupendous in his new role as Casanova. He dealt out tokens of attention with a light hand, conjured up shy smiles on their faces, but it interested him too little to really do much about it.

Like Joe, he had become fascinated early on by natural scientific phenomena. At home one day, having opened the medicine cabinet in the bathroom too brusquely, a bottle of mouthwash, a strip of vitamin pills and an old toothbrush fell to the floor; though up to his knees in an explosion of glass and glycerine, Engel noticed that the bottle, the strip and the toothbrush all hit the tiles at the same moment, despite their differing weights.

'Newton,' was all Joe said when Engel told him of his discovery.

'Oh,' Engel said, 'too bad. I really thought…'

'Listen, forget Newton. The guy wore a wig. Goodyear's our man.'

No one knew what he was talking about.

'Charles Goodyear,' Joe said, 'was the first person to vulcanize rubber. It was a revolution. Copernicus made the world round, Goodyear made it drivable. Back then rubber was a real problem, it got too soft when it was hot and hard as a rock when it was cold. There wasn't much they could do with it, but Goodyear was nuts about it, about the idea of rubber. He experimented for years but couldn't get it right. Until one day he mixed sulphur with the rubber and accidentally spilled some on a hot stove. Then it happened: it got hard, it vulcanized. That's what they'd all been waiting for, that was the start of the whole thing, after that rubber made the world go round. On rubber tyres! But it didn't do Goodyear much good, he couldn't even defend his patent. He died without a penny. Martyrs, that's what they are, they give their lives for a cause.'

That made us feel sad and a little quiet, the same way you feel when you hear about jazz musicians whose playing was out of this world but who never got a cent from royalties. You wished it could have been their own stupid fault, just so you wouldn't have to feel like that.

On those afternoons, when they were all sitting around back in Joe's garage, India would roll me out to them. India was good to me. Ever since the day I came by to ask Joe help me get Sam down out of the tree, she seemed to have developed a fondness for me. When I would come down Achterom on one of those vacant afternoons and see their bikes standing out in front, I'd pound on the door with the flat of my hand till she opened up. She'd roll me out back with a kind of breezy helpfulness and park me in between Joe, Christof and Engel. The garage was always full. There was only one chair, for Engel. In any case, he was the only one I ever saw sit in it. He probably wanted to keep his duds clean; I never met anyone else who wore tailored suits at the age of sixteen. Joe would sit on the workbench, Christof on the engine block. That garage was the smithy of their plans. In that smoke-brown shack that smelled of welding rods and burnt oil they dismantled the world, in order to put it back together as they saw fit.

'But rubber tyres won't do you much good if the roads are rotten,' Joe said. 'You need roads: asphalt roads, not the kind of sandy paths and broken stone they had back then. Those were bad for cars, and everyone you passed choked on your dust. Which brings us to Rimini and Girardeau.'

Joe looked at Christof, who was twiddling his fingers absent-mindedly.

'It's also the story behind Bethlehem Asphalt, Christof. Your people owe it all to them. The engineers, ah yes!'

He made a clacking sound with his tongue. Engel nodded to him to go on.

'It was easy as pie, really. Rimini and Girardeau came up with the idea of taking all the rocks out of the road and filling the potholes. After a steamroller smoothed the whole thing out, men with huge watering cans would sprinkle boiling tar all over the road. A thin layer of sand over that, let it dry for a couple of days, and you have the first highway.'

'You forgot the internal combustion engine,' Christof said. 'That seems more important to me than rubber and roads.'

'Ooof,' Joe said, as though someone had punched him in the stomach. 'That's a different story altogether. Horse and wagon, steam turbine, internal combustion engine. Here's how I see it: you've got four elements, OK? That's what man had to tame: fire, water, earth and air…'

That caught my attention right away: those were also the names of the first four chapters of Musashi's book: 'Earth', 'Water', 'Fire' and 'Wind'. (The last chapter consists of only one page: 'The Void'.)

'Fire is the first element,' Joe said. 'Fire brought light into the darkness of prehistory.'

He waved his hand over his shoulder, as though prehistory were back behind the hardboard dividing wall with the shapes of tools outlined on it in marking pen, the way traffic and murder victims are outlined in chalk. You never saw the tools themselves hanging there; in the workshop behind Joe's house, the tools went their own way.

'Then you've got fire, which is the start of civilization. After that comes water, important for farmers, water is. Irrigation means greater productivity and prosperity for many. Then earth: soil for the farmer, roads for the merchant. From the road comes the wheel. The merchant and the soldier are the ones who profit most by the wheel, and each wheel is a little cog in the big gearbox of the Earth. After a manner of speaking. Together, the two things form a mechanism. The wheel leads to the combustion engine, which goes along with the wheel. The combustion engine sets the wheel in motion, the wheel makes the world go round. That's three.'

I thought about my own form of propulsion, which I owed to wheel, rubber and asphalt. I, half man, half vehicle, saw myself for a moment as a tiny link in Joe's view of world history; my wheels rolled across the surface of the earth and contributed to making the world go round.

'OK,' Joe said. 'So air was the final element they had to force their way into.' The airplane was the crowbar they needed. In the late nineteenth century, the first person to really fly was an engineer too: Otto Lilienthal. He just kept picking himself up and dusting himself off, until finally he flew with a pair of wings on his back that he'd copied from the birds. That was the mistake they all made, every single person who tried to fly; imitating the birds is ridiculous of course – in proportion to its body, a bird's wing muscles are so huge that you could never reproduce that with your arms, no matter how strong you were. That mistake in their thinking kept people on the ground much longer than necessary. But Otto flew fifteen metres, which is incredible! Within a couple of years the first zeppelin was floating in the sky, silent and beautiful, but also a flying bomb. No, the real potential lay in the marriage of the combustion engine with a pair of wings. The first time the two kissed was in America, when one of the Wright Brothers flew thirty-six metres: more than twice as far as Lilienthal – a revolution of *twenty-one* metres! After that it was wide open; aviators started popping up everywhere, breaking one record after another. A one-kilometre flight above Paris – world news! Crossing the Channel in a monoplane – England went bonkers. Anthony Fokker flying above Haarlem – the end of days!

When he got excited like that, Joe seemed more and more like some nutty sorcerer's apprentice.

'It's weird to think that, at the same time atomic science was being developed, planes didn't amount to much more than a little bamboo, ash wood and canvas.'

'No, that's normal,' said Engel, lighting a gold-rimmed cigarette. 'The mind always has a head start on the invention. An idea is weightless; it floats out in front of matter. We can think up all kinds of things, but try carrying them out. That's the bitch.'

'Engineers are patient, though,' Joe said solemnly.

'Did you guys know that P.J.'s mother is a nudist?' Christof broke the train of thought.

'P.J.?' Joe asked.

'Picolien Jane,' Engel said. 'New girl? Blond pin-curls? South Africa?'

Joe shrugged. Christof hopped up onto the engine block.

'You mean you've never seen her? I don't believe you!'

'I probably have,' Joe said, just to calm him down.

How did we find out that P.J.'s mother, Kathleen Eilander, was a nudist? Perhaps it was the postman who delivered *Athena*, the club magazine of the naturists' association of the same name, to a 'Mrs K. Eilander-Swarth' every three months? Or was it a barge captain from Lomark who claimed to have seen her naked on one of the beaches between the breakwaters? Or then again maybe it was only a rumour, a bit of gossip congealing into such solid factuality that one day Kathleen Eilander felt the irresistible and hitherto unknown urge to go down to the river, take off all her clothes and go skinny-dipping. However it happened, we knew. Never in our lives had we seen a nudist. But the term smacked of *very serious* nudity indeed, and of things for which we had been waiting for a long time.

Engel looked at me. His eyes were the same colour as the ink in my favourite fountain pen. He knew how much I liked those afternoons when Joe climbed onto his soapbox and pronounced theories with their feet on the ground and their head in the clouds.

Bright and early each morning, Christof claimed, Mrs Eilander jogged down to the river to go bathing. He also said she walked around naked in the garden behind the White House. Her legs, Christof said, were long and kind of strange, but legs hardly played the leading role in my fantasies about the nudist. No, I saw other things. Things that took my breath away. She was a mother, and therefore an old lady, but after hearing the news about her nudism I noticed she was transformed into a sexual creature with a secret to which we just happened to be privy, and which filled our heads with burning questions and our guts with melted sugar.

Reluctantly, Joe descended to the subject of Mrs Eilander's legs.

'Can we get a look?' he asked, but Christof shook his head.

'Wall around the garden,' he said, 'and it's still dark when she goes swimming.'

Joe toyed pensively with a screwdriver, twirling it in the fingers of his good hand like a majorette. Wednesday was dozing on my shoulder. The wrinkly membranes were pulled down over his beady eyes. He had become a beauty of a bird, a jaunty, proud creature trained to come back whenever I whistled. Joe had made a lucky pick, I don't think a more handsome jackdaw could be found. The feathers at his neck and on the back of his head were silvery-gray as graphite; when he walked the bobbing of his head lent him a certain consequence. It's not like with starlings, birds that seem to radiate a sort of lowliness. Starlings fly in spectacular eddies and shimmering spirals, that's true enough, but in such huge numbers that you can't help but be reminded of big cities where people hate and tread on each other, but strangely enough can't get along without the others.

Wednesday possessed an inner nobility that placed him above inferior garbage eaters like starlings and gulls. He would be able to see Mrs Eilander walking naked in her garden, but jackdaws weren't interested in things like that. I often tried to put myself in Wednesday's place as he flew over Lomark, to imagine what the world looked like from a bird's-eye view. It was my dream of omniscience – nothing would ever be hidden from me again, I would be able to write the History of Everything.

We all looked at Joe, waiting to hear his thoughts. Joe looked at Wednesday as the screwdriver propellered faster and faster through his fingers. It was amazing how fast he could do that. When the screwdriver fell at last and all four of us, wakened from the spell, looked at the concrete floor where it had landed with a clear tinkle, Joe raised his eyebrows.

'It's actually quite simple,' he said. 'If we want to see her naked, we'll need our own plane.'

The airplane was the crowbar that man needed to force his way into the air, the final element; that's what Joe had said that afternoon in the garage. But it wasn't until he came up with the idea of building his own plane that I realized what he meant; the plane would be the crowbar with which we would part the heavens between Mrs Eilander's legs. The plane would allow us a view of that *terra incognita*, and Joe was the engineer who would make it happen.

I watched the airplane grow, starting with the eighteen-inch moped wheels we found at the junkyard right up to and including the fine, varnished propeller Joe wangled from a nearby airfield.

They started work on the high-wing plane in a shed at the edge of the factory grounds, amid black mountains of broken asphalt scraped from old roads and dumped there for reuse. The big grinding machine had broken down years ago. Now it stood in slow collapse between chunks of unprocessed asphalt on one side and the pointy hills of a finer structure that it had spit out on the other.

In the mineral world of the asphalt plant, bulldozers trundled back and forth between piles of blue porphyry, red Scottish granite, bluish quartzite and sands of many varieties. The ground stone came in by ship from German mills along the

Upper Rhine. A sharp eye might find among it pieces of mammoth bone and tusk, and the occasional fossilized shark's tooth. Christof had a sharp eye. Pointing at the piles of sand and gravel, he would speak of himself as the curator of a ragtag collection of prehistory, what he called the 'Maandag Museum'. And Christof was the boss's son, so no one interfered; the three of them could do whatever they liked, as long as they didn't get in the way.

There came a day when the plane was a full eight metres long: a fuselage of steel wires, tubes, cables and crossbars, schematic as an articulated insect's rump. Structural elements, Joe told me, were always arranged in the form of a triangle.

'Geometrically speaking, the triangle provides a solid construction,' he said. 'A square will shift, change its shape. But the triangle is the basis of every solid construction.'

The thing remained wingless until the end. I could never really believe that the plane was actually meant to take off, especially after I found out that the gas and choke handles were made from the gearshifts of a racing bike. Had foreman Graad Huisman of Bethlehem Asphalt known the real purpose of their activities in the shed, he would definitely have kept the boys from coming there. But they talked about their plans to no one else, and no one ever asked me a thing.

The hangar floor was littered with sketches, blueprints and manuals. Dunhill in the corner of his mouth and one eye squeezed shut against the smoke, Engel pored over sheets of paper covered in calculations. For shock absorbers they had pulled the suspension springs off an old Opel Kadett at the Hermans & Sons junkyard and welded them between the fuselage and the wheels. Then the plane was hoisted on a rope a metre and a half off the ground and Joe climbed into it. We held our breath. Joe yanked on the rope, the knot slipped and the plane crashed to the ground. Everything remained intact, except for Joe, who climbed out with a 'goddamn sore back'. Thereby demonstrating that the plane would not fall apart during the landing.

'OK,' Engel said, 'now we can put the canvas on it.'

Each new phase in construction was preceded by a rash of thievery. What was needed now was tarpaulin.

'Blue tarp, and nothing but blue,' emphasized Engel, who was in charge of the plane's aesthetics. 'Sky blue or nothing at all.'

The stands for the Friday street market were always set up the night before, the tarps laid in readiness on the tables where the stallholders could find them the next morning. But one Friday morning in October the market superintendent found himself besieged by a group of unhappy vendors. Where were their tarps? How were they supposed to set up their stands? Was this what they paid stallage for? That day they were given last year's ratty old tarps, and that week's *Lomarker Weekly* ran a little article about the theft.

Meanwhile, at a secret location, the tarps were sewn together with angelic patience. Engel was the right man for the job; his father, the last of the Lomark eel fishers, had taught him how to mend fish traps and tie knots that would never come loose. Engel cursed regularly as he worked, but the final result was stunning. Using tie-rips, he stretched the tarps over the fuselage until they were tight as the head of a drum.

Joe was in charge of the wings. The frames were made from fourteen aluminium strips attached to the main girder of each wing, which presented the difficult task of bending twenty-eight ribs into exactly the same silhouette. Without being asked, I took over right away; a strong hand that knows its own strength is a more delicate instrument than any bench-vice or pair of tongs. Taking each rib between thumb and fingers, I bent them to the right curvature. Twenty-seven and one for good luck makes twenty-eight, there you go, sir.

They were flabbergasted.

'Jesus, talk about a vice-grip,' Engel mumbled.

'Frank the Arm,' said Joe.

From then on I was called on more often when it was time to bend things or to tighten them so they'd never move again.

At Pa's yard they tore an aluminium engine out of a pleated Subaru and installed it in the nose of the plane. The fuel tank was the kind used in small boats. The plane, they had calculated, needed to produce 130 kilos of pull in order to get off the ground. A weigh beam was attached to the wall and linked to the tail with a steel cable. Joe climbed in and started the engine. Holy Toledo, it ran like a dream. The cable went taut, the pointer on the weigh beam shot up to eighty kilos, then ninety. The propeller flailed, one hundred, the motor roared and papers flew through the shed. Wednesday left my shoulder with a panicky caw-caw, at a hundred and ten Engel put his hands over his ears, the engine was approaching 5500 rpm and making a horrible racket.

'HUNDRED TWENTY!' Christof screamed.

The pointer kept crawling along, Joe gave it a tad more throttle and Engel shouted, 'STOP!'

A hundred and thirty kilos of traction: the plane had passed the test.

One day Joe asked me to help him with a little experiment. He rolled me over to the workbench in the hangar, then sat down on the other side. The workbench Engel used for his drawings was between us. Taking my right hand in his he moved our elbows to the middle, so that our forearms formed sixty-degree angles with the tabletop. In one quick move Joe pushed my arm down, making me lean over crookedly in my cart. He brought my arm upright and pushed again, but with less force this time, so it took longer for me to tilt over. The back of my hand touched the tabletop. I looked at him, wondering what it was he wanted from me. He set me upright again.

'Put a little muscle into it this time,' he said.

I put a little muscle into it. So did he. We sat there across from each other like that for a while. Then he threw his shoulder into it and pushed harder. I didn't budge, he pushed harder and his eyes bulged. I gave a little.

'Put some muscle into it, damn it!' he groaned.

I buckled down and brought our hands back to the middle of the table.

'Push!'

I pushed him down. He groaned and let go.

'Was that difficult?' he asked.

I shook my head.

'A little bit difficult?'

Not very difficult. Joe nodded contentedly and got up. He went out of the shed and came back with a couple of rusty iron bars under his arm. The bars were of different thicknesses; he clamped the thinnest one between the jaws of the bench-vice at the end of the table.

'Bear with me here, Frankie,' he said, and rolled me over to the bench-vice. 'Now, can you bend that?'

I grabbed the bar and bent it. Joe put the next one in the vice. This one was thicker. When I bent it back at an angle I didn't feel much resistance, but the dent of the iron still glowed hot in my hand. Bending things felt good.

Joe fastened the final bar in the vice. It was a lot thicker than the first two. I wrapped my fingers around it and pulled, but the bastard wouldn't budge. I went at it, I didn't want to disappoint

Joe. A weird noise came from my throat, I pulled like my life depended on it, but nothing much happened. What I did hear was the sound of breaking glass, and metal clattering against stone. Then it gave – it came slowly in my direction. What was that running out of my nose; was it blood or snot?

'Whoa, big fella!'

I let go and, to my surprise, the bar sprang back like elastic. There was a loud crash. I groaned in disappointment: the iron hadn't bent, it was only the other side of the workbench lifting off the floor – the sound I'd heard was falling beer bottles and tools. I had failed.

'Fantastic,' Joe said, 'really fantastic. Do you have any idea how much that bench weighs?'

He squatted down beside me. His face was close to mine, he didn't blink, and I noticed that his left eye shone differently from the right one – the left eye was shooting fire, tempered in turn by the right one, which held a sort of compassion greater than I could grasp.

'That arm of yours might take you places,' he said. 'Keep it in good shape, you never know.'

I t was winter, the river left its banks. Around Ferry Island the current rose, and metre by metre the washlands disappeared beneath grim, sloshing water.

Then the Lange Nek went under, and before long only the traffic signs, lampposts and trees still stuck out above the water. Piet Honing brought the ferryboat to safety in a quiet inlet a ways north and ran the service between Lomark and Ferry Island with the amphibian that belonged to Bethlehem Asphalt.

Every morning and every evening the shivering asphalt men waited for him, the managers with their attaché cases and the workers with lunchboxes in hand. Most of the asphalt men were on bad-weather leave, though; once it was no longer possible to travel by regular means between Ferry Island and the shore, production had halted. Repairs and administrative work were all that went on. Piet Honing steered standing at the back of the amphibian and didn't mind the cold – his face had that leathery texture that weathers but doesn't wear out with the years.

In winter the inhabitants of Ferry Island, like Engel and his father, became real islanders. They did enough shopping in Lomark to last them a week, then locked themselves away in their restored isolation. The island used to be full of real anarchists, radical folk who drank potato moonshine and hunted hares with impunity, for the arm of the law wasn't long enough to cross the water. They were notorious for smacking each other over the head at the slightest provocation. That's all changed, though, people aren't like that anymore. They've grown tame. Everyone can afford a bottle of store-bought gin, and when you see them out walking their dogs you wonder who's been domesticating whom.

The river lapped against the winter dyke now, an expanse of water so vast it made our hometown look like Lomark-by-the-Sea. When darkness came along the drowned stretch of the Lange Nek, the streetlights would pop on and leave regular rings of light on all that hectic water bustling toward the sea.

Ferry Island had been cut loose from the rest of the world, but I was the one who felt adrift. I was outside the circle of light, missing the final construction work on the plane. Joe and Christof crossed with the amphibian, I patrolled the dyke like a nervous watchdog, looking out across the water from the winter dyke to the plant. Most of the time they stayed inside and out of sight. Wednesday perched on my shoulder. He stuck his beak in my ear.

A cold front was coming in, and before long even Piet Honing and his amphibian would be landlocked. Only the courageous would venture out onto the sea of ice then, two by two, roped together at the waist and carrying a pair of ice picks in case one of them went through. 'Raise the water, add lots of ice and then shut the lid on it': that's what they say here when the washlands freeze over.

What I kept wondering, though, was how the plane was supposed to take off; you needed more or less the length of a football field for that, and it just wasn't there.

The factory grounds were quiet, the bulldozers idle among the piles of gravel, the sky was sharp and clear. Finally I spotted movement on the other side. Looking through my telescope I saw Joe sliding open the doors of the shed. Christof and Engel pushed the sky-blue, wingless fuselage outside. Even knowing that the wings were coming later, it was hard to imagine the thing ever leaving the ground. For me, seeing it was like seeing the first airplane ever built. Over yonder, the pure desire to pull a fast one on gravity had materialized in the form of a long, kind of chunky box on wheels. There was a tailpiece, a propeller and an engine, and whether the thing ever left the ground or not I felt something for which I would find the right words only later, when reading about the history of cinema: the triumph of the will. Joe was the one who'd had the creative flash, Engel had stylized the idea into a sky-blue spacecraft… and then you had Christof, who checked the oil. And me? I was the one who'd bent the ribbing into the right shape.

Wednesday polished his beak on my shoulder and I set my cart rolling.

After going home to warm up a little beside the fire, I came back. They still didn't have the wings on it. Joe was driving the plane around the grounds with Engel and Christof running along behind. Over here on the dyke, I could almost hear their excitement.

Joe had said he needed a football field in order to take off. Now there was a plane, but still no runway. For the first time, seeing Joe driving around in circles in his watch cap and ski goggles, I began having doubts about his foresight and – let me be honest – his genius as well.

Once he'd learned how to work the rudder, which took a couple of days with a three-axle steering system, they put the wings on it. After that there wasn't much room to manoeuvre amid the piles of asphalt; the plane was now almost twelve metres wide.

Then, sitting there on the dyke, it suddenly dawned on me – I saw at last what Joe had seen long ago: the solution to the lift-off problem. It was every bit as simple as it was stunning: Joe had been waiting for the freeze to set in – the ice was going to be his runway! It was brilliant, and I couldn't help being amazed by his technical ingenuity. Once the plane left Ferry Island he could maybe park it somewhere else, somewhere in an abandoned shed or an underground bunker; in the presence of that great, calm soul who could plant bombs or build planes or do God knows what else without batting an eye, anything was possible. I mean, he was *fifteen* at the time, there was a whole world of unsettling ideas left for him to carry out with the unflappability of a bicycle repairman.

It wasn't even so much that Joe was an unusual kid: he was a force unleashed on the world. When he was around you couldn't help but feel a tingle of expectation – energy coagulated in his hands, he juggled the making of bombs, the racing of mopeds and the building of airplanes like a merry magician. Never had I seen anyone for whom ideas led so naturally to their own implementation, a person on whom fear and convention had such a shaky grasp. He dared to think the impossible, and noticed nothing of the disapproval going on behind his back. There were, after all, were plenty of people who didn't like Joe, because there was too much about him that defied under-standing. Most people are average, some even downright substandard; all of them, however, are extremely sensitive to the higher concentration of energy or talent in the above-aver-age person. If they have no access to that which makes you shine, they don't want you to have it either. They have no talent for admiration, only slavishness and resentment. They steal the light.

Regina Ratzinger is in the front room showing us her pictures. She's tanned and skinnier, even though it's winter. She went on holiday to Egypt on her own – which is to say, with a group of people she didn't know, led by a couple who acted as their guides. The pictures she made of the pyramids were taken at the hottest hour of the day; the clearest thing about them is the triangular shadows. Chefren, Cheops and Mykerinos are the names she rattles off, or is it Cheops, Chefren and Mykerinos? – she can't remember.

'A whole stack of man-hours went into those,' Joe says.

She tells us about a man with a turban and tobacco-colour teeth who helped her up onto a dromedary, after which she went for a knee-knocking ride in the desert. Then they had to climb back into the bus; there was so much to see, Egypt had so much to offer that you simply couldn't keep track of it all. On the west bank of the Nile, close to Luxor, the whole group was boosted onto donkeys and they rode through all kinds of ruins and necropolises and you never had to ask directions because, as the owner said, 'donkey knows the way'. The animals stopped on cue in front of a little shop with brand-new antiquities, stopped again beside the ice-cream vendor in the shadow of a crumbling temple, then trotted the rest of the way home with the rattled tourists holding on for dear life. Donkey knows the way!

There were adventures in the bus as well. Regina Ratzinger tells us about the man who turned green.

He was a retired teacher from the southern Netherlands, travelling with his wife. They'd spent most of the time nodding off with their cheeks flattened against the window of the bus. Two weeks before they left Holland the man had started taking Imodium, to keep from getting diarrhoea. Every guidebook you came across talked about the country's poor hygiene, and he didn't want to run the risk of having his holiday ruined by dysentery. After the bus had been on the road for about a week, dark spots began appearing faintly on his cheeks and around his mouth. He grew restless, started carrying on non-stop monologues and pacing the aisle. The dark spots broke through to the surface, a sort of moss began growing on his face – a fibrous, dark-green mould that turned to powder when he touched it. It had been three weeks since he'd had a bowel movement. The moss soon covered his neck as well and seemed determined, in some primitive, single-celled fashion, to spread right down into his shirt. His fellow travellers were concerned. Nothing to worry about, the teacher said, it would go away at some point, he'd probably just eaten something that didn't agree with him. By this time he had turned completely green and apathetic, all he did was loll in his seat and let the Aswan Dam and the temples of Abu Simbel pass him by. By the time they had crossed the Eastern Desert and reached the Red Sea the teacher could no longer stand upright. As three men carried him off the bus at Hurghada, his wife flitting nervously around them, all he did was smile benevolently. The fungus had now taken root on his tongue as well, making it look as though he'd been sucking on a green jawbreaker. The other travellers who saw his swollen belly said it looked like the bloated stomach of a drowned man.

At Hurghada's general hospital they gave him the maximum allowable dose of laxatives: he almost exploded. Three and a half weeks' worth of food had collected in his stomach and intestines, kilos of half-digested clay had piled up before a port hermetically sealed with Imodium. During the ensuing stampede of old shit, his anus and part of his rectum ripped open. 'Mr Brouwer has given birth to a golem,' someone in the group whispered, and they hadn't laughed so hard in ages.

'What's a golem?' Christof asks, but Regina Ratzinger has already moved on to the next stack of photographs.

Mr Brouwer remained behind in Hurghada while the rest of the group crossed the Sinai to the Gulf of Aqaba. In the village of Nuweiba, the last stop before flying home from Cairo, they stayed at the Domina, a luxury hotel with a swimming pool, a disco and a 130-kilo pianist in the lounge.

In Regina's photos we see a dark man with a moustache like a guinea pig. His skin is the colour of potting soil. Three pictures later we see him puffing on a water pipe and grinning through the clouds of smoke. A little later he's standing fully dressed beside Regina in a bikini on the beach.

'Who's the moustache?' Joe asks.

His mother slides the next photo over that one, but this one's got the moustache in it as well, standing now beside a campfire on the beach, against a dark sky with a few stripes of sunset in it.

'What's the moustache grinning about?' asks Joe, but his mother says nothing.

Joe gets up, Engel and Christof follow him. Regina stares at the photo.

'You can tell me some other time,' Joe says. 'OK?'

After Joe's father, not many people were buried in the old graveyard along Kruisweg, which runs behind our garden house – my current residence. On nice days, when the windows were open at our place, we always used to hear the funerals. Father Nieuwenhuis's voice through the loudspeakers, a member of the family coming up to the microphone to read a letter to the dearly departed, and finally the funeral director thanking everyone on behalf of the family and calling their attention to the buffet afterwards at 'Het Karrewiel' restaurant: right at the end of the street, the second left and all the way down, parking at the back.

For years I listened to this depressing business. More perhaps than Death itself, Father Nieuwenhuis's bland little talks made all men equal. No matter who you were, whether you'd climbed the highest mountains, brought twelve children into the world or set up a successful contracting firm, the apostles John, Paul and Nieuwenhuis were the Great Equalizers. The immutable dead earnest tone, the same meaningful silences, the searching gaze sweeping over the heads of the flock – it was almost enough to make you swear off dying altogether.

One Bible text still stands out clearly in my mind, and that's because of the time of year at which our windows opened for the first time – Easter. Along with the hum of bumblebees and the downy warmth of early spring, it was Nieuwenhuis's favourite reading that always came through those open windows, from Paul's first letter to the Corinthians:

Behold, I show you a mystery;
We shall not all sleep, but we shall all be changed,
In a moment, in the twinkling of an eye,
at the last trump: for the trumpet shall sound,
and the dead shall be raised incorruptible,
and we shall be changed.
For this corruptible must put on incorruption,

and this mortal must put on immortality.
So when this corruptible shall have put on incorruption,
and this mortal shall have put on immortality,
then shall be brought to pass the saying that is written,
Death is swallowed up in victory.
O death, where is thy sting?
O grave, where is thy victory?
The sting of death is sin;
and the strength of sin is the law.
But thanks be to God,
which giveth us the victory
through our Lord Jesus Christ.
Amen.

When the new cemetery opened, the old one behind our house became run-down. It was a gradual decline, in the end the municipal workers only came by for the most crucial of maintenance work. I wondered how long it would take before they dug the whole thing up.

Most people buy burial rights for ten years. That gives you at least ten years of peace and quiet, there where you and eternity meet. After that all you can do is hope they won't be too stingy to pitch in for another ten years, otherwise you'll be exhumed. Not that it really matters, but still; hardly a pleasant idea, is it, an eternity that lasts only ten years…?

Then again, how long does your memory still cause others to grieve? Two years? Three? Four or five at most if you're *very* well loved, but mourning rarely lasts longer than that. All that comes after is remembrance. Remembrance has its emotional moments, to be sure, but not the raw grief of those first few days and weeks. You begin to wear away, my friend. You're slowly eroded right out of them. There are moments when they can no longer remember your face, or how you kissed, your smell, the sound of your voice…Then it's pretty much over and done with. And one day someone else comes along and takes your place. That's a bitter pill, of course, but then *you* were the one who dropped out of the game, remember?

There she lies, your wife, beside someone else, the pleasure radiates all the way down to her toes, she can't remembering ever having…

Well, all right, there are other differences between you and him…The fact, for example, that he's as black as my shoe. She had him brought in from Egypt and paid for his ticket, and now he's lying on your side of the bed, looking at the gray light falling through a crack in the curtains. Maybe the new man is thinking about you right now as well, about the one who went before him. He knows the spot beside her in bed has been cold for a long time – he didn't exactly wrest that spot from you, no, but he is making the best of your worst-case scenario, and he wonders whether he would ever have had a chance if you were still—

He turns brusquely to this woman in love, the link between the dead man and the living, eyeing each other distrustfully in the shadows.

Here's what went before:

'What are we supposed to call him?' India asked when her mother said she was going back to Egypt to retrieve her lover for his first visit to the Netherlands.

'Mahfouz, that's all, that's his name,' Regina said.

'I'll call him "Papa" if you want.'

'Why would I want that?'

'Because it can be very difficult for a woman when her children don't accept her new husband. The mother may feel torn between loyalties, and that can sometimes prove a divisive element with the family.'

'Where on earth did you ever come up with that?' Regina said.

Regina Ratzinger went to Egypt to marry Mahfouz Husseini, out of love, but also to provide him with the documents needed to visit the Netherlands. In Cairo she met with a swarm of lawyers, the hours spent in the waiting rooms of blistering hot administration buildings were a torment, but by the end of the week they were man and wife.

They took a two-day cruise on the Nile, then caught a plane to Holland. It was 10 December; the sky, gray as a pigeon's wing, hung low over our heads.

When the Egyptian climbed out of the taxi on Achterom, the first thing he did was sniff the air like an animal. Did he smell the comfort of the delta? Of washlands that flooded at set times, as the Nile once had? His little suitcase contained a Koran bound in gazelle skin, a carton of Marlboros for Joe and India, a picture of his father taken in his shipyard and another one showing the whole family. For the rest a few clothes, but not many.

Joe came outside in his stocking feet and held out his hand. Husseini sighed deeply, as though a wish had been granted him.

'My son!' he said, locking Joe in his arms.

He hugged him like that for a time, held him at arms' length to look at him, then drew him back into his embrace. India appeared in the doorway. Her mother shrugged at her apologetically, as though to say, 'So many countries, so many customs.' Joe came out of the embrace a little rumpled. The Egyptian then turned to India and shook her hand. Later, India said that she had felt deeply insulted.

'Why didn't he…*grab* me like that? Has he got something against girls? Was there something wrong with my hair? Could he smell that I was having my period? Does he think menstruating women are *unclean*?'

'Quit it, would you!' her mother shouted. 'Mahfouz did that out of respect. Arabs have a lot of respect for women.'

Mahfouz Husseini was to become Lomark's first official Negro. Even though he wasn't really a Negro at all, he was Nubian; but hey, what did we know? White is white and black is black. Around here we can't tell the difference.

Husseini stayed until just before Christmas, then flew back to Egypt to arrange his definitive departure. One of his brothers would take over his shop in the Sinai; in Cairo awaited the bureaucratic hell through which one had to pass before receiving the right stamps and emigration forms. Regina pined, Joe and India were left to their own devices – their mother neglected the housekeeping and smoked more than she breathed.

'Mom, you have to eat *something*,' India said.

'I've already had two rice waffles.'

She shuffled out of the kitchen. Three weeks to go. India shouted after her.

'If Mahfouz sees you like this he won't think you're pretty anymore! Jesus, Joe, why don't *you* say something for once?!'

'What do I know about it?'

And with that he had spoken a great truth. For what *did* he know about it? He and Engel Eleveld shared a colossal contempt for love. I never heard him talk about it, but it seemed as though he saw love as a less-than-worthy pastime. As spinning one's wheels. Christof felt differently about it; like me, he had a crush on the South African girl.

I remember one time in the garage that summer, when

Christof drew Joe's attention to P.J.'s existence. A few days later we saw Joe looking at the new arrival as she sat with her girl-friends on the low wall around the schoolyard.

'So, what do you think?' Christof urged.

Joe slapped him on the shoulder.

'Good eye, Christof. It's definitely a girl.'

The freeze set in, the water in the washlands was higher than I'd ever seen it. Then one evening at the table I heard Willem Eleveld's voice on national radio. As an 'inhabitant of the disaster area', they'd called him to hear about the 'alarming water levels' in the big rivers. Eleveld was interviewed live, you heard him pick up the phone and say, 'Hello?' real slowly.

'Good afternoon, am I speaking to Mr Eleveld from Lomark?'

'You are.'

You could hear this horrible feedback in the speakers, because Willem Eleveld happened to be listening to the same station.

'Mr Eleveld, it's good to hear that you're listening to our program, but could you please turn off the radio?'

Engel's father put down the phone, fumbled around a bit, and the feedback vanished.

'And who would I be talkin' to?' he asked.

'Joachim Verdonschot from IKON radio, you're on the air live, Mr Eleveld. If I understand correctly, you live in the middle of the disaster area. Could you tell us what things are like there?'

'What do you mean?'

'Well, the flooding, for example.'

'Oh, not much to tell.'

'No water in your basement?'

'No more than usual.'

There was a rustling of paper in the studio in Hilversum.

'The high water has been causing a lot of problems, you and other inhabitants of your municipality are surrounded by it on all sides. When will you finally leave your house, Mr Eleveld?'

'Ferry Island,' Willem Eleveld said.

'Excuse me?'

'Ferry Island isn't a municipality.'

'Ferry Island. When will you leave your house, Mr Eleveld?'

'It'll go down again. No bother for us.'

'Well, then that's a blessing in disguise, as it were. Thank you very much, Mr Eleveld of Lomark, I hope you all stay dry out there!'

'No problem.'

January 1 arrived, there'd been a little drinking the night before, a few fireworks had been shot off, and now everyone was sound asleep, ready to wake up later in a shitty mood in a new year. The river had gone down some and was frozen hard, and the washlands lay beneath a layer of perfect ice on which the sun conjured up deep-golden flames by day – but now it was still night, and I was on the dyke, straining my eyes in the dark. Joe and Christof had just skated away into the blackness, shoes in hand. Today Joe was going to try to get the plane off the ground for the first time. Murmuring in the darkness they had pushed off, until all I could hear was the scratching of their blades growing wispier and wispier.

When I got cold I started rolling the chair back and forth, back and forth. The sun was taking a long time to come up. I decided to go for it: the other shore, I wanted to be there, to see the takeoff up close. I rolled down to the Lange Nek, to the red-and-white-striped barrier gate where the road disappeared under the ice, and out onto the river there. I'd never wheeled on ice before. No wonder it made me a little nervous at first, but once you got out there it was no big deal – just the feeling that you could skid at any moment, and your tyres slipping every time you yanked on the handle. In the almost complete absence of friction, progress was easy. A fuzzy strip of purple light was rising behind the Bethlehem Asphalt grounds, and I was all alone on that huge expanse. I might as well have been a downed aviator in the desert. The silence was bewitching, and I was in no hurry to get to the shed.

Lately I'd noticed a few more signs of life in my own body; I'd even made a deal with myself to get out of the chair and start learning to walk a little. It may sound strange, but my plan was to jump-start this old wreck of a locomotor apparatus – I was about to turn seventeen, had an erection now and then, but I was so damned spastic that self-gratification was almost out of the question. Somehow, though, I sensed that my body held a certain potential – limited though it might be – for finer motor development and, who knows, maybe even a form of non-wheeled propulsion. I had actually started a secret exercise program a while back that consisted of holding onto the table or my bed with my right hand while shuffling across the floor on my knees, keeping my torso upright all the while. That may not seem like much to you, but it's important to realize that what I was doing here, in fact, was re-enacting the entire course of evolution, all by my lonesome – this was what one might call the amphibious phase. I had just emerged from the primal ooze and could start thinking about holding my head up higher.

When I moved around the room like that it looked like I was doing some kind of penance; if Ma had seen me I know she would have rejoiced at another of her prayers being answered, quoting Isaiah and saying, 'Then shall the lame man leap as a hart, and the tongue of the dumb shall sing,' and so on, because some people would rather see wonders than willpower.

Whatever muscles I had left had to be revitalized. For years my body had been lying around in bed and slouching in its chair with no idea whether it was capable of more. My rehabilitation specialist hadn't held out much hope, it's true, but that was such a long time ago. I was older now, and sometimes you have to hand yourself an assignment. And when unreasoned optimism starts coursing through your bloodstream, that's the time to do it.

The ice was fantastic. The light on the horizon grew steadily brighter, and I was going where I had never been before. All around me was glassy blue light, the turquoise heart of a glacier. So smooth and so vast, why hadn't I tried this a long time ago?

Jet-black ice was sliding by beneath my wheels now, my sights were set on the extreme northerly point of Ferry Island.

But allow me, if you will, to withdraw the earlier image of the glacier's heart: what I was in was the heart of a winter-wonderland paperweight, one of those fluid-filled plastic universes that start snowing after you turn them upside-down. We had one on top of the dresser at home, it contained a rearing unicorn against a royal-blue background. Whenever you shook it it snowed all around the unicorn, whose mouth was open in a whinny.

Beneath the ice floor were the fields of summer and the winding road to the riverside. Down there the grass swayed in the slow current.

I was steaming like a workhorse; somewhere an engine coughed and roared. My ice palace fell into tinkling shards.

I turned and saw the plane moving across the ice. It was still more night than day, and from this distance the airplane looked like a sinister vehicle from the workshop of darkness. Two shadows that could only have been Christof and Engel ran out onto the ice. The plane had stopped and they were talking to Joe, whose head was all I could see above the fuselage. They slid the plane around until its nose was pointed at the village. Once the two of them had retreated a respectful distance from the prop, Joe revved it. I loved that sound, which grew higher and angrier the harder the engine was torqued. Joe shot off across the ice. As soon as he hit top speed he tried to lift the nose into the air. Every time he pulled up, the plane would leave the ice for a moment, then bounce back down. And again. Barely rising each time, then falling back. Like it was skipping.

Just short of the winter dyke Joe braked, swung around and came back in our direction. Now I was only a couple of yards from Engel and Christof, who stood riveted to the ice, watching every move Joe made. The airplane barrelled across the frozen flats, it was a joy to behold. There he was, coming straight at us, doing eighty or ninety now. Christof murmured, 'Come on, man,' and Engel flicked away a cigarette butt that sparked once and died. Behind us the curtain of dawn slid open further and further, lighting the sky in an orange and purple glow.

It must have been ten below zero that morning, but I don't remember the cold. Right before he got to us Joe swerved to the left, eased back on the throttle and cut the engine. The silence felt good. Engel and Christof ran to the plane, where Joe was shaking his head and peering at the controls; the hand throttle, the brake, the oil pressure, the fuel gauge and the thermostat. He still had the joystick clenched between his knees.

'It won't nose up,' he said when they got there. It was hard to make out exactly what he was saying, though, his lips had turned blue.

'I think I need more flaps, I'm not getting enough lift.'

Wearing those ski goggles and that old-fashioned red-white-and-blue-striped skater's cap, Joe looked like some kind of insect. Placing his hands on both sides of the cockpit, he wriggled his way up out of the plane's embrace. Before jumping onto the ice he squatted for a moment on the edge of the fuselage. On his back I could see a dark, wet spot about the size of a bicycle seat. The sweat had gone right through his layer of sweaters and his coat. Joe was too cold to stand up straight, all he could do was ask for a cigarette. Engel handed him his smokes and a lighter and they talked about what the problem might be. All three of them had been working toward this moment for so long, and now it wasn't happening. Engel walked around the plane, cursing quietly. Joe puffed on his cigarette like an old-fashioned flying ace on some remote north African air strip. Then he spit on the ice and climbed onto the wing and back into the plane, the cigarette still dangling from his lips. The engine fired, the prop began to spin, and an icy cold wind hit us in the face. Joe turned the plane around and taxied back to the shed. He saw me, and grinned.

'Happy New Year, Frankie!'

The next attempt was made on 4 January. They'd changed the angle of the flaps and adjusted the rudder. That didn't help either.

The weather was about to turn. By the weekend the cold front would make way for warmer air, and they worked non-stop; without the ice they would be lost. It was a race against the clock. January 10 arrived and with it the thaw; my tyres left wet tracks on the ice. For the umpteenth time Joe rolled out onto the frozen river, and now it was do or die. I joined Engel and Christof, watching tensely as the plane picked up speed in the distance. Faster and faster it went until, at top speed, it traced a flat line between the town and the old factory grounds.

'Pull the nose up, man!' Engel said breathlessly. 'Pull that goddamn thing up!'

If ever there was a right moment, this was it – it was still early morning, the air was clear, cold and 'thick', as Joe had called it, perfect for a takeoff. He went thundering across the ice; at this rate, unless he pulled up quickly, he would go crashing into the row of willows in the shallow ice of the washlands.

'What the *hell* is he doing?!'

Joe was racing flat out toward the trees; he'd never pushed the plane this hard before, but he wasn't even trying to lift off – if he didn't turn fast or brake, he was a goner. I closed my eyes, then opened them right away and saw him pull back at last. The rear tyre was off the ice, the plane hung wonderfully level and kept bouncing up and down, any other plane would have been airborne by now…Oh my God, oh my God…There he went! He was off!

The plane shot up a few metres, fairly brushing the tops of the willows as it went. Joe could never have calculated that, he'd simply taken an idiotic chance and had enormous luck. Pure luck, I was sure of it. If the plane hadn't done exactly what he hoped at that point, he would be dead now. But he wasn't dead, he was flying…

'Yeah! Yeah!' Engel was bellowing beside me.

Christof jumped up and down and threw his arms around Engel. Now the two of them were jumping up and down together, shouting at the top of their lungs. My own face was covered in tears. He had done it, he was flying away in a westerly direction, the throbbing of the engine fainter as he grew smaller on the horizon. He had performed the miracle of the Wright Brothers all over again. Nothing could stop him anymore.

*

If Mahfouz Husseini hadn't come back, Regina Ratzinger would probably have died of starvation. The way Mahfouz put it in his fractured English was: 'In years of dryness, flowers are first to die.' At least that's what Joe made of it.

Regina had trouble getting the housekeeping back on its feet. Something had changed in her, a degree of world-weariness in her behaviour and appearance that never went away again. She seemed not to change her clothes as often, and the knitting purists of Lomark noted testily that tiny glitches had appeared in the patterns of her sweaters.

Mahfouz often did the cooking now, so dishes with lamb and coriander began appearing on the menu, prepared with a sharp red paste of hot peppers and spices that sowed confusion on your tongue.

'Very tasty, Mahfouz,' Joe said.

Mahfouz looked up from his plate delightedly.

'Tazty, no?'

Five times daily Mahfouz rolled out his rug on the sun porch of the house on Achterom to murmur prayers in the direction of Mecca. He was not overbearingly religious, and never bothered Joe and India with his beliefs. They considered his faith as harmless as another man's habit of eating a fixed number of bananas each day, or automatically knocking on wood to ward off disaster. He took a correspondence course in Dutch, and after a few weeks he could ask the way to the train station or order a pound of beef and pork mince at the butcher's. Not that this was of any use to him; the village had no station, and no self-respecting Muslim would touch pork mince. But he felt at ease in Lomark, walked around the village a great deal and always greeted us politely.

Regina showed him off in public and seemed to glow softly in his presence.

'Nubians are a very handsome people,' she said. 'The handsomest in Egypt, they say. But as handsome as Mahfouz...'

'Right, Mom,' India said, 'we got you. Take it easy.'

Regina took her husband to the city: he returned with a linen suit and handmade leather shoes. He moved as easily in them as he had in the Indian off-the-rack goods he'd arrived in. Because he was in the habit of waxing his moustache, and because Regina dressed him as a tropical dandy, he was something of an anachronism in Lomark, a man lost in some strange corner of the world.

The first time Mahfouz Husseini saw me he leaned over and looked me deep in the eye, to see if I had all my marbles. I didn't try to stop him. When he'd had a good look, Husseini straightened up and laughed; apparently he'd seen something there. Then he said a few words in Arabic and moved around to the back of my cart. Hey, tenthead! Let go, I need to train that arm! I'm not your old auntie! But he seized the handles without asking and started pushing me around the village exactly like an old lady. I was embarrassed. It was all a bit too much. I sat in my chair glowering, with no idea where he was taking me. In one fell swoop he had shattered my carefully cultivated isolation. People were looking at us. At the dinner table that night they'd say, 'Did you know Frankie Hermans has a nurse with a moustache?' We looked like jerks together, Husseini and I.

But unless I was mistaken, we were heading for the Lange Nek. The Arab hummed little snatches of some tune and was really putting them down, his soles creaked on the asphalt. I could smell the river from a long way off, the water had a smell I couldn't describe but that made me calm down. Maybe it was all the impressions he'd undergone on his way here.

'There is Piet,' Husseini said.

The water had gone down again, Piet Honing's ferry service was running as usual. The boat was in midstream and coming our way. Piet was tearing off ticket stubs and handing them in through open car windows; the change he received in return went into the pouch around his waist. Then he went into the pilothouse and reversed the engines. Two cars and a cyclist came on shore. I didn't look at them. Piet came over to us.

'So, buddy, I haven't seen you for a while.'

I grunted.

'Lots has happened, nothing's changed – you know what they say. Had some damage this winter, though, the river took a whole bunch with it. But we're back in business, aren't we, Mahfouz? Am I right?'

He gave Mahfouz a shy little slap on the shoulder and went back on board. Mahfouz pushed me to the edge of the quay, I pulled hard on the brakes. The Arab squatted down, the elbow of his left arm resting on his knee, the fingers of the other hand plucking at his moustache.

From that day on, Mahfouz and I sat together pretty often at the Ferry Head. I enjoyed having him around; he would talk and I would listen. Whenever Piet was having mechanical problems, Mahfouz jumped right in the thick of it. At his father's shipyard in El-Biara, a little place just outside Kom Ombo, he had learned how to take apart an engine and put it back together again. He was the youngest of six brothers and three sisters. His father owned a yard on the banks of the Nile, and at a bend in that river Mahfouz had learned how to build a felucca, the characteristic ship of the Nile. His father had groomed him to work in the family business, but with so many siblings Mahfouz decided to seek his fortune in the tourist industry instead. Far from home, in the village of Nuweiba on the east coast of the Sinai, he had opened a little shop fifty metres from the beach. He sold rugs, Bedouin silver and pharaonic statuettes that could pass for antique if the buyer was blind and retarded; because so many tourists met those criteria, business was brisk. His shop was in a long row of others selling exactly the same items. Above the door was the print of a hand in dried goat's blood: the hand of Fatima, devout daughter of the Prophet. Each morning Mahfouz hung the rugs and cotton clothing outside his shop, and flapped the dust off them each evening.

Nuweiba consisted of three loosely connected districts: most tourists went to Tarabin, a burgeoning strip along the beach full of hotels, restaurants and shops. A few kilometres to the south lay Nuweiba Port, where the ferries left for Jordan. In Tarabin Mahfouz had led an uneventful life. He slept about ten hours a day and spent the rest of the time in his shop or with friends. They played backgammon beneath the fluorescent lights, a waiter from the nearby restaurant brought them countless trays of tea.

Husseini felt strong, and believed that his diet of fish and rice and the sea air he breathed improved his blood. In his opinion, a person's soul was in the blood. Blood travelled all around the body and infused with spirit the framework of flesh and bones that called itself Mahfouz Husseini.

Sometimes he would fall asleep in a beach chair and wake

the next morning just as the sun rose above the mountains on the far shore. He lived with his face to the sea and his back to the desert, free of the great desires that make life a living hell. After someone told him that the Sinai was sliding away from the Arab Peninsula across the way at the rate of a centimetre and a half each year, he thought he could see the distance widening.

The day a bus from Piramid Tours came rolling into Nuwei-ba, he was sitting in his armchair outside the shop. Later that afternoon the first tourists from this new bunch appeared in his street: three women. Dutch. Mahfouz could tell right away. It was possible at times to mistake Dutch people for Germans, but the latter tended to have a kind of belaboured modesty, as though they could be arrested any minute. Germans also *did* talk louder than the Dutch, it's true, but they didn't walk around as though the world belonged to them. Dutch people moved with a heavily self-confident tread, as though they knew their way everywhere.

Mahfouz's colleague, Monsef Adel Aziz, shouted, 'Lookie-lookie-no-obigation' at the women, the sign for the others to approach them as well, rubbing their hands and preening their feathers. Mahfouz saw a tired smile cross the face of the youngest woman. One of the older women, he could tell, had come to his country in search of physical love; one developed an eye for such things. Women like that had something hungry in their gaze, something insatiable. More and more of them had started coming each year; sometimes you saw white grandmothers with amazing lavender hair walking hand in hand with young boys. The story had it that these women had been abandoned by their husbands in their own country, or that they had come to Egypt because their husband was ill and could no longer fulfil his conjugal obligations. Monsef Adel

Aziz consorted with such women and was none the poorer for it. The young men of the village didn't care whether the women were old, young, fat or pretty. Mahfouz himself had had an affair with an American woman; when her vacation was over she had asked him to go home with her, but in his eyes a house in Iowa was no better than a shop in Nuweiba. Catherine O'Day had therefore started spending a few weeks each year in Nuweiba. It had been a few years, however, since he'd seen her. He'd received a postcard from her once, with greetings from America. The postcard hung on the back wall of Husseini's shop, half covering a photo of him with his arm around the popular actress Athar el-Hakim, who had once come to Nuweiba for a day to shoot some scenes on the beach.

The women were coming toward his shop. Concerning the oldest, the one Mahfouz had recognized as sexually needy, he heard later that week that she had started a torrid affair with a bellboy at the Hotel Domina; an attractive young man who, in response to her elaborate praise for the ease with which he had carried her luggage, had immediately dropped his trousers to show his sizeable dong. Mahfouz took a good look at the youngest of the three – there was shadow around her. He felt the need to comfort her.

'Hotchachaandoolalabathingbeautywithoutabra!' Monsef Abdel Aziz shouted after them, knowing full well that he had lost the battle for their attention.

The women had almost reached Mahfouz's shop. Stroking his moustache in one fluid motion with the back of his index finger, he said with his most winning smile, 'Welcome, welcome…'

The women had run his clothing through their hands, each of them had tried on a few rings bearing semiprecious gems and bought a few postcards. Then they walked on. But anyone travelling down the road in a southerly direction had to pass back that way again. When they reached the end of the shopping street the women turned, the woman with the shadow walking on the inside now. Mahfouz ran into his shop, grabbed a souvenir and flew back outside, where he was just in time to hand his present to the woman with ash-blond hair. She took it, confused, not knowing whether it was a present or whether he wanted money for it, and tried to give it back.

'It's a gift, for you,' Mahfouz said.

It was a little model boat, a felucca with an alabaster hull and a sail with the Eye of Horus painted on it in blue and gold. The woman thanked him awkwardly and walked on.

Nuweiba was little more than a hamlet. It was certain that Mahfouz Husseini and Regina Ratzinger would meet again.

The next day they saw each other beside the swimming pool at the Hotel Domina. He had delivered a box of leather wallets to the hotel's souvenir shop and was about to walk back down the beach to Tarabin when he saw her.

'Ah, the beautiful lady,' he said, bowing his head slightly.

'Wait,' she said. 'I wanted to… a little something… for that lovely present.'

She went back to her recliner at the poolside, wrapped a sarong around her body and tied it with a knot between her breasts, bent over and took a couple of Egyptian pounds from her bag. She walked back to the man and said, 'Here, for you.'

Mahfouz shook his head and smiled sadly.

'I understand,' he said. 'You don't want my gift. I am sorry.'

'Of course I want it, but…'

But it was too late: the Egyptian raised his hand briefly to cover his heart, took two steps back and was gone.

Later that afternoon she took a taxi to his shop to apologize. He agreed to meet her that evening for a meal.

'Oh,' she said as she left the shop, 'my name is Regina Ratzinger. What's yours?'

'Call me Mahfouz.'

They had fish on the beach in Tarabin. A Sudanese man, his skin black as ink, sat smoking in the shadow of a fishing boat; wagtails were hopping on the sand. The evening sky wrapped itself around them like the lightest of woven fabrics. A Bedouin came by leading a camel by a rope. The Bedouin tried to interest her in a ride along the beach; Mahfouz said something and the Bedouin left. After dinner they walked along the water to the Temple Disco at Hotel Domina. Regina danced with her eyes closed; around them the other members of her tour group swayed tipsily.

Later, back on the beach, Mahfouz built a little fire. He pulled a pack of Cleopatras from his shirt pocket and stuck a cigarette between his lips. His hands went to his pockets but found no lighter. Regina took a burning stick from the fire and held it up to him with shaking hands. He touched the tip of the cigarette to the wood and drew fire into it. Neither of them noticed the glowing ember that fell on Mahfouz's Terlenka trousers. When the material began to smoke and he leapt up with a shriek to slap out the fire, Mahfouz realized that something had changed for all time.

Look,' Joe said, 'Mrs Eilander.'

The Peugeot station wagon belonging to P.J.'s mother was racing along the dyke in our direction. She was kicking up a lot of wind and we watched her go by in a flash, looking grim. She didn't even respond when Joe and I raised our hands in greeting.

'Pissed off,' Joe said.

We had seen her car parked at the police station manned by Sergeant Eus Manting. Why she was there was not hard to guess: she was complaining about a strange airplane that sometimes flew frighteningly low over her garden; Joe had recently started carrying out reconnaissance missions over the White House.

Joe climbed down the dyke, into the washlands, with the words 'Need to think a bit, Frankie.' The little clouds of smoke rising up above the sea of stalks and overgrown poppies told me where he was lying. Swallows swooped over him, and insects went whining low across the land in the face of an approaching low-pressure zone.

Flagpoles with book bags on them had been hung out in front of some of the houses in the village. One more year and it would be our turn. And then? Then they would go – Joe, Christof and Engel – to some other place. To study or to work, in any case to do something that didn't require me. I had, it seemed, become a deeply embedded anchor that would always remain in place. My horizon was blank and I tried not to desire much, like an animal or a Buddhist.

Or like Joe.

I saw Christof on his bike, cycling toward me like a madman.

'Seen Joe?' he asked as he pulled up.

I pointed to the field, where the little rings of smoke he produced faded into nothingness as soon as they rose above the grass. Christof leaned his bike against a post and took the barbed wire along the dyke road gingerly between thumb and forefinger. He pushed it down carefully and stepped over, first his right leg, then the left. As he walked down the slope he shouted, 'Joe! Hey, Joe!'

A hand stuck up out of the grass.

Christof waded over to him and was soon up to his thighs in green, as though sinking slowly. A gust of wind rolled through the grass, behind me the dry leaves rustled as they blew across the road. Not so long ago they had skated down below us there and made an airplane take off, now you could occasionally see an oystercatcher disappear into the breathing sea of grass and flowers, above which swallows performed their daredevil dives. After a while Joe sat up, a little irritated maybe at being disturbed while he was thinking. He got up and walked in my direction. Christof had no more business staying down there, and followed him.

'So what did you see, Joe?!' he shouted. 'Don't be such an asshole, man, I have a right to know, I helped too, remember…'

Joe held down the barbed wire to let Christof step over. 'I saw her,' he then said slowly.

Christof almost exploded.

'And what was she doing?'

He seemed to think that nudists did something, some kind of sexual rite or something.

'There was nothing to see,' Joe said. 'There was hair all over it.'

It was like someone had turned down all the sound in the world without saying anything, that's how quiet it was. You could see Joe thinking. I was disappointed by the announcement; I couldn't imagine much of anything specific with all that hair, but the effort taken seemed way beyond the results achieved. I had been expecting more.

'God damn it,' Christof said. 'I figured as much.'

Another long vacation was on its way. One of those that slowly melts you away and leaves you to baste in your own juices. The summer holidays were always a bad time for me. There wasn't a whole lot to do if you weren't messing around with mopeds and pimply girls. It's true, I spent my summers in the short trousers and the loud Hawaiian shirts Ma bought for me, but that only drew even more attention. I would rather have bundled myself all up and pulled the gray leatherette plaid up around my neck, but in the summertime that gave me a terrible rash. So instead I sat there like a bump on a log and people looked at me like I was an imbecile. That's the first thing they think, of course, when they see someone in a wheelchair, that he's not playing with a full deck. I stopped trying to prove the contrary long ago.

What I liked most was sitting by the river with Mahfouz, to whom I didn't have to explain a thing. The sun glanced off the water; the light was so bright that it lit up the inside of your head and everyone could look right in.

We sat there like that often, the Egyptian and I, drifting off into the soothing narcosis of daydreams that comes over you when you stare for a long time at waves or a fire. Piet came and

Piet went, a car honked as it passed, and from the willows on the shore white fluff blew out across the river, settling on the water or floating to the other side. Housewives complained when the willows gave off their fluff, sometimes there was so much that it piled up in their doorways and blew into the house as soon as it got the chance. Mahfouz's mind was somewhere completely different, maybe he was thinking about where he came from and the strange wind that had carried him here, to these basalt blocks in the company of Frank the Arm.

Out on the river there were lots of private boats, those floating fridges that illustrate to us how general prosperity and bad taste go together like salt and pepper. Sometimes an old-fashioned saloon boat would come by too, with people on board in sporty clothes with blue or aubergine-coloured stripes. They came from another world and drifted past ours with conspicuous lightness. There was a kind of yearning in the way the people looked from their boats at the shore, just as there was a kind of yearning in the way I looked back. They often waved.

I knew that boating enthusiasts liked to wave to each other and to people on the shore. Drivers and cyclists never waved to each other, but motorcyclists did. Because of that waving, boaters and motorcyclists enjoyed some secret connection. Once in a while Mahfouz would wave back, without interrupting his musings. Sometimes he also made muffled sounds, as though agreeing with himself in some inner conversation, and when he did the plucking at his moustache grew more rigorous. I could see why Regina was in love with him – he had lustrous black hair and deep, dark eyes with lots of white around them, like the Tuaregs in *National Geographic* with their blue scarves that leave only their eyes uncovered.

'In Nuweiba there was a pelican,' Mahfouz told me once. 'Big, white. One day he came out of the water and never went back. Maybe he'd had enough of living at sea and decided that he wanted to live among people. He ate of our meat, our bread and our fish. Tourists came who wanted to have their pictures taken with him. Sometimes we would build a fire at night and he would float close by, so he could keep an eye on us.'

At this point in the story the Arab pulled out a ragged pack of Cleopatras and patted the filter against his left thumbnail. He lit it, then remembered that I was there too. We smoked. Some smokers exhale smoke like it's coming from a plane, a straight, gray contrail, but I'd never seen anyone smoke the way the Arab did – he smoked, how shall I put it, to *vanish*. He took a dollop of smoke in his mouth and let it eddy up around his face the way clouds rise to hide a mountaintop from view. Is that the way they smoked where he came from? It was something to see. He seemed to have forgotten what he was saying about the pelican, in any case he'd squatted down again and was watching the boats with his face regularly eclipsed in cloud.

After some time had passed in that way, Mahfouz started talking again, about back when the tourists had avoided his country because of the situation in Israel, and how all of them grew a lot skinnier as they waited for better days.

'Imagine you are a sailor,' he said, 'and suddenly the wind is gone. Your ship just lies there in the middle of the sea and all you can do is pray for wind…That's how it is with the merchant, too; he tightens his belt and looks on high until Allah remembers him. We waited like seeds in the desert for rain, for better times. And our pelican waited too. But we had to eat first. After all, he had the whole sea full of fish, no? But then he stopped waiting until he got something, and started stealing.'

Mahfouz looked at me sternly.

'Dependency turns you into a thief. He had become an evil old

94

thief. We chased him away but he kept coming back, maybe he had forgotten how to fish. One evening he committed a crime for which Allah punished him. Monsef Adel Aziz was roasting a chicken on the beach, and the pelican tore the chicken from the spit and swallowed it in one gulp. One hour later he was dead.'

Mahfouz ground out the cigarette with his heel and shrugged. I looked at him, baffled. Was that it? I hadn't been expecting such an abrupt and fateful ending. But Mahfouz himself seemed to think it was pretty nifty, he looked at me as though awaiting my approval. He could keep waiting. I thought the story sucked.

It was in that same week that I saw Joe worried for the first time.

'She took his passport,' he said. 'The crazy bitch.'

I raised my eyebrows in a query.

'My mother. She's hidden Mahfouz's passport. She's afraid he's going to run away or something.'

Regina was going to great lengths not to lose her Arab.

'She hid his fancy suit too. She thinks he attracts too much attention. From women.'

I'd already noticed that Mahfouz was looking a bit less natty lately. The people on the ferry no longer stared in amazement when he collected fares for Piet; an ebony Arab with a fragrant moustache and a linen suit tearing their tickets – that was something worth seeing!

Now that love had pitched its tent at his home, Joe was not at all pleased with the way things were going. India interpreted the events for him; he himself was still less than sensitive to the myriad possibilities of love.

'You mean it's sort of like your tastebuds?' he asked India. 'Sweet at the tip of your tongue, sour halfway and bitter all the

95

way at the back? Is that what you're saying, that love is sweet at first but gets more and more bitter the more she loves him?'

Even though the perception of saltiness was missing from his simile, I found the comparison rather apt: infatuation as the gateway to gullet and intestinal tract. It squared with what I'd read about it, and with things I'd noticed with my own parents. And somehow I couldn't stop thinking about that ridiculous story about the pelican and the roast chicken.

As the grass smouldered in the fields and the sheep were rushed to the slaughterhouse with heat exhaustion because the farmers were too lazy to plant them a shade tree, I learned to drink. It's the only thing Dirk ever taught me, oceanic drinking, drinking for as long as it takes to strip you of all dignity and make you a beast among beasts, braying for love and attention and too filthy to handle.

How does something like that get started?

You pass by the Sun Café and your eldest brother comes outside, because he saw you rolling by. You're surprised that he's even allowed in there, because they banned him, didn't they? Whatever the case, Dirk's already had a few and his mood is treacherously buoyant. He shouts, 'You look a little hot under the collar, Frankie, come on in!', and before you know it he's pushed you into the Sun and shouted, 'A beer for me and one for my little brother, Albert.'

Albert is the man behind the bar, otherwise it's all men whose faces you know but whose names you've forgotten. What the hell are you doing here?

'Stop looking like you're going to bite someone, Frankie!'

Dirk is dangerously jovial and, to your deep disgust, has now referred to you as 'my little brother' for the first time in your life. The worst of it is, you know exactly why: today you're his circus animal, he's going to profit from your existence at last by having you drink your first beer in front of everyone and then laughing along with them as the beer runs down your chin and into your shirt. He's getting the laughs and I'm getting the pity, but no one protests because 'it's his big brother, he knows what he's doing', and there's the next beer already, and why not: if you want me to drink, you chump, then I'll drink till that rotten smirk is wiped off your face, because this isn't what you had in mind, having me change from your trained sea lion into your shame and fury, because you can't keep anything under control without rage and bullying… All right, Albert, my throat's dry as dust and my brother's footing the bill… and if I take a bite out of your glasses it's only because I'm spastic as all get out, but hey, the way I spit out the glass in a glistening stream of slivers and blood, that's pretty nifty, isn't it, guys?

That's how something like that gets started.

And how far do you have to go to be purged of their pity? Not very far. I drank till I fell on my face, lowing like a cow, and they lifted me back into my cart and bought me no more beer. By that time Dirk was already so pissed off that he would have whacked me one if it hadn't been so unseemly to punch a cripple in public.

What surprised me most was how much noise I made. They thought that was funny at first. The alcohol kindled a fire under my usual soundlessness. It was as though my gullet ripped open, oxygen swirled around and I screamed, man, I screamed. It had been a couple of years since Dirk had heard me make a sound, he couldn't believe his ears. Once the novelty had worn off, the men just grimaced a bit uneasily as I blasted my foghorn.

'That'll be enough of that,' the barman said.

Dirk yanked on my arm. He could fuck off. The men turned

back to the bar, one of them said, 'They're all the same, the lot of them.' And although Dirk knew exactly what he was referring to, he was glad to be able to turn his attention to something else.

'So what's that supposed to mean?'

'What? What are you talking about?' the man said without turning around.

'That we're all the same.'

The man looked at him as though he smelled something foul. This was Dirk in due form, this was what he was known for. I saw the iron descend into his body and the rage darken his eyes; this was the Dirk I knew: old Dirk If-you-can't-pound-the-shit-out-of-it-then-try-fucking-it Hermans.

'What's eating you, asshole?' the man said.

'That's what I thought,' Dirk said. 'You dirty piece of shit.'

And before I knew what was happening Dirk had slammed the man's forehead down on the bar. Blood spattered from his wrinkles. The man came off his stool with a roar and threw himself on my brother, but got such a hard thump that the glasswork tinkled on the shelf. The others jumped up, apparently compelled somehow to act as a unit in the event of an attack from outside, and now Dirk had five on him instead of only one. But, like I said before, he couldn't count past three anyway. The bastard went down like a drowning man. Two of them dragged him toward the door and the others kicked and punched him so hard that they hurt themselves. They ignored me. When I saw that crowd of mechanics and masons piling onto Dirk, for whom I'd never felt one millisecond of sympathy, let alone brotherly love, something weird happened: I got angry. Almost too angry to breathe. Raging inside me was something you might call 'the cry of blood', in any case something I'd never counted on. Reeling under this new sensation, I threw off the brakes and rammed my cart as hard as I could into the scrimmage.

I smashed into a guy who had his back turned to me as he whacked away at Dirk. My cart hit him behind the knees, buckling his legs forward and throwing his upper body back so that I could grab him by the throat with the only weapon I had: my hand. It found his windpipe and squeezed. His arms flailed but found no purchase. The hand squeezed harder, the fingers sinking into flesh. I felt muscles contracting in mortal fear, and the wild pounding of blood. I remember pleasure and the need to kill him. It was going to be easy. Just don't let go and squeeze harder, that was all. Tear out his gullet. My fingers were tingling. The others let Dirk go and started in on me, they yanked on my arm with that purple head and lolling tongue attached to the end of it, and punched me in the head without mercy. Amid the rain of blows I saw the face growing darker all the time. Oh God please let me murder him—

That's all I remember.

Only that face, which I remember as being black. And after that day, there were two things I knew:

1. that the man I had wanted to kill was a roofer by the name of Clemens Mulder, and that he would never be my friend;
2. that I had found a new love, namely the release of alcohol, and would be true to it for the rest of my days.

It's like a chain of little spiders,' was India's comment when she saw the stitches on my eyebrow.

She brought me to the garage behind the house, where Joe was jabbing at his arm with a needle.

'Joe, what are you *doing*?!' India said.

Along the length of his left forearm he had tattooed the letters of his own name: JOE – still bloody, but a clear aquamarine beneath. It was August, the dog days had us all in their grip.

'What's up, Frankie, been in a fight?' Joe asked.

All you had to do was look at me: both eyes blackened with old blood, six stitches across my brow. Joe never got into fights, things like that didn't happen to him. I realized that I'd crossed the line into the bastards' domain, joined the ranks of the murderous and, what's worse, of a family in which the boys started swinging their fists as soon as they came of age. (The Hermans have no girls; ours is a bloodline of gnarls and knots, not of soft things.)

I, who had vowed never to become like them, had plunged headfirst into the first brawl that came my way. If no one had stopped me I would have strangled that roofer. I had fallen, and Joe could tell. He didn't say much that day, just sat there jabbing more ink into his arm. His jaw muscles pulsed each time the needle pierced his skin.

I left after a while and didn't see him for a couple of weeks.

In the days that followed I worked on my diaries more than ever, going back to do some necessary checks and amendments.

My thoughts went back to the years before I'd met Joe, before I'd left the world behind for 220 days. So many questions back then. So many that it made me dizzy. There had to be more to it than this, I was sure of it: people couldn't *really* be content to live and die the way they did. Some secret was being kept from me, some thing they knew but weren't telling, something a thousand times more real than this. Wondering why, they say, is the start of all philosophy. For me it was the start of a kind of hell.

'No whys about it,' Pa would say. 'That's just the way it is.'

And when I kept asking he would smack me up against the side of the head. He was the wrong person to ask, in other words, but that didn't mean there was no answer; I wasn't too ignorant to know ignorance when I saw it. So I waited. Somewhere a door would open, someone would explain how it went, and until then I would keep my eyes wide open and keep asking why.

People, I knew, liked to think of life as a stairway. You started at the bottom and kept climbing as life went on. Nursery school, kindergarten and then primary school, where they told you that 'higher education' was the answer. That's where you'd find out about the things you couldn't see from here.

I believed them. But I was consumed by impatience, so I went on asking why until it started getting really irritating. In their eyes I was just being cheeky, overplaying my hand. As though I was asking to speak to God himself.

I wouldn't want to pretend that I, with all those questions of mine, was the kind of kid you'd have found endearing. More like autistic. Back then my thinking had an aggravating sever-ity to it that I've never even approached since. The same kind of barebones austerity I later came to admire in the philosophy of the samurai.

And the answer didn't come. I'd expected a lot from high school. Biology, history, literature...that's where it was going to happen. It had to be buried somewhere inside that pile of books I lugged around each day.

But the books spoke with the voices of teachers, or the teach-ers spoke with the voices of books: how that worked was never quite clear to me. They taught me skills, but provided no answers.

Until then, my 'why' had always been referred on. But this, for the time being, was where the buck stopped, this was where I was going to stay for the next five years; these same mouths would speak to me the whole time and, to my horror and dismay, I discovered that my question wasn't particularly pop-ular here either. Things *were* what they were, and it didn't do to go poking around in it too much – just like Pa said.

I caught a glimmer of an abysmal truth. The people here wanted to pass the time as comfortably as possible, without having to deal with questions that couldn't be answered with a simple 'yes', 'no', or 'I don't know'. No one around me was doing anything except the best imitation they could of what they'd seen other people do before. Parents imitated *their* parents, kindergarten teachers other kindergarten teachers, pupils other pupils, and clergymen and educators each other and their books. The only variation was in what they forgot to imitate.

None of them knew the way, rank amateurism was all it was. And I lay awake at night, my eyes wide open, more afraid of the things that weren't there than of the things that were.

Some people say they were born in the wrong body; I,

however, was born not only in the wrong body but also in the wrong family in the wrong village in the wrong country and so on. I read a lot, and in those books I thought I sometimes perceived a shimmer of light. I devoured every book in the Lomark library, except for the large-print section. When I discovered the samurai, I was impressed by their Spartan self-discipline. They at least saw the need, when you had lost your honour and life was rendered meaningless, to stick a knife in your own belly. *Seppuku*: the clean, straight cut you could never practice, because the first time was also the last. More people should give it a go.

At church I sat in the back pew playing cards, while up in front Nieuwenhuis was saying 'He that searches for the truth comes to the light,' but I still couldn't see a thing.

Nieuwenhuis's conviction was born of the need to be convinced, that much was clear to me. But exactly what he was convinced *of* was less clear. Repression was the only thing that could have kept that trap spring-loaded for two thousand years. But now that the internal combustion engine and social democracy had taken some of the tension out of it, you saw repression making way for tolerance and guitars in the church. It was like the way old people who had been real bastards all their life would suddenly break down and weep over nothing when their number was almost up.

Looking back on it, I think I wasn't even searching for the truth or anything, just for something that shed a little light.

My first year of high school was one huge disaster. It made me sick. Everywhere I looked I saw mediocrity and submissiveness. And an innocence that ruined everything, because it meant no one could really help it. If we were, in fact, the measure of all things, what hope was there of redemption?

By the end of my second year I was furious. A long vacation

followed, and I watched July go by. Then August came, and I waited for nothing. I lay on my back in the tall grass that was already turning yellow. The dryness rustled, little bugs crawled over my arms and legs. I let them. Somewhere I heard the pounding of a galloping horse, the corn was still half high and the rust-brown sorrel stuck out above it. I looked up at the blank sky. A lovely blue and all, but otherwise nothing. Growling monotonously, a little plane crossed the void.

At the edges of my vision the woolly thistles were bursting their buds, butterflies fluttered aimlessly and I had the feeling I was sinking. I sank to a dark and quiet place.

It was a day for cyclomowers.

I must have heard it, the tractor pulling the snapping blades, cutting through grass and flowers. Whack whack whack. No sleep so deep but that you would hear that. Who could fail to hear the roar of a 190-horsepower John Deere? Who would lie down and sleep in the grass at mowing time? Who would do something like that? Then you've got only yourself to blame.

You're right, all of you.

Who would lie down in the grass at mowing time?

The front wheel of the tractor crushed my sternum and broke my back, but the blades missed me. The man up on top saw me, but too late. Some call that luck, others misfortune. Musashi says: the Way of the Samurai is the unflinching acceptance of death.

As to what happened afterwards I can only guess. Although I was clearly on my way to the end, sometimes I think I waited – for some reason to come back, a single reason to grasp at a branch along the river of death and start in on the road home, inch by inch, back to where I came from.

Maybe Joe was that reason.

That was a long time ago, and I can't really get to it anymore, I was too far gone for clear-cut memories. Sometimes it's so far away that it seems as though I made it all up – the tractor, the dream of the hero, the return to that brighter place.

The memory of my dreamtime.

The body floats just below the surface. There is no pain, no one is missed. Close to the surface, where the light breaks through the water, it is clearer, you can taste the sun.

'Look,' someone says, 'he's dreaming.'

The hero's dream. A hero will come, the sound of his heavy footsteps precedes him, those who are outside go in and close the doors; heroes never bring only good fortune. It's cold, we smell woodsmoke. It tumbles from the chimneys and mixes with the mist that has settled over the fields and roads.

The newcomer whistles a quiet song. He will bring good cheer and sow confusion. He bears new times like a sword. He will shatter our illusions and break through our terse backwardness. His feat will bring beauty, but we will chase him away; this is no time for heroes.

There are hands that lift you up, there are hands that put you down. The body approaches the surface, it has grown lighter, a little lighter all the time. That light, oh hell, it breaks through my forehead like a thermal lance. I am born for the second time. Blind and helpless, I wash ashore. Around my bed they're talking about Joe.

I've learned to shuffle around on thin, crooked legs, always holding onto something with my good arm to keep from falling. I wait, in the little house at the back of the garden, for my parents to die. I live in a rectangle. There is a twin electric hotplate, a microwave oven, a table and a toilet. The bed is behind the table, against the wall. Ma's the one who put the plants on the windowsill. You don't have to do much with them, they stay green all the time anyway. At the back I look out on the old cemetery, at the front I see my parents' kitchen and dining room. At meals they sit with the lamp on above the table; every day *The Potato Eaters* is called to mind at least once. I eat at my own table, I don't like being watched. For me, eating consists largely of waiting: waiting for the spasms to go away and then quickly taking a bite. Sometimes that works, other times not, you can't always feel the tremors coming.

Every morning Ma waves to me from the kitchen across the way. Then she brings Pa his coffee. I don't have to be there to hear what that sounds like. After breakfast she comes over and helps me dress. I get coffee and a sandwich. When I go out I roll over the tile walkway in the garden to the bike gate, which leads to the street. At lunchtime Ma brings me a warm meal, at night I heat up a pop-top can of hot dogs and eat them with lots of mustard.

Sam built the shelves for my diaries, I like the looks of them. I see order. Artificial order imposed on everything that's happened.

Every word I write, I write between spasms. During an attack the biro sometimes goes flying through the air.

The inside walls of my house are covered in light-brown plastic panelling with a wood pattern. That's easy to clean; in the winter the garden house is humid and a speckled mould grows on the walls like barnacles on a ship's hull.

Dirk has already moved out of the house, he prefers to live alone with his covert filth. Sammie's only home at the weekends, the rest of the time he stays at a boarding school for young people with learning disabilities. The junkyard is doing well, business there always runs in direct proportion to the general prosperity. Dirk works there full time and someday he'll take over, although Pa doesn't seem anywhere near stopping.

'Good morning, dearie,' Ma says when she comes in in the morning. 'How's about a nice cup of coffee?'

To that end she brings with her a faded plastic vacuum flask from which she pours strong Java. I drink my coffee with a straw, just like all other hot beverages that can cause second-degree burns when you knock them over in your own lap. My favourite straws are the flexi ones you can bend to a forty-five-degree angle. Ma makes my bed, then sits down at the table.

'Oh, that's nice. It was time to take a load off.'

That's just the way she talks, her words are pure comfort. And that's how she keeps the peace around here. Ma's kind of small, but still she's a mountain of a woman. Her flanks are covered with a floral-patterned dress. She tells me things she's heard from other women. Usually about disasters. She likes disasters the way she likes cookies with her coffee. I listen to news of accidents, illnesses and bankruptcies. By talking to each other all the time about other people's misfortunes, women pass fear along. Fear with a capital F. And although they feel compassion for the luckless bastard in question, they're thrilled that it happened a few doors down; the volume of suffering in the world is divided into unequal portions, and the bigger the neighbours' portion the smaller yours will be. Sometimes there's information in there that I'll be able to use someday for my *History of Lomark and Its Citizens* (don't laugh). Looking at Ma as she talks, the melancholy love I feel seizes me right by the throat.

We're condemned to each other; me, her damaged fruit and very personal catastrophe, and she, who, like old horses, carries the world's suffering on her back.

From this side of the table at least she seems to be getting smaller. I'll be around long enough to see her grow completely translucent and then disappear without protest from the face of the Earth – good mother Marie Hermans, née Maria Gezina Putman. Always there to lend a helping hand, a good woman and a loving mother. God rest her soul.

At the registrar's office in the town hall I once tried to find out about the background of the Putman family, but got no further than Lambertus Stephanus Putman, the first Putman to live in Lomark. He came here in 1774, betrothed to a local girl. They didn't marry in the village itself, but just across the border; in those days after the Reformation the Catholic Church was banned around here. Lambert drowned in the great dyke-break of 1781, but with five children he had scattered enough seed to become the patriarch of a new Lomark family.

Not a family that made much of an impression, though. Only a few things have been preserved in the 'Old Judiciary Archive of the Right Seigniory of Lomark', such as cadastral drawings, deeds, *procès-verbals* and baptism certificates. Whenever a Putman had to sign something it almost always says, 'This cross being the signature of So-and-so Putman, having declared the inability to write.'

Even the crosses weren't very good.

They worked at the brickyard or as fishermen or farmers with a few fruit trees in the orchard, and that was pretty much it.

I think about them often. The air I breathe contains molecules they must have inhaled too, I look at the same river they did. It's been partly channelized now and there were no breakwaters back then, but it's still the same water with the same cycle of rest and flood. I sometimes wonder whether all the Jakobs, Dirks, Hanneses, Jans and Henriks felt the same way I do, whether they also hoped so badly that it would all turn out better someday.

Sometimes at night they stand around my bed, the cousins from way-back, speaking quietly to each other in a language I don't understand. They look at me with big eyes, like African children seeing a missionary for the first time. I look back helplessly, they're so dingy, so innocent, I don't know what they want from me; they just stand there and laugh like the ringing of a bell, as though I'm the weirdest thing they've ever seen.

I was scared of them at first, I thought they came from the old cemetery behind my shed-house, but that's nonsense. They don't do any harm, they just stand there and are amazed at me the way I'm amazed at them.

Maybe I should note here that I'm not the first person in our family to see such things. Grandma Geer, my mother's mother, used to live with us. She was a widow and had the room that became Dirk's after she died. I must have been about eight when, at breakfast one morning, Grandma Geer laid her knife on her plate and looked around the circle of faces.

'He's a-come,' she said in her thick Lomark dialect. 'Our Thé's a-come. He sayed: "It'd be all over, girlie, I'm comin' ta fetch ye."'

And she went back to eating her breakfast.

'Our Thé' was her late husband and my late grandfather, Theodorus Christoforus Putman, who had come to sit on her bed that night and promised to fetch her soon.

One week later Grandma Geer was dead; she died in her sleep, seventy-one years old but seemingly fit as a fiddle.

The Hermanses are another story altogether. Pa's family lived here already in the Middle Ages – maybe before that, they may even have arrived with the troops of Claudius Drusus. But when the Vikings showed up they were sitting in the church along with all the rest, praying to be saved while 'the cock that showed its pluck' did their dirty work for them. In the archives I found Hendricus Hermanus Hermans, better known as 'Hend', who was beaten to death with a 'pry of iron' by the bailiff of Lomark in the summer of 1745. Afterwards, his head was 'removed from his bodye with a sharpe ax' and impaled on an iron stake 'in recompense for that committed and as fereful Exampel to all'.

This Hend was found guilty by the magistrate and aldermen of Lomark of the murder of Manus Bax, a fisherman. Hend tortured Manus for three hours to make him confess to the theft of some fishing nets, then beat his brains out with an iron crowbar.

Hend Hermans was married to Annetje Dierikx, who bore a son in the winter after Hend's execution. That son, Hannes Hermans, appears in court records describing the theft of fire-wood and illegal fishing. Hannes sired four children before his first wife died. The second also bore four children, two of whom died in the same flood of 1781 that killed the above-mentioned Lambert Putman. The children who drowned were girls, and after that no girls were born to the Hermans family. Not even stillborn. Only boys. Pa and his brother both have three sons. Like I said: a bloodline of gnarls, and not of soft things. And somehow they all find wives as well, to keep the whole thing going in perpetuity.

Although the Putmans and the Hermanses must have known each other, it took almost two hundred years before a Hermans married a Putman: Pa and Ma. We are the product of that union, descendants of Lambert but especially of Hend, from whom Dirk gets his rage and his thirst for torture. Dirk knows that that's what we're remembered for. That only makes him even more furious.

Sammie is sort of the exception, maybe he's more of a Putman, they're not like that.

And although I had promised myself never to become a Hermans, I know now that I'm just the same. Hend is in us. You can't get him out just like that.

The November before our final exams a pile of junk appeared in the garden, undoubtedly brought there from the wrecking yard. The focal point was a washing machine, around which Pa had piled planks. On top of it all was a kind of cake tin with a lever attached. I didn't want to know what it was supposed to represent, once assembled, because I sensed it would not be to my advantage. A few days later Pa threw a tarpaulin over the whole thing. Now it was a work of art awaiting its unveiling. I kept acting as though I hadn't seen it. Some things go away if you ignore them, while others come bearing down on you.

Ma didn't say anything about it either, so I knew it was bad news. She usually told me everything; her silence now told me that she felt badly about it.

At supper I could see Pa and Ma discussing subjects that I could tell had to do with me; sometimes, when the spark of disagreement jumped the gap, I would see Pa shove his chair back abruptly and raise his voice as he pointed an angry finger toward the garden. I could see that Ma was defending me, but after a while the subject became snowed under – literally as well, for the carload that fell around Christmas covered the garden and the thing along with it. In the morning Ma would defrost a little circle on the kitchen window and wave to me through it.

I went outside less than usual; exams were coming up in May and I planned to pass them without a hitch and graduate with honours. I wanted to deliver one proof of intelligence. I would not go on to university, would not learn a trade, would remain outside the arena of competition, and so I wanted to finish off one thing so that people would say, 'Did you know that the Hermans kid, the poor sod, passed his exams with an 80 percent average!?'

After the fight in the Sun Café, the summer before, a certain distance had grown between me and Joe. It wasn't that he condemned me for it, it was more like I felt bad about it. I had failed to live up to an unspoken but important agreement about the kind of people we were going to be. It had to do with purity, with making sure no one could claim that we were part of a defective world or that we helped increase the volume of idiocy in it. We would form a disdainful fifth column, that was the agreement. But before you knew it, you had blood on your hands.

I had, that is. Not Joe.

That he continued being an example to us, that was a comfort. Sometimes I wondered whether he really saw things as clearly as it seemed; at such moments I thought he was simply indifferent to most things and just sort of laughed at them. But most of the time I was sure that Joe was good at holding people and situations up to the light. Ever since I'd met him I had tried to look at the world through his eyes and weigh it in the balance. The brawl had ruined things, but I really wanted to do better and get my purity back. No matter how Joe laughed at Catholics and their methods, I would do penance and cleanse my soul of the filth I had inherited from Hend. I would go through the fire of purification, come out clean at the other end, and while I was at it I'd cut out the cognac and cola at the weekend, when there was live music at Waanders' roadhouse out along the highway.

But oh, it was a great temptation.

When I'd had a few I stopped caring what people thought, as long as they kept raising that glass to my lips. Until my blood alcohol had risen far enough for me to hold my own glass, that is; alcohol relaxes the muscles and makes the spasms less intense. I was the only person in the crowd who got a steady hand from drinking. I drank therapeutically, as it were.

It would be hard to stay away from Waanders'. People acted different when they were in there. They dared to say more and didn't look past me so skittishly. Others had no problem with feeding me like a lamb raised on the bottle. Sometimes I felt positively cheerful. Elvis or Dolly Parton was playing on the jukebox, outside night had fallen and smoke rose from the copper ashtrays. We were passengers aboard the drunkards' ship, we had slipped our moorings and were drifting to where no one could ever find us. But when the whole thing was over there was always someone who pushed you out the door, cart and all, because they wanted to sweep the floor and turn off the lights. After all, what would become of the world if everyone stayed drunk all the time? I would put up a struggle, swat at the hands that pushed me, yank on the brakes, but they just pushed the whole thing out the door anyway.

'Hey, Frankie, take it easy, man!'

When they laughed, it was in annoyance at the struggle against what was always an untimely end to all things good and easy.

It was a bad winter for Mahfouz. He'd taken on the tint of unvarnished garden furniture.

'It's my blood,' he complained. 'It's not good.'

He was wearing three sweaters and a ski jacket and had a wool cap pulled down far over his ears. All you could see was his moustache and a pair of rheumy eyes.

He wasn't the only one who'd been feeling poorly. Christof's grandmother had died, even though she must have expected to see the daffodils come up one last time. But March arrived too late for her, and she remained behind in February. February is a real bastard.

The day they put old Louise Maandag in the ground the heating in the church was turned up high; the east wind cut through your clothes like a scythe. The people actually kept their coats on inside to save up a little heat for the procession to the grave. The church was filled to the rafters. A dead Maandag always receives a lot of attention, because so many people are dependent on them in one way or another. Nieuwenhuis gave it everything he had, he sprinkled his water and swayed his incense with the holiest of holies he had in him.

I was parked in the aisle, Joe was sitting beside me at the inside end of the pew. Beside him was Engel, his legs crossed in godless elegance. Two rows up ahead I saw the blond curls belonging to P.J., who was sitting ridiculously close to Joop Koeksnijder. Old Look-at-how-cool-I-am Koeksnijder, finished school two years ago and the proud owner of a Volkswagen Golf. Outside you could hear a truck backing up; my eyes traced the contours of P.J.'s shoulders. She had the broad, straight shoulders of a swimmer.

Sometimes the sight of her would suddenly enrage me. I'd never had that with Harriët Galma or Ineke de Boer, who had been the very first in our class to bear fruit and already went bowed beneath their weight. Sometimes I stared at P.J. for the longest time, just to see whether there was something not quite right there, something ugly or weird to make it hurt less, and sometimes I drove my cart along right behind her to see if she stank. But she didn't stink. Then I would grow furious and feel like crushing something. But the angry flame always leapt to the inside.

Up at the front of the church, Nieuwenhuis was blaring, 'And when You call us to You, we bow to Your majesty!'

Joe leaned over to me.

'So you finally get around to being dead and you have to god-damn bow all over again!'

He leaned back in the pew, then thought better of it.

'If He'd wanted us to do so much bowing, why didn't He make us with a hinge at the back?'

I burst out laughing. A lot of people looked around, I simulated a spasm. Joe sat there, keeping a straight face. Christof stood up stiffly from a pew at the front and walked to the coffin with his grandmother in it. A couple of nieces and nephews followed him, they all put a rose on the lid. Men came to lift the coffin onto their shoulders and carry it up the aisle and outside, and with that the whole thing was pretty much over. The visitors crowded out behind the bearers. Piet Honing gave me a friendly nod.

It was hard for me, having Piet be so nice all the time. I could never have been that nice back, simply because I didn't have enough of it in me. It would always be a transaction in which I found myself short of change, and that left me feeling guilty.

I was the last in line and rolled down the little ramp at the side entrance. There were a few people standing around out there, lighting cigarettes and commenting on the service, the rest were walking behind the hearse. We were bathed in the light of a limitless blue sky. I watched the tail of the procession disappear and had to take a shit. I went home.

There was no one out on the street, and the shops, usually filled at that hour with housewives with little children, were empty. I turned right on Poolseweg and heard footsteps behind me. Joe passed me, he was running toward his house. He waggled his eyebrows at me as he went by. At the bottom of Poolseweg he suddenly stopped and turned around.

'Hey, Frankie, how much do you weigh anyway?' he asked when I got up to him.

A year earlier I had weighed a little over fifty kilos, and I hadn't put on much weight since. I held up five fingers and saw his lips moving along with his thoughts. He seemed to be calculating something.

'Fifty kilos, right?' he said. 'How much difference can it make? You feel like taking a little spin in the plane?'

My eyes grew big in horror. And I still had to shit real bad. It made my stomach hurt.

'Not a long ride,' Joe said. 'Just a little spin, to get the feel of it.'

Between that moment on Poolseweg and the moment when he climbed into the cockpit in front of me, all swaddled up like a samurai, a little more than sixty minutes went by. I could have used each of them to change my mind. Like when he took me home first, where sunlight fell through the windows like fire, and stood at the back window for a while looking out at the dishevelled General Cemetery where his father was buried – all that time I could have said no.

I hoisted myself out of the cart and grabbed the edge of the table. Like a drugged chimp with one short leg I lumbered across the room, holding onto chairs, tables and cabinets. Joe turned around and looked at me in dumb amazement.

'Hey, man, you can walk?'

If walking was what you'd call it. I crossed from the dresser to the toilet door and disappeared behind. I pulled the door closed hard after me and sat down on the pot with my trousers still fastened. I had to go so bad that I broke out in a sweat. I clenched my teeth and wormed my way madly out of my trousers while my intestines did their best to rid themselves of their freight. Sometimes you have to go so bad and you can still keep it up for a long time, but as soon as you get close to a toilet you need superhuman willpower to keep it all in. It seems like intestines know when there's a toilet around.

Just in time. I couldn't do anything to muffle the dull, heavy farts.

'Well, well!' Joe said from the other side of the door.

That door was nothing more than a framework of slats with lily-covered wallpaper, so the voice of my intestines was as clear to him as it was to me. A second wave came rolling out.

'Man-oh-man!'

I felt like dying. Just like with Engel and that urinal. Maybe that's the way women feel at the gynaecologist's, butt up in the air and legs wide while a cold ice-cream scoop grubs around inside them.

When I came back into the room, I didn't look at him. The

light lifted the ramshackle objects in my house and examined them from all sides – wear, poverty and age had nowhere to hide. I gimped my way over to the dresser beside the bed to wrap myself up for the flight.

'If I had a dog that smelled like that,' Joe muttered, 'I'd take it out and shoot it.'

We went to his house to fetch a bike and, for better or worse, lugged my suddenly-six-times bulkier corpus onto the baggage carrier.

'OK,' Joe panted, 'and now don't move.'

He seized the handlebars and tossed his left leg over the crossbar. Standing with his right foot on the pedal he used his full weight to get us rolling. At the end of the street Joe stood on the pedals and accelerated, but made it only three-quarters of the way up the long slope to the dyke before he had to hop off. I almost flew off the baggage carrier.

All things considered, the whole operation had already cost so much effort that I wished there was some way I could get out of it. It was so damned cold that it turned your face hard and sullen, the wind whipped tears from my eyes that I couldn't wipe away because I had to hold onto Joe. Like a warm, heaving animal he fought his way upwind along the dyke to the spot where he'd stashed his plane. My legs with those black leather circus shoes at the ends of them dangled alongside the baggage carrier, I couldn't rest them on the frame and so I had to sit the whole damn way with my full weight resting on my nuts.

Halfway between Lomark and Westerveld we coasted down off the dyke and onto Gemeenschapspolderweg. Along that road were three isolated farms. The wind was finally behind us. To the left and right the black fields lay fallow, ploughed for the winter into frozen furrows with frost on their backs. We cycled up a private road, gravel chirped beneath the wheels. At the end of the road was the farm that belonged to Dirty Rinus. So this was where the plane had been hidden all this time! I saw no trace of Rinus himself or his brown Opel Ascona. In the yard stood a wheelbarrow, its handgrips the only things not encrusted with a layer of dried manure and straw, otherwise the thing seemed covered with it. Joe rode to the shed all the way at the back and leaned me, bike and all, against the wall.

'Wait here for a minute,' he said, as though I had any choice.

He disappeared through a little stable door. It wasn't hard to figure out why he'd parked the plane at Dirty Rinus's; Rinus didn't give a shit – the one thing he had plenty of – about anything. Sitting there against the brick wall like a sack of potatoes, I could see into one of the stalls where a row of Belgian Blue cattle stared back in despond. They were up to their knees in manure. Along their bellies I could see horizontal scars. Caesarean sections: Belgian blues are mutants with a birth canal that's way too narrow; their calves have to be cut out from the side.

I was cold and my balls ached. Somewhere a pair of doors slid open, followed a moment later by the strangled cough of an engine that had been standing still for a while. After the first few tries it caught. I recognized the sound: a 100hp Subaru engine. Joe let it idle for a few minutes to warm up the oil and water.

Until that moment I could have changed my mind. We would have gone back home, Joe would have shrugged in puzzlement but forgotten it quickly enough, and I would have been relieved not to have to go through with it. But once the plane came around the corner, it was too late.

I don't think I had fully realized that I was going flying. Only when I saw that sky-blue monster appear again after a whole year did a wave of fear and excitement go coursing through me. Joe circled around the yard and turned the plane with its nose toward the pasture. Then he turned off the engine, stepped out onto the wing and climbed down.

'Like a charm,' he said, sounding pleased.

He went around behind me, put his arms under my armpits and locked his fingers across my chest. He pulled me off the baggage carrier like a drowning man. His breath brushed my face, I could smell Mahfouz's cooking.

'Help out a little here,' he grunted, 'you're too heavy for me.'

I hung in his arms like a baby learning to walk. With my good hand I grabbed hold of the wing and nodded to him to let go. It was the first time we'd ever stood beside each other. I was more than a year older than Joe, but a head shorter.

'Let's see, how are we going to do this?' Joe said.

He found a ladder with liquid-manure spatters on it and leaned it against the side of the plane. He himself stepped up onto the wing and into the belly of the machine, then held his hand out to me.

'If you just...yeah, the first rung, then I can give you...give me your hand...now put your foot up, your foot! One more... hold on...'

And so I arrived breathlessly in the plane's rattan bucket seat. Joe pushed the ladder away and sat down in front of me, half on the metal superstructure because there was only one chair. Together on a bicycle built for one.

'Can you see all right?'

My head stuck up just above the edge of the cockpit.

'Here we go, Frankie.'

He turned the key in the ignition and started the engine. We taxied through the open gate and into the pasture, a strip of frozen grassland stretched out before us. Joe put the plane into neutral and pulled on the handbrake. Then he opened the throttle the whole way. Thunder rolled, a frozen hurricane roared around our ears. I was chilled to the bone.

'Flaps out!' Joe shouted.

He popped the handbrake and we leapt forward. I grabbed him around the waist and we shot ahead with a deafening din. I felt his body working the pedals and the joystick, which he pulled all the way back when we reached full speed.

We were off. The ground disappeared beneath us, I screamed. The plane shivered, the wings swept left and right but we were already twice as high as the tallest poplar, with nothing more to worry about. There was a cheerful tingling in my scrotum. Behind and off to one side I saw the river and the washlands. Joe turned ninety degrees to the right and flew parallel to the river, heading for Lomark. The icy cold wind made my eyes and nose run and paralyzed my lips, but I ignored it. The plane stank of petrol.

From the looks of it we were going to hold at this altitude. It was hard to say how far up that really was. Below us the world reeled past like a slapstick film. Every rise and every hill that usually cost me so much effort was now nothing but a bump. My entire biotope, including all the things ordinarily hidden behind houses, hedges, ridges and dykes, was laughably flat and obvious from here. At this height there were no more secrets, and that was sad and lovely.

Every once in a while Joe looked back over his shoulder and shouted something unintelligible. The plane shuddered across the blue-golden sky and I was reminded of those old monster movies where Godzilla and all kinds of other dinosaurs moved just as unnaturally and jerkily as we did in mid-air.

In the milky distance I saw the electrical plant blowing its vertical plume of smoke. Joe pointed down. We were above

Lomark. In the depths lay the cemetery, where Louise Maandag's funeral seemed to be over. I tried to trace the road to Het Karrewiel where the funeral guests should now be eating their sandwiches. I found the restaurant, in the parking lot I saw the last few people in black on their way to the big dining room for coffee and sandwiches with salami and cheese, with no idea that we were up above them.

Joe shoved the joystick to the left, the left wing plunged down and the right one came up as he banked toward the river, back where we'd started. In my stomach I felt the jubilant sensation of falling. We were going to put the plane down before they had to saw us out of the cockpit like two frozen primeval hunters. The plane levelled out. I picked out the ferry landing and the old shipyard and then a wee little man who looked like he was dragging something much bigger than he was. Joe saw him too.

'Mahfouz!' he screamed over his shoulder.

The river gleamed and the cars' roofs glistened along the dyke. I tried to take it all in at one go in order never to forget.

When I saw Rinus's farm coming up fast, I was stunned – the landing! I didn't want to think about the landing, I'd never watched Joe make a landing before, the landing was the hardest thing of all about flying! I thought about death, about how, together, Joe and I...and suddenly I wasn't so afraid of it anymore. We passed over the farm and now I saw Dirty Rinus's Opel parked in the yard. The plane turned and lost altitude fast. The pasture was right in front of us and Joe was starting his approach. He was going to try to be as close as possible to the ground when he got to the field, I felt his body go tense, the wings shivered nervously and we were still going way too fast...Pull up! Pull up, man! But he headed on in, with the pasture looming like a wall. Joe pushed the throttle all the way in and pulled the flaps all the way out, the noise dimmed but the earth was still coming up at us like a fist. Then the wheels smacked the ground. The plane hopped and came back down again, we raced across the field and I saw chunks of dirt flying up. We were losing speed fast.

Right before the fence Joe brought the plane to a halt.

The landing had taken an alarming number of metres more than liftoff.

When he killed the engine, Joe's body relaxed. The silence came pouring into my ears.

Two metres in front of us, Dirty Rinus was leaning against the fence, a rollup dangling from his lips and his index finger raised in minimalist greeting. Joe turned to me and gave me a purple-lipped grin.

'That was a tight one,' he said.

The edges of his ski goggles were rimmed with ice.

Things are looking up. The washlands are almost dry, the willows bend over the pools left behind. Their lower branches are hung with flotsam, between them the coots paddle in search of nesting material. At dusk the bats come swarming out and at night, when you hear the first frogs, you know the weather will be getting better soon. Mahfouz could use some spring sun as well. Sometimes we sit on the quay together, soaking up a little warmth while he scans the sky to see what all that trumpeting could be about.

'Nile goose,' he says.

Two Egyptian geese go squabbling low overhead. That's late March. Then comes April and the fist you made against winter unclenches. But too soon. In April the wind starts blowing like you'd forgotten it could ever blow. Your house shrinks beneath the hammering. Out on the street people shout to each other, 'Weird, this wind, huh?!', meaning that it crawls into the cracks in your brain and drives you raving mad. It goes around yanking liked a spoiled kid on whatever it finds. You thought everything was battened down but the whole world is flapping and moaning. Including, of course, shutters, gutters and decorative elements. The wind changes pitch and volume all the time and you can hear church bells and children's voices in it. It feels to me like it's coming straight off the Russian tundra, a filthy east wind that humps against the back of my house and makes it impossible for me to study.

The geography book I've buried my nose in speaks of permafrost and tundra landscapes ('agriculturally, such soils are of no significance') that remain eternally frozen. Sometimes to a depth of hundreds of metres. Finals are in May, I have a 7.8 average for my exams but I've still got the jitters. I long for the moment when it's all over – it's not the thought of it but the longing that's so nice, that every day brings you closer to the moment when you stand on the banks and watch Jordan calmly roll by. My fervent longing is one I share with twenty others who, at this same moment, are all struggling with extracts, workbooks and low bacteriological activity in the tundra. We long collectively for *thereafter*. But when all this is behind us they will enter the promised land, and I will remain behind. I'm very much aware of that.

When the wind finally dies down it starts raining so hard that the streets foam. That goes on for days. But one morning you wake up with the feeling that something is missing – the noise is gone! The rain has stopped and the wind has blown over. Somewhere a wood pigeon is cooing. The branches outside are motionless, they drip and glimmer in the early sunlight. You hear jackdaws happily tumbling through the sky above the cemetery.

That is late April.

From down by the river comes the sound of handiwork.

I know now that it was a keel beam Joe and I saw Mahfouz dragging along the day we flew over the river. He's building a boat.

'It's a felucca,' says Mahfouz, who's too busy to talk much these days.

Joe says the boat symbolizes the love between Mahfouz and

his mother. Other people have their own song, they have a boat. The first time they met, Mahfouz gave her a model boat, a felucca, which is now on the windowsill in her bedroom.

They have something with boats, those two. After they got married in Cairo they took a short cruise on the Nile. One night they stood on deck and looked up at an uncommonly clear sky full of stars, and that was when Regina had a vision. She saw a wooden ship being driven by bent-backed rowers; she and Mahfouz lay on a bed of pillows on the afterdeck while girls in white stroked the air above them with ostrich-feather fans. He was a prince of great beauty, she a lady from the highest ranks of society. Regina's eyes shone with tears when the vision faded. 'We've done this before, Mahfouz,' she'd said. 'This isn't our first life together.'

Joe shakes his head. 'She married my father as a Hindu princess and Mahfouz as Nefertiti. She's the whole history of the world rolled into one.'

At the spot where the Demsté shipyard once stood – the firm went bankrupt in 1932, but when the water's low you can see what's left of the slips – Mahfouz has built a framework of planks in the form of a ship. It's not very long, six metres or so, and it's shaped differently from what you usually see around here. The frame is only the rough form of what the boat will be, but it looks broader than our sailboats. The front and back curve up only slightly, more like a cargo ship than a yacht. Here and there along the quay are sawhorses with planks laid across them, and weights to slowly bend the wood into shape.

Regina bikes down along the Lange Nek to bring Mahfouz tea, bread and cigarettes. She devours him with her eyes, her Nubian. The colour that our winter wiped from his face is gradually coming back. He's building her a flagship, she lights his cigarettes and pours him tea with enough sugar in it to knock the enamel off your teeth. Reluctantly he lays aside his plane and sits down beside her. From her bag she produces sandwiches wrapped in silver foil. Ferryboat passengers stop and look at the shipyard's small-scale resurrection. Mahfouz works amid the paintless sloops on their trailers with flat tyres and the green river buoys twice a man's height, all waiting to be hauled away by Hermans & Sons. He works hard, he wants to launch the boat this very summer. The steam box he's built to bend the stubborn rib beams consists of a length of pipe; he hangs the rib in the pipe, boils water on a small fire under it, and the steam disappears into the pipe and softens the wood.

'Wow,' Joe says as we watch him from the top of the landing, 'he's pretty good.'

'He could make a living at that,' Christof says.

Engel is thinking about it.

'If it was me I'd paint it blue.'

In response to a mysterious kind of magnetism, Christof and I turn our heads at the same moment in the direction of Lomark and see P.J. coming along the Lange Nek. That kindles a flame in the two of us, but the company she's in creates a cold countercurrent: Joop Koeksnijder.

'Dirty Nazi,' Christof hisses.

That never dies out. Of course Look-at-how-cool-I-am Koeksnijder isn't a Nazi, but his grandfather was, and that's still the first thing that comes to mind when you see his grandson, especially when he's with P.J. Eilander. The prick. We hate Jopie with a hatred fed by intense envy. And we hate that even more. He possesses the object of our dreams – look, she gives him a shove and he hops away, you can feel their obsession with each other all the way over here. Like disgruntled old men, we turn back to Mahfouz and his boat.

It takes forever for P.J. and Jopie to get six feet away from us, where they stop to view the activity down in the old shipyard. Koeksnijder nods to us, Engel and Joe return his greeting.

'He's building a *boat*,' I hear P.J. say in amazement.

Her Afrikaans has worn away to a faint accent.

'Enough of those around, I'd say,' Koeksnijder says.

I don't look at P.J., because she can read my thoughts this way too.

'Joe,' she asks, 'isn't that your mother's husband? The man from Egypt?'

Joe nods.

'Papa Africa,' he says, and that really makes her laugh.

Koeksnijder moves behind her and a little to one side, in the attitude of a man protecting something.

'Papa Africa,' P.J. repeats. 'So what does that make me?'

'The daughter of the man who hurt me last week. Two cavities.'

Koeksnijder lays a hand on P.J.'s lower back, the way impatient husbands do on Saturday afternoon as they propel their wives past the shop windows.

'We're going across the river,' P.J. announces. 'Bye-bye!'

Christof mumbles something dull, Engel says, 'Good luck with your finals.'

The gates of the ferry close behind them, we watch them go.

'She likes you,' Engel says to Joe.

'You're the one who deals with the women around here,' Joe says. 'I'll stick to things that run on petrol.'

Engel, accustomed by now to his own electrifying effect on girls, shakes his head in disbelief.

'She never looked at me even once…'

In preparation for their lives to come, Joe, Engel and Christof attend the orientation day for higher education. Joe comes home from the polytechnic looking disappointed.

'Worthless,' he says, 'I could teach myself that just as easily. That place smells of nothing.'

It's only when he goes along with Engel to the art academy, just for a lark, that he finds what he wants. The Applied Arts section has exactly what he was looking for: lathes and CO_2 welders. The studio is full of mysterious constructions in various stages of development, and the walls are hung with the most minute working drawings.

'The whole place smells like machine oil,' he says.

Only then do I realize that his comment about the odour of nothingness at the polytechnic was meant literally. He follows his nose, and that's new to me.

Engel signs up for a major in illustration, Joe for the applied arts. In order to be admitted, they have to present work that demonstrates both their talent and their motivation. Engel shows up with a portfolio full of work that qualifies him immediately, Engel is a natural born artist if ever there was one. I've never thought of Joe as an artist, though, and as far as I know he never has either. He could just as easily become an instrument maker or a technical engineer. But although he admires engineers for giving the world its motor skills, when he thinks about it he finds himself better suited to a freer curriculum.

On the day of the entrance exam he unbolts the wings of his plane and lashes the whole thing onto a trailer. Dirty Rinus drives him to the academy; when they go in the porter says, 'You're not allowed to smoke in here, sir,' effectively banishing the little farmer out of doors for the rest of the morning. Joe rolls the fuselage into the building and installs it in the room where the evaluation will be taking place. Once the wings are back on it, all the space is taken up. And does it really work? a professor asks. Joe climbs in and starts the engine. A tornado tears through the classroom. He's accepted.

But let's go, time is running short, next Monday will see the start of the big test to show who's ready for the world and who isn't.

There's cruelty in the fact that the exams take place on the loveliest day of the year. The fields are groaning with vigour, trees unfurl their leaves with the pleasure of a person stretching his limbs. Above it all shines a tingling spring sun that urges everything on to more, while we sit row by row in the assembly hall and have no part in it. We shuffle our feet restlessly, cough faintly and chew on government-issue biros. Cursed be the first to finish and turn in his exam with serene superiority. Cursed too the man on rubber soles who sneaks along the aisles. And completely cursed be P.J., with whom I share the same electives, leaving my mind eclipsed sevenfold by things other than anaerobic dissimilation and the pseudopodia of amoebae. Shame on her for the lustiness of such a body. It emits signals of nothing but plenty. I ogle the white flesh of her rounded upper arms like a starving cannibal, and feel little and evil at the deregulating message of her hips as she leaves the room while most of us are still hard at work. A few weeks later I will look first under the letter E on the list of candidates and see that she has passed with a 9 for biology, and nothing lower than an 8 for the other subjects. I myself prove to be a solid 7.8 man, but let me blame that on her presence.

Joe and Engel chose maths, chemistry and physics, which to me is like decoding a message from another planet. The only one who chose two full years of economics was Christof – in order, I believe, to learn the tenets of the entrepreneurship in store for him by birth.

All three of them pass their exams too, but Joe forbids his mother to hang out the book bag and flag. Even Quincy Hansen passes at last, albeit only after resits in Dutch and English.

And so you've finished school, and then this happens:
'It's a solution,' Pa says, 'a solution.'
'We've talked about it a lot,' says Ma. 'If it doesn't work out, we'll think of something else.'

'Let him *try* it first. There's no harm in *having* to do something. You think we used to be able to do whatever we liked? Working hard every day, and you didn't ask yourself whether you liked it: you did as you were told.'

'Frankie, you don't *have* to do anything. It's a start.'

'A solution is what it is! Just the thing for him. The best for everyone.'

'But don't you go thinking…'

'He knows that already.'

'That we want to make money off it, all we want is for you to be able to stand on your own two feet. When we're not around anymore.'

'Is he asleep?'

'From all that studying, sure, the boy's worn out.'

'He never misses a night at Waanders' though. If he can do that, he can work too. I'm telling you, it's a solution.'

Pa removed the plastic tarp from the pile in the garden and stood there looking at it for a while. It resembled nothing so much as a tangled mountain of pickup sticks, and I saw doubt creep into his movements. He pulled on a few loose ends and leaned a couple of parts up against my house. He avoided looking inside, he knew I was peering at him from the shadows. One hour later he had the pile sorted out: bars with bars and grids with grids. These he used to build a scaffolding against the side of the house. Left over now was a washing machine and what I knew by then was a press for making briquettes. That machine was to be the start of my career as a briquette presser. Paper briquettes, for the fireplace.

Here's how Pa figured it: I would go door to door collecting old newspapers, and because I was a charitable cause in and of myself, people would be pleased to help out and we would have loads of paper from which to press briquettes.

The garden had now become a workshop. The paper was rinsed and pulverized in the washing machine, after which I scooped it into the press. On the side of the press was a handle I used to press the metal lid down onto the paper pulp, squeezing the water out of it. Then I laid the moist briquettes on the scaffolding against the wall. Pa would take the dried lumps to the wrecking yard, where he would sell them to customers in wintertime, or use them to heat the canteen, don't ask me. 'I tell you, it's a solution…'

Summer was in full swing, the exams seemed far behind me now, and on some days I actually felt – how shall I put it? – useful. I pulled on the press plate so hard that my hand hurt, from the bottom of the grillwork trickled a greyish sludge, water mixed with pulp and printer's ink that had been used to report the birth of a polar bear or sixteen people killed in Tel Aviv. Headlines flashed by each time I loaded the machine, sometimes I found myself immersed in newspapers that were a year old. They weren't very different from today's paper, in fact; news articles were as hard to tell apart as Chinamen.

As in a sort of time machine I rocketed back and forth between an armed insurrection in April and the fall of the president in October, and looked through the window of the washing machine at how the world's events sloshed around a few times before decaying into gray porridge. Load, fill, press, dry – mechanical and efficient. On a good day I could press about forty to fifty briquettes. Load, fill, press, dry. It was simple, and it made me happy. In some strange way I felt a connection to Papa Africa – as Joe, Christof and Engel now called him – working on his boat at the old shipyard.

When I had some strength left in my arm at the end of the day, I would ride out to see him. I liked the work around a boat, and shivered whenever he planed the wood away into a tight curl. He worked himself into a lather, standing amid a sea of light yellow wood curls that smelled heavenly. A long telephone pole that would be the mast lay on a set of sawhorses and was planed to fit. Whenever Papa Africa straightened up from his work, the pain in his back made him moan and he would rest his hands on his hips as he stretched.

He walked around his boat, surveying it critically.

'This is what I use to make my ship,' he said, holding up his ten fingers.

Then he pointed to his head.

'And this is for the mistakes.'

I also liked the pounding of the chisels, which sounded from a distance as though someone were beating out music on a hollow tree.

Papa Africa began building the hull with overlapping planks, working from the keel up and hammering the wooden skin into place against the timbers. When he was finished, a real boat was there, not quite finished but also not too far from completion. The curls went flying from the yardarm.

Christof, who knew a bit about boats, said that a felucca like this one used an 'Arab lateen rig'. I'd never gotten used to his know-it-all tone. He displayed his incidental knowledge with so much aplomb that sometimes I went home and looked it up afterwards. I was never able to catch him out.

Christof would be going to law school in Utrecht. I wouldn't miss him. But yet, when I stopped to think about it, he was as much a part of my life as Joe or Engel. I'd had a few years to watch him closely and would have been surprised to find anything that had escaped me. I knew his tic, a contraction of the muscles around the right eye that pulled the corner of his mouth up with it. It was only slight, and it went very quickly, as though he were winking at invisible things, and I wondered whether he knew that his tic only appeared when Joe was around. Otherwise I knew that he countenanced absolutely no onions on his fries-with-the-works, and that at the age of sixteen he'd had a wet dream that featured his mother with three breasts.

Even if I didn't like him very much, maybe you could still call it a kind of friendship when you know someone that well, like a part of yourself that you'd rather not face.

My working days began on foot. The machines and scaffolding offered enough places for me to grab hold and move around. By seven I was already up and about, early enough to hear the roosters crowing at the farms out in the polder. The first hour was too serene to ruin with washing-machine noise, I spent it reading old news and smoking cigarettes others had rolled for me. Around eight I began operations. The briquettes, gray and fragile when I took them from the press, dried within about a week into firm, light-brown loaves. After noon my legs would start hurting; then I would plop down in the cart and work like that for a few more hours in the afternoon sun.

I felt healthy and strong, I had my first real wages in my pocket, and sometimes I would sit with Joe down at the ferry landing and drink the beer I'd brought along in the saddlebag on my cart. He, Christof and Engel were still around, and if you stopped thinking about it you could imagine that things would always stay this way, that we would always form a kind of community and that I could occasionally sit at the quayside with Joe while he flicked bottle caps into the water and Papa Africa stretched his back and moaned.

P.J. had already left; she had enrolled in the literature program in Amsterdam and found a room there. Someone told me that Joop Koeksnijder had gone to visit her once, and that she had treated him like a stranger.

I saw Koeksnijder at the street market one afternoon and suddenly understood what I'd seen before, the time he and P.J. had crossed the river and stopped to talk to us: a man about to lose his most valued possession. In essence he was already braced against the pain back then, it was already in his movements, but his awareness had continued to put up a fight. Now that she was gone, what we saw was a pauper who'd once been made king for a day.

I felt sorry for him – he had grown smaller, a figure from the past, not half the self-assured titan he had once been, but I'd be lying if I said that my relief wasn't greater than my pity. I didn't want to see anyone with P.J., and particularly not him.

She was my most valued illusion.

The situation was less than ideal: in the realm of fantasy I had to share her with Christof, who was subject to the same visions. I eliminated him from my daydreams with axes, trucks and heavy objects that fell on him at my behest.

*

Each Saturday I went door to door collecting scrap paper. After a while everyone knew what I was coming for, sometimes they had the bundles of brochures and newspapers waiting for me. The brochures were no use to me, but I let it go, it was touching to see the care with which some people tied up handy packages for me, bound with lengths of twine and knotted at the top. They seemed pleased to be able to do something like that. I wasn't quite sure how to deal with it.

Some of them made me wait outside, others said, 'Come in, Frankie, do come in!' and gave me a cup of coffee or a cigarette. Until then I had seen those houses only from the outside. This gave me lots of new insights. Now I could write my *History* from the inside as well. How do we live? What happens behind closed doors? What does it smell like? (Shoe polish. Furniture wax. Buttered frying pans. Old carpet.) Here in Lomark we listen to a transistor radio on the kitchen table, beside it a copy of the radio guide and lying on top of that a set of keys and a giro slip from a Catholic charity. In the living room, family photographs on the mantelpiece (Catholic families always taken from far away because otherwise they don't all fit in the viewfinder) and the eternal houseplants on the windowsill.

But what does that tell you? That things have gone well for us, during the second half of the twentieth century? We drive comfortable cars and heat our middle-class homes with natural gas. The Germans are long gone, after that we were afraid of Communists, nuclear weapons and recession, but death is worse. No one tells us what to do, but we know what's expected of us. Don't talk about a thing, but never forget anything either. We remember everything, and in silence we hoard information about those who surround us. Between our lives run invisible lines that separate or connect us, lines an outsider knows nothing of, no matter how long he lives here.

I've heard and seen a lot in those houses. I've heard the voice with which we speak around here of present and past, I'll do my best to let that be heard as well. About the National Socialist Movement, for example. When the Dutch National Socialist Movement received 8 percent of the popular vote during the parliamentary elections in 1935, we here in Lomark shouldered our share of the load. Some of the things-aren't-what-they-used-to-be men remember real well. If they would talk about it, it would sound like this:

He came here to give a speech, Anton Mussert, born beside the big river just like us. He was there for us, for the shopkeeper and the market gardener still reeling from the Crisis, who never got a penny of government support. He was a former head engineer with the Utrecht Province Department of Roads and Waterways, a man of the delta. We, who wanted nothing but a return to the old certainties, applauded loudest for the man who promised to restore Faith in God, Allegiance to People and Fatherland and the Love of Work. The meeting was held in the Ferry House down by the river. It was a winter evening, and they arrived from Utrecht in a couple of cars, they drove there along the Lange Nek. It was a small army of men in hats and long overcoats who climbed out and lined up beside the entrance, in the weak light shed by the lamp above the door. As though on cue they raised their right arms in the fascist salute and shouted a powerful '*Hou Zee!*' You could see their breath steaming, when they went into the Ferry House they were silent and disciplined.

The party was doing us a great honour with the Leader's visit. More than two hundred people had gathered in the pine-panelled Peace Hall, they came from far and wide to hear him speak. Mussert was a round man, actually kind of short. I guess maybe we felt a little disappointed at first when we saw this man whose dark hair had receded to the back of his head, leaving only a tuft at the forehead that he combed to a jaunty quiff. But we were so mistaken! A voice shouted, 'The Leader!' Then Mussert marched to the front out of a dark cloud of storm troopers and looked us over with his strikingly pale eyes. His body had moulded itself to the task history had laid on him: his chin jutting, his shoulders thrown back, like the first runner to cross the finish. When he raised his right arm, as though driven by a powerful spring, he kindled awe and pride in us, and we rose as one to return his salute. That is how we stood, facing each other. Then his arm dropped, pushing us as it were back into our seats, and he administered the following jolt of electricity.

'Brothers of our nation!'

We shivered with an obedient kind of pleasure, with warmth and reverence. His right eye spit fire, but the rational left eye weighed each word that crossed his thin lips. In unbending earnest he spoke to us about the degeneration of the modern age. About the Red Menace. About the farcical regime of the anti-revolutionary Colijn.

'We see the continuing decline of trade and industry, terror- ization by an army of presumptuous civil servants, and impoverishment. We shall free the people from the yoke of the political parties! The farmers will pursue their calling again as of old; workers from high to low, from director to errand boy, will once again come to realize that they have a task to fulfil in harmony on behalf of their people! A new prosperity shall be established; strict, powerful, but loving... Our able-bodied folk will defend our soil, our fatherland, our empire with all of the strength at our command, against all those who would mar the lustre of our independence or our territory!'

This was no political will-o'-the-wisp, not the way his opponents said, here stood a statesman. He was the one we would follow, he was the right man to lead us out of the Crisis to better days. Even the hearts of the doubters went out to him. His voice soared, the volume was raised.

'The Netherlands shall be independent of all foreign powers, a bulwark of peace, prepared to defend itself against all attackers, prepared to help build a federation of European states between whom confidence has been restored, who will prove a worthy instrument for the preservation of European peace and European culture!'

Our applause rained down on him. He was visibly pleased to be the object of our cheers. He spoke for an hour, then someone else came up to instruct us in how we ourselves could contribute to the restoration of our nation. After that we sang 'A Mighty Fortress Is Our God' and the national anthem, and then it was over. Buzzing with new hope we left the Peace Hall. Many of us bought copies of *Volk en Vaderland*. Far away, on the dyke, the red tail lights of Mussert's convoy disappeared into the night.

For Papa Africa, all the world's rivers were the same. They may have had different names, but all fed one and the same current. The Nile was the only river on earth, and at some point all the earth's waters flowed past his father's shipyard in Kom Ombo.

'He doesn't really think this is the Nile, does he?' Engel asked.

'Rhine, Nile, same-same,' Joe imitated his stepfather.

'If you look at it philosophically, I guess,' Engel said.

'Didn't he ever have geography at school?' Christof asked.

'He can't point to Cairo in the atlas. He doesn't know exactly where he is right now. And I don't think he cares much, really.'

Silent with incomprehension, we looked at the phenomenon that was Papa Africa, pencil tucked behind his ear, plucking at his moustache as he walked the yard. The boat's hull had now been painted red right up to the waterline, the rest was white. The mast still had to be raised and he was waiting for the sail, which Regina was sewing from stretches of canvas. The maiden voyage would be held in late August, and Regina wanted to throw a party at the wharf that day. She had big plans; she wasn't going to let this chance for attention and admiration go to waste.

The day itself was coming up fast, but I had a bad feeling about the whole thing. After that weekend Joe, Engel and

Christof would be leaving, classes started in September and I would remain behind in the realm of the dead. With a briquette press. I had truly been giving that thing hell, pressing far more briquettes than the drying racks could hold.

'With so many of them the price will go down,' Pa said.

Ma heard him say that. She pursed her lips, her arms folded across her chest.

'Twenty-five is what I'll give him from now on,' Pa said, apologetic but determined. 'Twenty-five is still a good price. When you've got overproduction, the price goes down, that's the way it is everywhere.'

'You have to keep your word,' Ma said.

'Well then he shouldn't make so many of them. If you don't have a lot of something you pay more for it, and if you've got a lot you pay less. Ask anyone.'

'He's your son.'

'He just spends it all at Waanders' anyway.'

Whatever the case, from that day on I got twenty-five for fifty briquettes and Ma made up the difference from her house-keeping money. And indeed, most of it I brought to Waanders'. Waanders' roadhouse had the advantage of being along the national highway, outside the village, which made a difference in both clientele and atmosphere. It was better than the Sun, where the mood was often, how shall I put it, *testy*, the sleeping dogs there sometimes woke up and busted right out of the kennel. The Little Red Rooster, on the other hand, was more like a bingo parlour for old people, you only went there for wedding parties or to get in out of the rain. Waanders' was the best. Trucks and cars stopped there with people I'd never seen before, which gave me hope, the way a certain kind of woman derives hope from an influx of enemy soldiers.

An example.

'What will it be for the gentlemen?' the barwoman asks a truck driver who comes in spreading the smell of warm asphalt.

He has his little boy with him, his son who's allowed to ride along in the cab today.

'What do you want?' the man asks the boy in a voice you wouldn't expect from him. He's wearing mules with white socks.

'A Coke,' the boy says.

'And something to eat?'

'French fries. With mayo.'

'French fries for the boy and I'll have ... a gravy-roll sandwich. Heavy on the mustard.'

'I'll give him a little salad along with his fries,' the barwoman says. 'For the vitamins. You want anything to drink?'

'Yeah, a Coke for me too.'

OK, maybe it's not the greatest example, but things sometimes really do happen at Waanders'. At the weekend they have live music and Ella Booij, the barwoman, is your girlfriend as long as you pay your bill. She has the professional gung-ho of a go-go dancer, but as soon as she gets to the kitchen you know that smile falls from her face like an old scab. She's not from around here. She comes to work from somewhere else around noon, driving a white Mazda automatic, and she goes back there when her shift is over. No one knows whether she has a family, she doesn't look like she loves anyone in this world. I appreciate it that she doesn't act nicer to me than she is.

She brings the truck driver with the white socks and the little boy two glasses of Coke, one in each hand. They're sitting over by the window. Out on the highway a truck goes screaming past.

'Good thing they're putting in that E981,' the driver says.

Ella looks outside, where the sun is making everything shiver.

'Yeah, good thing,' she says.

'The way it is now, it's getting out of hand. The question, of course, is how it will affect you folks.'

The truck driver looks at Ella, hoping to hear her opinion on the E981 that will connect this neck of the woods with Germany.

'You never know how it will go with those sound barriers,' the man continues. 'Whether you'll end up on the front of it or the back, that makes all the difference, right?'

'We don't have much to say about it.'

'No, I guess not, no.'

'Wouldn't mind, though...'

'But that's not how it works.'

Fifteen minutes later the gravy rolls and fries arrive. Contented, father and son leave Waanders' and continue their circle around the sun.

For the time being at least, Lomark's future added up to little more than the code name 'E981'. I'd read about it in the paper; it was a plan that deserved our attention. My impression was that some people were enthusiastic about it because they thought a four-lane would bring the village economic prosperity, but the general reaction was a shrug. In any case, the old road to Germany wasn't enough anymore, it was choked with a rising tide of vehicles. No one was thinking about reducing the number of cars, of course, only about widening the road. MY SPORT IS TRANSPORT I read on the bumper of one truck, and WITHOUT TRANSPORT EVERYTHING PILES UP.

My favourite was the sticker saying I ♥ ASPHALT, which had been pretty much the motto of every government since World

War II, and so the asphalt came pouring in. In stupefying quantities. Joe was right, the world ran on kinetic energy. 'The greatest minds in the world are working on that,' he said, 'and don't ever forget it. Basically, the combustion engine hasn't changed in the last hundred years; what they're working on now is how to refine it, how to make a car run as economically as possible with the lowest possible emissions.

'The automobile is being perfected all the time, but in a way that keeps it affordable for everyone. That's the miracle of our times: that we can rocket down the road for next to nothing. But don't believe in anyone who calls that progress. There's no such thing as progress. Only motion. That's the great claim of the twentieth century, that we can move. We'd rather surrender our right to vote than give up our cars. So if those environmentalists really want to change something, they'll have to come up with something better. And there isn't anything better.'

The route the E981 would follow hadn't been staked out yet; every once in a while the subject came up at Lomark Town Council meetings, but the questions posed were as insipid as the answers. People just don't deal very well with threats that lie too far in the future.

The day Papa Africa's felucca was launched, Regina Ratzinger's party gown got more attention than the whole damned ship. Someone called it an 'Arab wedding dress'. It was a sort of intense blue, with mysterious patterns embroidered on it in gold and silver thread. A pair of shiny slippers poked out from beneath the hem. She was wearing a goodly amount of makeup, and the sequins on her headscarf shimmied as she welcomed the guests.

'I didn't know it was a costume party,' Joe mumbled.

India made the rounds carrying a tray with glasses of beer and cava. She was wearing an olive-green T-shirt and a pair of faded jeans. Her skin was brown and shiny, on sunny days she rubbed lemon juice in her hair and it had turned blond. It was like we were seeing her for the first time. We couldn't take our eyes off her.

Little clumps of people were coming along the Lange Nek, on their way to the inauguration of Papa Africa's boat. It was a mild August day, not too hot, with a whispering in the poplars. The party got off to a slow start, the guests didn't mingle, they clotted. Some people felt uncomfortable with Regina's extravagant presentation and Papa Africa's somewhat tense aloofness. But of course he was tense, who wouldn't be? His ship's design was based on old memories and not some detailed plan, and that suddenly caused him to doubt. Had he remembered correctly, were the proportions right? He had put on his linen suit at Regina's insistence, but he would much rather have worn overalls, for this was a workday, not a holiday.

There was a bit of laughter among the guests now and then, but mostly they just waited. The things-aren't-what-they-used-to-be men were there as well. They stood close together, fluted glasses of sugared gin in hand, looking all around. Nothing escaped their attention; later on, back on their bench, all of this would be reviewed in minute detail.

Here and there people picked at the hors d'oeuvres laid on long tables. Regina had spent days preparing the little snacks. Seasoned meat on skewers lay beneath foil, for roasting later on. There were flat Arab loaves and bowls of red and green tapenades, and for the children – none of whom were there – she had baked almond cookies in the form of Lomark roosters. There lay a woman's love, and not a hungry soul in sight.

Piet Honing tied the ferry to its moorings and came on land. He shook Regina's hand.

'A fine-looking vessel, ma'am, isn't it? Yes indeed. A real beauty.'

His gaze cruised over the tables of food behind her back. She took him by the arm and said, 'Come on, Piet, help yourself. Please, people, do have something to eat!'

The Eilanders' Peugeot station wagon came roaring in from Lomark, Kathleen Eilander at the wheel. She parked with two wheels up against the embankment and yanked on the emergency brake. Julius Eilander climbed out, his hair tousled, looking like an escaped hostage.

'Kathleen!' Regina cried. 'How wonderful to see you!'

'Oh, you look divine, Regina! Is that the boat? What a jewel, simply gorgeous! Where's Mahfouz? I just have to tell him how much I admire it!'

'First have a drink, have something to eat! Eat! Oh, there's going to be so much left over.'

Julius Eilander followed in the wake of his wife's warlike enthusiasm. Piet Honing and Papa Africa were down by the boat, speaking the wondrous abracadabra only they understood. Running their hands over the wood, their lips formed words regarding the ship. Until a squall blew in between them.

'Mahfouz, how wonderful! I'm so proud of you…'

The Egyptian grinned sheepishly at Kathleen Eilander. Her husband seized Mahfouz's hand and cranked it forcefully.

'Good job, good job. You will take me out for a spin soon, won't you, old boy?'

About fifty people had gathered by the waterside. The ship was ready, waiting in the chocks to be pushed over the rubber mats and into the water. Papa Africa took off his shoes and socks and rolled up his trouser legs to just below the knee. Joe, Engel and Christof did the same, and even Julius Eilander sat down to untie his laces. Three more men removed their shoes as well. John Kraakman of the *Lomarker Weekly* took pictures.

'Are we going to be in the paper?' India shouted.

Kraakman licked his lips.

'Wait, don't move, that's right…'

He took a photograph of India smiling at the camera with her big, strong teeth, behind her the men discussing the way to go about it. The sides of the ship were waist high and their bare feet made them vulnerable. Papa Africa slid out of his jacket and handed it to Regina, who draped it carefully over her forearm to keep it from wrinkling.

'A kiss, my love!' she said theatrically.

She gave him a real film kiss, full abandon, eyes closed. With one arm she held him loosely around the middle, the other, on which the jacket hung, she held prettily outside the embrace. He returned her kiss with a more workaday one, a kiss alloyed with embarrassment; where he came from, intimacies between the sexes were not displayed in public. Then he turned and went back to the others. The men took hold of the gunwales, Papa Africa moved to the stern. 'On "go".'

'*Yalla!*'

They heaved as one.

'*Yalla!*'

The ship slid a few inches. This was how the pyramids had been built, the Sphinx, the royal tombs...Papa Africa shouted, the men leaned into it, an observer might have been reminded of a stranded whale being pushed back into the waves. Slowly the boat slid toward the water, the men in front already up to their ankles.

'*Yalla! Yalla!*'

Two, three more times they pushed, then the felucca slid into the water with remarkable lightness. Papa Africa was standing up to his waist in the water with both hands on the stern.

'Darling, your trousers,' Regina said, but he couldn't hear.

He climbed into the boat, loosened the halyards and lowered the sail into place. The ship almost rammed against the side of the ferry ramp. Everyone held their breath. Joe waded in up to his knees to help, but it was no longer necessary, Papa Africa secured the sail and fastened the boom. He ran to the helm and steered, away from the ramp, toward open water. Then he lowered the leeboard.

The ship drifted calmly into the stream. Kraakman's camera clicked, Papa Africa brought the ship around on the wind. People sighed as the sail billowed and unfolded like a dragon's wing. The ship was heeling, leaving a trail in the water. Papa Africa peered tensely at the top of the mast, then back at us. We couldn't see the expression on his face, but when we applauded he waved. Sometimes pleats appeared in the sail and Papa Africa steered to catch more wind. A little further and he would be out of sight, past the Bethlehem freight docks.

The guests were cheerful. They had witnessed a victory; the launch had gone as well as one could hope, and that lent the afternoon a symmetrical beauty. Papa Africa disappeared around the bend in the river, the people went back to the table with soft drinks, beer and snacks. Mr Eilander remained barefooted, waiting at the waterside for the ship to return. Sparrows bathed in the dust beneath the poplars, the world was at peace. Regina's gaze kept returning to the river.

'So you'll be attending polytechnic?' Kathleen Eilander asked Joe.

Joe shook his head.

'But I thought your mother said you were?'

They were silent for a bit. Then Kathleen, who was taller than Joe, leaned over to him again.

'So what *are* you going to do?'

'Become an artist. I guess you can't really say that. You're either an artist or you're not, so you can't really become one. The way I understand it, you go to art academy to figure out if you are one. Engel, for example, he's an artist and everyone knows that. But me? I'm good at making things, but that doesn't necessarily mean anything.'

His gaze travelled over her face, his mouth headed toward a laugh.

'What is it?' Kathleen asked. 'Is there something on my face? Here?'

She wiped her lips with her fingers.

'Now there is,' Joe said. 'A little bit of lipstick, higher...yeah, there.'

Kathleen dug into her handbag and pulled out a compact. She turned her back to him and dabbed vigorously at her mouth. Across the washlands, crooked columns of dust were rising up behind the threshers.

'Is it gone now?'

He nodded. 'It's gone.'

'Why do you let people call you Joe Speedboat?' Kathleen asked pointedly.

'Because that's my name.'

'But you don't own a speedboat, do you?'

Joe shook his head.

'And what about your real name?'

'There is no real name, only a mistake my parents made.'

His smile placed the conversation in another, warmer light.

'Joe Speedboat, that's just my name, Mrs Eilander, really.'

'Oh, please call me Kathleen. It makes me feel so old to be called "Mrs".'

Kathleen looked toward the waterline, where her husband and a few others were waiting for the boat's return like believers awaiting redemption.

'He should wear his hat,' she said. 'He'll get a sunburn like this.' She sniffed. 'Your stepfather has been gone for an awfully long time, if you ask me. I would be worried sick if I were Regina. After all, a boat *can* sink, can't it?'

Regina and India were standing down by the water as well, apart from the others. India spoke words of comfort to her mother, who was bent over with worry. Julius Eilander came up the ramp, shoes in hand, and suggested they drive downriver a ways to see if they could find Papa Africa. He asked his wife for the car keys. The things-aren't-what-they-used-to-be men didn't wait to see what would happen, they thanked Regina clumsily for 'all the hospitality' and headed off to their bench.

Julius Eilander returned half an hour later. He had driven all the way down to the New Bridge but hadn't seen the big sail anywhere. Faith in a happy ending had faded. A mood gray as a cloud of ashes settled over those still at the landing.

'We should call the police,' Julius Eilander said.

'Not that they'll do much around here,' his wife said.

No one dared to look at Regina, as though just looking at her would hit the percussion cap of her fear and pain and result in something you couldn't oversee. Julius Eilander drove back to Lomark; his wife stayed behind at the old shipyard, along with a few others who were saying, 'Have you ever seen anything like it?' and 'if I hadn't seen it with my own eyes'. The flames went out under the hot trays, no one bothered to relight them, the waiting took on the character of a wake. The blue hour was rising up around us, the blackbirds sang and chased each other through the bushes. Mrs Tabak, whose house Regina cleaned, turned to leave. She said, 'Try to stay optimistic, Regina, no matter how hard it seems.'

Two cars approached along the Lange Nek, Julius Eilander out in front and Sergeant Eus Manting's police cruiser bringing up the rear. They parked on the landing. Manting climbed out slowly and shuffled toward the group like a worn-out circus bear. He nodded to Kathleen Eilander, whom he remembered from a complaint about obnoxious air traffic.

'You're Mrs Ratzinger?' he asked Regina.

He took a notepad from his inside pocket, flipped it open and held it at bent-arm's length.

'The situation was explained to me by this gentleman. I've contacted the river police and reported missing a wooden sailboat, approximately six metres long, in the colours red and white. Is that correct?'

Regina and India nodded.

'Good,' Manting went on, 'and on board is a certain Mr…'

'Mahfouz,' India said promptly, 'Mahfouz Husseini.'

'Mr Husseini. And where is Mr Husseini from, if I may ask?'

'He's Egyptian.'

'Does he speak Dutch?'

'He understands it better than he speaks it.'

'And did he provide any information concerning his destination, leave anything behind…?'

Regina opened her mouth, her breathing came in fits and starts.

'Mahfouz was just trying out his boat,' she said. 'That's all. A little jaunt. Up and back, no more than that. So where is he *now*?'

She poked her finger accusingly at Manting.

'So where is he *now*?'

'My colleagues are looking for him, Mrs Ratzinger, at this point there's nothing else we…'

'*Where* is he *now*?'

'Now don't get worked up, ma'am, my colleagues are combing the river for him right now.'

At those words something snapped. Regina turned and walked away, weeping for the first time that day, with the howling ups and downs of a chainsaw. With her eyes, Kathleen Eilander heaped flaming reproach on Sergeant Manting for his lack of tact and went after her. Manting climbed into the cruiser and backed away from the landing. As he made the turn, his headlights swept over a shape down at the waterfront. Joe.

That was how the day ended, with Regina choking on her tears as she leaned against the Bethlehem Asphalt amphibian and Joe coming up the boat ramp and stopping beside the table that still held enough food to sate Tamerlane's hordes. He stuck a soggy rooster-biscuit in his mouth.

'Donkey knows the way,' he said quietly. 'Donkey knows the way.'

October came and Papa Africa still hadn't returned. In Regina Ratzinger's eyes there smouldered a plaint against a world in which people lose the thing they love most. She became a woman people looked past in order not to have to see that.

Her first husband had a grave she could visit, the second hadn't even left behind a body to which she could say goodbye. Once the sun had risen from the morning mist and was climbing quickly in pale and brighter light, Regina would walk along the Lange Nek to the river. There where the ship was launched she stood like the statue of the sailor's wife looking out to sea. She lived with one foot in hope and the other in sorrow, without being able to give in fully to either of them. The sound of the telephone ringing was never the same to her again.

When you saw her standing there, your heart shrivelled like an old apple. You prayed with her that the drab dragon's wing would come sailing around the bend any moment. That Papa Africa would moor his boat and say, 'I am sorry, it was more far, and the wind was low.'

And Regina stank. Oh Jesus, she stank with sorrow. India did her best to care for her, but to provide care you need someone who wants to be cared for. Regina might as well have moved to a cave in a barren mountain range, she had reached a degree of

self-denial that would have made saintly Anthony the Anchor-
ite shake his head in pity. She ate only the minimum needed to
keep the organism going, and she fell silent. After school India
would cook copious meals, but her mother only scratched at the
edges of her plate. Sounds of domestic tension were heard, of
something that could break any moment.

They were completely overspent and condemned to each
other. Sometimes, for no real reason, Regina would summon up
childhood memories and then, for a moment, you might have
thought you were seeing a mother and daughter living
together on an even keel.

After his stepfather disappeared, Joe waited two weeks before
leaving for the art academy; he had tried to comfort his mother.
'Maybe he just sailed back to where he came from,' he suggested, 'out of homesickness.' Regina's resistance to that idea
was bitter. To Joe she was an abandoned woman, to herself a
widow all over again. She wouldn't let anyone console her or
change her mind; Joe had no reason to stay any longer. He put
on his father's old army rucksack and went to Engel, who had
found a room in a working-class neighbourhood in Enschede.
Engel had told him there was always room for him on the sofa.
Joe left on the 6.45 bus, and I went with him to the station. He
didn't say much, nothing really. We were headed for an important moment in our friendship, which would reach its
conclusion with Joe waving to me through the back window of
the bus and me rolling home with a huge lump in my throat,
convinced that an epoch was drawing to a close.

Somewhere in November, Joe came back to Lomark. At least, that was when I suddenly saw him standing at my window, grinning from ear to ear. I waved to him, he came in trailing cold air. He looked bigger, standing there in my room with his heavy army coat and his rain-drenched hair. I was happy as a pup to see him. I had also run out of cigarettes, and now he could roll me a bunch. He hung his coat over the chair and sat down across from me.

How's it going? I wrote on my notepad, and he shook his head.

'It was about time for me to come home.'

Things were not going well, his mother and India were both on the verge of exhaustion. I looked at him as he rolled my cigarettes and dropped them in the empty mustard pot. His hair was longer, but that wasn't what gave me the feeling something had changed. I squinted hard and tried to take him in carefully, but I couldn't put my finger on it. Maybe I just wasn't used to him anymore.

'I was in Amsterdam for two weeks,' he said.

He licked the cigarette paper and rolled it into place.

'With P.J.'

I looked the other way. Jealousy's as visible as a solar eclipse.

'She's got something going with a writer. A real nutcase.'

Joe gave me a rundown of the last few months, starting at the moment he'd left that morning on the bus.

They were going to be fellow artists there in Enschede, Engel and he. They were going to show people a thing or two. But one day in late autumn, Joe and his classmates went on an excursion to the Van Gogh Museum. During the ten minutes he stood there, the queue advanced only a few metres. Right in front of them was a busload of Japanese tourists, behind them a group of disgruntled day-trippers from Groningen who were doing their best to keep spirits high. Joe looked around. His feet were cold. Fuck this, he thought suddenly, stepped out of line without a word and disappeared in the direction of Museum Square.

And there he stood, far from home and with no reason to go back. He took a deep breath, looked around and decided to stay in Amsterdam for a while and see how things worked out.

Around dinnertime he started thinking about a place to stay. He knew only one person in the whole city: P.J. Eilander. He phoned P.J.'s mother, who gave him her daughter's address on Tolstraat, just above a coffee shop. The coffee shop was called Babylon, if she remembered rightly.

Joe took the tram. He experienced giddying happiness – no one knew where he was, life could go any which way, there were as many possibilities as combinations on a fruit machine and every direction he chose was the right one, because it was time for the machine to pay out.

P.J. wasn't home. Joe waited in Babylon Coffee Shop, sitting by the window where he might see her come by. Meanwhile, he had all the time in the world to feast his eyes on the economics of soft drugs. In Lomark it had been sport for a while to smoke a few quick joints and then cross the border into Germany – to come back with stories of a different planet. That was just for laughs, but smoking here was serious business. The users seemed to avoid daylight as much as possible, and applied themselves with cultish dedication to the rolling and routine firing up of huge bombers. It was truly something to see. A native from the jungle who was dropped here and saw this for the first time would think he was observing an official religious rite.

'Hey, man, want a drag?'

Joe looked up. A man with black curly hair beneath a red cap was holding out a trumpetlike joint.

'No thanks,' Joe said. 'I'm waiting for someone.'

'Don't be an ass, man, that's what it's made for.'

'No really, thank you.'

'You look like you could use a toke.'

Joe accepted the joint.

'My name's George,' the man said. 'The Urban Indian. But you probably picked up on that.'

Joe reappeared from behind the cloud.

'My name's Joe Speedboat,' he said in a squeaky voice.

'Joe Speedboat! You're all right, man, you're all right!'

Like tens of thousands of tourists, on his first day in Amsterdam Joe got stoned ('Jesus, man, you know, if I could just build all the things I see…'). It was completely dark outside when George the Urban Indian left, from outside the window he had shouted, 'Good luck, Joe Speedboat! Good luck, man!' and cycled away on his delivery bike. Joe remained behind in the blessed dreams of his first, second and third joints ('I was really dying for a strawberry yoghurt drink, so I ordered one. That stuff ran down into my stomach like a cold mountain stream. You never tasted yoghurt drink like that').

It will never be clear what would have happened had P.J. not run out of cigarettes that evening. She had returned home at around seven, and now she went downstairs without a coat to buy a pack at the coffee shop. The men at the pool table looked up; walking over to the counter with the jar of tobacco, rolling papers and lighters she said, 'Could I have a pack of Marlboro, please?'

'Anytime for you, baby, anytime.'

On her way out she saw, in the shadow of the rubber plant by the window, a familiar face. The boy, his eyes half closed, was sitting at a table littered with empty bottles of strawberry yoghurt drink. P.J. went over to him.

'Hey, Joe,' she said. 'You're Joe, aren't you?'

His eyes opened a little further.

'Hi.'

'It's me, P.J., we went to school together.'

'Oh. Hey. I. Know. You.'

'What are *you* doing here? No one from Lomark…'

That was how Joe made his arrival, floating in a basket of reeds and encircled by feminine attention and lots of questions. Where he was staying? Nowhere? He could sleep in her bed. She always spent the night at her boyfriend's place, she'd be back in the morning. He must be hungry, she started talking about something she called 'the munchies', triggered by the smoking of marijuana. But it would have been wiser for Joe not to have touched the pasta she prepared for him. He made it to the toilet just as the geyser of rosy-pink yoghurt drink, commingled with tagliatelle and tomato sauce, came rocketing up, spreading a sweet-and-sour dairy smell throughout her toilet and living room.

'Oh. Shit. Oh. Sorry.'

'Jesus, Joe, what did you do? Smoke the little plastic bag along with it?'

His eyes were bloodshot, his body as wobbly as on the day

his father had been lowered into the grave and grief had forced him to lean against his mother.

'You need some sleep, Joe. Lie down. You don't want to get undressed? No? Well, OK.'

'Hey. Thanks. A. Lot.'

The next morning he found a note.

Hey Chief Smoke 'm up
Back at noon
Breakfast is
in the fridge take
whatever you want
x P.J.

In his memory, the night gone by had lasted a hundred years. Tepid light came drizzling through the cracks in the curtains, he went back to bed and lay there with one arm under his head, smoking a cigarette. There were dead houseplants in the corners. His gaze slid over the shadows on the ceiling, which was higher than the room was broad. Breakfast, as he had seen it by refrigerator light: half a container of cottage cheese, a crescent sliver of hard cheese and half a litre of skimmed yoghurt.

When P.J. came in a few hours later, he was sitting straight as a ramrod in a chair by the window, which provided him with a view of paintless balconies and gardens where the sun never shone. The bed was made up so tightly you could bounce a coin on it, and the gas fire was turned off.

'Wow, cheerful as the grave in here,' P.J. said. 'Have you been sitting in the dark all this time? Didn't you get yourself some breakfast? Oh, I'm sorry, I'm always tense when I come back from Arthur's place.'

'Arthur,' Joe said.

'That's right, you don't know, how could you? Arthur Metz, the writer. He's my significant other. Or I should say, my boyfriend; Arthur hates euphemisms.'

'Euphemisms.'

'Arthur Metz,' she repeated. 'Never heard of him? This is his latest novel.'

She pushed a book into Joe's hands. *My Gentle Demise* was the title. P.J. stood at the counter making coffee, she looked over her shoulder at Joe.

'He's a poet too.'

Infatuated pride radiated off of her. On the back cover of the book was a photo of a handsome man with premature wrinkles on his forehead, bags under his eyes.

'I'm always at his place at night, during the day he needs to be alone. He can't write with anyone else around. After ten o'clock he wants to see me again. Arthur needs that solitude, he's very sensitive. Anything that disturbs his rhythm upsets him terribly. When I'm ten minutes late he starts asking where I've been.'

'Wow,' Joe said.

'I'd love to introduce you, but he can't handle new people. It scares him. Sometimes it makes him aggressive, you never know. He finds it very difficult to be touched, sometimes he shrivels all up when I touch him.'

'Is he, uh…'

'Oh, Arthur is as psychotic as they get. He's tried to commit suicide three times. But the things he's taught me! It's amazing, the things he teaches me! With him it's totally different from anything I've ever known, I'd never thought that existed, you know what I mean? It's hard to explain.'

'Even better than Jopie Koeksnijder?'

At that P.J. laughed so hard that the coffee splashed over the sides of the mugs.

'And what about here, Frankie? Anything happen around here?' Joe asked when his story was finished.

I frowned. I couldn't come up with anything worth telling. It had been quiet without him, without Engel and Papa Africa, even without Christof. Almost everyone I knew had left, and the ones still around didn't interest me. Quincy Hansen had stayed, of course; I wouldn't be shot of him as long as I lived. He was working at Bethlehem Asphalt, doing minor administrative work. What a waste of all those years of valuable learning.

I was still pressing briquettes myself, although production had taken a dip since the rains had set in.

'Really, nothing?' Joe asked.

I shook my head and wrote: *Papa Africa?*

'Shit situation. Anything's possible. Theoretically, he may even have sailed back to Egypt, but...'

Joe's expression reflected the incredible hardships of such a journey.

'It's possible, though,' he said. 'Stranger things have happened. What do you think, would he have tried that? I mean, you two got along.'

Difficult.

'Difficult, but not impossible! I looked at the map; he could have gone right out to sea. Along the New Waterway to the North Sea, through the Straits of Dover. If he stuck close to shore, then along the coast of France toward the Atlantic, the Bay of Biscay, northern Spain, I mean, why not?'

He dug into the tobacco and pulled out a honey-coloured wisp. I scratched my chin and tried to imagine the route, but Europe's outer boundaries were fairly vague in my mind.

'Imagine it, all the way past Portugal to Gibraltar, it's possible! If Thor Heyerdahl could cross the Atlantic on a papyrus raft, why not Papa Africa in a felucca all the way to Egypt? He was a good sailor, that's for sure, and if you had a little luck with the weather, why not?'

I nodded, despite all my petty objections.

'Think of all the things he must have seen once he was past Gibraltar... Algiers, Tripoli, Tobruk, and then you turn right past Alexandria and sail straight into Egypt. I could see him doing that, really.'

Joe needed that faith, it was as hard for him to accept the loss of his stepfather as it was for his mother. But where she submerged herself in gray mourning, he created the heroics of an odyssey. He had thought the whole thing through, he seemed capable to me of making the journey himself just to prove that it could be done. And preposterous or not, it cheered me up, the possibility of a happy ending. If Joe thought it was possible, who was I to say it wasn't? He was the can-do man. But if Papa Africa truly had tried to sail back, there was one thing Joe hadn't mentioned.

Why? I wrote.

'You remember her hiding his passport?' he asked.

I nodded.

'There were other things, too,' Joe said. 'One incident I remember was after Ramadan, right before Christmas last year. Maybe it had nothing to do with it, I don't know, but I've never forgotten it in any case. You know Papa Africa never ate pork, he seriously thought it would kill him, or at least give him hives. Things like that were *haram*. He had lots of things like that; if India had been his daughter, for example, he would have had her circumcised. Or he believed that the left hand belonged to the Devil, so you should never eat with it, because that was *haram* too. They used to argue about things like that, or at least my mother did, he never argued back. He was too calm for that, you remember how he was. "She has a hot head," he would say, and leave it at that. The day before Christmas, though, my mother made lamb meatballs for dinner. The next day, on Christmas Day, she asked him how he was feeling. Fine, he said, why did she ask? You don't feel sick or anything, she asked, no different than usual? He shook his head no, everything was fine. Then she hit him with it: "Because yesterday you ate *pork*. Not lamb, pork. You see, it doesn't give you hives! Allah didn't punish you!" And she went on like that, while we just sat there stunned.'

Joe licked the gummed edge on the final cigarette and wormed it into the mustard jar along with the others.

'I mean, go figure. India was furious with her, but he didn't say a word. Talk about a fucked-up Christmas.'

That Joe had come back to Lomark to stay was something I realized only in late November, when he found a job as a hod carrier. Every weekday morning at six he would be freezing his butt down off at the dyke, where the van came by to pick him up along with a couple of other guys. They took the back roads into Germany, where they worked on the construction of new apartment complexes and industrial estates. Illegal cross-border labour was nothing new, it had existed for centuries on both sides. Through a complex network of contractors and sub-contractors, construction workers were funnelled through to Germany, where no taxes or social premiums had to be paid for them. They received their wages by the week and it was their tough luck if they fell from a scaffolding or if a U-beam landed on their foot. Joe had seen a man who had gone into a coma after being hit on the head by a concrete element that was swinging from a crane. His buddy went to the office to complain, but they told him it was the man's own fault, '*Man soll aufpassen an der Baustelle*,' et cetera, and the friend had grabbed the contractor and started strangling him with his own necktie. Stuff like that.

At the end of the week the *Gastarbeiter* drank potato schnapps in the van, went out to dinner at a dingy, steamy restaurant with *gutbürgerliche Küche*, and came home pissed as newts. When the frost settled in the work stopped, and that was the end of Joe's construction career; when the new year came he got a job at Bethlehem.

He began driving bulldozers.

Now that the Ratzinger family had handed over a son to the asphalt plant as well, you might think they had become naturalized. But Lomark doesn't open its arms that easily, things like that take generations around here. And even then...But Joe was back on the grounds where he'd once built an airplane, working this time for Christof's father, Egon Maandag. Production was still on hold because of the high water, but foreman Graad Huisman taught Joe what he needed to know. He received bulldozing lessons. Sometimes at coffee break Huisman would suddenly start weeping. The maintenance men sitting around the canteen didn't even bat an eye, Joe said; since he'd been diagnosed with cancer of the knee, Huisman cried almost every day. The canteen smelled of oranges and tobacco smoke.

Joe was now one of the men in orange overalls, on the grounds themselves he had to wear a white hard hat. It had never occurred to me that someday he would have to work for a living like everyone else. When the water went down he walked to work; sometimes his mother walked with him, on her way to the river to see if Papa Africa had come back yet. They would say goodbye at the gates, Joe with lunchbox in hand and a lump in his coat pocket where he kept an apple or an orange. The day crew would gather in the canteen to run through the production schedules, then they all went to their posts. Joe climbed into the cab of the Liebherr, slid his butt back and forth in the seat until he was comfortable, then started the engine. The machine coughed thick, black smoke, Joe revelled in the way the engine throbbed. The heating and the radio he always turned all the way up. Radio, Joe said, is the opiate of the working man.

The grounds were dotted with hills of sand and gravel that had been brought in by barge. In accordance with the operator's directions, it was Joe's job to continually fill the dosers: huge, partitioned hoppers that held the ingredients for the asphalt. He drove back and forth between the dosers and the piles of minerals, which he bit off in chunks. From the dosers the material went by conveyor belt into the bowels of the asphalt machine.

Lunch was at twelve-thirty.

'What's up?'

'Aw, nothing.'

'Got in late last night, I guess.'

'No, not this time either.'

'Oh. So what else is up?'

'Aw, nothing much.'

And so spring came. But east wind and spring storms came as well, to punish those who had rejoiced too soon. The trees in the cemetery drummed their wooden fingers against the back of my house. The windows were steamed, I read in the piles of newspapers that the E981 would almost definitely bypass Lomark completely. The municipal newsletter said that a committee had been set up to protest against the decision. The members feared that the village would be caught between the two transport arterials into Germany: the river on one side and the E981 on the other, especially if Lomark had no exit of its own. That was crucial. The only way to reach us then would be to get off at Westerveld and drive along the dyke to Lomark. It was a monstrous plan.

Signs appeared along the national highway in the pastures of farmers who sympathized with the protesters. LET LOMARK BREATHE was the most poetic one. It was the brainchild of Harry Potijk, chairman of the committee of the same name. Potijk compared the walling-in of Lomark with suffocation; this imagery had more impact than any subtle argumentation. Harry Potijk was the ideal spokesman, and this was to be his finest hour. For twenty years he had been chairman of the local historical society, and he could orate like the old-fashioned books he had digested during countless hours of autodidactic effort. With the arrival of the E981, his life – uneventful till then – took on the glow of an ideal. He was given the opportunity to advance the committee's arguments during a Town Council meeting.

'And if a sound barrier is built, as indicated in the plan before us,' he said, 'and the river rises, what then? We will be trapped like rats. There will be nowhere for us to go, the dyke road is flooded, our homes are filling with water and the only route of escape is hermetically sealed with a sound barrier.'

He paused to allow his words to sink in with the council and the public gallery.

'My question then, Mr Chairman, is this: do you plan to equip each household with a rubber boat?'

Scornful laughter rose from the gallery.

'Please stick to the facts at hand, Mr Potijk,' the chairman said.

Potijk gave a servile nod, but that was a ruse.

'And if you say that the water will never reach such heights, what do you know of climatic change around the world? Of the ecological imbalance now blamed on global warming? Of the melting icecaps?'

At this point in his speech he pointed dramatically at the wall, on the other side of which rivers churned and the earth hissed with heat.

'Has it slipped your mind that the river this summer reached an all-time low, and that a few years back the water was higher than it has ever been before? Have you forgotten so soon? Even Mr Abelsen, a man known to you, now ninety-three years of age, has never in his life seen the water so high. There are forces at work about which we know nothing and which we cannot predict, so that we must take into account today what seems only a doomsday scenario in the distant future...'

The committee's proviso was clear as a bell: the motorway

could be tolerated as a *fait accompli*, but not the lack of an exit and entrance ramp at Lomark. Lomark must be given its own exit and entrance, a windpipe, an asphalt smoker's lung.

When Harry Potijk realized that there was little he could expect from the mediocre-minded town fathers, he piloted his supporters along a more radical tack: one Wednesday afternoon they left in a hired van from Van Paridon Rentals for the houses of parliament in The Hague. In their imaginations the demonstrators may have been preceded by the sound of fife and drum, but reality consisted of the cobblestones of the Binnenhof beneath a gray sky, and no one who listened. A few attempts were made at the yell they had practiced on the bus, but the war cries fell to the earth as mutely as insults in a foreign language. A man with a briefcase and umbrella passed by at one point and inquired politely about the purpose of their gathering.

'An MP,' whispered Mrs Harpenau, the librarian.

Harry Potijk rose to his full height and began rattling off the group's mission statement, but was soon interrupted.

'Oh, so this is about a highway? But then you're in the wrong place, you should be at the Ministry of Transport. On Plesmanweg. It's quite a way from here.'

Dazed, the group left the Binnenhof and headed for the address he'd mentioned, which was indeed a long walk. They stopped along the way for coffee and sandwiches, then it began growing dark. Mrs Harpenau and two of the others wanted to start home, because of the children...and that was the end of the march on The Hague.

The photo that appeared in the *Lomarker Weekly* was taken from so far away that the signs were unreadable, and the huddle of protesters looked painfully small there on that huge square.

I've kept that photo. It shows how laughable we are, even in the pursuit of good.

The spring fair brought us something new: Mousetown. As an attraction it was fascinating, precisely because it was so dated. You passed through a black curtain and found yourself in a darkened, unpleasantly hot space where the bitter smell of mouse piss and sawdust snapped at your nostrils. What awaited you there was the rather static spectacle of a wooden castle, at eye level for children and wheeled pedestrians like myself. The castle itself was two stories high, lit from the inside by clumsily sunken lightbulbs. The streets around it were illuminated by Christmas lighting, with bright yellow sawdust scattered on the ground. The entire fortress covered about ten square metres and was surrounded by a moat, its water as opaque as that in the water bowl of the guinea pigs Dirk used to keep – all of whom, one by one, had died a death as hideous as it was mysterious.

The element of motion in Mousetown – a fair, after all, is the celebration of flying, spinning and/or swaying movement; little wonder, therefore, that Joe could be found there almost all the time – consisted of a few hundred mice. The visitors watched the rodents swarm with a kind of fascinated horror. The animals pissed, shit and screwed in what in the human world would be called public places, which produced a great deal of laughter. There was a drawbridge leading to an island in the moat which, along with the back wall, formed the edges of the mousy world. The city was rectangular, you could walk around it on three sides, and the back was a plywood barrier crudely painted with clouds and a sun. The city itself was well lit; the area around it, where the people stood and stared at the storybook plague of rodents, was dark as a haunted house.

Of course I saw Mousetown as a parable for Lomark, that stinking nest in which we were trapped in each other's company, caught between the river on one side and the future sound barrier on the other. Harry Potijk's committee, however, failed to underscore their arguments with that particular metaphor.

One day I saw Joe and P.J. at the fair. They were standing at the Spider, their backs to me. P.J. was waving to someone being flung around in one of those seats, and Joe was counting the money in his wallet. God, it had been a long time since I'd seen P.J. Had she lost weight? I looked at her golden blond curls and heard myself sigh like a melancholy hound.

After Joe had gone to Amsterdam he and P.J. had sort of become friends, and they saw each other whenever she was in Lomark. Which wasn't very often. The last time had been at Christmas, but I hadn't seen her then because I hadn't felt like going to midnight mass. That made it almost nine months now – months during which my time had stood still and hers had sped up.

I rolled along behind them in the direction of Mousetown. The noise coming from all those rides grated on my eardrums. It was tough going on the flattened grass, the fair was probably the only time I left the asphalt and paving stones behind.

I didn't want to be seen. I was suddenly furious at the thought that I didn't live on my own two feet but could only look up at her, speechless and stunted. I had to force myself not to think about what I might have grown to be…the height from which I might have looked in her eyes, the words I would have used to make her laugh, the way Joe did, the way that asshole of a writer made her laugh. (Since becoming aware of his existence I had run across his name a few times in the papers. When I did I mocked him and crumpled the paper into a ball. Somewhere, he had someone who hated him.) In P.J.'s presence my defects were aggravated, I became as crooked and little as I already was. There was no salvation from that.

In one of the most frank, most personal entries in my diary, the kind that simply has to be true because it's about feelings (tears tell no lies, haha!), I talked about the nasty predicament in which I found myself.

> …allowed to dream, but don't kid yourself into having any expectations. I dream the colour of my love for P.J., the staggering orange of a rising sun. I won't be able to tell her that. This is completely fucked. I mean, when it comes to my life touching hers I might as well be dead or a Chinaman from Wuhan. Sometimes it feels like I'm going to cry, but that's nonsense, I'm going to turn to stone. Work on that. Never stop practicing, Master Musashi says. Do not think P.J. thoughts. That weakens. Practice practicing. Become stone. This is my Strategy.

I closed myself up in the darkness of Mousetown in order to think diffuse thoughts, about how they transported an attraction like this from town to town, for example, or what you would have to do to keep the population from exploding. If the mice were allowed to reproduce at will, before you knew it the whole city would become a roiling blanket of soft little

mousehides, they would form factions, the struggle for resources would begin, all against all and each one for himself,
a bloodbath…

Maybe the owner got rid of the nests with a spade or a Dust-
buster. It was also possible that the baby mice were eaten by
the adult animals, a phenomenon I had seen once with Dirk's
guinea pigs, who had exterminated their entire nest one night
in an inexplicable fit of fury. We found the hairy babies the
next morning: bitten in two. Those otherwise so daffy guinea
pigs had in their hearts a horror you would never expect. Not
long afterwards the adult animals met the same fate. The culprit was never brought to justice.

I sat in my cart in the dark by the back wall, because it
amused me not only to look at the mice, but also at the people
doing the same thing. They were so intent on the sparkling
light source in the darkness that they usually didn't see me. It
was the vantage point I liked most: looking without being seen.
Creeping into their minds and trying like hell to figure out
what was going on in there.

From the sniggering you could tell that mice were doing it,
otherwise it was mostly women complaining about 'that smell,
it's like ammonia', and children growing ecstatic at the pileup
of hundreds of filthy animals.

The black curtain opened and some of the twilight leaked in,
I saw the sheen of P.J.'s hair. Joe was behind her.

'Oh, that smell!' P.J. said.

The curtain fell heavily into place behind them, and P.J.
approached Mousetown with the enthusiasm of a child.

'Oh, look, what a darling! The one with that crippled leg.'

She stuck her arm over the moat and tried to pet some of
the mice. Her finger scared the daylights out of dozens of little
animals.

was written on at least six pieces of cardboard.

'Picolien Jane!' Joe said in mock rebuke.

I breathed as quietly as I could, the longer they were in here the more painful it would be to have them spot me. My heart was pounding. People I knew seemed very strange whenever I eavesdropped on them. I drifted far away from them; paradoxically enough it wasn't the intimacy but the alienation that grew.

P.J. wouldn't stop teasing the mice. She leaned far over the moat and was busy trying to cut off one particular mouse from the rest. She succeeded in manoeuvring him toward the drawbridge, then blocked the road into town with her right hand, her fingers spread slightly like the pickets in a fence. All the animal could do was cross the bridge to the island in the moat.

'Come on, Robinson, there you go.'

In a panic he ran across the bridge onto the island; P.J. raised the drawbridge and isolated him from the rest.

'That's kind of mean,' Joe said.

'Nooo, Robinson's always been kind of a loner.'

Joe laughed a little reluctantly and followed her to the curtain at the other end of the room, where the EXIT sign spread its soft green glow.

'Bye, Robinson,' P.J. said. 'Be a good boy now!'

They went out through the curtain, P.J. laughing at something Joe said, and I was alone again. I took a few deep breaths and looked at the castaway mouse, who was now on the verge of a nervous breakdown. He sniffed around at his new surroundings, and I noticed then that mice have lovely beady little eyes.

Although it was early spring and the heating season was almost over, I jacked up my daily production of briquettes. Working helped ward off bad thoughts.

'You'd think they were eating those things for breakfast,' Pa said each time he loaded a new batch onto the trailer.

We could be outside now without freezing to the ground or being washed away by rain; the greenery in its pots shot up high. Each day the rushes in the ditch grew a few centimetres as well. The silhouettes of trees, hard in winter, were coming into light-green bud and the chestnuts were full of pale candles. Sometimes a happy feeling started swirling around inside you that had nothing to do with good news or anything that had happened. 'It's in the air,' that's what they always said, and because I have no better explanation I'll leave it at that.

I was in the garden, waiting for the newspapers to spindry.

It was eleven o'clock, Ma had already called out, 'Coffee, Frankie?', when Joe suddenly appeared at the bike gate.

'Welcome,' he said, 'on this glorious Day of Labour.'

It was indeed 1 May, and Joe had a bee in his bonnet: I'd known him long enough to see that. Hands in his pockets, he took a look around the junk store that I had secretly started thinking of as Briquetterie F. Hermans & Son, the son being the result of a glorious union between a certain Ms Eilander and yours truly.

'Yup, today's a lucky day,' Joe said.

He took the aluminium ladder from its hook at the back of the house and asked for a claw hammer. Then he began prying at the horseshoe above my door. Ma came to the kitchen window, waving and pointing to ask me what he was up to. I shrugged. The door opened.

'Good morning, Joe! What are you doing?'

From his perch halfway up the ladder, he looked at her over his shoulder.

'Mrs Hermans, good morning. I'm turning the horseshoe around. It brings bad luck if you hang it upside down. It's sort of asking for trouble, if you know what I mean.'

With a couple of blows that made the windows rattle in their frames he hammered the horseshoe back in place, with the points up. Wednesday began cawing and jumping around in his cage. I'd been neglecting him for the last few months, and I promised myself to do something about that.

'Are you serious?' Ma yelled back. 'Has that poor boy been living all these years…?'

I hissed at her to make her shut up. She stood in the doorway wringing her hands, our Marie Hermans, laden with guilt and motherly love.

'Don't worry,' Joe said as he hung the ladder back in place. 'Today's a lucky day anyway, Mrs Hermans.'

He pulled out a pack of Marlboros. Since he'd started at Bethlehem he smoked cigarettes from a pack; it was too much trouble to roll them while he was working.

'Smoke?'

Oh yes, something was definitely up. He had that Half-

a-league-half-a-league-half-a-league-onward look in his eye
that held a promise, a Change of Gear.

I waited. For a while we sat across from each other like that
in the crystal clarity of the first May morning, blowing clouds
of smoke into air so fresh you felt like licking it up. The neighbours had the blankets hanging out the windows. Joe looked at
the briquettes drying on their racks.

'How many of these things have you made, anyway?' he
asked suddenly. 'A thousand? Two thousand?'

I nodded. A thousand, two thousand, how should I know?

'And how many are you planning to make?' Joe asked.
'Another thousand?'

I held up five fingers.

'Five thousand! You're kidding me! Jesus Christ, Frankie, are
you going to keep squeezing newspapers for the rest of your
life?'

I nodded solemnly. Pressing newspapers into fuel was my
mission. I couldn't imagine anything better. Joe pushed his
cigarette butt into the ground with his thumb. It left a little
planting hole.

'You know, I don't believe it for a minute. What I wanted to
say, Frankie, is that I've had plenty of time to think in the last
few months up on that bulldozer, and I'm going to tell you why
this is our lucky day. I think your arm means something. A lot
more than you even realize. And I've figured out how we can
put that special arm to use to obtain the two things for which
all humans are condemned to strive: money and prestige.
Because you, Frank Hermans, are an arm wrestler.'

Joe's joy beamed all the way into the garden next door.

'Isn't that what friends are for, to see things in you that you
never saw before?'

I frowned, took a newspaper from the pile and a pencil stub

and scribbled *What do you mean, arm wrestler?* in the margin.

'Arm wrestler, you know, two people sitting at the table with their arms in the middle and trying to push the other one down. You're a natural! They way I see it, you've been at training camp for about ten years now, with that cart of yours and squeezing those briquettes and stuff, and now it's time to put that to good use. You remember out in the hangar, when I asked you to bend those metal rods? When I was working in Germany I saw steel benders, these guys were real monsters, who couldn't do half what you did! You're pretty much unbeatable, Frankie, all we have to do is get started. There are competitions all over Europe. I'll be your manager: we split the take, and have fun doing it.'

He looked at my arm with something close to infatuation, as if I wasn't attached to it, making me feel a kind of confused jealousy toward my own limb. This was his plan: first I had to go on a balanced diet of protein shakes, carbohydrates and fats. At the same time I would start a daily training program in the techniques of arm wrestling, based on the information he'd looked up at the library on the Internet. He was going to be my coach. We would spend the whole summer studying and training, and our very first tournament would be in Liège in October. The main prize was about seven thousand smackers. Second place got five thousand, third place took three.

'Fat city,' Joe said contentedly.

He'd already drawn up a tournament schedule that would take us all over Europe. Eastern Europeans in particular were crazy about arm wrestling. Two men, one table and then push until one of you lands on his ass.

'But make no mistake about it,' my self-appointed coach and manager said, 'there's more technique involved than you ever dreamed possible.'

The first six months of the season we'd spend warming up, a tournament here and there, finding out where I stood in the arm wrestling hierarchy. And because Joe was irrationally optimistic about it, in May of next year we would take part in the world championships in Poznan, Poland.

'The only thing you lack is weight; weight is our Achilles' heel. Shoulder, chest and arm, that's what we've got going for us. Trapezium, biceps, triceps, pectoralis major and forearm, they all have to be in harmony, but then we're off like a shot. The way I see it…'

I held up my hand to stop him.

'Right, now you.'

I picked up the pencil and wrote two letters at the edge of the newsprint: *NO*.

Joe pursed his lips, as though he'd stumbled upon an interesting chess problem.

'No?'

I shook my head.

'Why, I mean, think about it…Why no, why so fast?'

Don't feel like it.

And after a while, when Joe went on waving his hands wildly and giving me a bug-eyed explanation of the advantages of his plan, I got tired of listening to him.

Piss off.

Behold if you will what happens when someone comes by on a good day and offers to expand your world ten thousand times over: you panic. Joe offered me competition. I, the man-of-no-contest, who had always seen himself as unfit for the struggle, who had placed himself outside the arena as observer and commentator, was being asked to arm wrestle. They would look at me, judge me and boo or cheer. What Joe was offering was nothing less than a place in the world, a freedom of movement I couldn't comprehend. It was horrible. So I said no. And I didn't just say no, I clammed up. Everything had to stay the way it was, because the way it was was good. And if it wasn't good, it would get better. Suddenly I found myself bitterly defending the value of a converted garden shed, a briquette installation and a few hundred square metres of room in which to move. Anyone who shook a finger at that risked having it chopped off.

I watched Joe walk out of the garden. He left in dumb amazement at my choosing the beaten track instead of the thrill of adventure. I was relieved and disappointed to see him give up so soon.

So I had become fused with my immobility. I explained that to myself as a kind of harmony with my surroundings and the people in it. You can't call that happiness, happiness burns brighter than that; it was more like the absence of revulsion and the longing for death.

A couple of days after Joe had shown up in the garden, Wednesday flew off. I let him out of his cage and for the first time he didn't come back. Ma said it was because it was springtime, that nature was like that, but I felt sort of heartbroken. Whenever I heard a jackdaw I thought it was Wednesday, but the cage remained empty.

Joe seemed to have abandoned his arm wrestling plans, or at least he'd stopped talking about them. Instead he occupied himself with buying a car, his first: a long, black bomb that had served for years as Griffioen's hearse. Christof's grandmother had ridden in it to her final resting place. It was a real Joe car, an Oldsmobile Cutlass Cruiser, all straight lines and an impressive quadrangular grille. It needed a little work but it had been kept up well and didn't have a lot of mileage. Joe put in a huge stereo installation, so you could hear the stamping bass long before he himself showed up.

'It gives me the shivers,' Ma said. 'It's like having Death pull up in front of your door. I knew everybody they ever took away in that thing. Couldn't Griffioen have sold it somewhere else? For the sake of the next of kin?'

Joe unbolted the passenger seat so I could go out cruising with him; there was enough space there for me, cart and all. We drove back and forth along the dyke, tooled along the state highway and stopped in for soft ices at the roadhouse like a couple of old fogies. At least he did: I got beer with a straw, because we all know the joke about the spaz who tries to eat an ice-cream cone. We looked at the traffic and the reflection of the setting sun in the windows. In the little playground a father was waiting for his daughter at the bottom of the slide.

'One more time! One more time!' the little girl shouted each time she got to the bottom, and she kept it up until the tears started.

Christof and Engel had been gone from Lomark for a year already, Joe had come back and found a steady job at Bethlehem. He seemed content with that. I mean, how was he supposed to have *become* something when he already was something: Joe, a three-dimensional, mint-condition product of his own imagination. I was thankful he'd come back.

In July they came trickling in, though, one by one. First Engel, then Christof, and finally P.J. too. The periods away from home had grown longer and longer, just as they had with Wednesday, until finally he never came back at all.

Engel had made it through his first year with ease; he was considered an exceptional talent and had received a grant to attend the Ecole des Beaux-Arts in Paris in the second semester of next year. Things like that, things that in anyone else's life would have resulted in a proud banging of the gong, he merely accepted with an impassivity that drove me mad with envy. I saw the same kind of impressive stoicism in Joe. As far as that went, Christof had a chicken heart more like my own: we were always on the lookout, reading the omens and judging them fair or dangerous; we lived with nervous noses sniffing the wind, so to speak.

After Papa Africa disappeared, the meeting place at the ferry landing had gone out of style. During the last summer all of us were together, Joe's car became the nexus; in the mild early evening hours we drove out to Waanders' to drink (me) and exchange anecdotes about the year gone by (them). Christof had joined a fraternity, and he introduced us to a new world. Among the subspecies of frat-rat the laws of the barracks were adopted voluntarily, and the newcomer ('fresher', Christof said) had to quickly learn a new jargon in order to survive. The malicious tyranny of the senior members resulted, according to him, in 'friendships for life'. He was proud of having endured those humiliations. Christof didn't seem angry at his tormentors; instead, he seemed to long for the moment when he himself could administer such afflictions.

Engel looked at him in mild horror.

'You mean they *stood* on your face?'

'Well, they didn't really stand on it, it was more like putting your foot on it, for a little bit.'

At that, everyone fell silent.

'But everyone does it,' was how Christof defended the customs of his brotherhood. 'You just have to grit your teeth and bear it. After Christmas it gets a lot better. It was fun too, in some weird way, an ordeal you all go through together.'

He sighed.

'It's hard to explain to someone who wasn't there.'

Perhaps, Joe suggested, that was the whole idea: to cultivate a conspiracy in which only the members knew what it took to belong. Christof nodded gratefully. Whenever he got in a tight spot, Joe came to his rescue. For as long as I'd known him, Joe had always watched over Christof.

'It's getting chilly,' Engel said.

That day he had on a beige suit and white shirt, the tips of its collar worn over his lapels. The world of the artist had done little to change him, although it was easier now to see the kind of man he would become; the kind you saw standing at the rudder of a yacht in magazine ads, with that brand of eternal boyishness from which greying temples and crow's feet from peering at the horizon could do nothing to detract.

He had sold his first work – a gigantic triptych, ink on paper, showing a horse hanging in a tree in a attitude so twisted it made your stomach turn – to a gallery in Brussels. When asked, Engel didn't mind explaining where the idea had come from: a little World War I museum close to Ypres, in West Flanders. In a stereoscope there he had seen photographs of horses blown into treetops by the force of an exploding mortar; he had never been able to shake the image.

Engel turned to Joe.

'By the way, are you going to come by and pick up your stuff sometime?'

'Is it in the way?'

'No, as long as you pick it up before December. After that I'll be in Paris.'

'I'll come by with Frankie sometime,' Joe said.

I saw Ella Booij clearing glasses from the terrace tables and caught her attention with a great wave of my arm.

'More beer, Frankie?' she shrilled over the heads of two customers, a gray-haired couple so vital they might have come cycling out of a Geritol commercial.

When Ella brought the beer, she referred to Engel no less

than three times as 'the young gentleman', which produced great hilarity. Ella couldn't keep her eyes off him.

'God's gift to lonely ladies, you are,' Joe said to Engel once she'd left.

Summer broke out like an ulcer. Ma complained of swollen ankles and fingers that made her wedding ring pinch. I had a furious rash on my back and arse, as though I'd been rolling in a patch of nettles. Then P.J. came to Lomark. And what did Joe do, the jerk? One Saturday morning while I was pressing briquettes in the sun, bare-chested (after Ma had announced in her farmer's-almanac voice that sunlight was good against rashes), he brought her to my house.

Joe and P.J. came through the bike gate without me hearing them, and suddenly we were standing there face to face, all three of us speechless somehow. I looked for something to cover myself with, but my shirt was on the bed. Withering under P.J.'s gaze, I crippled my way through the briquette machinery and into the house. Joe came after me. I frantically tried to pull on my shirt, but the little sparrow claw was unwilling and the other arm was spasming out of control.

'Don't act so pissed off,' Joe said. 'How was I supposed to know you were walking around half naked? Here, let me...'

I slapped his hand away. It had to be on purpose: the only, the really one and only time I went outside uncovered and he had exposed me to *her* eyes. Outside, P.J. seized the handle of the press and pulled it down. She was less pale than usual, her skin was now the lightest shade of beige, her eyes an even more whopping turquoise. Later I heard that she'd been to a Greek island with Lover Boy Writer.

Joe had come by to ask me to go along to collect his things in Enschede. P.J. would be going too. We had to pick up Engel first, at Ferry Island. He buttoned my shirt for me, murmuring, 'Mean-tempered bastard' as he did. The black T-shirt he wore had DEWALT written on it in yellow letters.

'Hello, Frankie,' P.J. said when I came outside. 'Sorry if we gave you a fright.'

It was the first time she'd ever spoken directly to me. I saw Ma looking out the living-room window and waved to her. When she appeared at the kitchen door I made a drinking gesture. She said hello to Joe and introduced herself to P.J., 'but I've seen you before, of course'. They were an unlikely contrast, this worldly girl and Ma, that rough monument of care and industry. Although they seemed to speak the same language, I was sure that if you sat them down for an hour at the kitchen table together an abrupt end would come to the vocabulary they both understood, they would reach the outer limits of the things both of them could imagine.

I repeated the drinking gesture.

'Would you like some coffee, or tea? Or something else? Something cold? Both coffee? I'll just make a little then, it will be done in a jiffy, no, no problem at all. Cream, sugar? Both black? Well, that should be easy to remember.'

I felt like scratching, my back was itching badly, aggravated by Ma's blank inertia and the cross-examination that had to go before a plain old cup of coffee. P.J. asked me a jumble of questions about producing briquettes, the answers to which I wrote on my notepad without meeting her eye.

'You have nice handwriting,' P.J. said as Ma brought the coffee.

'He writes everything down,' Ma hastened to say. 'You name it. He sits there writing all day long. Frankie, come on, show the young lady your books! His whole wall is covered in them.'

I hissed at her like a cornered serpent, but P.J.'s curiosity had been aroused.

'That's pretty special,' she said, 'a guy who keeps a diary.'

Ma, who had backed off to the kitchen door, nodded and wrung her hands in that way of hers that made me feel bad about myself. P.J. asked if she could see the diaries. I led her into the house and pointed to them.

'Are these the ones?' she asked.

Her finger, the same one with which she had scared the day-lights out of Mousetown, slid across the bindings of ninety-two chronologically arranged hardback notebooks, for which I was the sole customer at Praamstra's bookshop. She turned to face me.

'I don't suppose I could...?'

I shook my head.

'I didn't think so.'

She knelt down beside the shelf containing the earliest years and sighed.

'What's in them – I mean, is it all personal or is it also about the outside world?'

I made a sound of assent.

'Both?'

I nodded. She stood up.

'My boyfriend, did you know that he's a writer? I bet Joe told you. Arthur would love this. Oh, Frankie, can't I look at just one page, please?'

There was a predatory glimmer in her eyes. She was warming me up to dangerous heights. I knew that nothing would be impossible for her, no one can resist beauty with a will. I pulled out a notebook at random, laid it on my lap and flipped through it until I found an innocuous passage: lots of Joe, the start of winter and a difficult day at school. I handed it to her. She sighed again.

'It's beautiful,' she said after a while, 'really beautiful. Your handwriting, so much…orderliness, and a whole bookcase full of it. I've never seen anything like it, this has to be the book of everything. That you, I mean who would have thought, that you just write and write, that you see everything but don't say a thing.'

Definition of God, I scribbled, and for the first time tasted the delight of her laugh. She closed the book and put it back between the other two.

'And what about me, is there anything in there about me?'

What could I say? If I confirmed it she would want to know what I had written about her, if I denied it I would be denying my love and disappointing her. A spasm came and ebbed away, I wrote:

The facts
arrival in Lomark 1993
grade-point average: 8.4
Jopie K.

'You looked at my grades! But, by the way: it was an eight point five.'

I shook my head, made a column with her final marks, averaged them and came up with 8.4. (Yes, she was impressed.)

Ma watched from the window as we pulled away. I was sitting up front in my own cart, P.J. sat on a blanket in the back because there was no seat there, only the rails they'd used to slide the coffins in and out.

'Your mother's so sweet,' she said.

We picked up Engel and drove out of Lomark. Combines were bringing in grain from the fields, swarms of gulls followed the machines like a fleet of fishing boats. Light-yellow wisps of dust hung in the air.

P.J. asked Joe to open the back window (electric), then stuck her bare feet outside. She lay on her back, resting her head on her arms, her sweater had slid up and left her tummy bare. I saw the shape of her breasts. Engel was listening to Joe's theory about Papa Africa's odyssey. The hypotheses had now been further refined: on the Internet Joe had looked at the weather maps and traced his stepfather's possible route. There had been no major storms in August or September of last year.

For the duration of that drive I was dazed by the recurring sense that something good was about to happen. I rolled down the window a little, the earth smelled of hot dust and grass. Engel talked louder above the wind.

Somewhere in the course of that slow, fluid day we got to his house in Enschede, in a working-class neighbourhood built entirely of red brick. Fat people were sitting on the stoop in garden chairs, unreal numbers of washed-out children were slurping at soft drinks.

'Welcome to the barbecue barrio,' Engel grinned. 'The grease pit for all your super-discount shopping needs.'

P.J. was horrified.

'Haven't they ever heard of calories around here?'

A neighbour raised a swing-top bottle of Grolsch in greeting, I could see the wet plucks of hair in his armpit.

'Hey, Engel, them's friends a yurn? Take a load off, mister, join us f'r a wee Pilsner.'

Engel lived on the second floor, when he opened the doors to the balcony we saw back gardens full of plastic furniture and obnoxious piles of toys.

There was a half-litre of supermarket rosé in the cupboard, but no straw. Engel poured it into teacups. P.J. said, 'Come on, let me help with that' and held the cup to my lips like a mother. I drank and looked greedily, she was so close that over the edge of the cup I could see the light summer freckles on the bridge of her nose. I drank it all at one go.

'Boy,' she said.

'It's medicinal,' Joe explained, 'it keeps him from shaking. I bet you'd like another one, wouldn't you, Frankie?'

I grinned.

'Well, you heard the man.'

There was an unmistakable rumble of thunder in the distance, and Joe began collecting his things. A sleeping bag, his father's knapsack, a folder with sketches and two clay sculptures representing machines you'd expect to see on a building site.

'Your pans,' Engel said, 'don't forget your pans.'

Joe put everything in the car and said we had to get going.

'We need to be home by dark, the headlights don't work yet.'

P.J. tossed the last glass of rosé down my gullet, the way she cared for me did me good. Engel was staying in Enschede and waved to us as we drove off. The thunder and lightning were close now, the sky above the city had turned to mica. Engel waved until we turned the corner. It was the last time I saw him alive.

The next weekend Joe came by to pick me up on his way to the junkyard: he needed parts for the hearse's cooling and electrical system. With a sort of dramatic affirmation I realized that this was the first time I'd been to the yard since the accident. The operating capacity had grown by 50 percent in the last couple of years, there was a new press for car wrecks, and the waste-separation methods had become more sophisticated. That might sound high-tech, but the basic business was the same as ever: wrecks and old junk. Still, it wasn't the kind of *bidonville* you might expect; all the waste was separated and the used oil was neatly collected and disposed of. ISO 9000 certification, Hermans & Sons, let there be no mistake about that. I always thought that was funny, that Pa wanted to have the kind of proper junkyard that people would feel good about coming to, like a slaughterhouse without the bloodstains.

Joe parked close to the front office. There, inside, was the social heart of the enterprise: the coffee and powdered-soup dispenser. Joe opened the door on my side, I swung myself out of the cart and he unloaded it. He rolled me over the rusty metal plates into the yard. I looked around, but nowhere did I see a sign reading BRIQUETTES FOR SALE, which made me wonder how Pa actually brought them to people's attention.

Dirk was running the mobile crane. In its jaws was a freshly crushed wreck, which he manoeuvred into place with pinpoint accuracy atop a pile of other wrecks. The press flattened the car bodies until they were only thirty centimetres thick, the noise it made was like an accident in slow motion. When Dirk caught sight of us, the wreck stopped, swaying, in midair.

'PA'S IN THERE!' he roared.

'Man, has he ever gotten fat,' Joe said quietly.

We were at a safe enough distance for unfavourable remarks about Dirk's appearance. My brother *had* grown fat, not in the gradual way that makes the skin glow a friendly pink, but explosively fat, without giving his surroundings a chance to get used to his new shapes. He had red spots on his neck and acne rosacea on his cheeks from the high blood pressure. Old Dirk had at last started resembling what he had always been: a weird, cracker-barrel alcoholic who smelled faintly of loneliness.

We went into the stripping shed. Coming from a mezzanine floor covered in metre-high crates we heard the sound – amplified to the power of ten – of someone searching irritably for a little wrench at the very bottom of a metal toolbox.

'Anybody home?!' Joe shouted.

The racket stopped, Pa appeared.

'Boys.'

The tail end of a rice-paper rollup was stuck to his lower lip. I'd once seen him toss a butt like that on the ground, where it landed on the wet nicotine gob and remained standing upright. Pa came down the steps on his leather clogs.

'What can I do for you?' he said to Joe.

His false teeth radiated light in the dusky shed.

'Well…' Joe began.

That was when I saw Pa stiffen in fright. Not a big fright, just an explosion on the seabed far below. I was trained in reading such micro-expressions. His eyes darted to and fro between me and something behind me. I turned my head as far as I could, but the angle was too sharp. Seizing the handle of my cart I twisted the front wheels around and turned ninety degrees. The back wall was in the shadows, but I could still see it with paralyzing sharpness: a tower of paper briquettes…piled up against the brick wall. One thousand, two thousand, ten thousand, who's to say.

A long, cold shiver ran through me. The briquettes were neatly piled up, as though to form a wall of insulation. All this time Pa had barely sold a single briquette, but he had kept paying me for more and more of them, 'It's like they're eating those things for breakfast, Frankie,' and the price he paid for his failed business instinct had been my weekly wage – to give me a goddamned sense of self-worth or whatever it was those two had tried to palm off on me.

Pa coughed like an engine on a cold morning. That was the most horrible thing about it, that he was as embarrassed about the situation as I was. I heard Joe ask him something about a radiator, so far away that it sounded like he was in a different room. Pa was silent with despair, I saw my own shame reflected in his eyes, and we stood there gaping at each other in that hall of shameful mirrors.

'OK,' said Joe, 'then I'll just wait for a while.'

I left the stripping shed and went to the car. Dried mud crunched beneath my wheels. A few minutes later Joe came out of the shed carrying a hammer and a screwdriver and gestured to me that he'd be there in a minute. The car radio was tuned to the weather report. They were talking about rain.

Sword

What was left but to try and become an arm wrestler? I went into training; Joe and I set our sights on the first tournament in Liege, in late October. Dumbbells were brought into the house and Joe got a good deal on a batch of protein supplements in the flavours strawberry, vanilla and lemon. In powder form, to mix with milk. The flavours had more to do with colour than with fruit; they were all identically sweet and creamy, with an aftertaste like chalk.

The most important weight training I did while sitting on the floor: with my elbow on a low table and a dumbbell in my hand, I curled the weight up toward me slowly, then lowered it again until right above the tabletop, keeping up the tension all the time to stimulate the muscles to maintain maximum force. I had to keep doing that until flames shot out of my arm. We'd started with sixteen kilos and three sets of twenty repetitions, with a thirty-second break between each set. Gradually the number of reps decreased and more metal discs were added to the dumbbell. Five weeks later I had thirty-eight kilos hanging on the thing, which is a lot of weight for an exercise aimed only at the biceps. My forearm I trained with wrist curls, a minute flexing of the wrist with weights in hand.

I lived on a diet prepared by Ma and strictly monitored by

Joe. My face grew thinner (Ma's perception: worried) and my arm and upper body grew heavier (Joe's perception: enthused). Because there were only so many repetitions I could do, I also propelled myself each day back and forth between Lomark and Westerveld. That was a journey of 4.2 kilometres out and 4.7 back, because on the way home I always rode past the White House, where P.J.'s parents lived. The house hadn't been white for years, though, and the thatched roof was dark brown, mossy and in need of replacement. Even after all this time, my primal fantasy concerning the women of that house seemed possessed of an auto-regenerative force. One could say that I went sniffing around there each day like a dog, drawn by lures more powerful than any visual stimuli. One could also say that I was bored to death and wanted to fill my head with sweet illusions, and that I hated myself for it afterwards because it violated my abstinence from deranging 'P.J. things'.

As a result of all the heavy training, my sleeve now contained an elephant's leg in miniature. It was completely out of proportion to the rest of my body, but then again: symmetry had gone out the window years ago. Joe did a lot of reading-up on ways to make me not only stronger, but also heavier. That resulted in an additional eleven kilos. Eleven kilos. That added up to a total of sixty-four, which meant that my heaviest opponents could outweigh me by more than twenty kilos, for the lightweight category went up to eighty-five. Even if I stuffed my face morning, noon and night I would always remain an extremely light lightweight. I consulted Musashi about this, but nowhere did he say anything about the ideal weight of the true samurai.

I concentrated on rereading the essays 'Water' and 'Fire' in *Go Rin No Sho*. They're not so much about strategy, but are of a more practical nature in instructing the reader in the way one should fight. Written by a man who, at the age of fifty-nine, had never lost a single fight.

When I'd read the book as a youngster I had revered it as a kind of Bible: this was the world of Kensei, the Sword Saint. But I had also understood only the topmost layer of what he was talking about, the things that stimulated knightly fantasies, if only because of the names of the tactics you could use to defeat your enemies. The Fire and Stones Cut, for example. That one I had tried out on Quincy Hansen in the schoolyard, and with my broomstick sword broke the defences of his book-bag shield. And, lest I forget, there was the Body of a Rock, which I practiced without an opponent: 'When you master the Way of this strategy, your body can suddenly change to rock. The Ten Thousand Things are then powerless against you. That is the body of a rock. No one can move you.'

I was practicing the Body of a Rock on the day of the cyclo-mowers. I thought I had found the liberating gravity of which he spoke. The tractor approached, I remained in place. I should have known better; Musashi himself says that unripe strategy produces sorrow.

Now, these many years later, I read it all again but it seemed to say something very different. *The Book of Five Rings* was like a gobstopper that changed colour all the time. Now I could apply it to defeat arm wrestlers. Wherever it said 'sword' I took the liberty of reading 'arm'. That wasn't actually so far-fetched, for what is a sword if not a sharp and artfully styled extension of the arm? With 'sword', Musashi himself probably meant other things as well, for he defeated his most daunting oppo-nent, Sasaki Kojiro, with an oar. The whole point is the spirit of things, the word is merely a beast of burden with ever-changing meanings on its back.

Joe was taken with my fascination for the book. He walked

around the house as he read about Holding Down a Shadow or, better yet, Scolding Tut-TUT, and he kept saying how fantastic it was. The Scolding of Tut-Tut was, in fact, very special:

> 'To scold' means that, when the enemy tries to counter-cut as you attack, you counter-cut again from below as if thrusting at him, trying to hold him down. With very quick timing you cut, scolding the enemy. Thrust up, 'Tut!', and cut, 'TUT!' This timing is encountered time and time again in the exchange of blows. The way to scold Tut-TUT is to time the cut simultaneously with raising your long sword as if to thrust at the enemy. You must learn this through repetitive practice.

'Tut-TUT!' Joe said. 'Tut-TUT!', and laughed himself silly.

The admonition to practice repetitively, he realized, meant that I needed opponents, for it made no sense to shout Tut-TUT at the dumbbells. I longed deeply for someone on whom I could unleash my growing strength and insight.

To make a long story short, Joe found Hennie.

Hennie Oosterloo was a dishwasher at the Little Red Rooster and had been in Lomark for as long as anyone could remember. He lived in one of those wooden houses you can buy for next to nothing at the garden store, at the back of the Little Red Rooster's parking lot. Hennie and I had more things in common than the garden houses we lived in: he was, second only to me, the most uncommunicative person in the village. He must have been in his fifties, but he seemed innocent as a baby. And even though he was strong as a bull, people said he wouldn't hurt a fly.

A few years earlier Hennie had been the talk of the town after he had let the waiting staff at the Little Red Rooster corral him into taking part in the July tractor-pull. These days there was a photo on the wall of the restaurant showing Hennie holding a gift certificate and an engraved silver plate and wearing a tight-fitting sleeveless vest with the logo CAFÉ REST. THE LITTLE RED ROOSTER LOMARK. In the picture he was holding the gift certificate and plate the way a savage might hold a vacuum cleaner.

I don't know whether light ever penetrated into the brain of Hennie Oosterloo, whether he'd experienced pleasure at his victory or felt a gnawing dissatisfaction at wearing his life away in the washing-up room, but none of that was reflected in his face. He always wore the same, even-tempered expression, which was in fact no expression at all; his face, as it were, was always in neutral. He had a wispy beard and flabby lips, otherwise his face had no dents or bulges and his skin seemed stretched too tightly across his skull. Hennie was such a natural part of the landscape that I'd always looked past or through him, and now suddenly he walked into my life in a pair of blue jogging pants that looked like they were cut from terrycloth. His T-shirt read HARD ROCK CAFÉ CAPE TOWN, but I was sure he'd never been that far from home. He wormed his way through the door of my house.

'Hennie, this is Frankie,' Joe said. 'Frankie, Hennie.'

Hennie turned his head left and right. I was located somewhere halfway through that sliding gaze, but he seemed to draw no distinction between a transistor radio, a pile of newspapers and my head. Joe stood between us a bit uneasily; by now he'd grown used to one silent type but two such enigmas must have been social agony, even for him.

'Let's get started, Hennie; if you'd just sit down here, opposite Frankie, that's right, here.'

Joe placed us straight across from other and pulled two identical pieces of wood from a plastic bag.

'These are handgrips,' he said. 'Is it OK if I screw them to the table? I want to show you what the real competition setup is like. These things are to keep you from using your weight unfairly.'

He put the grips, which were attached to two metal brackets with two holes each, upright on the table between Hennie and myself. From the plastic bag he then produced a cordless drill and ran four screws right through the tabletop. I slid up in my chair and, using my good hand, seized the spastic sparrow claw. I had to pry open the clenched fingers one by one and wrap them around the peg. Tight as a vice. The elbow of the other arm I placed in the middle of the table, and opened my hand.

'Just one more thing, wait a minute.'

With a big piece of chalk Joe drew a square around our arms.

'That's the box,' he said. 'You have to stay inside it. If your arm moves over the line, you forfeit the match. OK, Hennie, if you'd just…that's right, yeah. And then put your other arm down, just like Frankie…thanks.'

Hennie's right forearm came down like a railroad barrier, somewhere in the middle of the box our hands locked. Both of us clutched the pegs with our other hand, producing a compact, symmetrical whole. It was a strange and intimate sensation to be holding the warm, dry hand of someone I barely knew.

'Go,' Joe said.

He pushed the chronograph button on his watch. Our hands clenched: I made sure mine was on top of Hennie's right away, so he had to bend his wrist back; being on top gave you a big psychological advantage. The question, though, was whether psychology had any impact at all on Hennie Oosterloo's tortoise brain. He kept his arm where it was, unmoving, in the middle of the table. That meant he had chosen the strategy of biding his time, letting me attack and awaiting his chance. I made sure I kept the pressure on, not to be caught out in an unguarded moment, and thought about Becoming the Enemy ('In large-scale strategy, people are always under the impression that the enemy is strong, and so tend to become cautious'). But what was Hennie's point in doing nothing? Did it mean something? I mustn't think too much, I mustn't place myself too much in the enemy's shoes – attack him like a stone from a sling. The table creaked and I felt him give a little. Maybe my attack had encouraged him somehow; he rounded his shoulders and applied a kind of offensive counterpressure. It started slowly, but I felt it mounting like bad weather. I heard myself groan with a kind of comic-book sound and lost the Stance of Strategy ('Your forehead and the space between your eyes should not be wrinkled. Do not roll your eyes nor allow them to blink, but slightly narrow them'). Slowly, as though melting, I lost ground.

'Hey, Frankie!'

Oh, I didn't want to disappoint him, not him, not in my first match…I squeezed my eyes shut and, rising up out of the defeatism, I felt a blood-cloud of rage, the same as when I'd tried to strangle that roofer: a hot, red glow behind my closed eyes.

'And…three minutes are up!'

We both let go at the same time, my first round was over. Matches end after three minutes if neither opponent goes down. Arm wrestling is always about the best of three rounds. If your hand is even a fraction above your opponent's, you've won. Hennie Oosterloo and I had ended our first struggle in a draw, that's how I saw it. But even though Joe tried not to let it show, I sensed he'd been hoping for better.

'OK?' he asked. 'Ready to go again?'

I nodded.

'How about you, Hennie?'

Hennie grabbed the peg and planted his elbow on the table. I shook the fatigue out of my arm and resumed my position. This time I abandoned the Stance of Strategy right away and closed my eyes – I had the impression that actually *seeing* my opponent cost me strength. I went straight into the offensive with the Fire and Stones Cut, striking with everything you have in you. I felt my arm and shoulder shake from the power being released, the raging red glow spread at the back of my eyes like ink in water. From my deepest parts there unrolled a stifled, pained cry. It sounded like Tut-TUT!, and when I opened my eyes again I saw Hennie's torso leaning at a strange angle. My hand pressed his to the tabletop. From that bent, defeated position, Hennie looked up at me impassively with his dull, watercolour eyes.

'Jesus,' Joe said.

I let go, and Hennie's upper body swayed back into place.

This was my second match. I had beaten a man who had at least forty kilos on me. Joe pounded me on the shoulders in delight.

'Fantastic, man, fan-tas-tic!'

When I smiled Hennie started smiling too, without knowing why. The leaden cloud that had hung over my house ever since the disaster with the paper briquettes made way for light and air.

A third match followed, which I lost because I was still caught up in the violent rush of victory from the second. In the next weeks, many followed; Hennie received two-fifty a match and each time we wrestled I learned more about 'Knowing Collapse' and the 'Release Four Hands', as well as the principle that released a jolt of adrenaline at the mere thought of it: the 'Spirit of Crushing'.

*

Fall arrived, the tournament was drawing near. Sometimes I felt unbeatable, at other times I thought we should never have started. In late October we drove to Liège. Along the state highway, a few kilometres outside Lomark, I caught a portent of things to come. Standing in the field were men wearing fluorescent orange vests over their dress clothes: surveyors. Joe slowed. The men shouted to each other from the far sides of the field, then bent back to the theodolite. The land was being divided along invisible lines, somewhere a map had been spread out on which our future was traced like a dress pattern in a ladies' magazine.

'There's no stopping it,' Joe said. 'I've only started to understand since I've had my own car. In fact, I think that if you don't have a car you can't understand it at all. Holland has picked up a kind of momentum that only makes it go faster and faster, like a wagon crashing down a hill. Standing still is losing ground, that kind of thinking. Everywhere, really everywhere you go, highways, suburbs and industrial estates are spreading like a cancer. This country can only change that quickly because it barely stops to think about itself, or because it thinks badly of itself, that's why it's in such a hurry to look like something that could be anywhere. A soul like a coin: folklore on one side and opportunism on the other. Folklore, that's the cock of Lomark, being proud of an imaginary past. And opportunism, that's the enthusiasm with which people accept a motorway like the E981, because they think they're going to profit from it. You don't hear anyone protesting about that, except Potijk's clique, but that's a kind of folklore in itself. Hopeless, this place is completely hopeless.'

It was the first time I'd ever heard him talk like that – like an outsider. Of course I hated the scrawny boiling-fowl on the Lomark arms just as badly as he did. It was the cookie cutter from which every Lomarker was stamped, predestined to weakness and a whole lot of cackling. We knew that when the Vikings came the bird had crowed in fear, not because it was brave. But hearing Joe talking so aloofly about Lomark made me feel uneasy, as though it was no longer the two of us who were condemned to this village and could laugh out loud at its backwardness, but that suddenly he was criticizing things from the outside while I was still stuck in the midst of it. Maybe, before long, he would start seeing me the same way…how long would it take then before he judged me to be a hopeless case, a clodhopper covered in red river clay? Why was he suddenly acting like an outsider when, in my thoughts at least, I had always come to his defence when people in Lomark spoke mockingly of 'foreign elements' like him and his family? If he suddenly started wearing his outsidership like a medal, all that did was confirm the kind of *Blut-und-Boden* mentality I despised so much: the mentality that meant newcomers always remained outsiders, mistrusted and mocked behind closed doors. Didn't he realize how fragile the whole structure was, and that by doing this he was making it even shakier? That he and his family were the harbingers of something new, a point of departure from the age-old bitterness and a history you could only be ashamed of? When he put himself on a higher plane like this, it only proved them right – how could I explain that to him?

We moved onto the highway. I stared out the side window: this was the road we used to take when Ma brought me to Dr Meerman. What I remember best was the temperature of the metal objects with which Meerman tapped and probed me: as if he kept them in the fridge just for me. Of our journeys home I remembered the panicky optimism with which Ma passed Meerman's words along to me: keep at it, don't give up, do lots of exercises, don't fret – on and on like that, until I felt like opening the door of the speeding car and rolling out.

Joe punched a few buttons on the car radio but couldn't find anything, which was fine by me, I was equally content to listen to the engine's soothing hum. I longed for the end of the day, when my matches would be over and I would know my place in the hierarchy. Joe had printed up a list of the forty strongest arm wrestlers in the lightweight category (a clutter of names, dates of birth and kilos), but what really mattered of course was the Top Ten, and within that the man who was Number One. I can still remember exactly when I'd heard his name for the first time. Joe had stabbed his finger at the list, as though pointing to a coveted enemy stronghold on a map.

'Islam Mansur,' he said. 'That's our man, the ab-so-lute king of arm wrestling. Only one metre seventy-seven tall, but oh what a monster. What do you think, might that be something for Frank the Arm, just by way of something to shoot for?'

We both laughed in relief at that: from Hennie Oosterloo to Big King Mansur, that was a good one. I couldn't wait to see him in action, though: Islam Mansur, the Libyan who beat heavyweights with ease. During our training period Joe had regularly come up with tidbits of information about him: he was said to have been born in a tent in the Sahara, but the date and year were unclear. He had discovered arm wrestling in the Foreign Legion, while stationed in Djibouti. In cafés he had sometimes won from four men all at once. After his second tour of duty he left the Legion and started bodybuilding in Europe. Arm wrestling was something he did just for fun, on the side, and it was with the same nonchalance that he became world champion. Mansur was a hero in his own country, but these days he lived in a Marseille suburb. It excited me just to hear his name; I associated him of course with Musashi: Islam Mansur was the Arm Saint who, just like the Sword Saint, had never lost a contest.

We stopped at a Shell station. The Oldsmobile was a guzzler, so we'd be pulling into plenty of gas stations before this trip was over. In the outside mirror I saw Joe put the nozzle in the tank and turn his head to watch the digits roll around on the pump. A couple of minutes later he stuck his head in the window.

'You want something to drink, Frankie, or a Mars bar or something?'

I watched him as he went into the station. Again I felt that empty melancholy I'd been having lately, whiny feelings, as though something bad had happened. Like now, when my eyes suddenly started smarting at the sight of Joe's jeans sliding off his hips. His trousers were always loaded down with all the things he had in his pockets, so full they almost fell off, but at that given moment, when the sliding doors opened and he passed through between the cut flowers and the windscreen fluid, I couldn't help being moved. There was a connection with the Strategy of Becoming Stone. Strangely enough, since I had started trying to achieve greater distance from P.J. things, I actually felt moved much more often. Sometimes I experienced things as though they were already in the past, and then I got this way. The rest of the time, though, I was like stone. Or tried to be. Which was hard work.

Joe came back and climbed in.

'If you need to piss, just tell me, OK?'

The Oldsmobile's lazy motor made a deep thrumming that worked its way up through your tailbone. We only braked again when we got to Maastricht, because for some crazy reason the motorway there was interrupted by stoplights – after that there were signs saying that Liège was only twenty-seven kilometres. I was having trouble keeping my foot still.

'You need to go to the toilet?'

I shook my head. Neither of us said anything for a bit.

'It's only a game,' he said then. 'All a game. If we come home with a good story, that's plenty.'

We looked at each other and smiled the way old people do at a shared memory. The only thing I wondered was: what made something a good story? Going down in disgrace in Liège was definitely not one of them. There was more at stake here. Something that had to do with believing, about whether we could turn an idea into flesh and blood, whether we were slaves or masters, even about 'fighting for survival, discovering the meaning of life and death, learning the Way of the Sword', as the *kensei* says.

We drove into Liège. I was jittering terribly now. Joe asked for directions a few times in his schoolbook French, and the closer we came to our destination the worse the nervous cramp in my limbs became. We were really going to do it, and no matter how many matches I lost that day, I was going to sit down at a metal table and pit myself against men I'd never seen before. Joe repeated the last set of directions he'd heard and steered the car – generally known in Lomark these days as 'Speedboat's gravemobile' – down the gloomy streets. We took a wrong turn, Joe tried to remain calm and murmured, 'Three times to the left is also right.' He seemed as nervous as I was. OK, not quite, but definitely nervous. He had a lot riding on this.

One hour before the tournament started we got to the Metropole Café with its meeting hall for billiards, darts, dance parties and arm wrestling. It took us a long time to find a spot that was big enough for the Oldsmobile. Parked around the café I saw number plates from France, Germany and England.

My left arm had convulsed into a stick, the other one kept twitching up and down, making it look at times like I was doing the fascist salute.

Joe rolled me across the street, up onto the curb and through the swinging front doors. We found ourselves in a narrow hallway with a set of stairs going up in front of us and the open door to the café on our right. Behind the bar a man with an oversized moustache was polishing the mirror. Joe asked the way, he pointed up. I tilted myself out of my seat and began climbing the stairs. Step by step, I worked my way up. Joe had folded the cart and was carrying it up behind me. By the time I got to the top the sweat was running down my back – all beer and tobacco toxins leaking from my pores. The stairwell was filled with the odour of smouldering cigars and old carpet.

I found myself in a shadowy entranceway with brown panelled walls. At the end of it a door opened and a wave of noise came rushing out. We heard the tinkling of glassware, raised voices and heavy objects being slid across a wooden floor.

The meeting hall was a low room with dozens of chairs scattered around, and there were at least a hundred people in there. A mist of cigarette smoke hung just below the ceiling. I saw tattooed men with bulging muscle groups beneath their tight mesh vests and sleeveless T-shirts. At the centre of the room stood the altar of this fringe cult: the metal table with its upright pegs. Joe went looking for the organizers in order to sign in. I squeezed the armrest of my cart to stop the uncontrollable jerks rolling through my body. Oh cigarette, oh beer…I didn't seem to remember anything about having come here of my own free will. When Joe came back I gestured for a cigarette, he lit one for me and wedged it between my lips.

'Knock-out system,' he said. 'Lose once and you're finished. They start with the lightweights, then the big boys. The betting begins right before you do, and you start on "Ready? Go!" How you doing?'

I nodded.

'You start against...look here, Gaston Bravo is the guy's name. I heard someone say he's a hometown boy, so don't let yourself be distracted by the cheering. I'll help you onto the stool, all you have to do is concentrate on that first match. Tut-TUT, OK?'

He took the cigarette from my mouth and knocked off the ash. Waiters were running back and forth with trays, everyone was talking loudly to be heard above everyone else who was talking loudly, the atmosphere was like a sideshow. Right before the first match started the noised swelled even further, two men left the crowd and sat down at the table. There was some heavy betting going on. The referees assumed their positions on both sides of the table, and at 'Ready? Go!' the men went for it. The room was too small for the noisy tempest that burst loose then, it was enough to wake the dead. One of them was obviously a bodybuilder, the other a stocky farmhand with a tanned, healthy face. I was pleased to see the farmhand win the first match; he hadn't looked like the strongest of the two, and it was in my own interests that appearances be deceiving.

The ease with which he won threw the bodybuilder into a poisonous rage, the same kind that overcame Dirk whenever someone got in his way. The second round took longer, but the farmhand won again and went on to the next round. The loser stalked out of the room, pushing a slender, good-looking girl rather heavy-handedly toward the door.

There were another five contests to go before it would be my turn. I saw crude-bodied, potato-faced bastards who you could tell had ploughed on through to this competition table by means of dirty schoolyard tricks, men whose entire lives had consisted of leaning on others, of which arm wrestling was the literal expression. Those who lost had to stifle their swagger for the moment, but you sensed that would be only temporary; before long, to salvage their injured self-image, they would be blaming it on the bad shape they'd been in that day, on a cheating opponent or a referee who was blind as a bat. And their wives and children would go along with the ruse, to avoid incurring worse.

Well OK, maybe they weren't all that bad, but half of them were for sure. It was a pleasure to see a number of them hit the table.

'You ready?' Joe asked at one point.

Yes, that's why we'd come – for a moment I thought about refusing, or about throwing the match right away. Joe pushed the cart up to the table. It grew quieter, we could feel the people around us hesitating about which of us was the wrestler. And if it was Joe, what the hell was I doing here? When I lifted myself out of the cart, leaning on the stool for support with one hand, a whisper ran through the ranks and grew in volume as Joe helped me onto the hot seat.

'*Mesdames et messieurs!*' the announcer reverberated, '*François le Bras!*'

François le Bras, was that me? Apparently it was, because he went on to announce the other man as Gaston Bravo. I looked at Joe, he was laughing. What a scream. The only problem was, my opponent didn't come to the table. I could see him in the front row. I knew it was him because the other men were pushing him forward.

'*Allez, Gaston!*'

I made a quick estimate: an immigrants' son, too young to have worked in the mines and therefore now holding down some menial job (later I heard that he worked on the line at a munitions factory in Liège). He was what they called 'good looking' (black hair slicked back and big, sentimental eyes).

One of the judges went to see what was keeping him. Bravo pointed at me and gesticulated wildly. I understood, he didn't want to go against me. Not against a wheelchair case, the same way footballers wouldn't want to play against a girls' team. I tried to make eye contact with Joe, who signalled to me to stay calm; confusion worked to our advantage. After some coercion, Bravo came to the table. He didn't meet my gaze, just sat down and planted his elbow in the box. I did the same and seized his hand. It was a frightened hand, and a wave of disappointment rolled over me. Because of his opponent, the man sitting across from me was no longer taking the game seriously. It was painful and insulting. I had counted on plenty of setbacks, but not this one. I kept myself from looking to Joe for support, I had to do this on my own.

'Ready…Go!'

I struck hard, to avenge the insult. He was already halfway to defeat by the time he seemed to wake with a start and tried to resist, but it was too late: 1–0. The howling of the crowd was terrible to hear, they had all put their money on Bravo, they egged him on with the fury of floor traders at the stock exchange. For the second round, Gaston Bravo seemed prepared to do things differently.

'Ready…Go!'

And there he was, his hand on top. He certainly had impressive biceps, my, and oh, such a finely sculpted torso to put behind them; I had to surrender almost ten degrees, but that was it. Without anger I forced him slowly and without a smidgen of doubt onto the table. Then I held his hand beneath mine for a couple of tormenting seconds before letting go. François le Bras 2–Pretty Boy 0. My first official victory, and I felt no joy. He hadn't looked me in the eye once, he hadn't evaluated me as a person but as a defect, and I had defeated him with the power of hatred. I think he didn't even care; my entire person was *hors concours* to him.

'François le Bras!' Joe crowed, 'the man of the hour! He didn't have a goddamn chance, not a chance…What's wrong?'

I averted my gaze, which was full of rage and frustration. Joe gasped.

'You don't get it, do you? He wins his first fight and he's disillusioned about the way it went…Frankie, listen to me, the only reason we're here is *because* you're in a wheelchair, do you understand? Without that thing you would never have had a miracle arm, it's a direct result *of*, so if some prick draws that to your attention in his own pricky fashion, that's nothing new to you, is it? Think about the Strategy! Jesus, by the time they get used to a guy in a wheelchair it's already one–nil! You just fought against some dickhead from the barbell club and you kicked his ass! Would you please try to understand that?'

I tried to smile. Maybe I shouldn't resent being seen as a freak in these surroundings. Maybe I needed to make that my forte. A bitter pill, but there you had it. 'Today is victory over yesterday's self, and tomorrow is victory over what you are today' – *Go Rin No Sho*. When would I really start understanding things like that, instead of just toying with the words because I found them so impressive?

'You want a beer?' Joe asked. He could see that the arm had started shivering again.

Yes, I wanted a beer, and again I felt that fathomless friendship.

The next match was against the farmhand I'd seen doing his stuff earlier. His kind of strength was different from that of

Hennie Oosterloo or Gaston Bravo: more sinewy, as though he could keep it up for hours without getting tired, like a pack animal. The only thing was – and I noted this with a mixture of triumph and regret (because he seemed like such a nice guy) – it wasn't enough. I crushed him in less than one minute. He sort of smiled, slid around on his stool until he was comfortable, then put his arm back in the box for the second go. Once again, I got on top right away.

'You must learn the spirit of crushing as though with a hand-grip.'

Again I pushed through his resistance.

'It is essential to crush him all at once.'

He was three-quarters of the way to defeat.

'The primary thing is not to let him recover his position even a little.'

This is How to Crush, as Musashi prescribes it: 'If we crush lightly, he may recover.'

I had crushed the farmhand, but he showed no sign of disappointment. He got up off his stool, walked around the table and grabbed my hand to congratulate me. He wore his defeat like a saint, and by shaking my hand seemed to forgive me for having crushed him. I would have liked to say sorry or something, or do the whole match over again and let him win, just to stop feeling so shitty about it.

'Man oh man,' Joe said, 'the semi-finals. You understand now?'

Fifteen minutes later or so, what I understood best was this: my next opponent was going to be a Walloon who I'd seen win before, a man who wore at least one gold ring on each of his oily fingers, as well as on both thumbs. Right before the match he would take them off one by one, then slide them back on again when he was finished. One of his front teeth was framed in gold as well. He gave the impression of being built entirely of soot and motor oil. His strength was hard to judge.

We fell into the referee's 'Go' at exactly the same moment. After thirty seconds I was almost certain we were applying the same strategy. I let him come, there was no hurry. Haste comes when you're afraid of losing. All this time the soot-and-oil man was staring at me with eyes slightly narrowed. He was doing an awfully good imitation of the Stance in Strategy, but in a natural sort of way; he didn't seem like the kind of person who would study Japanese techniques. He maintained constant pressure on his half of the triangle, and that gave me the feeling he was holding back. He was saving something to use against me at a certain point, and with his hand on top he already had the advantage. The first thing I had to do was correct that situation.

I closed my eyes and bowed my head, and right away I felt the soothing influence of the Glow, that invisible instrument for explosively multiplying power, and brought the triangle back upright. I should have noticed that he was giving in too easily, though, because the moment we reached starting position he struck. He had been waiting for me to take the initiative, and had applied the principle of *Tai Tai No Sen*, 'to accompany him and forestall him', in masterly fashion. When I opened my eyes his golden grin was beaming right at me, and I was leaning over sideways and powerless.

Stay calm, I told myself. Nothing's been lost yet. I sucked in air; breathe in, breathe out. This was an opponent I had to fight like stone. Going into our second round, I withstood his initial attack. He was feeling sure of himself now, and exerted much more force than he had before. With that, in a certain sense, he had become me during the first round, and I was able to anticipate what he was going to do. When I looked up I saw his eyes closed in great effort. Yes, this was a glorious reversal of the first round!

Before I continue, it might be useful to explain that when you're arm wrestling you feel a continuous flux of muscle tension, ranging from the very slight to the extremely pronounced, and it's important to pay close attention to such changes in pressure. You can feel them, like the dying down or rising up of the wind. Musashi writes that in a duel we must make sure that our opponent changes position, and that we must profit from his irregular rhythm.

It was a joy to feel the soot-and-oil man's power increase, he wanted to beat me quickly. At the moment his pressure crested I yielded just a tad, only a couple of degrees, just enough to cause a minimal modification, and that was the One Right Moment: I threw everything I had into it and pressed him past deadlock at a single go. He groaned in dismay but there was no stopping it, his hand smacked down on the table.

The crowd bellowed indignantly, from one corner of my eye I saw Joe drop back in his chair in relief. The soot-and-oil man grimaced at his supporters, a crowd of gold-bedecked caravan dwellers who made noises that sounded like they were rounding up a herd of bison.

We assumed our positions for the third and decisive round. I looked at him from a kind of inner distance, and saw something I had never seen before in someone I had beaten: humiliation. You could see it around his nose and mouth, little twitches that spoke of a wounded ego. I knew now that he would go for the full offensive, he would show his fellow caravanners that the second match had been nothing but a stupid mistake and, with a total blitz, erase his defeat.

Then I did something that startled him; I brought my lips

down to my upper arm and seized the sleeve of my sweater between my teeth. I snapped at it four times to raise the cuff up above my bicep, then put my arm in the box. The twitching of his face had grown worse, he had completely lost the composure of our first match. It had been only veneer, glued on from the outside, not enlightened from within. I was seeing 'Knowing Collapse'. All things can collapse, Kensei noted in the final weeks before he died. 'Houses, bodies and enemies collapse when their rhythm is disrupted.' His advice then, when one sees the Collapsing happen, is to pursue the opponent without mercy. 'Focus your gaze on the enemy's collapse, chase him, so that you do not let him recover.' And he adds: 'The chasing attack is with a strong spirit, you must utterly cut the enemy down so that he does not recover his position.'

Thank you, Kensei.

We attacked at the same time. He tossed his head to the side and his upper body shot forward wildly. It was the charge of a bull. I closed my eyes, the Glow rolled in like a dark sea, completely at my service. I knew that this was the same rage that had possessed my ancestor Hend Hermans before they smashed his brains out with a crowbar. It ran in the family, the way some people have red hair or stubby fingers. In Dirk and me it had blossomed in full.

I began wrenching my arm back and forth, the way you rock a heavy cart to get it over a hump, to and fro, tut-TUT, to and fro. We shot past perpendicular and back again like a poplar in the wind, I toyed with him until I had enough room for the final push, and on TUT! he went down. Broken at the base, as it were. When I let go, I fell off my stool as well.

For the first time that day I felt a rush of well-being. Joe jumped up from his chair and gave me a powerful hug.

I had tasted blood.

I would go looking for more. I had penetrated to the ecstasy at the core of human existence: struggle and conquest.

All Joe could do was shake his head and say, 'Super, ab-so-lutely super,' and I floated to the ceiling, warm and light as a feather. We had reached the finals, the top two…

'Here, man, have another beer', Joe said. 'You're shaking like a leaf.'

For the first time, I heard someone place a bet on me. Money was changing hands like lightning, someone said it was a ridiculous long shot, there was no way I could win from the last man standing, Mehmet Koç, a prizefighter *par excellence*. I'd already seen him at work against a black powerlifter from Portsmouth, and it had stunned me a bit. Koç was a kind of Turkish wrestler with chest hair that seemed to grow out of his shirt like an upside-down beard.

'So, what do you think?' Joe asked in hushed earnest.

I pursed my lips to show that I was less than confident.

The announcer called Koç's name, then mine, I heard shouts of dismissal and encouragement. Even though the aficionados all agreed that I didn't stand a chance, in the course of the last few matches I had won an ambiguous kind of favour.

About what happened next I can – no, I want to – be brief: I was blown right off the table twice by a Turkish Hulk. After having been mistaken during the rest of the tournament, this time the aficionados had it right. There was no strategy one could bring to bear against Mehmet Koç, he was simply much too strong. I put up all the resistance of a bicycle pump. It was even sort of exciting to be crushed the way the Turk did it, it was the power and beauty of a wave that crashes down on you and leaves you tumbling underwater.

So I needed to become stronger. To practice repetitively. To never let up. But I'd won my very first second prize! After we'd changed the money at the border, Joe split the take with a big casino grin. Five thousand down the middle: I'd never had so much money in my life.

When we got home the briquette installation had been removed without a trace, leaving only the dark spots on the tiles where the washing machine and press had stood. The racks against the walls of my house were gone too, all of it taken away. Without a word. Good, excellent. Fine by me, let's pretend it never happened.

The burning pain that arose in my forearm thirty-six hours after the tournament was nothing but muscle soreness that would last a few days; more serious and longer-lasting was the inflammation of the biceps tendon. I sat at home immobilized, unable to move myself in any direction. Even the tiniest effort brought on agonies like the paralyzing stabs of pain one felt during the growth spurt of adolescence.

'That can't be good for you,' Ma said, 'just look at you.'

I made her even more worried when I slid ten hundreds across the table.

'What is *that*?' she said severely. 'I don't want your money, you're my child, I would never…'

I slapped my hand down on the table. Then I wrote: *Take. It's nothing*.

'A thousand! That's not nothing! I'll put it in your savings, otherwise someone we know will spend it all on God-knows-what.'

Mother, it's for you. That's the way I want it.

She looked at me long and hard, I looked back coaxingly, mixed with a kind of anger. She nodded, folded the notes one by one, made a bundle of them and said she hoped it wasn't 'bad money'. She slipped the bundle into her apron pocket.

Joe came by during his lunch break to see how things were going. He massaged my arm and rubbed it with Tiger Balm. Then, after filling the mustard glass with rollups, he went back to work.

Sun and clouds came and went in a restless pattern that made the house light at times, dark at others, a phenomenon that had made me feel sombre even as a child. At a quarter-past five, Joe returned.

'Man, this place is like a haunted house. Have you been outside today?'

A little later he was pushing me along the dyke. The sky was the colour of zinc, heavy clouds were squeezing all the light out of the washlands. A final, pale crack of sunlight stood ajar on the horizon. A swarm of starlings was searching for a place to roost, gulls argued above the dark fields, and far in the distance veils of rain brushed against the greyness. The prospect of another winter weighed on me.

Twelve days later I was ready at last for a light training session. It came as a relief: using my muscles intensively had become a remedy for the darkness inside. The dumbbells, the arrival of that neutral soul Hennie Oosterloo, the tournament in Liège; it had kissed awake the man of action in me. Wearing out my locomotor apparatus freed my mind, because of the endorphins it released. That was the first conclusion to be drawn from arm wrestling. The second was that I was a temple of burning ambition. That had nothing to do with Kensei's philosophy; it was all rage and bloodthirstiness, and I understood now why some sports were symbolic massacres.

I racked my brains over how I could ever defeat colossi like Mehmet Koç. How one sweeps away a mountain of sand with a feather, that question.

I could see only one solution: hypodermic redemption. I suggested this to Joe, but he never added such rough remedies to the training program. 'If we can get as far as we did in Liège with just a few months' training,' Joe said, 'then you're nowhere near the limits of your natural ability.' We did increase the volume of protein supplements, though, and the number of repetitions, and he gave me a jar of creatine, a controversial performance enhancer made from animal tissue. 'An advance on your birthday present,' he said.

They say lots of activity boosts your testosterone. Maybe that's why I dreamed so immoderately of P.J. during that period. Lewd dreams, with no fucking whatsoever. Can you dream of copulating when you've never actually done it? What I remember of those dreams are violent, exhausting scenes between me and other men before she and I even touched. That touch brought on feelings so ecstatic that I knew they had to exist in real life as well. She twisted her body in such a way that, in the course of things, I could never see her cunt. That was the trick my dream mind played, to camouflage my lack of anatomical insight.

But the truly special thing about those dreams was this: that I walked upright, ran and leapt. And when I made love to her, it was with a body that was whole.

It was Joe who arrived with the news that P.J. was at her parents' and that she was 'not doing well'. Not doing well meant: beaten up by Lover Boy Writer. In a fit of psychotic rage he had damaged home and garden, as well as the temple of his beloved. She had been at her parents' place for days without showing her face. I saw a disturbing correlation between the violence in my dreams and that of her slaphappy Lover Boy Writer.

Joe and I went to Acacia Florist's on Breedstraat and had a red-and-white bouquet put together for delivery to the White House.

'It's actually more the season for autumnal tints,' the noodle of a shopkeeper said.

We ignored him.

'Would you like to add a text for the recipient?'

Joe looked at me.

'You're the writer around here.'

The shopkeeper handed me a folded card with a hole punched in it. I wrote:

We're around.
Your friends
Joe and Frankie

'What kind of a text is that?' Joe said. 'Don't you have to write something like "best wishes" or something?'

I shook my head. I had full confidence in P.J.'s ability to decode the message; she would read that we were here if she needed us, and that we were thinking of her without imposing our presence. That's the way it was.

The very next tournament, in a backstreet district of Vienna, was a fiasco. I won't go into it in depth because it was a glitch, an isolated dip in another otherwise steadily rising curve. There's no sense boring people with things like that, I think. It was a paradoxical defeat, because it came in a period when I was experiencing exponential muscle development. That produces greater strength in the long term, but deep depressions in muscle capacity in the short term. That, in short, is how we lost Vienna. One thing, though: my picture appeared in the paper for the first time. What you saw was mostly that arm with the veins bulging out along it, and the beautifully defined muscle groups. Above all that, a head that looks like it's about to explode. Until that picture started making the rounds of friends and family in Lomark – Joe had bought a whole pile of the *Wiener Zeitung* – almost no one knew what we were really up to. Once they found out, though, they erupted in a sort of boundless curiosity about our doings. With his story Joe became the man himself in the canteen at Bethlehem. A match was organized on the spot between the operator and Graad Huisman. Huisman won and, before long, began weeping again over the tumour in his knee.

At coffee the next morning Ma said people were driving her mad with questions. Whether it was really true that I had beaten men twice my weight, and whether I had actually won a tournament in Antwerp. In the Sun Café, where the incident with the roofer remained unforgotten, the rumour went around that I could never have become so strong without the use of 'pills'. I noticed that people were looking at me differently – that people were looking at me. It was very invigorating.

Around that time I started smelling different. I don't know whether it was just perspiration or something else as well. I don't know, for example, whether you can smell testosterone. In any case, both Joe and Ma started throwing open the window whenever they came in. Joe even bought me a stick of deodorant, Beiersdorf 8x4, which to this day stands unopened on the kitchen shelf as one of the countless memories of him.

I still rode past the Eilander residence each day, on the way back from my training route to Westerveld. I flew by so quickly, in fact, that I barely had to time to peek in. Sometimes, when Joe had told me that P.J. was at home, I didn't peek at all. I hoped she would see me and come outside and call my name, and invite me into that mysterious house which I had never seen from the inside. I wanted her to feed me beer the way she had fed me rosé that summer day, I wanted her to say intelligent things and pass along to me exciting details about the world of writers she now knew from up close. When she would ask me how my own writing was going, I would inform her that I had stopped, which was true: I no longer wrote.

I had spent years constantly painting the view from my own head, and then it was over. I would announce this with the romantic decisiveness of the artist who doesn't believe that his talent obliges him to anything, but who sees it as something he can leave behind like an old pair of gym shoes. As casually as possible I would then draw her attention to my wrestling arm, and she would realize that I had become a man of action. Times had changed, other things were required of me. And after all, wasn't writing an extremely unmanly activity? One to which arm wrestling was vastly superior? She would understand that. She would admire my stance, and think about Lover Boy Writer, who I imagined as a deeply neurotic pen pusher with puny limbs. The comparison would work in my favour. And then we would – we would, we would…

I can't claim that the Strategy of Becoming Stone was always successful.

We heard nothing from P.J. about having been beaten up, it remained a wild supposition. Joe said he had seen contusions next to her ear and above her eye, bruises that were already getting better by then and had faded to a yellowing glimmer. She hadn't said a word about it.

Before long, though, it became clear that it was no isolated incident: once again, she came home damaged. We heard that she had refused to go to the police. The manhandling of girls with pin-curls and lovely broad cheekbones is, of course, forbidden by law, but without a police report that's not much help. The White House became her rehabilitation centre. This time Joe and I sent a funny get-well card showing a dog with its tail all bandaged up.

Now she responded – by knocking on my door one wet and muddled Saturday morning.

'I'm not intruding, am I, Frankie? Regina said Joe might be here.'

But Joe was probably out working at Dirty Rinus's. He had bought a marked-down bulldozer from his employers at Bethlehem Asphalt and was fixing it up. All I knew was that he was planning to enter some race with it. I gestured to P.J. to sit down across from me. Then I saw it: her bottom lip was split. Two stitches held the rip closed, and there was a disfiguring red lump on her chin. My eyes filled with tears of rage, but P.J. shook her head.

'It looks worse than it is. It was such a sweet card you two sent me. But how are you doing, Frankie? I've been hearing lots about you, that you take part in contests? With your arm?'

Arm wrestling, I wrote. The pegs and the square of chalk were still on the table; I assumed the starting position and motioned to her to do the same. She planted her elbow across from mine in the fading box, our hands folded around each other.

'And now?'

I pressed a little and she pressed back.

'That's it?'

I nodded and let go. That was it.

'No, show me! I want to feel how strong you are.'

She laughed, then winced at the pain in her torn lip. I put my arm back in the box and pressed her with great composure against the tabletop, as though lowering her onto a bed.

'I couldn't do a thing,' P.J. said in amazement. 'No wonder.'

Tournament in Rostock next week, I wrote. *Come along.*

'Rostock? Where's Rostock?'

Mecklenburg-Vorpommeren, on the Baltic.

The stakes were high at Rostock, and rumour had it that Islam Mansur would be there.

'That's where you and Joe are going? Maybe I will come along. I don't want to go back to Amsterdam, not for a while anyway.'

She laughed again, this time more carefully.

And so it came to pass that Joe and I stopped by the White House on Friday morning to pick up P.J. Her upper lip was a bit less swollen now, the stitches had been removed from the lower one. She was carrying a floppy brown shoulder bag. For a girl, she travelled light. Joe opened the tailgate for her, she climbed in and said good morning to me. Kathleen Eilander came out of the house in a duster shiny with wear, but even in that old rag she was still attractive, her breasts showed only a hint of sag.

'Take care of my daughter, Joe,' she said with that strange accent of hers, 'she's the only one I have.'

I think Kathleen Eilander sensed that I was staring at her through the window, for she suddenly crossed her arms as though she felt cold. I'd been staring in order to collect material for masturbatory fantasies in the future, and quickly averted my gaze. Kathleen watched us pull away, but didn't wave.

No one said much for the first few hours. It was hard to tell whether or not it was a painful silence.

'I'm starving!' Joe said, once we were well into Germany.

We stopped at a gas station. In the toilet a cleaning lady was mopping the floor, outside the traffic hummed rhythmically across little bumps in the concrete roadway.

'I ordered *Kartoffelsalat* with a curry sausage for you,' Joe said as I slid into the booth. 'You have to keep your strength up.'

My gaze moved to the glass doors of the fridge beside the counter.

'Beer's on its way.'

The man at the table beside us was polishing his cutlery with a napkin. P.J. was in a quiet mood, we couldn't get her out of it. Joe stood up and went through the swing doors into the petrol station. He came back with a road map of Germany, unfolded it halfway on the table and ran a finger along our route.

'Hey, a village called Lilienthal, here, close to Bremen. You remember Lilienthal?'

Of course I remembered Lilienthal: Otto, the engineer with wings on his back who had flown a few metres back in the nineteenth century. Joe's index finger travelled on along the E37, which became the E22 at Bremen, and then on past Lübeck. The Baltic! From there a stretch along the coastline, past Wismar, and then Rostock.

It was late afternoon when we drove into the docklands of Rostock. Darkness had almost settled in. We saw huge ferries, glistening palaces waiting to set sail for Kaliningrad, Helsinki or Tallinn. We drove past supermarkets where Scandinavian passengers were buying cartloads of alcohol and tobacco. Joe turned down a quay and we passed a wall of pine logs leaking tears of sap. The smell was overpowering. At the end of the quay, blindingly lit by huge halogen lamps, a ship full of scrap metal was being unloaded. A mechanical claw bit off chunks of the residue of the industrialized world, out of the hold there came crushed car bodies, refrigerators, wheels and nondescript household appliances. With a sweep of its arm the crane brought the junk on land and dumped it atop an apocalyptic mountain of scrap.

'Ah me,' Joe said, 'look at that: the end of all motion.'

We heard a sound behind us. P.J. was awake: her head appeared between the front seats.

'Where are we?' she asked in her sleepytime voice. 'Oh, wow.'

We watched the salvaging and fantasized about the world coming to an end, a judgment day that nibbled quietly at the back door while up front consumer squandering continued apace, and no one was any the wiser for it. Joe backed up a ways, closer to the wall of pine logs, where we had a view of the next step in the evolution of scrap. Another crane was swinging a magnet the size of a Mini Cooper, using it to pick out chunks of metal and load them onto trucks. As soon as the crane operator turned off the magnetic field, the metal fell into the truck beds with a nasty tearing noise.

Parked on the asphalt flats to our right was a lonesome Trabant with a handwritten sign in the back window: ZUM VERKAUF. A ferry blew three hollow blasts for departure.

We drove on slowly past the docks, trucks stood lined up at attention to one side in massive car parks, along some of the quays we could see the sharp silhouettes of dozens of articulated cranes against a sky full of artificial light. When we stopped and Joe turned off the engine you could hear the blissful sound of diesel motors and generators. We entered that sublime state of mind you encounter whenever you see something grand and massive. P.J. leaned forward.

'I'm so happy to be here with the two of you,' she said. 'I just wanted to say that.'

I stared straight ahead at the black water that glimmered like oil. Joe started the car.

'Let's see if we can find that harbour restaurant.'

We drove past Nissen huts, a little power plant and more petrol stations than we'd ever seen in one place. Ost-West-Strasse was easy to find; in fact, it was the main drag along that part of the waterfront, where the *Hafenrestaurant* was too. Names in this place served only to indicate function. The *Hafenrestaurant* was a low, rectangular building, with every-thing on the ground floor. MITTAGESSEN AB 2.50 read the sign in the window, and hanging from the building itself was a neon sign advertising Rostocker Pils. Yes, please.

Inside, under the suspended ceiling with sunken fluorescent lighting, we found two competition tables and a crowd of men. Hardly any women, which meant that suddenly all visual attention surged in aggressive, uncontrolled waves in P.J.'s direction. Most men would broadcast signals of desire upon seeing a woman like her, but in the harbour restaurant it was a tad worse: we were dealing here with truck drivers and seamen, a group that had little contact with the fair sex. Still, P.J. didn't seem shocked by the hormonal turbulence she caused.

For the first ten minutes or so, after hearing that Islam Mansur wasn't going to show, I was very pissed off; I had hoped to see the Arm Saint at work, to catch an analytical glimpse of his strategy. But the place was full of Asians, blacks and count-less Bohunks, fellows tough as nails, as well as pipsqueaks of whom you wondered how they stood up to life at sea or on the docks. Joe and I knew that we were witnessing something unique: a place at the edge of the world, full of men from every continent who spent their lives circling the globe just to earn their monthly wages. P.J. offered to fetch drinks. In order not to further aggravate the place's steamy atmosphere, Joe said, 'No, let me do that.' I got my Rostocker Pils at last; it even had a straw in it. It had taken us almost nine hours to get here; P.J. was the only one who had slept, Joe and I were running on a jacked-up kind of antsiness.

At eight-thirty I moved into position for the first time that evening. I was more accustomed now to being, at least briefly, the centre of attention, and that helped my concentration. In fact I had no desire to even see my opponent, I would rather have fought blindfolded; thoughts and expectations of him only distracted from the Strategy.

My first opponent seemed to be taking part on a bet, as a joke that had gotten out of hand. Without wanting to be blasé about it, I crushed him completely. P.J.'s delighted applause made me feel good. Wait until I really get rolling, I told her in my thoughts. Joe helped me off the stool and into my cart, we moved to a vantage point in the lee of the swarming crowd, between the yellowed, mordant potted plants beside the entrance. For the first time that day P.J. crept out of her shell of silence.

'That arm of yours! It looked like someone's thigh, it was almost scary...those veins!'

Joe nodded, well pleased.

'Like a thigh, that's right. Months of work went into that.'

I grinned awkwardly and sucked beer through my straw. On this day, every match would be dedicated to her, I would crush them one by one until there was no one left.

Meanwhile the contests went on, lightweights and heavy-weights, each at their own table. The blood-drunken screaming in a host of tongues drowned out all thought. Joe tried to point out my next opponent, a Russian, who was continually obscured from view by the mass of bodies moving wildly to the rhythm of the struggle. Then I caught sight of him: Vitali Nazarovitch, pale skin and eyes of faded blue. Beneath his T-shirt he had a torso like something from a men's health magazine. I rotated my wrist, round and round. Pliability is a living hand, says Musashi.

Not long afterwards I was staring at Vitali's neck muscles, which bulged like the roots of a great tree. I liked arm wrestling so much, I guess, because of the cheerful stupidity of the whole thing. There were no hidden agendas or intentions. No words were spoken, yet still it involved an intense primary contact. Nazarovitch had a workingman's strength, unlike the bodybuilder's strength which pops like a balloon if you put too much pressure on it.

The first match went nowhere. We used up the entire three minutes and ended in a draw. During the pause I noticed Nazarovitch looking at P.J. Not furtively, not with a pseudo-accidental glance, no, openly and self-confidently. I didn't dare to look whether she was responding to his flirting.

Until that moment the Russian and I had shared a symmetrical rhythm. Now that was shattered. Just before the big push a flash of light went off in my mind, a bolt of lightning. I came out of the corner with such force that I was afraid for a moment that my muscles would tear from their ligaments. The Russian groaned as he hit the table. Hurrah for creatine.

Joe gave me the thumbs-up. The Russian shook his head in the direction of two of his buddies. I wanted him to toss and turn on his cot that night, trying with all his might to deal with a defeat he couldn't understand, I wanted him to be too disgusted to even masturbate. In his dreams he would relive his childhood fears, the next day he would be tired and irritable.

At the start of the third round Nazarovitch stuck his jaw out aggressively, but I had gauged his strength by now: he couldn't beat me. A draw was the best he could hope for. In that knowledge, I attacked.

'... with your spirit calm, attack with a feeling of constantly crushing the enemy, from first to last. The spirit is to win in the depths of the enemy. This is *Ken No Sen*.'

And that was the end of the third round. The Russian could slink back on board his filthy steamer. He wouldn't forget me for a while.

'You moved way up on him,' Joe said. 'I've never seen you go way out like that. It did the trick. Be careful you don't shoot out of the box, though, watch your balance.'

Number three was a Czech truck driver in leather clogs. His breath stank like water that had been left standing in a vase, which wouldn't have been so bad if he hadn't been in the habit of exhaling forcefully as he wrestled. I heard a German behind me say that I had 'the body of a child, but the arm of a heavyweight'. I could live with that.

The Czech bit it in two rounds.

Around me there grew a kind of admiration, fuelled by puzzlement and awe. One of the heavyweights, a 120-kilo giant, came over unannounced and shook my hand. He said something to Joe, we thought it was Polish.

'I think he said something nice,' P.J. said after he was gone. 'He didn't seem angry, I don't think.'

Suddenly we felt a bit out of place in the *Hafenrestaurant*, amid that crowd from the fringe, from a world that seemed realer – because harder – than our own. We smiled at each other encouragingly and resolved to remember it down to the smallest detail.

There was some fantastic wrestling going on, and the smell of garlic and beer-breath grew ever stronger. Joe fetched three sausage sandwiches and two half-litres for P.J. and himself, a bottle of Rostocker for me. I preferred the bottle whenever possible. And no one, except Ma, knew my peculiarities the way Joe did. He almost never had to ask, most of what he knew about me was a result of his own attentiveness. That's the way it had been ever since he blew up that substation that supplied the fair with electricity: no fair for Frankie, no fair for anyone.

The crowd in Rostock had more confidence in me than the one in Liège, where only a few people had bet on me. Here things went much better, money flitted back and forth each time the announcer called out the name they had given me: '*das Ungeheuer*', the Creature. This was the next-to-last match: if I won this one, I'd be in the finals.

I found myself seated across from a stoic. Stoics were what I feared most. 'If you think, "Here is a master of the Way, who knows the principles of strategy," then you will surely lose.'

He was a stocky Asian, not very tall but with impressive shoulders. I was particularly on guard, of course, because I assumed that Asians by nature were closer to the Strategy of the samurai.

He had an iron grip, but I attacked just a little faster, putting my hand on top. His counteroffensive threw me completely off balance. He pushed with everything he had in him, groaning like he was shitting rocks.

'Come on, Frankie!' P.J. shouted, sounding rattled.

There was no way I could keep this up, I was losing horribly. All he used was the Fire and Stones Cut, pounding as hard as he could in hope of a sudden victory – and that's what he was getting. Until a miracle happened – a miracle, and nothing less than a miracle: I felt a violent shiver pass through his arm into mine. The Asian gave a sharp little cry and suddenly relaxed all his muscles, bringing us back to perpendicular. He yanked his hand away and grabbed at his forearm with the other one, making sounds of pain quite different from ours: the sort of high-pitched, wailing cries that ninjas make in cartoons. Joe was beside me in a flash. 'What happened?!' After a few minutes my suspicion was borne out: with the force of his own attack, the Asian had torn a tendon in his forearm.

I had passed through the eye of the needle.

'How lucky can you get?' Joe said.

'I thought I was going to die,' P.J. said, squeezing my good shoulder. 'He looked so... mean, as if there was no difference between this and murdering someone.'

The final was going to be between me and someone called Horst, last name unknown. But first we watched the heavy-weight semi-finals, in which the same Pole who had shaken my hand pulverized his opponent. It was a real *tour de force*, the alpha silverbacks at their best. It bothered me to know that I had to follow an act like that. The audience had come here to be entertained, to spend a few hours void of thought. So when it was my turn, I – for the first time in my life – laid on my handi-caps a little thick. Horst, looking like a Viking with his blond beard, was a bit taken aback to find himself sitting across from some Quasimodo. The audience did what it needed to do: they lapped it up. I looked around the crowd. The mood was tense, something could happen any moment. A little man screamed at me, flecks of foam flying from his mouth. Horst took up his position. My hand disappeared in his.

'Ready... Go!'

Without blinking an eyelid, Horst pushed me past the criti-cal forty-five-degree limit. I heard a muffled shriek from P.J. and tried with all my might to get out of my predicament. I tapped into reserves I had never touched before and made it back almost to perpendicular, at which point Horst simply attacked anew. I never left the defensive and Horst won the round, but he seemed disappointed at not having slammed me against the table.

I flexed my wrist back and forth. Fixedness means a dead hand. We started all over again.

'Tut-TUT!' Joe shouted.

'With very quick timing you cut, scolding the enemy.'

Come on then, you blond bastard. But my attack was neutralized by his. The Nazi swine. I realized that I had only one chance: to bend his wrist, which meant I had to pull him toward me a little in order to get past dead centre. Pliability is a living hand. I looked at Joe, who glanced quickly at his stopwatch.

'Thirty seconds!'

Thirty seconds. Fuck you, *Kartoffelsalat*.

'Fifteen!'

I had worked him toward me very slowly, in accordance with the principle of Knowing the Times, now was when it had to happen. His hand was bigger, but mine was stronger; all physical performance in my life until now had been the product of manual effort. I put so much pressure on my wrist that my molars cracked, his wrist bent far over backwards. It coincided perfectly with the final whistle and both referees awarded me the round. I had won on a technicality; it was my most strategic victory to date.

One round to go. My arm was still feeling good, no cramps or stiffness, I felt capable of breaking his morale. Horst Worst began the third match with barely visible reluctance. He had been counting on finishing up in two rounds, and now he was faced with a draw. And with an opponent whose muse was looking on. (Can you see me, P.J.? Do you admire me?)

OK, Horst Wessel, this won't take long. I'm going to burn you down, pizza face. With your faggy beard. Does it hurt? This is

Frank the Arm calling, are you ready for the ultimate humiliation? It'll only hurt for a moment. Here it comes: in the name of the Father... the Son... and the Holy Ghost...

Horst went way down, but not all the way. I wanted to crush him completely, and the thought of shouting occurred to me. 'Shout according to the situation. The voice is a thing of life. We shout against fires and so on, against the wind and the waves. The voice shows energy.'

The first time I shouted there was something hoarse about it; it had been so long since I'd shouted. The second shout was already fuller, stronger. The third time, though, it was a shout I believed in myself: rounded and powerful and the embodiment of the struggle. And Horst buckled. 'We shout after we have cut down the enemy – this is to announce victory.'

Die, dog.

We went out to dinner at an Italian place in the centre of Rostock. It was almost midnight, in the Burger King across the street they were busy mopping up. The waiter put a bottle of red wine and a beer on the table. I had been sensational, my arm was twitching from the energy still being released. P.J. fed me *quattro stagioni* and tomato salad with basil. Meanwhile I smoked and drank – all at the same time and in indecent quantities. We were feeling like free agents, heroes. We thought about Lomark and laughed, because we were out conquering the world. We would become travelling *ronin*, landless prize-fighters without a lord, free beneath the living sky. I was ecstatic and wanted it to never end, which is usually about the moment closing time arrives. We were allowed to take with us one more bottle of wine and a couple of beers in a plastic bag, but then it was really *Schluss*. We exited laughing and noisy, it was grand to feel that something had gone the way we'd dreamed.

Now we had to find a hotel. Someone pointed us toward the station, which was bathed in unreal, green light. Close by was the InterCity Hotel, but it was full of visitors to a trade fair for the offset industry.

'I could always just drive home,' Joe said.

Still cheerful, we headed out of the quiet city. At the

commuter village of Kritzmow we got our last chance: along the highway lay 'Kritzmow Park' with a supermarket, a bank, a *Spielparadies* and a hotel. We parked the car and wandered around the empty amenities centre until we found Hotel Garni.

'All right,' Joe said, 'you never know.'

He rang the bell, and did it again after a couple of minutes. The intercom produced a rattling sound, then a woman's voice.

'*Ja?*'

The door remained shut; the desk closed at eight. Joe had an ace up his sleeve, however, and announced that we were travelling with a handicapped person who was completely exhausted. Where he came up with the word '*Behinderte*' was a glorious mystery to me. The voice on the intercom had to think about that one. From the corner of my eye I saw a curtain move on the first floor, and to illustrate my defects I swayed back and forth a bit in my cart. The electronic catch on the door buzzed open.

The woman at the top of the stairs was businesslike, but not unfriendly. Breakfast was served until ten in the morning; P.J. got a room of her own, Joe and I would share a double. In the room we sat around having a few more drinks, but the thrill did not return, the experience had started wearing thin. After half a bottle of beer P.J. said good night and went to her room. Joe collapsed in an easy chair, I fell on my back onto the bed.

'I saw what you did,' he said with his eyes closed. 'You pulled him toward you slowly, but without him noticing. It was brilliant. I knew that when you looked over you were asking me how much time was left, I knew it right away.'

He raised the bottle to his lips, but it was empty.

'How's yours?'

Mine was empty as well. He sat up and looked around the room, searching for the plastic bag with bottles from the restaurant.

'Fuck, I guess P.J.'s got it.'

He went out of the room and closed the door quietly behind him.

When I woke up the clock radio said 03:52. In alarm-red digits. The light was on, I was still dressed, and Joe's side of the bed had not been slept in. The shock came after the perception: he had been gone for almost two hours. A crippling realization spread through my body: Joe and P.J....

I sat straight up in bed, beset by images of Joe and P.J. who had entered a world where I was no longer needed. A single bed was enough for them. That I was lying alone on the double bed only thickened the poison. I had brought it on myself; I had asked her to come along, out of vanity, because I wanted her to admire me. For her I had won the tournament – and Joe had walked away with the main prize. The hot beast of jealousy gnawed at my innards. He knew what I felt for her, how could he not know! Technically speaking, that made him a traitor. Joe Turncoat. Our affinity, my everlasting deference to him: meaningless. The disaster couldn't have been more complete, this was a crisis the ramifications of which could not be overseen. I would be tossed back into deepest loneliness. Never to wrestle again, never to see P.J. again, or Joe: to avoid the two of them like the plague for the rest of my born days. Never to say a word about it, but to be consumed from inside by prideful bitterness.

04:37 and he still hadn't come back. Joe and P.J.; I had never thought it was really possible. I swear. Even though it was so obvious. And it went so easily: Joe closed the door behind him and everything changed. Should I go and look for him? Wait in front of her door, sneak in, find them? Naked, asleep?

Strangle them.

WHEELCHAIR ATHLETE EXTERMINATES LOVE NEST

05:20. Outside, the traffic had started rolling.

We got back on Saturday afternoon. On Sunday morning I turned on the transistor and left it tuned to Radio God; I wanted to hate. A marriage was announced, between Elizabeth Betz and Clemens Mulder. The groom's name, as it happened, was not entirely unfamiliar to me: it was the roofer from the Sun Café.

'The vows will be celebrated at two-thirty,' the man of God said in a Vaselined voice.

The roofer, too, had found a female of the species with whom he could produce little roofers. And no one raised a finger to stop them. The man of God continued with the week's deceased.

'Mrs Slomp, having passed away at the age of eighty-two.'
Organ, lento.
'Mrs Tap, having passed away at the age of fifty-seven.'
Organ, andante.
'Mr Stroot, having passed away at the age of seventy-three.'
Organ, allegro moderato.
'Let Thy light shine upon these families in their hour of mourning.'
Organ, allegro con brio.

When the man of God said it was time to bring the Lord our gifts of love, I switched to Sky Radio.

On Wednesday my picture appeared in the *Lomarker Weekly*. I was wrestling with the Czech, the two of us listing like   a ship. INTERNATIONAL SUCCESS FOR LOMARK DUO was the headline above the article, which dripped with local sentiment. The information was correct but caricatural; Ma, however, was so proud of that story. She was, if I'm not mistaken, more interested in the newspaper report than in the way it really went. Pa's silence was deeper than ever. After the discovery of the briquette fraud we had been living with our backs to each other, both of us with different kinds of shame in our souls. Ma said he had hung the clipping beside the coffee and powdered-soup dispenser. For weeks, 'the newspaper story' served as point of departure for most of her conversations; she didn't know that Joe had lost his virginity only a couple of hours after that picture was taken. That his hands, accustomed to gears and drive shafts, had never felt anything so soft. That he had been walking around ever since in a sort of loathsome glow, while at night I sweated the love out of my system like a fever. I masturbated myself silly, as the only remedy against fits of jealous frenzy.

My friend and my dream lover had broken the triangle, the triangle that forms the basis for every sound construction. I had lost contact with the new connection, become a floating point in the darkness. Ever since Joe had come back to Lomark and started work at Bethlehem, I had believed in the illusion of unchangeableness. Now he was in love.

But how could I shove Joe and P.J. out of my life? They were the only people with whom I felt any kinship. I was confronted with a crucial moment in the process of growing up: the capitulation.

It took a lot of willpower when I was around Joe to act as

though nothing had happened. We attended tournaments, and I kept looking for Islam Mansur. I think Joe never noticed anything of the cold depths between us. I doubt whether he ever knew that I loved P.J., that I had longed for her from her first day in Lomark. He had never been particularly receptive when it came to affairs of the heart. He told me all about it. About how, when the violence in their relationship became habitual, P.J. had left Lover Boy Writer. The writer had gone on pestering her for a while; his own pathetic narcissism wouldn't let him accept anyone leaving *him*.

'Sometimes I'm glad it happened,' Joe said, 'that he fucked up like that. Not the punching and stuff, but you know. Otherwise this never would have happened.'

His expression actually went all *soft* when he said things like that.

'Everything's different now,' he said, 'even though nothing much has really changed. Except the thing with P.J. I wake up with the feeling that something's waiting for me, something good and important. Every day is a promise. And when I go to sleep that feeling's still there. It's a kind of perpetual motion, an uninterrupted flow of energy that doesn't need any fuel. Except for a telephone call, sometimes, or a kiss.'

I nodded, the bile rose in my throat. I was capable of hating him. I was vaguely shocked by the ease with which I could accept that idea. Somehow, though, the thought wasn't unwelcome; it would be easier, after all, to hate the man who possessed what I wanted most in the world. Meanwhile, with masochistic pleasure, I let him tell his story. I always encouraged him to tell me more. Only never about sex, he never talked about that, maybe out of reverence, or maybe it was simply discretion.

He had taken her to the Dolfinarium, in Harderwijk. The dolphin show in the big tank had been set against the background of a story with witches and fairies. The actors were laughably bad, the dregs of the profession. The whole thing revolved around a magic pearl, which the fairy queen consistently referred to as the 'magical poil'. The dolphins themselves were completely irrelevant to the story; all the animals had to do was a little synchronized jumping out of the water, for which they were rewarded with a herring. At the end the fairies and the witches had sung a song of reconciliation. The dolphins jumped through a hoop. Joe and P.J. were beside themselves with laughter, the story of the 'magical poil' was to become one of their pet memories.

The November sky was clear and cold, full of orange contrails that lit up like fireworks. Down here on the ground everything was in its naked form. Disorderly clouds of lapwings rose up above the washlands, slow explosions of thousands of specimens heading southwest before the freeze rolled in.

Joe spent all his free time in Dirty Rinus's barn, working on his bulldozer. Once, when I went down to visit him there, I saw the plane again for the first time in years. It stood against the back wall, damaged and dismantled. There, in such miserable condition, stood the object that once filled me with such mad hope – of there being a way out that had to do with the will and the ability to think big. And it no longer interested Joe at all. I felt a lump in my throat. I made my way between a stripped Citroën 2CV, an antique hay tedder and a few other machines from the early days of industrialized farming. Dirty Rinus never threw anything away. He was so frugal that he even locked the garbage can when he left the house. People in the village weren't particularly fond of him, but he was still remembered for his pronouncement during the oil embargo in the Seventies: 'Oil crisis? What oil crisis? I used to spend twenty-five at the pumps, and I still do!'

The wings of the plane were leaning against the wall, with

nasty rips in them. I reached out and tapped my index finger against the tail. The canvas was as taut as when Engel had first fastened it with tie-rips. It made a pleasant sound. This plane belonged in an aviation museum, it was a miracle that a couple of boys had actually built something airworthy, it should have been the showpiece in some private collection. The worst damage was up at the front; rods were sticking through the torn fuselage, you could see right through it. The propeller had been taken off and was lying on the floor, everything was covered in a layer of sticky dust.

'Roofing tiles fell on it,' Joe shouted from the front of the barn.

I looked around, he was standing on the ladder of the bull-dozer, from up there he could see me amid all the rubbish. I saw the hole in the barn's roof, the sky above. Around the plane lay mossy, broken roofing tiles. It galled me that Joe no longer even looked at the thing, but that's the way he was. He made something, tested its possibilities, then let it fall from his hands. Conservatism was foreign to him; he let time and roofing tiles do their work while he started in on a new chapter in his study of mobility. He didn't think much about things that weren't there; neither tomorrow nor yesterday were there, and so of little importance to him. I wasn't like that. There were days when I bridled at the sense of standing with my back to the future: a river running back uphill into the mountains.

Joe had always been obsessed with motion. Motion driven by the internal combustion engine. I remember a dark hotel room that smelled of old overcoats, somewhere in Germany or Austria I think, with Joe lying on the other bed and orating about his favourite subject. Every once in a while I could see his cigarette flare up.

'Fear and overconfidence,' he said, 'those are the prime

movers of history. First you have fear, which is all the thoughts and feelings that tell you something can't be. There are lots of those. The problem is, they're often true. But all you have to know is what's needed, nothing more than that. Knowing too much leads to fear, and fear leads to stagnation. The drudges are the people who tell you that you can't do something if you're not trained to do it, but talent doesn't pay any attention to that. Talent builds the engine, the drudge checks the oil: that's how it works. What do you think, you think Anthony Fokker knew what he was doing? He didn't even have a pilot's license, only talent and a lot of luck. Overconfidence is every bit as important as talent: *I* can't *do it, but I'm* going *to do it anyway.* You see for yourself whether it works or not. Some people get lucky, others don't, that's pretty much all you can say. There was no way we could build an airplane, we didn't have the technology to do it. But I can do my arithmetic, and Engel can too. In fact, Engel is a giant at arithmetic. And that's what you need if you're going to build a plane. Together, the two of us did the strength calculations for the wings and fuselage. Calculating and weighing, weighing all the time. We fudged a little with the battery, it weighed something like thirteen kilos, so that was the last thing we put in, a little ways to the back because the plane was nose-heavy.'

I heard a deep sigh in the dark.

'I was more afraid of it not getting off the ground than I was of crashing.'

His face was lit up by the flame he used to find the ashtray.

'And one other thing, Frankie. Energy that isn't put to use, that isn't applied, reverts to heat. Heat is the lowest form of energy. Then comes kinetic energy, like in an engine, and then electricity or maybe nuclear energy. But heat is the lowest level. A person who's sweating is converting motion into heat, the way a stove does with fuel. And heat is loss. Entropy, Frankie: the law of irreversible loss. That's why the heated, high-entropic world is so simple, because it's all about loss. Anyone who doesn't know that doesn't know what's happening. People spend most of their lives looking for warmth. A little monkey that can choose between two artificial mothers – a steel one that provides food or a terrycloth one without food – will choose the terrycloth one. Warmth and affection: eternal babies is what we are. Fleaing each other. But too much warmth makes you dull, makes you drowsy. That's the oppressive thing about so many marriages – and once things get to that point, the spirit screams bloody murder. So what do you do? You buy a car or build a boat, the way Papa Africa did, because motion is the basis of all life. The molecular speed of an object determines its temperature – and if you add the factor of speed to that…Jesus, like having a rocket up your ass! For a lot of men the car is the only escape they have left, the only release from the cloying warmth of all the promises they've made: their marriage, their mortgage, the indignities tossed at them at work. Driving fast and fucking on the sly. That's why adultery is a bourgeois act, Frankie, something for people who promise too much, because the promise summons up its own violation. So watch out for people who promise too much. That's all I'm trying to say.'

He yawned.

'Man, am I ever tired.'

Joe had bought the bulldozer, a yellow Caterpillar of solid, functional design, in order to take part in the Paris–Dakar rally. No one had ever driven Paris–Dakar in a bulldozer before and, seeing as there were no rules against it, Joe was going to be the first to try. I didn't understand what he saw in it, but he considered the bulldozer the crown of his kinetic creation. It took a hell of a lot of work though to modify that heavy machine and make it suited for the rally.

Joe's biggest problem was how slow the thing was. It had engine power aplenty, he explained, but the gearing was too low, so it could never produce the kind of speed he wanted. He had ordered four larger gears from a machine plant, one for each wheel, and meanwhile he went on rebuilding the cab. The standard cab construction was too rigid to sit in during a rally, especially on the kind of stony desert substrates he was expecting. That's why he was putting the whole thing up on springs, and Joe had also added a pneumatic driver's seat from a truck in order to keep his kidneys in place while tearing at a hundred kilometres per hour or so across stones and through craters. In order to get to such speeds, which were insanely high for a bulldozer, he jacked up the revs by putting a heavier spring in the fuel pump. Now the engine could get up to 2500 rpm; parked there in Dirty Rinus's barn was a racing car that weighed almost nine thousand kilos.

We were in Halle, at the close of a nerve-racking tournament in which I'd barely squeaked into third place, when we heard about Engel. Joe phoned home from the hotel room. I remember that the window was open, letting in street noises and a breath of spring. After a while he hung up gingerly and looked at me.

'Engel is dead,' he said.

There was only one thing I was really sure of at that point: that I longed blindly for the moment before that announcement, when the world hadn't been wrenched from its pilings.

Joe wanted to go home right away. I would rather have stayed in the hotel, to let them refill the minibar so I could keep drinking it dry until the world recovered its old shape, but a little later we were driving wordlessly through the night. The radium dials on the dash spread their greenish glow, never before had I so felt the lack of a voice with which to speak hollow words of dismay.

All we knew was that Engel had been killed in an accident. I thought banal thoughts, about how his things would have to be brought home, how the price of his work would now go up, and about how long it would take before the remains would stop looking like Engel. It was a disappointment to discover that a friend's death produced no finer thoughts. At four in the morning we drove into Lomark. Light spots in the sky announced the new day, we drove down the Lange Nek to the Ferry Head, to Engel's parental home, where the lights were still on. Joe cursed, and I think it was only then that we realized what Engel's death must mean for his father.

'Come on, let's go in.'

Joe pushed me along the flagstone path at the side of the house. In the front room, under the lamp above the table, we saw a form hunched over. We both wished right then that we could turn around and leave. Nets were hanging in the backyard, the eels would start migrating soon, and the outboard motor was clamped to the edge of an oil drum. Joe knocked on the door to the pantry. We heard someone stumbling about, then the light went on and Eleveld opened the door. It didn't look like he had been to bed yet.

'Boys.'

Joe shuffled his feet hesitantly.

'Mr Eleveld, we were in Germany…we came right away. Is it true? About Engel…'

'It's terrible, boys. Terrible.'

He led us through the pantry, his head bowed. I'd never seen anything that broke my heart like that. Engel's racing skates were hanging from a nail, on the floor was the row of shoes he used to wear, arranged neatly pair by pair.

We sat down at the living-room table. Eleveld was alone, he had heard the news that afternoon when a policeman called from Paris.

'Whether I was Engel's father, the man asked, and he gave his description. "Yes, sir," I said. "That's my son." Then he told me he had bad news.'

Eleveld turned away from us. Lying on the table were prospectuses from Griffioen's Funeral Services. I pulled them over and, not knowing what else to do, began flipping through the booklet entitled *Ideas for Funeral Arrangements*. The suggested illustrations for mourning cards consisted of weeping willows, ships at sea, Christian pictograms, and doves carrying a wreath. At the back I found examples of texts beside which Eleveld had put an X:

6. Until we meet again
10. Words are not enough
19. No need to struggle anymore, rest is yours
21. A fine memory is so dear that only flowers can speak of it

A glance at the prospectus 'Recommended Price List Accompanying the Book *Ideas for Funeral Arrangements*' made it clear to me how Griffioen paid for his Mercedes S600.

'But how did it happen?' Joe asked hoarsely. 'Did they say?'
Eleveld shook his head.

'I'm not so good with foreign languages...from what I understood, a dog fell on Engel's head. From the balcony of an apartment building. A dog.'

I couldn't imagine that Eleveld really knew what he'd just

said: a dog had landed on his son's head, in Paris? It was so sur-
real that, if only for a moment, it opened up a hopeful prospect:
what if it wasn't true, what if Engel was alive and only scaring
people with *art*? But looking at old Eleveld you knew that
couldn't be right; Engel might have laughed at our reactions,
but he would never do that to his father. Two days from now
they were going to bring him home, the insurance company
had arranged for a funeral transport firm to pick him up from a
cold store along the Seine.

We left Eleveld as day was dawning. The clock in Lomark
struck five, birds were singing everywhere.

'Engel discovered the law of gravity,' Joe mumbled as he
loaded me into the car.

But he shared my doubts; when we got to my house, he said:
'I'll believe it when I see him.'

On Tuesday morning, that is what happened. Engel's viewing
was held at Griffioen's funeral home, I went there with Joe and
Christof. An attendant closed the door quietly behind us, we
were alone with the coffin in the middle of the cool, soundproof
room. There were four big candles around it.

'It's really him,' Joe said quietly.

I got up and had to lean on the back of my cart to see him,
lying beneath a stretch of cheesecloth spread over the end of the
coffin. Under his chin was a brace that kept his lower jaw in
place, his lips were colourless, his cheeks sunken. His cheekbones protruded in saintly fashion. This was Engel, my first
corpse. My arm started shaking, I had to sit down. The cooling
element zooming away beneath the bier was a monotonous
requiem to our friend's absence. In a chair on the other side of the
coffin, I could hear Christof weeping. I had never heard him cry
before. It annoyed me. The noises he made came in phrases, to
match the rhythm of his breathing. To me it felt like he was co-

opting Engel's memory by making more noise than we were.

Suddenly I realized that Joe, Christof and I once again formed a triangular construction, just like when we were younger and I only knew Engel as my silent helper at the urinal.

Joe lifted the cheesecloth frame from the coffin and laid his damaged hand on Engel's cheek. He stared in concentration at the face, which you could now see had been broken by the impact. We had no idea what kind of dog it was, only that the animal had fallen from the ninth floor of an apartment building in a Paris suburb, right onto the head of Lomark's next-to-last Eleveld. There was something about that family and things falling from the sky, be it dogs or Allied thousand-pounders delivered to the wrong address. I'd gladly have given a finger for Engel's last thoughts before fate struck him down in the form of *Canis familiaris*, man's faithful servant for more than fifteen thousand years.

That afternoon Ma took me to Ter Staal's to buy a suit. My arm had become too big for the sleeve – 'My land, it's the first time I've ever seen such a thing,' Ma grumbled – and my misshapen undercarriage was going to be a true test of her inventiveness with the sewing machine. Matching shoes were out of the question; it would have to be the same old wooden blocks, only shined to a polish.

'I suppose it's for the Eleveld boy?' the salesgirl asked.

I felt that the girl needed to mind her own business, but Ma joined in enthusiastically in the female choir that likes to sing of other people's calamity.

'Terrible, a thing like that,' she said. 'Some people just seem born for misfortune. Frankie spent a lot of time with him.'

'And the father? I guess he's all alone now? First his wife, now his son...'

Ma raised her eyes devoutly.

'The Lord moves in mysterious ways.'

'He never came in here,' the salesgirl said. 'I think he bought his clothes in the city, at least that's the way it looked.'

She tugged unpleasantly on the jacket, trying to get it off my shoulders, and I braced myself a little in the hope that she'd pull till it ripped. We left Ter Staal's with a black polyester suit so inflammable it should have had a NO SMOKING sign on it.

On Wednesday Ma came in with the *Weekly* containing the funeral notice. For some strange reason, Eleveld had chosen 'No need to struggle anymore, rest is yours', which seemed more appropriate for an old person who had died after a lingering illness than for a young artist hit on the head by a falling dog.

'The poor man is all confused,' Ma said, two pins in her mouth as she went to work taking in my new trousers.

They were glorious spring days, the sap was flowing in the trees, the tinkling chirp of sparrows could be heard in the bushes between the house and the old cemetery.

'Engel will be buried on Friday morning. He was fond of flowers.'

That was news to me as well, but on Friday morning his grave was indeed surrounded by piles of flowers in crackly cellophane bouquets. The service held beforehand was in true Nieuwenhuis style: the empty rhetoric of the resurrection and he-who-lives-on-in-our-thoughts. I couldn't imagine that people still found comfort in phrases durable as linoleum tiles.

I sat on the aisle in the second row, beside P.J., with Joe and Christof on the other side of her. I had a hard time concentrating on Engel's service. From one corner of my eye I saw that Joe and P.J. were holding hands, and I knew Christof couldn't have missed that either. His reaction would be pretty similar to my own. All we could do was accept it, gritting our teeth all the while; within a friendship, rivalry like that takes place beneath the surface, where the hot beast of jealousy gnaws at the bars and poisons our souls with unsettling whispers. In Christof and me in equal measure. The only effective antidote was masturbation, but with the gradual return of energy after orgasm the jealousy returned in full force as well.

It cut me in two like a river. On the one shore, Joe was the one I loved like no other; on the other he was my opponent, because he had hijacked my fondest dream. I didn't understand how those things could exist side by side and even trade places in the wink of an eye. How mistaken I had been: I had seen Christof as my greatest rival – and that was what Joe had become.

And P.J. grew only more beautiful. She wore a thin, light-gray woollen suit-dress, her black heels clicked on the paving stones as she walked out of the church in front of me. Beneath the waisted jacket her buttocks screamed to be caressed; above them, on her lower back, rested Joe's hand, just as the uncallused hand of Lover Boy Writer had rested there not long before, and Jopie Koeksnijder's before that. She had her mother's high waist.

Girls were weeping around the grave. I knew a few of them from school, Harriët Galama and Ineke de Boer for example, even the horrendous Heleen van Paridon – who, for as long as I'd known her, had resembled a neurotic housewife with a dusting obsession – and many others I had never seen before. Engel's fellow students. They wore mad outfits that probably passed at the art academy for expressions of highly individual taste; that they all looked pretty much the same in them was beside the point. One extremely tall girl in big yellow basketball shoes was taking photographs. Beneath her brown tweed jacket she wore an unnerving candy-pink skirt; the combination with her pretty face made my eyes hurt.

It was with such women that Engel had consorted since leaving Lomark – he had slept with them on mattresses on the floor, with background music by manic-depressive musicians with long hair and a death wish. After the deed they ate olives or chocolate and experienced a deep sense of uniqueness and irreproducibility. Now that Engel was dead, those girls came to Lomark and were amazed at his provincial roots and his father who looked like a bicycle racer from the days of black and white film. Eleveld stood in the inner circle and listened intently to Nieuwenhuis who, because it was Eastertide, read aloud from Paul's Epistle to the Corinthians. He again shared with us the mystery of eternal life: we will not all sleep, but we will all be changed. This was his outflanking manoeuvre, to assuage the pain and puzzlement of death. Diametrically opposed to this you had Musashi, upright and in full armour, for whom the Way of the samurai is the resolute acceptance of death. According to Nieuwenhuis, trumpets would sound before we were resurrected to immortality; Musashi says nothing of things of which he has no knowledge. What he does know is the way one should die: '…when you lay down your life, you must make fullest use of your weaponry. It is false not to do so, and to die with a weapon yet undrawn.'

What we do find, in the final section, 'The Void', is this: 'What is called the spirit of the void is where there is nothing. Man's knowledge cannot fathom this.' Musashi offers us one way out of ignorance: 'By knowing things that exist, you can know that which does not exist. That is the void.' That was precisely why Nieuwenhuis and the Apostle Paul rolled off me like water off a duck's back: they didn't start their reasoning with things that exist, but with a nutty kind of messianism.

I heard jackdaws flying over, by reflex I looked up to see if I could spot Wednesday. A fire of longing roared in my chest.

'But thanks be to God,' Nieuwenhuis said with a dying fall, 'which giveth us the victory, through Jesus Christ, Our Lord.'

Meanwhile, Engel was still dead, and the bottomless realization began to dawn that I would never, ever see him again.

At Het Karrewiel they were serving white buns with ham or cheese. There is comfort in the hunger we feel when we have lowered a loved one into the grave; hunger is unmistakably a sign that you're alive. The eating of white buns distinguishes us from those to whom we have said farewell; we eat, we live – they are eaten, they are dead. With white buns in Het Karrewiel we return with a feeling of relief from the gates of Hades; our time has not yet come.

I had hoped we would stick together that afternoon, but everyone went their separate ways. Joe walked P.J. back to the White House, Christof took off with grooves of bitterness at the corners of his mouth – he wasn't yet accustomed to this unusual rivalry at the heart of the friendship. I sat at home in that stupid suit and knew that the world had changed beyond recovery. And this wasn't the end, there was a great deal yet to come. With Engel's death, a crucial stabilizing force had disappeared from our social construct; I had a strong sense of more decay on its way, not much farther down the line.

At six o'clock I opened a can of frankfurters and shook them onto a plate, which I put in the microwave. Before eating them I dragged them through the mustard, because the taste of frankfurters always makes me think of morbidly deformed chickens in the death camps of the factory farms. Schnitzel or frying sausage produces the same disturbing awareness, with one phrase in particular haunting my mind: 'pig pain'. As I ate I listened distractedly to that art program on Channel 1, the one where the interviewers are primarily interested in the life of the artist and almost never probe into his work. The girls I had seen today around Engel's grave, I suspected, would end up someday on programs like that, reflecting with the earnestness of a child staring at its first turd in the potty. On the radio you almost never heard anyone talk about things like arm wrestling or bulldozers, those were worlds hidden to them.

Halfway through the frankfurters, an interview was announced with the author of a new novel, *About a Woman*: Arthur Metz. It took a couple of seconds for it to hit me: this was Lover Boy Writer. In my thoughts I had never referred to him by his real name, that would have implied that I recognized him as a man of flesh and blood whom P.J. had loved. The pseudonym helped me to keep my distance from that hated fact. First they played a song, then the female interviewer came back. I listened tensely.

'With us here today we have the poet and writer Arthur Metz, whose novel *About a Woman* appeared last week. He's here to talk about that book. Welcome, Arthur.'

A vague crackling in the mike.

'Come a little closer to the microphone, Arthur, so we can hear you. Maybe it's good to start off by noting that the narrator of your book is a writer who, I believe, resembles you rather closely. But the first question that came to mind when I read your novel was where you found the female character, Tessel. She's the tragic heroine of the story, and I had the idea that she stood for the modern woman with all her troubles: the demands of eternal youth, for example, and the constant struggle against overweight, which I think a lot of women will be able to identify with. Did you intend *About a Woman* to be a modern novel of manners?'

It took a moment before a reply came, the writer cleared his throat rather loudly. The first audible word was 'uuh'.

'I could have given the book another title,' he said then, '*Whore of the Century* or something, but my publisher, uuh, didn't think that was a good idea.'

'Why *Whore of the Century*?' the interviewer asked. 'That sounds like a personal vendetta. Is that what it is, a personal vendetta?'

'There *are* no great novels without a personal vendetta.'

'But did the events in the book actually happen to you, is that what you're trying to say?'

'I, uuh…I don't write anything that doesn't fall within the possibilities of my own existence.'

Metz seemed to squeeze his words out one by one, like a turtle laying its eggs in a hole in the sand.

'That's an awfully sweeping statement. Could you be a little more specific? What do you mean by the possibilities of your own existence? Do you mean that in this book you've described the facts as they could have taken place?'

'Uuh…Yes.'

'So you're saying this is pure fiction?'

'At a certain point, many writers have to deal with a woman who forces herself upon them as their muse. Tessel lives in the terrible realization that she is empty inside and, at the same time, that she does not fill anyone else's life with, uuh…love. She wants to be the most important thing in someone else's life, in order to forget herself. And then preferably a, uuh… writer.'

'But *why* does she want that?'

'She dispels her feelings of emptiness and, uuh…futility by, on the one hand, fits of bulimic gorging, and by seduction. On the other. She looks for a writer in order to be immortalized as his muse, in order to, uuh...recover her self-worth. Against the emptiness. A dangerous and extremely beautiful parasite...in fact.'

'Well yes, as I read your book I also had the feeling that she is both monstrous and helpless. Somewhere you write that she is a "muse by calling", a muse without an artist to immortalize her. Have you ever met anyone like that yourself, someone who perhaps inspired you in the writing of this book? I mean, it has such overwhelming autobiographical intensity.'

After a fairly long silence you could hear the spark wheel of a lighter scraping against flint, followed by cigarette smoke being inhaled with obvious pleasure into the tiniest branches of the bronchia.

'First we're going to listen to a song,' the interviewer said. 'Here is the lovely "Suzanne" by Leonard Cohen.'

It was much too nice a song for this shit day: full, welcome tears ran down my cheeks. Far too soon we returned to the interview with the writer.

'While the music was playing, Arthur, you told me that you wrote this book within a very short period. Was there a reason for that?'

Metz mumbled something about necessity and rage; in fact he didn't seem to want to talk about his book at all.

'You also deal here with a very controversial subject,' the interviewer tried. 'You state that physical violence is the logical conclusion of all intimate contact. The scenes in which the writer assaults the girl Tessel are among the most distasteful in the book, but perhaps even more shocking is that you seem to say that such violence is justifiable.'

'Violence, uuh...is much more multifaceted than many people think. Perhaps one would do better to look first at the conclusion, in other words at the results of human actions, before deciding what is violent and what is not. That imposes nuance on the, uuh… absolute distinction between culprit and victim.'

Then he repeated the word 'victim', more to himself it seemed, as though it were a new word to him.

'But there's no way to justify physical violence against women, is there?!'

'I, uuh… I'm not justifying anything,' was the weary reply, 'I'm recording a process. As a, uuh… Lover of the Truth.'

With this the interview was more or less over. The irritated female interviewer tried to bring the writer back to life with a few more of her surges of moral current, but he was sunk in the morass of gloom and contempt.

I was alight with curiosity about the book. I knew that the character of Tessel was made after P.J.'s image, and I had found it exciting to try to decipher the writer's messages across the airwaves. I strongly suspected that he had encoded P.J.'s surname, Eilander, in the first name Tessel/Texel, after the island. What's more, Metz demonstrated the see-through rhetoric of the chronically self-authenticating depressive, and that fascinated me.

Three cold frankfurters still lay on the plate, the mustard was showing traces of the dark crust that, within twenty-four hours, would begin to crack.

The next morning I went to Praamstra's bookshop, which specialized in the better Christian literature and had an excellent assortment of titles such as *A Personal Talk with God* or *The Gospel of Jesus in the Life of Your Child*, and ordered the novel *About a Woman*. Author: Arthur Metz. Delivery time: 'Usually two days, but it might take a week, just so you know.'

I f I hoped to make even a ripple at the international arm-
wrestling tournament in Poznan on 6 May, I was going to
have to be in top form. Joe was convinced that this time
Islam Mansur would really be there; a shot at the first prize of
fifteen thousand smackers was something he wouldn't want to
miss. I intensified my training program as I felt necessary, and
although I saw Joe regularly during the week – he often spent
the weekend in Amsterdam with P.J., or at Dirty Rinus's working on his bulldozer – I told him nothing about what I'd heard
on the radio. What is lacking cannot be counted, saith the
Preacher.

On Thursday, *About a Woman* was waiting for me at Praamstra's: 316 pages, that will be twenty-nine-fifty please, thank
you very much. P.J. would certainly see the book in Amsterdam,
and it was very much the question whether she would be
pleased about that – the advance radio review did not bode well
for her. It felt like I was toting someone else's confidential medical files around with me, and when I got home I started
reading right away. The story interested me least of all; I was
looking for the character of Tessel. I found her in the chapter
entitled 'Puke Girl', which began by sketching the socio-cultural
background against which eating disorders made their appearance:

In 1984, the readers of *Glamour* magazine were asked what it was that would make them happiest. We would expect their response to have been: wealth, pleasure and holiday destinations with guaranteed sunshine. But that is naïve: 42 percent said that weight loss was the key to happiness. It was in that same decade that Tessel was born to South African parents. She was sensitive, intelligent and fat. Tessel grew up in a society in which being overweight was condemned as a visible sign of weakness and a lack of self-control.

The cult of the low-fat body followed on the heels of the increased self-determination of women – the foodstuffs industry, clothing and cosmetics producers responded with a compulsory model that made slenderness synonymous with desirability and success. In the history of mankind, no other period is found with such rigid directives for the ideal proportions of the human body. No dictatorial system has ever succeeded in imposing such an all-inclusive *Körperkultur*; the bodily ideal of the Third Reich was made possible at last by modern industry. Within the commercial propaganda, a healthy, slender body with a well-balanced BMI (body mass index) is the only vehicle for positive self-awareness, friendships with other healthy, attractive individuals and professional self-realization.

When Tessel began awakening to her own sexuality, bathroom mirrors and reflecting glass surfaces in public spaces entered her life. With her blond curls and pretty, broad face reminiscent of Eskimo girls, she was not unattractive. Her locomotor apparatus, however, was swaddled in a layer of fat that was visibly thicker than that of the other (largely white) girls in her class. Her kneecaps receded further due to the girth of her thighs; when she looked down, her neck formed a fleshy bib. Her sexual awareness began with repulsion toward her own body.

Major events influence our lives only in small part; a casual comment or chance event often has a greater impact on one's life than does the first man on the Moon or the discovery of the structure of DNA. The decisive sentence in Tessel's life was spoken by her mother, one muggy afternoon as they were shopping for shoes in Cape Town. 'Look, just your type,' her mother said, and Tessel knew exactly what she meant. In front of them, a fat little boy was walking along with his mother. He wore a pair of short trousers that showed his chubby calves, he had a Springboks cap on his head. It was a pedagogical *faux pas*, and Tessel froze in horror.

The fat boy on the shopping street became her sole prospect for the future. She was doomed to kiss fat boys, sit beside fat boys at school and at university, she would marry a fat boy and give birth to fat boys. She considered suicide.

I looked up from the page and felt that my face was warm and flushed, as though I had stolen a look at someone's secret diary: P.J.'s secret diary, to be precise. Were these the things she had told Metz in her infatuation, before they split up amid hatred and violence? It was sensational reading and, thank God, Metz wrote much more fluently than he spoke. The writer continued:

Around the time that Tessel began considering the practical aspects of suicide, her parents decided to emigrate to the Netherlands. South Africa's future loomed before them as an orgy of violence, a national free-for-all. Tessel realized that she could make use of the interruption to leave behind her life as a fatty. Her new existence could be drastically less ponderous.

To start with, she skipped the meals on the plane. The pangs of hunger with which she arrived at Schiphol Airport she welcomed as the first victory over the old her.

For the first few months, the family was in transit. Tessel, with an impressive show of willpower, pressed on with her starvation diet. She ate only that which was absolutely necessary, and then only to put her parents' minds at ease. Within two months she had lost fifteen kilos, and then another seven before they moved to their new home.

In the new setting no one knew she had ever been a fat girl, and she never showed anyone pictures taken of her in South Africa. In amazement, Tessel noted that she was considered *pretty*, and not simply pretty but beautiful; she had girlfriends, boys fell in love with her. The metamorphosis was complete. She was, in fact, half her old size, but she still felt: fat. For years, upon entering a boutique she would first go to the racks of outsize apparel.

Tessel had stopped starving herself; that had met with too much resistance from those around her. Now she ate in accordance with a strict, clockwork regime of small quantities of low-fat, low-calorie foods. Her inner resistance to such stultifying discipline resulted in eating jags, moments at which she allowed herself a brief respite of complete excess, when she could let herself go and bury her sorrow beneath an avalanche of cookies, marzipan, chips, ice cream and chocolate. And, in regret at having violated her own rules, she then vomited it all out into the toilet.

A layman could have diagnosed it as bulimia nervosa.

Commonly, the image the bulimia patient has of her own body is out of synch with its actual girth. Those around her see normal proportions, but the patient herself looks in the mirror and sees a swollen monstrosity. Puking is the only way to control the monster, and the resulting feelings of shame aggravate the sense of loneliness. For women who suffer from bulimia, the world is a twisted mirror in which they constantly try to adopt the correct pose.

Those who only rarely vomit think this must be a painful, intensive activity, but it is very easy for the puke girl. She has trained herself to vomit in a way that remains hidden from the outside world: we see no red eyes, smell no sour breath. She sticks toothbrushes and spoons down her throat or, with no other means available, presses two fingers against her uvula. The toilet seat is raised, the view fills her with disgust, but she braces herself and thinks: OK, here we go.

In Tessel's case, the detrimental effects of gastric acid on the teeth (the rapid destruction of tooth enamel results in cavities) was only a minor problem: her father was a dentist.

With that, my final doubts were swept away; the only figure presenting itself from within this description was P.J. Eilander. Her secret lay spread before me on the table.

Tessel now controlled her weight with the most invisible form of self-mutilation: vomiting. Within her grew an existential void and a sense of her own intrinsic worthlessness. These were her last authentic emotions. In the outside world she reacted to the emotions of others with behaviour that she had copied: she knew that comforting went with sorrow, and that joy had to be met in turn with confirmation of that joy. She herself knew only the derivatives of emotions, echoes from the days when she was fat and miserable. Her inner world was a cold, blasted place; calling out to her from the ruins were pudgy boys and girls, drowning in their own fat.

The special thing about Tessel was that the course of her life had been cut in two: one part – far away, on another continent – in which she had been fat and miserable, and another in which she was desirable and where – outside her own family circle – no memory existed of who and what she had once been. Inside herself she exterminated every memory of the former character, of the life that had caused pain, along with feelings that were deep and real. None of this was visible on the outside: one saw only an intelligent girl with an above-average sense of humour, a pleasant person to be around.

Her sexual development was normal: she kissed boys on occasion and lost her virginity at sixteen to a young Turk in the resort town of Alanya, where she was on holidays with her parents and a girlfriend. Her first real boyfriend she found at the age of seventeen, a boy from her village without a ghost of a chance. She held him completely in her sway; Tessel had discovered the limitless power of beauty and unscrupulousness. When she went off to university she forgot the boy as carelessly as she might have lost a hairpin. He had served his purpose; Tessel had used him to reconnoitre and refine the possibilities of sex as a weapon. She was ready for bigger things.

This was Tessel when I met her. When she introduced herself to me at the annual literature meeting of the Faculty of Letters, there was electricity in the air. Four days later we slept together for the first time; lying in my bed was a perfectly beautiful, perfectly heartless monster.

I thought back on P.J.'s behaviour in Mousetown, when she had tormented that frightened mouse and isolated it from the rest. Independently of each other, Joe and I had both had our misgivings; that ungirlish cruelty had revealed a side of her we would rather not have seen.

I was happier than I had ever been in my life. Tessel combined a touching gentleness with pornographic sexual abandon. She was, without a doubt, the funniest woman I had ever met. She was a dream, because she gave me everything I longed for: she supplied to order. This was the miracle of which she was capable. To her parents she was the ideal daughter, to her teachers a talented student, and to her drinking friends a lecherous bitch who danced on café tables and wound men around her finger. And to me...to me she was Love with a capital L. She showed me what I wanted to see most, and I wanted to believe in that. She nourished hope – of love that was meant to be, of two separate halves that find each other amid a crowd of millions.

In every social situation she unerringly reflected that which was expected of her. Her mimesis was perfect, except in one regard. One area of life was inaccessible to her, because she neither knew nor understood it: intimacy. This she could not imitate, in the same way a chameleon cannot turn white.

Sex was Tessel's substitute strategy for intimacy.

How was I to know that, from the very first day, she slept with other men as well? When I found a text message one day that proved she had at least one other lover, I punched her in the face twice.

To be desired by many men was Tessel's magic charm to ward off her mother's curse: that her sexual market value was low and that she would attract only fat boys. When, by a complete fluke, I found out that that first act of unfaithfulness had not been the last, I hit her again and this time raped her as well. She wept as she came, and told me it was the best sex she'd ever had. There were nine other men. Each cock that penetrated her confirmed that she was wanted, and pretty. The liberation was always short-lived, for she lacked the inner conviction of her own beauty. She would go looking again, be desired again, again the wings of ecstasy would spread and again she would return disillusioned to the gorged, quivering image she had of herself. By way of necessary counterbalance she always had a lover to come home to safely, to uphold the appearance of normality.

Somewhere in those turbid times I told her: 'You could not have dealt me a harder blow.'

She thought about that for a moment. Then, in utter calm, she said: 'Oh yes, I could have.'

I asked no further.

Tessel was the Whore of the Century.

I had to stop reading, I was shaking too badly. Here was a man who was asking himself in despair how he could have loved a woman who was merely the reflection of what he expected from a woman. He had dissected the cadaver with a sure hand. It was fabulous and frightening.

First Metz, and now it was Joe's turn. And I was the only one who held all the pieces of the puzzle; I had known P.J. before she knew Metz, I knew who she was with now, and – although I experienced a moment of doubt – Joe *had* to read this, he was headed for catastrophe.

The next time he came to see me I slid the book solemnly across the table. He picked it up, looked at the cover (a detail of some fuzzy painting representing a female body), read the blurb and put it back on the table. He frowned.

'I don't know why you read shit like that,' he said.

That was all he ever said about it. In fact, Metz had predicted Joe's reaction to a tee: 'We don't want to see them for what they are, and thereby multiply the damage they will cause us with time.'

'By the way,' Joe said, standing in the doorway. 'Is it OK if P.J. comes along to Poznan?'

We left on 5 May, in the early morning hours. Lots of houses in Lomark already had their flags out for Liberation Day. It was one year ago that Joe had suggested I become an arm wrestler; from the very beginning, Poznan had lain in the future like a promise, it was the most important tournament of all. Despite the bizarre way everything had sped up since the events in Rostock, I had trained like mad and even sparred with Hennie Oosterloo. I had tried out a number of different openings on him, and sometimes let myself be pushed almost to the table in order to learn how to come back from hopeless situations. Oosterloo was useless otherwise, I was now in a completely different class.

I acted normal toward Joe and P.J. Everything fine, no jealousy, no revelatory literature: business as usual. Everything would have to run its course, and I would assume the role of clinical observer. Joe had ignored the warning and was fair game now. Someday he would come back and ask to look at that book and kick himself for having chosen to be blind.

It was at least a ten-hour drive to Poznan. Joe stayed behind the wheel the whole time, P.J. occasionally massaged his neck, we were witness to a perfectly harmonious love. At times everything that had happened seemed only a diabolical figment of the imagination: we laughed and Joe and P.J. sang songs, and it was as though Engel wasn't rotting in his grave and that damned omen of a book had never been written.

We reached Poznan before nightfall, steam coming from the radiator. Joe parked the Oldsmobile in front of the Hotel Olympia, an uninspired colossus from the days of socialism, with an endless number of floors and enough beds for an entire army.

'Look at that,' Joe said as we entered the lobby.

He pointed at the digital clock above the desk, which showed both date and time: 5.5.19:45. It took a moment before I realized that this was the exact date of Holland's liberation, a stimulating coincidence that lasted only a minute, when the clock hopped to 19:46 and the moment was over. Joe asked for two rooms, one for him and P.J. and one for me, for that was how things now stood.

After a knock on the door, Joe came in.

'Everything OK? Bathroom and everything?'

He dropped into a chair by the window and looked down at the street.

'Man, I'm exhausted. Tomorrow's the big day, François.'

And, after a while: 'I think I'm going to hit the sack, I'm still seeing the white stripes on the road.'

Oh Joe, please *look* at her the way you once looked at me and saw me on the dyke – Jesus, Joe, you don't know what you're getting into…

'I'll see you bright and early in the morning, Frankie. If you need any help, dial zero and then five-one-seven, that's our room number.'

The window provided a view of concrete and asphalt. Low sunlight coloured everything orange; here, too, Man was concerned only with himself. I closed the heavy synthetic curtains but opened them again a little later; darkened rooms while it's still light outside depress me, I think because they remind me of death. Since Engel died I also couldn't stand the smell of tallow, which had filled every corner of the funeral home. I tried to read a little in *Go Rin No Sho*, but couldn't keep my mind on it. Then I waited for darkness to fall, while down below the Poles lived their lives and inside me the multitude of things came washing in. There was nothing more I could do.

The tournament was in a gym on the south side of town. Two competition tables and fifty-seven wrestlers, about half of them lightweights. A strong entry. Right before the gong announcing the first two bouts, the man I'd been waiting for so long came in at last: Big King Mansur. Although it was as much a sensation as, for instance, an entrance by Muhammad Ali, and I had actually been expecting an even number of virgins to be strewing rose petals before his feet, it was in fact only a black man walking into a seedy gym. He wasn't very big either, more stocky, with exceptionally broad shoulders. His head was shaven and the light from the high windows of the gym reflected off his scalp. Beside him was a slender woman in sunglasses whose classic petiteness told me she had to be French. She was the kind of woman tennis players and football stars marry, the kind you see on TV sitting in the stands with her hand over her mouth when things get exciting.

Joe nudged me, I nodded that I had seen him. Mansur and the woman sought out a quiet corner, the only quiet corner in fact in the packed gym, and the woman was sent off to fetch two chairs. With slow, deliberate movements Mansur took off his jacket and T-shirt and fumbled around in a sports bag until he found a little vest. When he stuck his arms through the straps I saw his awesome latissimi dorsi, the muscle group referred to in the world of strength sports as 'wings'. Joe told P.J. who Big King Mansur was, that we were looking at the unassailable world champion, the fearsome Beast #1.

'And Frankie has to wrestle against him?' she asked.

'Maybe,' Joe said. 'If we're lucky.'

The crowd itself consisted of people with conventional bodies – smooth, fat and white, just like in Rostock. We figured out that if I won all my bouts the fourth match would be between me and Islam Mansur. The first two matches weren't much of a problem. The third one I almost lost to a guy I'd seen doing his stuff back in Liège, a black man from Portsmouth. But then I thought about Islam Mansur, how badly I wanted to go up against him, about how today could be the day, and I beat the Englishman just in the nick of time.

It took two bottles of beer to keep the spasms under control. P.J. rubbed my shoulders, Joe was on pins and needles. Would I be able to give Mansur a run for his money? Was there any sense in hoping he'd have a bad match, that his concentration would flag? P.J.'s hands produced shivers of pleasure, I was sucking up beer like a sump pump. Then it was time. From the corner of my eye I saw Mansur coming out of his corner and approaching the table, the consummate human machine. Joe rolled me over to the table and helped me onto my stool. Just briefly he laid his hands on my shoulders – I felt the missing fingers on the right – and looked me in the eye.

'I believe in you,' he said, and let go.

I was on my own, across from a force of nature. Mansur sat down.

Arm Saint, at last.

He seized the peg (damn, his left arm was just as big as his right, he really could take on opponents with both at the same time) and slid his elbow into the box. Only then did he look at me; bulging eyes, lots of white around them. His palms were white too. I put my arm on the table and we engaged. Solid as a wall, like laying my hand against a warm building.

From what I'd seen of Mansur's earlier matches, I knew that his openings alternated between the Fire and Stone Cut and the Red Autumn Leaves Cut ('The Red Autumn Leaves Cut means knocking down the enemy's long sword. The spirit should be getting control of his sword'); I readied myself. His palm was dry and soft, mine was little and clammy. Mansur kept his eyes on me the whole time, I knew it was part of his strategy to hypnotize his opponent with a penetrating, uninterrupted stare. In an interview he had once said that his greatest strength came 'from inside'. 'When your spirit is concentrated, you can block out everyone around you. Your opponent is the centre of attention.' Although that may sound rather banal, I could actually feel his energy grow solid and I was drawn into his gaze. I became the glowing core of his attention, sealed in a vacuum by his eyes.

'Go!'

Mechanically I tightened all my muscles and felt that enormous hand pulling all power toward it. For a moment I wrested free of those eyes and looked at his arm, lined with quivering muscles trying to break through the skin. Then I resumed my spot in his field of vision. In that way we had finally become the middle point of the universe, Mansur and I, and I felt a deep sense of gratitude and justice. I knew that the outcome was unimportant; all that mattered was the *fatefulness* of this moment, the collision of two heavenly bodies that had sought each other out in boundless space, forces coursing toward beauty and destruction. The moment of impact went slowly, without a sound.

I withstood his attack; my defence had improved in the course of time. The muscles in his neck were tight as snares, from his shoulder had grown a low hill that I'd never seen in another wrestler. Was that P.J. who screamed? With my eyes I traced the course of a vein on Mansur's forearm. All my life I had longed and sought for something without flaws, without contamination, and in my dreamlike state I remembered a story about perfection – about Chinese artisans, masters of the art of lacquer painting, who would board a ship and only start work on the high seas; on land, minuscule dust particles might contaminate and spoil the lacquer.

The triangular construction Mansur and I formed belonged in that category: perfect, superhuman – we were far beyond time and space now, the roar of the crowd I heard only as though it were coming from a valley far below. A great deal clearer was the sudden sound of a dry twig breaking close to my ear – I felt us losing balance, being slung back into the world, heading for the end.

Only then did I become aware of a raging, maddening pain in my forearm, the flames were shooting out of it, and I saw Mansur let go of my hand and look at me in amazement. Halfway down my arm the pain was bundled like a glowing knot. I knew the bone was broken. The muscles had stood up to Mansur's inhuman strength, but the radius or the ulna had not. Snapped like a twig; I bellowed in rage and pain. Joe was at my side.

'Frankie, what is it?'

I shook my head, this was the end of everything, it was the bone that turned out to be my Achilles' heel, I would have to start again from scratch. Mansur came over to us.

'I think he broke his arm,' Joe said.

Mansur nodded.

'I'm sorry,' he said. 'It was a good fight.'

He looked at me, thought about it for a moment, then corrected himself.

'It was a spiritual fight. You are a strong man.'

He raised his right hand to his heart, the same way Papa Africa had always done, and disappeared with the woman into the crowd of inquisitive onlookers.

'We have to get to a hospital right away, Joe!' P.J. said. 'He's turning all white.'

I suddenly went limp with pain and felt that I would throw up at any moment. The arm lay useless in my lap. My sole weapon: broken. Two taxis were waiting outside, the drivers leaned smoking against the grille.

'Hospital!' Joe barked. '*Krankenhaus!*'

The rest was exactly what you might expect: the shot of painkiller, the setting of the ulna, the splint, the sling, the whole shit thing. The only startling detail was that we had to pay the equivalent of almost 500 smackers, to which end P.J. loaned us her credit card. For that price we got to take the X-rays home with us. Now I couldn't do anything anymore, at most scratch out a few block letters with the fingers sticking out of my plaster sleeve. In the taxi on the way to the hotel, Joe turned to me.

'Two minutes and thirty-nine seconds, then you broke.'

Two minutes and thirty-nine seconds: I was amazed, it had felt like an eternity to me.

'You didn't give an inch, the others all went down within the first minute. Well, that's the importance of calcium. Just imagine if that bone hadn't broken? You had a chance, you really did. But OK, a couple of months, Frankie, then we're back on the road.'

P.J. groaned in disapproval.

'You guys are nuts.'

The nurse had given us a box of painkillers, the first of which was administered to me at five o'clock and washed down with beer.

'Sleep in our room tonight,' Joe said, 'for if you need to pee and things.'

I hadn't even arrived at that complication yet; Joe would be assuming Engel's old role... I decided to get sloshed.

All things considered, my arm left me less depressed that I would have thought. I took comfort in the fact that it had happened while doing battle with the Arm Saint: it was my Fracture of Honour.

P.J. showed her solidarity, drinking at the same pace I did. Our waitress's face bore an expression of boundless long-suffering. Out in front of the hotel entrance, Joe was bent over the engine of the Olds, repairing the leaky radiator with duct tape. The waitress brought more beer, P.J. stuck a straw in my bottle and set it in front of me where I could get to it easily. I drank with a vengeance, to calm the spasms; the arm was immobilized, but the contractions caused me hellish pain. She pulled the X-rays out of the envelope and held them up to the light one by one. When you looked at them like that, the bones were flimsy little things. A wonder that they had held up for even two minutes and thirty-nine seconds.

'A clean break,' she said, 'not jagged or anything. Does it hurt?'

Yes, dear Florence, it hurts. Will you ease my pain?

'We'll have to take care of you for a little while now, you can't do anything. My finals are in August, but I can study at my parents' place.'

P.J. slid the photos back into the envelope and said, 'Come on, let's see what's happening in town. I've pretty much had it with this place.'

She rolled me out of the dining room and across the lobby to the desk, a dimly lit niche at the end of the hallway. The clerk was reading a book.

'*Bitte*,' P.J. asked, 'do you have a map of the city? We're looking for a *gutes Restaurant*, or maybe a bar.'

The man looked up angrily.

'*Hier keine Bar!*' he snapped. '*Keine Bar in Poznan!*'

His Slavic accent sharply emphasized each syllable, his eyes glowed with a kind of anger.

'Here we have only *Arbeitslosen und Banditen*! Going into town is suicide.'

He demonstrated to us how deadbeats and bandits would knock us over the head and steal all our money. P.J. looked on in amusement. Then she tried a different tack.

'Would you mind my asking what book you're reading?' she asked sweetly.

'Ah, reading. Yes, of course.'

He handed it to P.J. and we saw that it was a comic book, with Vampirella in an SM suit on the cover. In the background, SS officers were torturing a blonde virgin.

'*Sehr gut!*' the desk clerk said.

P.J. flipped through it and showed me a page on which SS men with massive dicks sticking out of the trousers of their uniforms were raping a group of women, who looked rather like gypsies with their thick, dark locks and the hoops in their ears.

'They don't make them like this where we come from,' P.J. said.

The desk clerk's smile revealed a ruined set of teeth. He opened a drawer, pulled out another book and handed it to P.J.: a Polish edition of *Mein Kampf*. The idiot was reading *Mein Kampf...* P.J.'s eyes sparkled.

'What else do you think he has in that little cabinet of horrors?'

She gave him back *Vampirella* and *Mein Kampf* and leaned across the counter, trying to see what else he had. The man, rising to the occasion, pulled out a grimy little book of photos in which he appeared in heavily wooded surroundings, posing with one foot on the back of a dead bear. In his hand he held a huge hunting rifle.

'*Schiessen,*' he gasped, '*gut!*'

But the prize piece in his collection was yet to come: a *pistol*. Or a revolver, I can never tell the difference. He rested the bulky thing on the palm of one hand, and only gave it to P.J. after a good deal of cooing and wooing on her part. He was proud that we were so interested in his collection.

'This is getting better all the time, Frankie, look!'

She pointed the pistol down the hallway behind us and sighted along it with one eye closed. The cackling laughter from behind the counter gave me goose flesh.

'*Arbeitslosen und Banditen!* Bang bang!'

The last thing he handed us was the little bundle containing the passports we'd left at the desk the night before. P.J. traded the pistols for the passports. She opened the one on top, saw that it was mine and stuck it in the pouch on the side of my cart. Her own passport she put in her back pocket. The only one left now was Joe's. She glanced over at the door of the hotel, then back at the passport. Then she opened it; I sniffed in protest, I knew exactly what she was up to: she wanted to see Joe's real name. So even *she* didn't know! But that was forbidden, no one was allowed to do that! She looked surprised at the way I shook my head so adamantly.

'You mean you're not curious?'

Of course I was curious, but that wasn't the point. Fucking bitch, put it away! But her eyes were already scanning the front page. She raised her eyebrows and smiled. Then she turned the open passport to face me, I saw Joe's photo in a flash before I closed my eyes. I wasn't allowed to see this. Everything crowed alarm in the darkness, she had no right, it was blasphemy, *no one* was allowed to finagle him out of his real name, it was his only secret. As soon as I thought she'd understood, I opened my eyes, but there, twenty centimetres in front of my nose the front page of Joe's passport was still dangling. She was looking for an accomplice, she was luring me into her corrupt universe, the one Metz had warned me about, oh Christ, how could I refuse her? I focused on the passport in front of me. Joe's passport photo, a little tough, a little casual. Oh, Joe, I'm sorry, I'm so sorry.

Naam/Surname/Nom
RATZINGER

Voornamen/Given names/Prénoms
ACHIEL STEPHAAN

The passport disappeared from view, P.J. handed it back to the clerk.

'Would you please give it to him yourself?' she said. 'He'll come by in a minute.'

He nodded in amazement, he had no idea what had just happened. P.J. rolled me back into the dining room and set me down in front of my beer. A few minutes later Joe came in, wiping his hands on a soiled rag.

Achiel Stephaan Ratzinger.

The man at the desk called him over and gave him his passport. In the doorway to the dining room he smiled at P.J. and said, 'Do you guys have your passports? He says…'

'Yes, love, we've got them.'

'All right. And we've got wheels again.'

P.J. lit a cigarette for him. His fingers left oil spots on the paper. Achiel Stephaan. Why the hell had his parents given him such a retarded, Flemish name? Had they named him after a Flemish grandfather? A guru from Westmalle? Whatever it was, we were looking at a man without a secret. And that secret was a Belgian joke. Achiel Stephaan; handed over to the Philistines by his sweetheart, betrayed by his friend.

*

That night in their room I puked all over everything. Joe helped me into the bathroom, I screamed, I think I even begged his forgiveness.

'You were terrible,' Joe said on the way home the next day. 'You threw up all over me, you nut.'

That I had pissed all over his fingers remained our secret. In the back, P.J. remained as silent as the Sphinx.

I t's an X-raylike experience, knowing Joe's real name. Achiel Ratzinger is the fate he tried to escape; it caught up with him at last. I seem to recall biblical characters being given a different name, after some drastic change in their lives. I scribble a note to Ma, asking to borrow her Bible.

'It's never too late to start,' she sighs.

It doesn't take long before I hit pay dirt. In Genesis, God himself gives new names to Abram and Sarai. 'Neither shall thy name any more be called Abram, but thy name shall be Abraham; for a father of many nations have I made thee.' Abraham's wife Sarai also receives a new name: Sarah.

In the New Testament, Peter receives a new name as well, as seen first in the Gospel of Mark: 'And He appointed the twelve: Simon (to whom He gave the name Peter), and James, the son of Zebedee, and John the brother of James (to them He gave the name Boanerges, which means, "Sons of Thunder").' The same thing can be found in the Gospel of John, where Jesus says: 'You are Simon the son of John; you shall be called Cephas (which is translated Peter).'

In the Book of Acts, Saul – that fanatical persecutor of Christians – undergoes a change of name when a heavenly light appears to him on the road to Damascus. A voice revealing itself as that of Jesus shouts: 'Saul, Saul, why persecutest thou me?' Saul becomes a believer and, for the rest of his life, bears the name Paul.

It seems to me that the patriarchs and disciples were given a name to match their new, elevated status. Men of God who bore their name as a sign of distinction.

. Finally, in the Book of Revelations, I read that if we lend an ear to the Spirit, we will all be given new names. 'And I will give him a white stone, and a new name written on the stone which no one knows but he who receives it.'

Our secret name that is known to no one – P.J. and I, however, have peeked under that stone and are disappointed at what we find: the humiliating tag stuck to Joe's back, so that when you are around him you sometimes feel the urge to giggle. His Achilles' heel had lain tucked away inside his name the whole time: *nomen est omen*. The men of God were given names that made them greater; with Achiel Stephaan, P.J. and I have made Joe smaller and divested him of his dignity. Beneath his self-appointed name he has no clothes.

In the weeks that follow P.J. does a great deal for me, she takes me out for walks ('Do you want to wear my sunglasses? You're squinting so badly') and when evening comes she feeds me frankfurters with obvious distaste. After work Joe comes by and the three of us sit around, making Joe and P.J. seem like a couple with a pathetic child. When I have to piss, Joe helps me. Ma is the only one I let wipe my butt, I still will not tolerate anyone else behind my *anus horribilis*. That Joe sometimes takes my dick between thumb and forefinger in order to worm it back into my underpants is bad enough. He doesn't dry it off the way I always do, so Ma has to boil my underpants to get the piss flecks out of them. When Joe helps me I look the other way, as though I weren't there. I'd kill myself if I ever got a hard-on.

Joe's real name has brought P.J. and me closer together. Guilt

feelings rise to the surface when I'm alone again and lie looking at the dying light of day. Sometimes I see Engel, the
expression on his face with which he assesses this, and somehow it seems unlikely that any of this would have happened
were he still around. Joe stands alone in the face of a new three-
cornered construction of a woman without scruples ('She is not
depraved or bad, she simply lacks a conscience: that is all' –
from *About a Woman*) and two friends who quietly hate him at
times.

When I'm not in the mood to feel guilty I tell myself that it's
actually nothing more than an exchange of intimacies: he's
seen my dick, I've seen his name. So what if we know that
about him, he has P.J., doesn't he? It's only fair that I then take
back something in return. Compared to him, I'm nothing but a
petty thief. But when in my mind I again hear the hideous
laughter of the desk clerk at the Hotel Olympia, I can't defend
that train of thought. Joe Speedboat is more than an adolescent
whim, it's his destiny. The men of God became different people
because of their new names, and it's unthinkable that they
could have gone back to who they were as Abram, Simon or
Saul. But that is exactly what has happened to Joe. We no longer
see the beloved sorcerer's apprentice, but Achiel Stephaan
Ratzinger, like a kind of Christof who long ago tried to disguise
how pathetic he was by adopting Johnny Monday as his *nom
de plume*.

I see that P.J. in her thoughts has begun calling Joe 'Achiel'; a
certain nonchalance has crept into the entirety of actions with
which she expresses love: every kiss and every glance now poisoned by irony. Sounding brass, a tinkling cymbal. Agonizingly
slow, she's busy tearing him apart.

I believe every person must have a holy core, one area where
he is reliable through and through; the same holy core that has

become corrupted in me and that I have never been able to discover in P.J. Only that predatory opportunism that possesses a beauty of its own, definitely; when she takes care of me, she lets me feel like I'm truly important to her. This has bound me to her more intensely, the knowledge that she does not possess love but does her best nonetheless, for reasons we may never know. Metz writes: 'Perhaps she does have a heart, but keeps it in a thousand places.' I think P.J. really wants that, to be like other people, that she's envious of the abandon and loss of self with which Joe loves her, and that she despises him for it.

She is obviously still fascinated by the notebooks, my *History of Lomark and Its Citizens*. The day will come when she will ask to read them. I will give in, for if anyone is to be allowed it is she. She is as welcome in my world as I am in hers. But the day I'm talking about is this one, now, the day she makes a drawing on the cast on my arm. The drawing shows Islam Mansur as King Kong, who is holding me (tiny, but clearly wearing a sling) in the palm of his hand and looking at me with one bulging eye. THE GREATEST LOVE STORY EVER TOLD, she writes beneath it. She draws well, Mansur's incarnation as gorilla is striking. As she colours the gorilla blue she is very close, I hear her deep, quiet breathing, I feel the warmth of her body like a stove. Sometimes, when grains of plaster block the tip, the flow of ink stops. When the light falls in a certain way, her eyebrows are almost reddish.

'Sit still,' she says as a spasm rolls by.

I lean forward a little to muffle the start of an erection in the folds of my trousers. Who wouldn't be edgy, with her around? Even knowing who she is, you remain susceptible to that seductive ruthlessness that one could also dismiss as humorous naughtiness. That's the whole point: you can recognize her manipulative nature if you choose, but to close your eyes to it is an act of the will. That makes P.J. a self-imposed fate. And I, I do not wish to be spared.

King Kong is almost finished, P.J. looks up. I look the other way, fix my gaze on the tabletop and the things on it. The atmosphere is suddenly, how shall I put it, *charged*, making it difficult for me to swallow.

'What is it, Frankie?' she asks quietly.

I feel caught; sometimes my thoughts are like muffins you can pull right out of the oven. The next thing I know is that her hand, *her hand*, is at my crotch. If only she doesn't feel my hard-on, I think in a panic, before realizing that that is precisely what this is all about. It is the hand of God with which she gives me soft, dizzying little squeezes; never before has my dick in some-one else's hand been something to squeeze softly, only to shake firmly or scrub rigorously, but not this, not like this. She glances out the window and loosens my belt. I don't budge, deathly afraid of anything that will stop this. She opens the zipper and slips her hand into my underpants. Good hand, warm hand that closes around my cock, making me almost choke with bliss. P.J. pulls it out and slowly begins jerking me off.

'You're so hard,' she says, more to herself than to me.

Her hand moves a little faster, the fingers tightening their grip, greater joy cannot be imagined. I hear the cloth of my trousers rustling against her wrist, her breathing grows faster. A little pensive fold appears between her eyes. She slows, slides her thumb across the head of my cock and my vision darkens to the speckled image of snowfall at evening, I come all over her hand and my trousers. I stifle the scream, my upper body doubles over. Then the cramps ebb away and she lets go. She smiles serenely, gets up to fetch a dish towel from the kitchen and wipe the sperm off her hand. She cleans off my trousers as well.

A little later she walks to the door, holding her bag. In the doorway she turns and asks, 'Did I take good enough care of you today, Frankie?' and bestows upon me a little smile. Shattered, I lean back in my chair and know that there is no limit to what I would do for her. Her faithlessness was heralded, she has proliferated as naturally as lice on a child's scalp, and all the things I've thought about myself are true as well, it was only a matter of time before it came to the fore. That knowledge contains an element of freedom; facts are better than suspicions.

Today I have chosen to end my misery; the pleasure of P.J. in exchange for my only friendship seems like a fair trade. And if you didn't feel so shitty about it, nothing would be the matter.

Afew days later I look on in regret as the nurse cuts P.J.'s drawing right down the middle. Beneath the cast the arm has grown much thinner, for the next month or so I won't be able to do anything strenuous with it. Late in June comes the longest day, rainy and a gusty gray. Ma says it's going to be a wet summer, and that we'd be better off getting used to it; partial to heavy clouds with occasional rain or drizzle, daytime highs between nineteen and twenty-two degrees, and lots of earwigs.

The first time I open a can of frankfurters on my own I'm afraid the arm is going to break again, but after a while everything is back to normal. It takes some effort to get back into my training rhythm, I can't imagine that Joe and I will go on with everything like always, but for him there's no doubt about it. The doubt exists only in my own head, where the things of the last few months converge in the moment when I come all over P.J.'s hand. This is the life that comes after. All my innocence was only guilt that hadn't materialized yet.

Sometimes Joe says things like 'I don't know, man, sometimes I'm so scared. Since Engel died I keep having the feeling that something terrible is going to happen.' He sniffs his armpit: 'I can actually smell it. Fear.'

He works himself silly on that bulldozer, he goes in search of physical labour to counteract afflictions he can't really put into words. He too will become human, naked, afraid and lonely like all the rest.

The Paris–Dakar rally is costing him a wad; he's found a couple of sponsors, with Bethlehem Asphalt chief among them, and for the rest a few shopkeepers who are in for a laugh. They give him T-shirts with their names and logos on them. The arm wrestling has paid off well, and with that job of his he'll make out all right. On 1 January he has to be in Marseille for the start of the rally. Sixteen days later the whole circus will grind to a halt in Sharm el-Sheikh, Egypt; just because it's called Paris–Dakar doesn't mean it automatically starts and ends there.

One day, when Joe comes by with a big map of Africa and shows me the route, I suddenly realize that he has an ulterior motive: Sharm el-Sheikh is on the Red Sea, not far from the village of Nuweiba where Papa Africa kept shop when he met Regina. But Joe says nothing about that, and I don't press the point. He rolls up the map, then reconsiders.

'Shall I hang it up in here?' he asks. 'Then you can sort of see where I am.'

It's a nice, big classroom map on a scale of 1:75,000,000, a Wenschow relief-like map. Joe has traced the route with magic marker.

Outside the poppies stand out remarkably red against a seashell-gray sky, at times the sun breaks through at evening and colours the clouds. Wood pigeons and magpies hop about on the roof of my house, I can hear them clear as day. They pick at the moss growing on the corrugated asbestos.

I can move freely again, but Lomark feels different. The dyke, the streets have become foreign to me. The hope once prompted by Joe's arrival is extinguished, we are what we were

293

and always will be. Joe is a redeemer without promise; he didn't bring progress, only motion.

'We do our best,' he said a long time ago, 'we build an airplane in order to see the secret, but then you find out that there is no secret, only an airplane. And that's fine.'

He cast a spell on our world, but after it rains the colours wash right off again.

The E981 is getting closer all the time, you can already see the machines in the distance and after dark there is a flood of artificial light from over there. The provincial highway is one big obstruction, people complain, but too late. Egon Maandag is rubbing his hands in glee, the E981 means a mega-order for him. In the end, though, I think it will work out badly for Bethlehem too; the lack of an exit will hurt his company's logistics.

Summer blends into fall, I'm getting back into decent shape and sometimes wrestle against Hennie Oosterloo to keep the rhythm going. I don't think Joe and I will be attending any tournaments this year, he's too busy with other things. After Paris–Dakar we'll see how it goes.

One day I run into India on the dyke, she's moved out of the house and is studying 'something with people' in the west of the country. A light drizzle is falling from the yellow sky. India is pleased to see me, she's dyed her hair black, which makes her face very pale.

'Frankie, I haven't seen you for such a long time,' she says.

She looks like she's going to cry. I take out the notepad and write that she looks like an Indian, with that hair of hers. The paper grows soggy in the rain. India runs her hand matter-of-factly through her hair.

'This isn't hair,' she says, 'this is a mood.'

We move off together toward Lomark, when we part she seems very concerned.

'Keep an eye on Joe a little, would you, Frankie? He seems kind of…kind of lost lately. You know what I mean?'

I know very well what she means, and watch her go, in her olive-green army coat that Joe once wore and that belonged to their father, if I'm not mistaken. The coat is dark with rain and hangs heavily on her shoulders. She turns and gives me a little wave, the girl who you think smells faintly of peaches.

On 20 December Joe takes off for Marseille, to be there for the start of the race. He doesn't have enough money for a flatbed, he'll have to drive the whole way himself.

'Gives me a chance to test the thing right away,' he says.

He has meticulously traced out a route along the back roads; on the main roads there's too much of a chance of being stopped and asked troublesome questions. Once the rally starts, though, he's home free. I admire his stoic disregard for time, effort and gravity.

In the early morning hours the three of us – Joe's mother, P.J. and I – go out to wave goodbye. It's cold, it's raining, the world is full of blue shades. Regina holds her umbrella over me so that only my left side gets wet. She's dried up ugly, as we say around here when a woman doesn't grow old gracefully. Dull is what she's become, crushed by love.

The bulldozer is growling on the parking lot in front of the bank. Joe says, 'Well, I guess I'll get going now,' and P.J. cries a little. They hug and Joe whispers something in her ear that I can't hear. She nods sadly and bravely, they kiss. Then Joe holds his mother tight and tells her not to worry, that he'll come home safely because 'nothing can happen to you in one of these babies'. He shakes my hand and smiles.

'Don't forget your calcium, Frankie, OK? I'll see you next year.'

He hugs P.J. one more time, she doesn't want to let go.

'See you soon, girlie. I'll call.'

He climbs into the cab, it's an awesome sight to see him up on that thing. He touches the gas, the wipers sweep across the glass, the monster starts to move. Joe sticks his hand out the open window, rolls out of the parking lot, honks and heads down the street. This is the last we'll see of him until 1 January.

Then there is the TV bulletin on RTL 5, each night from eleven-thirty to midnight, with all the news about the rally. I watch in my parents' living room, we see the drivers in a park near a grandstand, there's a marching band and a cadmium-yellow bulldozer sticks out above all the rest – covered with stickers from Bethlehem Asphalt, Van Paridon Rentals, Bot's butcher shop and a few other lesser sponsors. He made it, he got to Marseille along the back roads, and that in itself is a miracle. Now he only has to drive 8552 kilometres to Sharm el-Sheikh. At the table, Pa mutters that Joe's 'not right in the head, ever since those bombs, too'.

The first day, the caravan heads to Narbonne; the next day to Castellon in Spain, close to Valencia. In the harbour of Valencia the whole shooting match is loaded onto a ferry to north Africa. In Tunis Joe drives into the sun, one day later he reaches the desert. Sometimes, when the rally is filmed from the air, we catch a glimpse of him with a huge cloud of dust fanning out behind. The drivers make a beeline south, and on the fourth day Joe gets in just before the time limit. If you don't make that, you can turn around and go home. I hear him mumble something about 'the nick of time'. It seems like he was mistaken, that the bulldozer isn't as perfect a desert vehicle as he thought. The landscape is beautiful but demanding, the first drivers become stranded in sand dunes and deep holes in dried-up wadis. The rest arrive in Ghadamès, a dot just across the Libyan border, in that part of the world where the map turns yellow with 6,314,314 square kilometres of desert. Joe is really in the Sahara now, with a bulldozer...

On the seventh day, and for the first time, he appears on the screen by himself, after a puzzling 584-kilometre stage along the Algerian–Libyan border. It's already dark by the time he comes in off the desert and drives up to the encampment.

'That'd be him,' says Ma, who's only half paying attention to the screen.

Joe's face is brown and dirty, the camera crew's lamps illuminate him against a royal-blue sky and a decor of tents, satellite dishes and men in motorcycle leathers bustling on and off. Joe looks over the interviewer's shoulder and says hello to someone we can't see. His T-shirt reads BETHLEHEM ASPHALT, LOMARK, with smaller letters underneath saying FOR ALL YOUR PAVED NEEDS. Why, the interviewer asks, did he decide to take part in a bulldozer?

'It's only a small step from a truck to a bulldozer,' Joe says. 'Except for a camel, I figured it was the best means of transportation in the desert.'

'And is it?'

Joe grins tiredly.

'No.'

'Are you having a rough time?'

'I'm sore all over, and it's a pity that you don't get to see much of the desert. I came here for the desert, but you have to concentrate on the road all day. Especially the ergs, dunes and stuff, sometimes that sand is like talcum powder. The landscape moves and you have to find your way through it.'

'You're taking part under the name "Joe Speedboat", what does that mean?'

'That that's my name, that's all.'

The interviewer sniffles.

'Really?'

'Yup.'

'Well OK, Joe. What do you expect from the drive tomorrow?'

'I haven't had time yet to pick up the road book, I still have to eat and fill the tank, and the clutch is slipping.'

'It's going to be a real killer, I can tell you that much already: five hundred kilometres to Sabha, lots of rocks and across the sand hills of Murzuk Erg. How does that sound?'

'It'll work out.'

'Good luck tomorrow, Joe. See you in Sabha.'

Joe walks away from the lamps, we see highlights from earlier that day, including a Dutch construction supervisor wrestling his motorcycle up a sand dune. He finally makes it to the camp two hours before Joe.

There's a clear difference between the amateurs and the professional entries; the pros always arrive early at the camp, where their backup crews are waiting. They shower, put on clean clothes and appear before the cameras spick and span. The amateurs don't have crews, often not even a mechanic. And because they usually arrive late at the camp, they're the ones who show the desert most. They're dirty, tired and rattled, and often sleep only a couple of hours a night. At five in the morning they're awakened by the first Antonov transport planes leaving for the next camp, where a little city – complete with kitchens, toilets, a press tent, huge satellite dishes and even a fully equipped operating room – arises in the desert within a few hours. One hour later everything is already covered in dust and sand, the cursing from the press tent knows many languages.

Joe holds his own, the race heads northeast, and he

completes one of the most difficult stretches of the rally with no real setbacks. Just after sunset he reaches Sabha. The camera crew is starting to warm to the idea of a Dutch driver in a bulldozer: that morning they filmed his departure from camp, and they're waiting for him when he arrives. The scoop is raised on the front of the dozer, high in the cab Joe gives them the thumbs-up. Two ladder-like constructions have been attached to the side of the machine so he can free himself from the sand if he gets stuck; hanging on the back are two huge spare tyres.

The drivers are exhausted, bruised and lame. There are lots of accidents, one driver has been killed.

On Saturday afternoon P.J. drops in unexpectedly. She's in Lomark for her mother's birthday on Sunday. She's wearing a coat with a silvery fur collar, and she shakes the water from her hair. I make tea and am grateful to see her.

'Are you following Joe a little?' she asks.

Glistening drops of rainwater are hanging from both ear-lobes. *Every night*, I write. *He's fantastic*.

Together we look at the classroom map of Africa. Yesterday Joe left Sabha in the Libyan desert: the map shows no human settlements until the oasis at Siwa, just across the border with Egypt, where hopefully he will arrive tomorrow. It's one vast, empty ocean, Joe is all alone between the sand and the stars.

'He's only called twice,' P.J. says. 'Once from France and the other time from Tunisia, or wherever it was. It feels like he'd be closer if he was on the moon.'

We drink tea, P.J. practices rolling cigarettes for me. The rollups are sort of wrinkly, but I'll smoke them with love.

'Do you write about him, about Joe?'

Indeed, I've started writing again, to ward off the emptiness. But I'm not sure I approve of my tone. The prose is as rectilinear as the border between Libya and Egypt, and perhaps equally void of illusions.

'Could I read it? What are you laughing about?'

Thought you'd never ask.

'Yeah, really? Is it OK?'

One condition – from start to finish.

'Oh, I'd love that, I want to hear you talk. Do you know what I mean? For me, those books are your voice.'

A few minutes later she's lying on her stomach on the rug with a pile of notebooks in front of her. The stove is lit, I smoke and watch her read, she's put my desk lamp on the floor beside her and flips the pages at regular intervals. When she laughs I knock on the table; I want to know what she's reading.

'The way you write is so funny', she says. 'Especially about Christof, you're really too hard on him. He's such a sweetheart.'

I think about Joe, thundering eastward at that moment through a world of sand and stone, alone with his thoughts and his eyes on the tracks in front of him. P.J. makes little noises as she reads. I wish I had written more in order to keep her here, this steady happiness should last forever. I try to figure out how much time she'll need, at least ten hours I reckon, maybe longer. On her left is the pile she still has to read, on her right the ones she's already had, the ones about the time Joe's bomb went off in the boy's bathroom at school, the warm glow of the early years, before she arrived. P.J. herself appears in book eleven or twelve. She won't get that far today; she asks me what time it is and is shocked when she sees the kitchen clock.

'Is it OK if I come by tomorrow, early, Frankie? It's so… fantastic, I wish I could read it all at once.'

That evening I see that Joe is still in the race; he's had a fairly easy day and looks content. The program has promoted him to the subject of a daily item called 'Speedboat in the Sand'. It lasts barely ninety seconds, recaps what he did that day and ends with a short interview in which Joe delivers a few pithy remarks. Tonight he's wearing a T-shirt from Santing Painters, with a logo advertising the discount winter rates.

'It's actually more a battle against boredom,' is how he summarizes the rally for us. 'You don't see anyone all day, the only person you can talk to is yourself, and at night you rub salve on your butt against the bedsores. Like living in a blind alley, if you ask me.'

The bedsore salve he got from me, I had a couple of tubes lying around that weren't too far past their expiration date.

'You don't feel all alone, now do you, Joe?' the interviewer badgers.

'As long as you don't lose your way, you're never alone.'

Ma, on the couch beside me, nods.

'Joe puts things really well.'

The next morning I shower at my parents', pick up around the garden house and wait for P.J. Whether I'm expecting visitors, Ma wants to know. Around four in the afternoon darkness begins to fall and my cigarettes are finished. I've just started in on my fourth bottle of beer when the door opens and P.J. comes in. She doesn't explain why she's so late, I signal to her to get herself a beer. She opens the fridge, takes a bottle and pops the swing-top like a real pro.

Congratulations on your mom's birthday, I write.

'Pfff, we've got family over, real Afrikaners, all they talk about is that country. It's completely exhausting. Hey, did you see it, "Speedboat in the Sand"?'

In his element.

'He makes me laugh so hard, everything he says is so atypical for that whole clique.'

She rummages in her bag, pulls out a book, Herodotus' *Histories*. She opens it and looks for something.

'My father looked it up,' she says. 'About the Western Desert in Egypt, where Joe is now. Here, from page twenty-four on.'

I read about Cambyses, a ruler in some age or other who sends a big army into the desert to enslave a tribe called the Ammonians:

> ... the force which was sent against the Ammonians started from Thebes with guides, and can be traced as far as the town of Oasis, which ... is seven days' journey across the sand from Thebes. The place is known in Greece as the Island of the Blessed. General report has it that the army got as far as this, but of its subsequent fate there is no news whatever. It never reached the Ammonians and it never returned to Egypt. There is, however, a story told by the Ammonians themselves and by others who heard it from them, that when the men had left Oasis, and in their march across the desert had reached a point about midway between the town and the Ammonian border, a southerly wind of extreme violence drove the sand over them in heaps as they were taking their noonday meal, so that they disappeared forever.

'A whole army gone, like that,' P.J. says. 'Imagine if archaeologists ever found them, mummified in the sand ... My father says it was something like fifty thousand men.'

Are you worried?

'A little: what if he gets lost? It's so incredibly huge and empty, I mean, if a whole army can disappear ...?'

She looks at the books lying on the floor, precisely as she left them yesterday, and says: 'Maybe I should get reading again, I still have a ways to go.'

A little later she's lying with a pillow under her stomach, reading my *History* while I leaf through those of Herodotus. I think about that vanished army, overtaken by a violent southerly wind, huge waves of sand...Joe is out there somewhere, maybe he's already crossed the Egyptian border on his way to the oasis at Siwa. He's been gone for three weeks and is already halfway through the rally, his equipment is still intact, on good days he keeps up with the truck class. In my eyes he's performing a miracle, but I can't shake the thought that he's being followed by a shadow that goes by the name of Achiel Stephaan.

'Hey, I didn't know you had a crush on me,' P.J. says from the floor.

She sounds surprised, teasing. It embarrasses me less than I'd expected, maybe because she's seen me come, you could say we belong together now, somehow. The look she gives me, it's the look that says something's on its way, I know it well by now. She gets up and takes her beer from the table.

'But you exaggerate,' she says. 'You guys here just aren't used to much. Durban wasn't really so special. And whether I am or not...'

Special enough to write a novel about.

'Your diaries, you mean?'

Metz.

She's startled; I don't know why I'm doing this, maybe I'm pissed off at her for being so late, maybe I don't want to be anything but helpless.

'Did you read that?'

A coolness has entered her voice, she's on her guard. I nod.

'What did you think of it?'

The man can write.

'That's not what I mean,' she says sharply. 'What he wrote about me, do you believe him?'

Belief is an act of love.

'What do you mean?'

So I believe you.

P.J. can't help laughing.

'You're a sophist, Frankie Hermans.'

My diary, his novel – who are you?

She looks, and thinks.

'This, Frankie, this, here, right now, that's all I can say about it. It's not all that mysterious, that's only what Arthur makes of it.'

At the end of the day, we're all named Achiel?

'Yeah, maybe you could say that. Achiel, yeah.'

It's the first time that name's been spoken out loud, and we laugh. She comes over and stands beside me.

'Have I ever told you how attracted I am to intelligent men?'

And so the mood has shifted to the kind of steaminess familiar to me from the time she jerked me off. She kneels down beside me and puts her hands on my thighs.

'Intelligence is irresistible.'

My head starts to glow, this is what I'd been hoping for, no, what I'd been praying for. She unzips my trousers but I point in alarm at the curtains; my parents can see us like this. P.J. gets up, closes off the darkness outside and bolts the door. As she walks past, she takes the dishcloth from its hook.

'Where were we? Oh, yes.'

I'm as hard as glass, she asks, 'Are you clean?' and I nod. Then she takes me in her mouth. I caress her hair, the inside of her mouth is wet and warm, her head moves up and down. I see her face from the side and my dick sliding in and out of her mouth, she smiles up at me, it's too much. The sperm squirts powerfully in her face. Sorry, sorry. Only when I'm completely drained does she let go and wipe off the cum with the dishcloth. Her hands, so unbelievably much warmer than the official thirty-seven degrees centigrade, slide under my sweater. My skin responds with uncontrollable shivers. She pulls my sweater up over my head and worms the sparrow claw out of its sleeve so that I'm sitting half naked in front of her. The light above the table shines bright on my white, asymmetrically curved torso, I rise to my feet and click it off. Paradise by the desk lamp on the floor.

'Come.'

P.J. helps me up and we move to the bed. I let myself fall onto it, she unlaces my clodhoppers. She pulls off my shoes and my trousers, I'm lying helpless before her. Under her sweater she's wearing a white bra. There are pale marks on her stomach, my hand asks for her. She puts her hands behind her back and unsnaps her bra, her arms slide through the shoulder straps and I see her breasts. I'm sweet on her.

She squeezes my dick, her jeans and panties fall to the floor. I see the shadow between her legs, there where I've never been. P.J. climbs up and straddles me, feeling around under her. 'Have you ever done this...?' I shake my head. Then she sinks down halfway on my cock, sighs deeply and shiveringly and impales herself on me. Her eyes are closed, mine are wide open. She leans forward and puts her hands on my chest while her lower body moves up and down, independent of the rest. Nothing more than this is needed, this is all I ask for.

Her head is bowed and a waterfall of curls is hanging before her face, behind it her loud breathing and sometimes a whining sound as though she's suffering a pain too great for words. Her pelvis slides powerfully up and down, our pubic hair grinds together, my hand slides over her buttocks, across her lower back to her stomach and her shaking breasts, 'Yeah, yeah, grab them,' she pants. The nipples are hard, my attention is divided and I no longer feel my dick that's melted away inside her.

When P.J. moans that she's coming I grab her by the back of the neck, spread my fingers across her scalp and feel the strong waves rolling through her body. She collapses on top of me, her breathing is a storm in my ear. She lies there like that for a long time. I remain motionless, slowly the feeling returns to my cock sticking in her down there. P.J. sits upright and slides off me.

'Jesus, that was great.'

She climbs down the front of my body.

'You're still hard.'

She starts jerking me off, my dick is shiny with her wetness.

'I want you to come, Frankie.'

She leans down over me and flutters her tongue across the head of my dick.

'Come now.'

Her hand slides up and down without pause, I wail and explode in her mouth.

At three in the morning I wake up, the stove is hissing and I pull a blanket over us. P.J. flutters her eyelids, smiles and sleeps on. I don't want to sleep, just look, but sink away again anyway. I wake up when I feel her body pulling away from mine and sliding out of bed. It's still dark, she's getting dressed.

'I have to go,' she whispers, as though there were someone else in the room.

She moves her hand lightly over my forehead, then she's gone. A wave of cold air from outside rolls through the room, I fall asleep again.

A couple of hours later Joe drives out of the camp at Siwa for a ride around the oasis. He goes thundering into the nearby sand dunes, the scoop sticking out high above the cab; a horned beast disappearing into the desert.

'It's so beautiful,' Joe says that evening on TV, 'when you come out of the dark and suddenly see that dome of light against the sky where the oasis is. Just punch it and head home through the date palms. You have to stay focused for so long; at the end of the day, for example, you can ask any driver you choose whether he saw that tire along the way, or a pair of shoes lying in the road, and he'll tell you. Everyone is so incredibly homed in all day on the tiniest deviation in that narrow strip of vision.'

On Tuesday morning the caravan starts crossing that part of the desert they call the Great Sand Sea, with dunes a hundred metres high. Joe's out of sorts, someone installed a generator behind his tent and the droning kept him awake all night. Around noon they enter the White Desert, a hallucinatory landscape of limestone and blinding white sand. Close to Dakhla they come down off the plateau to the oasis. Tomorrow they return to civilization. Almost one hundred drivers have already been eliminated in the desert, a few more will be added to that; only three out of every ten participants will actually make it to Sharm el-Sheikh.

On the fourteenth day Joe reaches the Nile. He crosses the river at Luxor and heads out the next morning into the Eastern Desert. The route bends north, the next-to-last encampment is at Abu Rish on the road connecting Beni Suef on the Nile with the Gulf of Suez. On the sixteenth and final day comes the longest stage in the whole rally: about four hundred kilometres on asphalt, by way of Suez to Abu Zenima on the coast of the Gulf of Suez, where they then go off-road again for another four hundred kilometres through the Sinai range and the sizzling heat. After crossing the Sinai, they come out at Wadi Watir. At the village of Nuweiba on the Gulf of Aqaba they will go back onto the road for the final kilometres south, to Sharm el-Sheikh.

*

The news that Joe had dropped out of sight in the rally a few kilometres before Nuweiba came as no surprise to me. He was last seen in the mountains close to the coast, and only noted as missing that evening when he failed to make it in under the time limit. That night on 'Speedboat in the Sand' the interviewer is on camera for the first time and reports in dramatic tones about the disappearance of Joe Speedboat and his race-dozer.

I die laughing; with Joe there's never a dull moment.

I t's late January by the time Joe finally shows up in Lomark.
Without the bulldozer. He chuckles a bit about all the com-
motion. He's as skinny as a rail, his hair is bleached by the
sun. His face and forearms are a reddish brown.

First he went to Amsterdam for a few days to see P.J., now
he's come back to put his mother's mind at ease.

'So how's things, Frankie? Anything happen around here?'

His standard question whenever he's been away for a while.
My throat is tight, visions of doom dance through my head. I
write: *Watched lots of RTL 5.*

'Yeah, that was funny. I don't think old Santing sold any
more paint because of it, but at least he was on camera.'

What did you do with the bulldozer?

He laughs slyly.

'Left it there.'

With whom, pray tell? Papa Africa?

'Let's just say that he can start his own earthmoving company now. Or something.'

Joe clasps his hands behind his neck and sinks back in his
chair contentedly. Suddenly I see it in a flash, an extremely
clear insight is what it is: he will always come out on top. The
treachery of lesser gods won't cause him to topple. He will
suffer for us, he will chop down a forest and change the course

of a river to help against the pain, but he will emerge unbroken. That realization makes me feel like digging a hole in the ground and disappearing into it forever.

Joe is going to see Christof this evening, on Monday he has to start work. He pats his pockets, takes his lighter off the table and smiles.

'All right,' he says, 'I guess I'll be moving.'

and then

This is later, many years later. A lot has happened, and finally I have come to understand the profound truth of the things-aren't-what-they-used-to-be men on their bench by the river: things are, indeed, not what they used to be. Even the dismay at that fact isn't what it used to be. You learn to live with such findings, like bleached bones.

After Joe came back from Dakar, Christof asked him straight out if it would be OK for him to invite P.J. to his fraternity's annual gala. He couldn't find another date. 'You'll have to ask P.J. about that,' Joe said, 'not me.'

And so P.J. went to the gala of the Utrecht Student Union in a close-fitting silver-gray dress, and no one could figure out how Christof had hit upon such a beauty.

That night he lost his virginity. All three of us had now converged in her loins.

The next summer, at a pavement café in Utrecht, Christof told Joe that he was having a relationship with P.J. too, and that she had chosen definitively for him, Christof. And that she didn't want to see Joe anymore, which is what it boiled down to. She had no liking for the ragged, painful nerve endings at the end of a relationship.

Joe didn't punch Christof in the mouth, nor did he break his neck; he hopped in his car and, just outside Oosterbeek, blew up the engine. He walked the rest of the way home, packed his backpack that night and left a note on the table saying he'd call, and that's all we know. People say he was seen in a bulldozer working on the E981, and that he had a black beard, so it could just as easily have been someone else.

Does it surprise anyone to hear that Christof got P.J. in the end? Not me, not really; he too was to have his chance, and when it came along he seized it. Christof could offer P.J. one thing her other lovers could not: order and certainty – throughout the centuries, the only demand placed by the citizenry on its authorities. That might have played less of a role, of course, if he had not made her pregnant. Christof's family moved heaven and earth to persuade her not to have an abortion, and not long afterwards a bulldozer (not a Caterpillar, but a Liebherr: Joe would have been horrified) began clearing the plot of land between Lomark and Westerveld where Christof and P.J.'s new house would stand.

Christof went into an accelerated program to get his law degree, and took a job at Bethlehem Asphalt. P.J. never finished college.

I have at last also discovered who it is that Christof resembles, the question that had become a sort of eternal obsession for me. I found him in the book *Hitler's Helpers*: he is the spitting image of Heinrich Himmler, I swear. That book had been on my parents' shelf for a hundred years. During a medical examination at the Lüneburg prisoner of war camp, Himmler, when asked to open his mouth, bit down on a cyanide capsule. The photograph was taken shortly afterwards. In the top left corner you see the shiny tip of a boot, Himmler is still wearing his glasses and lies wrapped in a blanket on the concrete floor. Christof all over, the way he's lying there.

I rediscovered that book the night after Ma's funeral. She

died after coming down with a rampant cancer of the lymph system. We had buried her and were sitting in the living room with relatives when I saw *Hitler's Helpers* on the shelf. I flipped through it and found the section with photographs. Dirk was looking over my shoulder.

'Looks just like that buddy o' yours,' he said.

There is one thing I still think back on with the greatest of delight, and that is the day Christof and P.J. married. The wedding was held in the church and P.J.'s dress was groaning at the seams from the child she would bear soon afterwards. Nieuwenhuis was all smarmy with Love, I was sitting in the aisle. When they left the church, P.J. glanced at me. The newly-weds drove off in a hired Bentley. The reception was held that afternoon at old man Maandag's place, the villa he'd had built outside the village after the Scania had destroyed the house with the gables on Bridge Street. It was a blazing summer after-noon, with plenty of poppies and cornflowers still in bloom. Christof was king for a day; his father gave a speech about princes on white chargers, the final words of which were 'Who shall buy her a white charger?' At that moment Christof came around from the back of the house leading a white mare, his wedding present for P.J. I have to give it to him, that was real class.

P.J. cried, the way she'd cried the day Joe pulled away from the Rabobank in his bulldozer. She kissed Christof and patted the horse's neck clumsily – she'd never really been much of a pony girl. The guests stood around admiringly, oohs and ahhs and so on, and Christof grinned from ear to ear. Then, at that moment, from out of the sky, came the sound of an engine: a lovely, purring growl that no one noticed at first, on lovely days like this one the sky was always full of small planes. This time, though, the sound became increasingly compelling, forcing itself as it were on the wedding party. Someone looked up, more and more heads turned in the direction of the noise that was suddenly very close. Then someone shouted, 'That thing's going to crash!' and the crowd blew apart as though someone had tossed a stink bomb in their midst.

A sky-blue airplane.

From low across the fields it came storming at the villa, trailing a banner behind it. Christof's mother was the first to knock over a table as she dove for cover, the clear tinkle of breaking glass made me shiver. The plane looked like it was still descending, then it roared right over our heads. A lot of guests made a dash for the house, the field behind was full of people running, but when the shadow blackened the patio I looked up; the association I had was that of a huge, ominous cross about to crush us. The pilot pulled up, I saw that he was wearing ski goggles and his teeth were bared in a grin. Around that point is when I started laughing and couldn't stop.

In the middle of the patio one woman stood frozen, staring at the shape the plane made against the sky: Kathleen Eilander. Her mouth hung open a little, she raised one feeble hand and pointed.

'There…' she said. 'That…'

I don't know whether a lot of people were able to read the words on the banner at that moment, but later the text buzzed its way around. I've said it before: with Joe there was never a dull moment. This is what it said:

WHORE OF THE CENTURY

in nice, neat letters. I almost choked with laughter. So he had read that book at last and, on this glorious day, put it to good use!

A pathetic note was that no one had thought amid the panic of holding onto the horse, which went galloping off across the fields to God-knows-where. The plane made a wide sweep and came back for a final salute. At that moment a furious, no, a *seething* Christof came running out of the house with his father's hunting rifle. His mother screamed as he cocked it, aimed and fired at the plane vanishing in the distance. He missed, or else the plane was already too far off in the direction of the village. Kathleen Eilander set a chair upright, sat down in it and watched the plane go. 'The horse!' someone shouted. Christof swore and took off after it with a few of the others.

Those who stayed behind stared at the wreckage in silent amazement. P.J. stood there like a billowing spinnaker of lace and silk amid the ruins of her wedding day. It was as though she couldn't decide between anger and hilarious laughter. My own laughter wouldn't stop, and in fact it has lasted until this day. P.J. looked at me, then at the colourful ribbon of wedding guests chasing a white horse across the fields, and shook her head slightly. She poured two glasses of champagne from one of the only tables left standing, ticked the glasses together, poured one of them down my throat and knocked back the other one herself in two gulps.

'Whore of the century,' she said pensively, wiping her lips. 'Whore of the century. Man oh man…'

Two weeks later P.J. gave birth to a son, that autumn they moved into the house where they still live. The little boy I saw for the first time as he was bicycling down Poolseweg beside Christof, an orange flag swaying from the back of his bike. Christof raised his hand in greeting, the fat little boy ploughed on. He didn't look like Heinrich Himmler.

Technically speaking, it's even possible that the little boy is my son, for P.J. and I never stopped sleeping together. And my balls are in perfect working order. Says P.J. She comes by when Christof is off travelling. Pa always closes the living-room curtains, on days like that she is there in full. P.J. is getting little wrinkles of age beside her ears, my love for her has never cooled. She is still my only reader.

The passages where I wrote about Joe, the things that happened and how we lost our souls make her uneasy. 'He was a dreamer,' she says, as though that explains or justifies anything.

Sometimes she asks me to pick her up with my good arm, I put my hand under her arse and she keeps herself in balance on my shoulder, so I can slowly lift her off the ground. Then she sits briefly on my hand like on the saddle of a racing bike. When I lift her I am, for a moment, as strong as a bear and she feels as light as a feather. This gives her a great deal of pleasure. After that we fuck like animals.

I still make my village rounds and occasionally drop in on Hennie Oosterloo in his garden house behind the Little Red Rooster. He sets his elbow in the middle of the table, because he will associate me with arm wrestling for the rest of his dim-witted life, but I shake my head and sometimes I almost start crying. I think about seppuku, the clean, straight cut, but in the end that is not in my line. I didn't lose my honour, I gave it away while in full possession of my senses.

The E981 has opened. A glacier of asphalt came grinding in, steamrolling new times before it, and we have disappeared behind a towering sound barrier of earth and plastic. And indeed, we hear nothing, just as little as we are heard. From the corner of their eye, drivers zipping by may catch a glimpse of the tip of our steeple poking up above the wall, atop it the cock that showed its pluck; otherwise the world has hidden us from view. But behind that we have not passed away, nor have we changed our shape. We are still here.

To find out more about our books, to meet our authors, to discover new writing, to get inspiration for your book group, to read exclusive on-line interviews, blogs and comment, and to sign up for our newsletter, visit **www.portobellobooks.com**

encouraging voices,
supporting writers,
challenging readers

Portobello
BOOKS